A Modern Journey

Derek Turner

© Derek Turner 2016

Derek Turner has asserted his rights under the Copyright, Design and Patents Act, 1988, to be identified as the author of this work.

First published in 2016 by Endeavour Press Ltd.

This edition published in 2018 by Endeavour Media Ltd.

To my parents, who are not at all like Ambrose's

Table of Contents

DELECTABLE MOUNTAIN	9
FIDELMA	16
DESCENT FROM THE CROSS	31
OLD MEDICINES	37
GETTING BACK TO BASICS	44
LEVEL 3	51
SISTERLY FEELING	61
ANGEL IN BEIGE	76
TRANSFUSION	88
MESSAGES RECEIVED	94
L-DAY	104
THE AMBROSE EFFECT	113
HIBERNIAN HALF-LIGHT	126
OPENING DOORS	137
PUTTING TO THE TEST	146
CAPTAIN OF THE NATIONAL SOUL	162
BOSCO'S PLAN	172
ORDER OF BATTLE	180
LIFE AND SOCIETY	187
COMETH THE HOUR...	200
A ROW IN THE TOWN	208
STREAM OF CONSCIOUSNESS	226
DUTY BOUND	232
MAGIC BULLET	240
IN ABSENTIA	246

REVELATIONS 261
Glossary of Irish Words 269

"Doth not wisdom cry? And understanding put forth her voice?
She standeth in the top of high places"
Proverbs, 8:1 and 8:2

"No doubt the townsfolk had been sunk in apathetic luxury;
the time was right for a Messiah. And lo! he arrived"
Norman Douglas, *Old Calabria*

DELECTABLE MOUNTAIN

Ambrose moved through the dying day, a carrier of diseases. He churned and seethed inside his clumsy self in empathy with the elements.

The storm that had squatted over the Irish Sea all day was capable of afterthoughts that could send people in the town below reeling, to teeter in a vortex of unease before hurrying for home. The great bay was a grey-blue-black maelstrom, lightless beyond the pounded promenade where strings of coloured bulbs swung nauseatingly, threatening to snap and strew the cowering town with tiny glass. The main force of the sea was broken by sucking, shining shingle, but the furthest-out rollers reared taller than the town, and even houses far from the seafront were crisped with salt. Up where Ambrose was, the force was even stronger, as if he were in the heart of an artillery battle - threatening to tumble him head-over-size-13s back downhill, or sneaking around behind to pluck him into the air like the rubbish he feared he was.

Ambrose had been up on the huge cape of the Head before - only once, when still a child, and by day - but coincidentally also in just such a mayhem of wind, a rogue front that had materialized unexpectedly out of an August morning, a black-browed beast rushing over the sea towards him personally. Even in his present extremity of feeling, he remembered exactly how it had felt on that day - what it had been like to have his five year old head protruding audaciously above the razor ridge, to stare into the saliva-strung gob of the gale - his abnormally large blue eyes at their largest, his lank black hair whipping back, the tips of his ears actually flapping, mouth agape in his pale physiognomy as if to swallow, but really so he could shout defiance at an adversary for once above contempt. Even now, in the middle of all his latest bitterness, he could taste the largeness and liberty of that lost moment - register once more the strength of the rock, the age and aliveness of the earth...

...but then...then...again the old denouement, the dimming of that day and of all days, as he heard yet again in imagination the sound that had so limited his life. The sound that had always crushed his creativity, basted him in guilt... The whinnying of his mother rose up from the past, straining from somewhere safe, slicing through the charged air - demanding as she had always demanded, needling as she had always needled.

"AMBROSE! What do you think you're doing? What is the point of climbing up there where it's so dirty and dangerous? Come down at once!"

He re-ignited with ancient hate, recalling how his eagerly extended antennae had shivered and stopped, like a snail touching poison - how he had felt himself shrinking back inside, when he knew he had been on the verge of something stupendous. She had been totally oblivious to his feelings. She had never noticed how small she made him feel, that day and all days. She had never noticed anything about him, in all the years. She had never noticed anything about anything.

She had always been so vilely practical, so ignorant of art and life - and clearly prepared to remain so, despite all his efforts to educate her, raise her out of her middle-brow miasma. She had always been, and would always be, obstinately at odds with her son - perplexed and infuriated by his refusal to do what she wanted him to do, what everyone else wanted, what everyone else did. For twenty-three years - twenty-three fucking years! - she had been trying to mould him, change him, break him...

There were times when he thought he had become inured to her awfulness and ignorance. There were even times he could feel abstract pity for her benighted state, of the kind he felt for famine victims in countries he would never visit. But what had happened earlier that evening had disproved this in the most painful way. The bitch could still cut! His uneven, unwhite teeth (kept that way, because it annoyed her immoderately) ground and grated together. She was to blame for the cataclysm of that evening...

An hour ago, or maybe much longer ago, Ambrose had found himself stomping away in humiliation and hate from giggling Philomena Cogaidh, as she stood with some of her many friends outside Fitzmaurice's pub, her brunette hair nimbused by light, her gamine figure even in that moment torturing him with its nearness and inaccessibility. Philomena had just taken advantage of a lull in the gale to express cogent views as to Ambrose's appearance, odour, oral hygiene, and probable potency, in response to his gabbled request for a date (the first such request he had ventured to anyone). He had only been able to summon the courage this time because he had needed so badly to prove he could do it - and because he had downed several whiskies, a drink he disliked. Now chemical bile burned inside alongside the emotional, threatening to bubble out over his clothes, puke over the stinking pile of life.

Philomena's cruelty, three quarters-expected though it had been, had sabred his heart. It had been so casual. He would almost have preferred if she had found him hateful, even frightening - because such statuses would at least have implied respect. But no - she had just dragged her beautiful, blasé eyes over him as if it was an effort and he had been an unwelcome stranger - a satellite salesman, or a charity mugger, or a Traveller. In that coolest of regards, there had been no acknowledgement whatever of six years spent in the same school year. Admittedly in all that time, she had only ever addressed one word directly to him (and that had been "Huh!") - and she had always joined in the many laughs at his expense raised by schoolmates, and some staff.

But he had always told himself - and at times almost persuaded himself - this was peer pressure, that there was interest in her eyes when he caught them, a subtle signal in the way she flicked her fine hair when she must have known he was watching, a shampoo-smelling cascade in the sunlight that streamed through the school's large windows as he ached. But it seemed she really had not been interested in him at all. Not at all! Even after what had just happened, he could not quite believe that she really had no idea of his sensitivity - his intellectual superiority. But it seemed she really did prefer, had always preferred, the oafs who sported her like a falcon on their beefy wrists for a few months before she once again took graceful flight.

But now, in a few seconds, with a few casual cruelties, that six year fantasy had been killed, and cremated, and its ashes scattered at the Community Recycling Centre. Like all of the rest of his dreams, like probably most people's dreams, it had been a delusion - nothing more than a by-product of neurochemistry, a symptom of psychosexual frustrations. At last he knew something he had always gnawingly guessed - his ideas were juvenile, mistaken, misplaced, a waste of time and mental energy. (At least he had never told anyone about them.)

Christ, how her lesson hurt! He had risked everything for her, like superheroes always did - and he had lost everything, a superzero. Not just the possibility of coition - not just his dignity, and credibility (such as they had been). She had stabbed to the core of his always shaky sense of self-worth - all his self-deluding claims to seriousness and profundity. He had extended his antennae again - and been poisoned yet again. All seemed salt, just as the storm that surrounded him was full of the tang of the sea.

And this had had to happen this evening! This evening, of all the evenings, when he had so badly wanted to prove he could do what even the stupidest of his schoolmates had done. Hideous words, hateful laughter, hammered behind his eyes, in her voice, a thing light and lovely as an angelic instrument - "You must be feckin' joking…look at the face on him, girls…you couldn't get it up…who in their right mind…"

Pound, pound, pound…

Other words heard that evening were whirling in there too, fluttering like litter caught in a cul-de-sac.

Useless…dirt…disgust…ashamed…useless…dirt…disgust…ASHAMED. ..Semi-blind with bitterness, despairingly half-drunk, he had rushed to get away, above this greatest, latest humiliation, and think – somewhere solitary, safe, very far from all this Vanity Fair... At that moment, as if it had just hove massively into view, the Head had suddenly registered at the furthest end of the High Street. It looked to him in that world-turning moment like the only really solid thing he had ever seen.

Like everyone else in the town, he had always been aware of the Head, a marker for the municipality visible for the last few miles of the journey from Dublin, a thing which had towered there countless æons before people came to bother it with cultural significances. But he was no outdoorsman, and it had seemed no more intrinsically interesting than the Bay into which he had skimmed so many emotion-relieving stones, the Mediterranean-looking promontory dotted with houses to which he would never be invited, the clay cliffs to the north that sagged brownly like old ladies' tights, the oak woods bisected and blasted by the bypass heading south towards Wexford. It had always been just another inert object, a prehistoric backdrop against which he dragged out a stagey life, a lump that defined the limits of local authority and imagination.

But now he saw with a kind of shock that the Head was monumental, beautiful. He wondered he had never seen those qualities in it before. So superb, remote – above the crowds, the clouds, transitional between earth and sky. It looked like land seen after a long and doubtful sea-journey.

Magnetized, impelled, he had chased along the road with gathering speed, the wind bowling him along - away, away, away, Ambrose, from dirt, humiliation. insensitivity, sublunary fears, secret hopes. Victorian villas rose up and fell away on each flank – Balaclava, Sebastapol,

Fairholme, Waverley – stodgy stucco substance, BMWs in drives, repro lanterns shining through fanlights. How he had always hated them! He had not been built for suburbs, nor had they ever taken him into account. He had always felt his ought to be a much Higher Fate - even (when he was extremely young) that he must be a changeling or princeling, fallen from great state by evil enchantment.

Cars passed, pushed briskly from behind, wind-watching drivers scarcely noticing the gangling, scowling, mouthing young man barreling along in thin glitter-flecked black jacket, T-shirt bearing the name of a musician no-one else in Ireland had heard of, skinny-fit jeans, thin-soled, pointy shoes that seemed to seek out sharp pebbles, and were now raising weals on both heels. Ambrose was only semi-conscious of such inconveniences, because now the wind had whisked him past the locked gates of Head House and over a failing wall into its bosky shelter.

As soon as he got over the wall, everything altered. Time slowed down, and sped up. The decayed demesne seemed a universe apart, and he was glad to be in it – particularly at a time like now, in such a pandemonium of thrashing trees, spears of sleet fired downhill into his face as he slithered up dubious tracks, glowering clouds sweeping down to hide all hideous things. He stood still and inhaled, more deeply than he had inhaled before...cold, wind, salt, earth, pines...but only for a few seconds before he hurried up and away, semi-ecstatic, semi-panic-stricken, as tiny and harried as Adam in an oil of Man's Fall.

Scots pines shook and creaked, roaring and rushing in their topgallants as if they were about to up roots and scud before the storm. Scrub oaks swished and rioted, gorse bent and relaxed, bent and relaxed, hawthorns shook and squeaked, and long grass streamed straight inland like the pennons of lancers. Brown-orange murk boiled in all directions, foreshortening lines of sight and making deeply significant the animal tracks that wound through thrashing trees towards secret lairs.

Ambrose had never been out in the countryside by himself - and this was night, and the most feral of possible nights. Such conditions, he could not help feeling, surely could be no coincidence. Such a night must signal something! How could all this energy be for nothing? He had recently been re-reading the Gothicks and Germans, and it seemed to him now that this was a truly Nietzschean night, a night for Alpine apparitions, a kind of Walpurgisnacht – one of those nights when time was a tunnel, and life raced in dark and dangerous directions - a night for great deeds, or appalling acts committed in secret amidst violent vegetation.

Things petty and portentous fought for mastery inside him, as they had always - but now as if they were being drawn to some conclusion. Self-pity, self-knowledge, arrogance, vanity, uncertainty, world-historical thoughts, outlandish theories, snatches of esoteric books and strains of discordant music, stinging memories, extravagant hatreds, contempt for himself and even more for everybody else, pulsating priapism and a desire to cut all dirt away… Tonight, heute nacht, on this exaggerated evening, this Mother of evenings, something huge had to happen, or he would surely explode. His heart felt like detonating in its skinny cage. Inside and out, all was the same vast barometric disturbance.

As he swore and stumbled amidst roots and rivulets, veins stood out all over his meagre body, and he found he was shouting grievances in his head or aloud, telling the pissed-on world below how much he hated it - that he was strong, and would defeat it. His fists (soft, white) opened and closed convulsively, and sometimes he lashed his arms out - once wincing as knuckles connected with rough bark. His past (frustrated) and his future (futile), cowered before him (pathetic), waiting to be punished – wanting to be punished. Society too. Because if he was a worm, it was a billion times worse. And all the while sobbing hamstrings and slipping feet carried him onwards and up – excrement and Excelsior in one package. He was aiming for the Cross.

On the highest point of the Head, placed there one 1960s August by sweating and cursing workmen, there was a twenty foot concrete cross with a self-deluding inscription – Christus Rex. It was unadorned and ugly, but on a clear day from its foot a vastness could be comprehended – down to the town with its tiny amusements, wider to several counties, out east to anchored ships, beyond them the City and the World and, for all the irreligious Ambrose knew, to any passing extra-terrestrials.

Earlier, as he had forced down whisky and stared at Philomena, he had noticed a framed black-and-white print of the Cross's unveiling on the pub wall - an image that made his lip curl in contempt. It was an Indian summer image of Holy Ireland, a sight to make the devout wish they had lived then rather than now - hatted, hand-bagged women, handsome young priests in soutanes, all in decorous attendance on a central Cardinal. It had been a great day for the Irish Church, a day of re-dedication, a counter-blow against the counter-culture, as a censer censed, a sermon was given, a mitre sported in the least likely of surroundings, and applause rippled out from the women who had raised the money. To at least some of the attendees, the elderly Cardinal's crozier had briefly seemed to pin down all of Nature, piercing the Head's granite geology as sorely and sweetly as Longinus had hurt Jesus, or Patrick had impaled the pagan's foot.

Since then - so recent, so long ago - the Cardinal had gone to his reward, and he had been joined by many of the attendees. Their Cross had weathered, gone down in the world's estimation – a seamark for men who dropped and picked up lobster-pots at the base of the cliffs – a turning point for summertime strollers – a graffiti easel and picnic place, visitors sometimes leaving glittering spoor of glass. Once, teenagers playing at Satanism had covered the base with graffiti. But all scars would always eventually be cleared away by someone – probably a council workman, but just possibly one of the rare pilgrims who came to climb the difficult north side as a forgotten sixth century saint had done, and sit for a while as he had done, considering the earth's manifold realms.

But nobody - that is, nobody else - would be mad enough to be at the Cross now. Caught unexpectedly by a great buffet of wind that rushed at him from around an outcrop, Ambrose almost fell down a steep scree - reminding him just how hazardous as well as exhausting it was to attempt ascent in these conditions. But then that was what he needed – an ache in his muscles to prove he had some, a task to show he had some worth, a dangerous place for dangerous thoughts, a wild place to escape all the tame people. Placing himself in peril helped him feel he really could be first among unequals. How powerfully alone and aristocratic it was - he was! To his uplifted eyes, the rock was a resounding Region, an echoing land, a great and ghosted place where everything was in motion, anything possible. It was a place for wind and wildness, inclemency and exiles – a place to stand and see things clear, a fulcrum with which he could overturn the world.

The gale was trying to push him flat, but he pushed back. Trees sought to surround him, but he escaped. Mud tried to make him slide, but he skimmed lightly over. Clouds hid the Cross but he knew exactly where it was. He gritted his teeth (uneven, unwhite) grimaced fiercely at himself and spat, before renewing his upward progress.

FIDELMA

Fidelma Sheehy-O'Connor perched in an immaculate interior, her obvious unease incongruous in so perfect a room. Here her most expensive possessions were ranged at magazine-informed intervals along cream walls set off by the kind of unblemished carpet only found in pet-free homes. Everything was faultlessly correct, from the skirting to the reproduction rose supporting a new chandelier whose faux-Murano glass droplets had been strung at quite extraordinary expense for such economy of effect. The just discernible theme was Gustavian, by way of Guangdong.

She was smartly dressed and fully made up, although it was late and she was expecting no callers. Who would be out anyway on a night like this one, when the wind was making the conifers outside quake and sway, hail was finger-nailing the glass, and the sea could be heard and smelt in all streets? Who, except…? Her eyes flicked again to the window.

In the reflection, she saw her new leather suite with ethnic throws. There was a neo-Nordic dining table with poor-quality ironwork and silk-shaded standard lamps spilling reservoirs of refulgence over silk flowers. A few shelves displayed books ranked equally with DVDs – once-read classics ranged alphabetically by author alongside often-watched period dramas and documentaries Fidelma believed combined uplift with irreproachable taste. (One had to be so careful what one watched on the vast screen that engulfed most of one pastel plane.) She also saw herself, tiny, yet in command of her ultra-organized environment. Everything one could want – much one did not actually need – was there, in its optimal place, mentally catalogued and budgeted, free from blemish or taint.

Fidelma was well aware how lucky she was. On the same date every December she would ritualistically write out a large cheque for a homeless charity run by nuns of the same order that thirty years ago had absorbed her younger sister. She switched her mind now to Mary. It was a relief to think about her instead of what was really on her mind.

It had been over two years since she and Mary had seen each other, and on that occasion Fidelma had had the feeling that her sister was only feigning interest in family matters - rather as if she were cutting cables.

She had been so distrait - sinking finally, it seemed, into comfortless sanctity in the huge hulk of the convent on the hill, along whose waxed, endless, echoing corridors the sweetest breeze became funnelled and freighted with the clamminess of death. On a night like tonight, Fidelma thought with a slight shiver, the place must rattle to its eerie foundations.

There had been other religious on both sides of the family – the Sheehys had almost become extinct on several occasions in the foregoing three hundred years – but Fidelma would never have expected this lifestyle-choice of Mary. Even now, she could still remember her as joyous infant, running along a country lane somewhere and sometime in their shared past, her arms full of the wild flowers that had become so rare, calling to Fidelma in squeaky joy, "wait for me, wait for me!" And Fidelma had always waited.

Funny the decisions some people make, she reflected. Funny how some seemed so determined to go against normality - to try to stand outside time. It must take great strength of character to be religious in a world full of such opportunities. Or was it simply self-delusion? Fidelma had always felt Mary had rather too much imagination. She could still see, with a compound of unease and some other emotion oddly like envy, the remote look on Mary's face when she had returned from a second visit to Oldtown Convent and announced that she would definitely be taking the veil. Mary's eyes had seemed simultaneously glazed and full, as if they had seen something too impressive ever to be described.

Fidelma had tried to ridicule her out of it, but there had been no one to back her up. Their parents had been dead several years by then - and in any case they might even have taken their younger daughter's side. They had both been quite conservative, even their mother - notwithstanding her local celebrity as medium and second-seer, which had elicited an embarrassing denunciation by the traditionalist parish priest. At any rate, Mary had stood her ground easily against Fidelma, and she and the idea had surprisingly quickly grown into each other. Now it was difficult for Fidelma to imagine her sister as anything other than deeply serious Sister with an upper-case S, stalwart of a dozen charities and hundreds of good works carried out for no reward, as the robust young woman transmogrified into skeletal self-denier. The rosy cheeks had started to look almost transparent, and Fidelma had had the horrible fancy that she could see the bones of Mary's jaw, see her teeth working, the tongue slithering up and down as she spoke. As for herself, Fidelma knew she could never have sacrificed all of this...

her eyes circumnavigated the room with *some* complacency... for something so insubstantial. A crown in heaven, indeed! How could anyone believe such childish things today?

But it was only some complacency. The room was too new and clean to feel easy in it, almost as if the house sensed that the decorative scheme was provisional, and would soon end up in a skip in the driveway, like two others that had tricked out this room in the last decade. The fact was that the room's occupant was never easy in herself, and nerves were always impelling her to purchase something so she could wall herself away from... Something. Or Nothing.

There were times when Fidelma could almost understand what had driven Mary into the apparent security of religion. Almost. The apparent security. There were things in the world she didn't like any more than Mary did - the sexualised culture, swearing, rudeness, aggression. She knew there was still a power in the flickering faith that guarded against social dangers. A sense, instilled at school, that there was such a thing as Deity-owed duty had helped in her own life, helped rationalize the fear and disgust she had felt for the offices of marriage and motherhood. She was gratefully aware that religion had always been a sort of shield against the random eros, a guarantor of slightly better male behaviour. And it was so pretty to believe the old metaphors at Christmas, when the tree-lights twinkled defiantly against the Great Darkness, lighting her all the way back to childhood.

But when it came down to it, for her old-time religion was essentially obscurantism - outdated, irrelevant, impossible, sometimes actually offensive in its divergence from today's accepted decencies. She was, she felt, alive and in the world, her head screwed on, her eyes open - finding her own path through positive thinking and independence from shibboleths, with occasional interventions by qualified professionals. In a world of possibilities, there were many ways to self-fulfilment other than Mary's well-trodden highway.

Fidelma's husband - whose name had been Fergus - had left her comfortable when he had so considerately widowed her after a mercifully brief and relatively dignified illness. According to his low-wattage lights, he had been a thoroughly decent man – capable, charitable, convivial, reliable, uncontroversial. (She had never allowed herself to whisper - boring.) He had laboured in the commercial property sector in order to pay for the house, done basic DIY tasks with different degrees of success, wheeled out dust-bins, brought her to strong-sunned, multi-starred resorts, and got perennially excited about football results as if they signified something meaningful. He hadn't conducted any clandestine affairs (she was sure, from monitoring his phone and going through his pockets). He had avoided politics. He had trooped to Mass at Christmas to fulfil vaguely-felt obligations, and in between would very properly never refer to religion. On very festive occasions, he had been known to hoist his slightly too well-fed frame onto the parquet, and lumber like a Guinness-brimming bear to 1970s tunes that for some reason had once been popular, and remained so among his generation as mementoes of less upholstered younger days. Fidelma would watch his caperings, and smile thinly as she sipped gin and tonic. It had been a good marriage, and a step up the scale - and yet when this paragon amongst paterfamiliases had died, her chief emotion had been relief.

Never again would she be compelled to endure those – a strong word, but the right one – loathsome embraces he would foist upon her from time to time. Even gin had never helped with this unpleasantness. But it was, she knew (thanks to the teacher-nuns), his right, and it had been her duty to submit, even as her body arced and could not help recoiling from his clammy hands, his chubby physicality, his sweaty seed passing between them like a dirty secret – them both falling away from each other afterwards, embarrassed and slightly appalled.

Then there was the torture to what this torrid thrashing had led, mercifully just the once – the shapelessness, sickness, dizziness, heaviness, headaches, backaches, irrational cravings, desire for darkness… and at the end of interminable months a mess of agony, blood, oaths and foam acted out in the blaze of halogen and cool strangers' eyes above white masks.

All that to produce a red and wrinkled goblin, with a crow-black corona of hair and a perpetually open mouth, wailing at the world into which he had just been induced at forceps-end, and which he had apparently hated from the outset. Begat in embarrassment, with the shifting eyes of a fox and the outsize ears of a bat, he did not resemble at all the golden-haired Christ-child of a thousand depictions. While gradually she had developed some of the obligatory maternal "instincts", she often couldn't help feeling that the whole business had simply not been worth the unhygienic inconvenience. She had consulted magazines, and when a year or so afterwards Fergus had made a half-hearted attempt to add a sibling, he had been met by squirms, sharp elbows, "Don't be silly!", "Stop this nonsense!", "It's my right...", and "Please...!" Even Fergus had seemed relieved, and soon afterwards, he had retired from the procreative field for good. Fidelma had been very pleased when this aspect of her life had finally been ironed and put away.

But her foray into matronhood had at least kept the family going for one more cycle. That would have pleased her father, at least. She had always so wanted to please him. Even now, with him gone more than three decades, she missed his quiet validations, and smiles for her alone. He had been so reliable, so strong, and so successful building bungalows - like the one he had built for his wife and daughters in West Cork, a few hundred yards away from the shell of the thatched cottage that was no longer good enough for twentieth century Sheehy-O'Connors. Yet he was proud of his heritage, and had with great labour drawn up a complex genealogy that descended them directly from the High Kings – nonsense of course, but Fidelma respected even this in him, because she was aware she had little imaginative faculty. Poor Fergus never compared with Dad! Would Dad might have seen something in Ambrose, she sometimes wondered? It seemed unlikely - although Ambrose was at least imaginative. (Way too much so!) Her mother would probably have liked him, though - she had always been perverse. Probably it was just as well Ambrose had never known his grandmother - she would probably have encouraged him, with all her rubbish about ghosts, and goblins, and second-sight.

Right from the start, Ambrose (the name her choice, to differentiate him from commonplace boys) had been a source of puzzlement and distress to both Fidelma and Fergus. Fergus had been spared much of it, because of his busy schedule, but she had always been expected to be there, to deal with soiled nappies, temper fits, lashings-out, bruisings, bumps and difficult questions. But even Fergus had started to feel early on that there was something odd about their child - and their relationship had never really advanced beyond this point.

A few days before Fergus had died, he had asked Fidelma to bring Ambrose to the hospice. He had wheezed he wanted to "give the boy a good talking to, man to man". She was sceptical about the value of any such proceeding, but she had badly wanted to please her soon-to-be-late spouse. The boy (boy... he had been twenty!) had complied sulkily. She had left them alone, as arranged. At the door, she turned, to see them together for the last time – Ambrose's black-clad rear elevation, lofty but narrow and slump-shouldered, his topography-less torso running straight down to outsize, splayed feet – looming like an anti-angel over the man in the iron-framed bed in that room tinged with disinfectant and undercurrent of colostomies.

What was said she would never know, because by the following day Fergus had deteriorated yet further, and he was muttering intermittently and unintelligibly. The waxy skin had seemed to shrivel back from his skeleton even as she watched, vaguely appalled. "Ambrose... bloody boy... I don't know..." was all she had been able to piece together from his meanderings in the four days remaining to their union. She still thought of him sometimes, with faint fondness and fading sadness, as he had been during those days – mouth opening and closing hesitantly in the coconut of his head, tiny on the puffed-up pillow, antediluvian hand scrabbling pathetically at the crisp sheets as he tried to hold onto something. It had only been in those last few days that she noticed how much his ears stuck out; so that was where Ambrose had got them. She had never really looked at Fergus before, she realized - only now, when all observations would soon be redundant. She had held her husband's cooling hand, dutiful, dry-eyed.

Ambrose, of course, never told her what had passed between him and his father. In fact, she couldn't think of a single time when he had confided anything to her. He had always just been there, on the edge of vision, edgy in every way, an eyesore she wished she could learn to love, a disconcerting and awkward shadow at the furthest end of tables, a gloomy constant in repeatedly refreshed rooms – hunched morosely over some ascetic cuisine – her catering treated with disdain, her attempts at conversation greeted by grunts or references to things, places and books she couldn't comprehend. *Nonsensical* things, places and books!

He never referred to people, though – he seemed to have no friends, and there had never been a girlfriend. Not a single one, in twenty-three years. She refused to think of another possibility, disregarding the malicious insinuations of parrot-faced Sandra Gulliver next door. Such things had never featured in the Sheehy-O'Connor universe, and never could (not that there was anything wrong with that lifestyle choice - far from it! It was just that... anyway, there was nothing wrong with it!) The reasons for Ambrose's lack of success with women lay closer to home. It was just that he looked so, so...how could she think it without disloyalty?...it was just that girls didn't seem to appreciate his special brand of difference. Maybe if he had looked after his teeth better, washed more often... There were also certain psychological shortcomings – although the doctors had never quite specified autism, Fidelma had read the newspaper supplements.

Ambrose could be clever, but only at useless subjects – and even here aptitude was never matched by application. She had been pleased to discover his nickname at school was "Catalogue" – a reference, she had assumed gratifyingly, to his bookishness. She was only part-right. Although it did allude to his greedy reading, it had really been coined by a surreally-inclined classmate to signify Ambrose's "catalogue of ears". (Ambrose knew, and had always borne a greater than usual grudge against that particular classmate. That was why he had carved his tormentor's name into various toilet doors at school; enjoying the fallout as the coiner tried to deny the vandalism had been one of school's few pleasures.)

As if to compensate for literary and other inutile aptitudes, Ambrose seemed almost a dunce at maths, science or anything practical. As for sports, Fidelma was painfully aware he had been a joke at his sports-renowned school – the last in any race, the last to be chosen for any team, the first to sneak off (alone) for a cigarette. This last habit appalled Fidelma, who was highly sensitive to smells, and one December afternoon she had made the then twelve year old stand in the garden for an hour after she had hosed him down with cold water. That had not worked. Nothing had worked. He had always been stubborn to the point of brutishness. Then there had been the night of the vodka party, when Ambrose had been fifteen… the memory of which still mortified her, and accordingly delighted Sandra Gulliver, who thought Fidelma a snob who needed to be brought down.

Fidelma had long suspected her son of using yet worse substances. He must, because why else would he behave as he behaved? Why else his rudeness, his multiple rejections - of her, her lifestyle, their neighbours, their lifestyles, society, the world? What else could explain the weird tastes, the day-long silences punctuated by sarcasms, the secret jokes that would occasionally make him laugh out frighteningly loud? Yet whenever she searched his room, she had never found any drugs. He was either more cunning than she gave him credit for - or his oddness had absolutely nothing to do with drugs, but was some kind of worm within.

Maybe it was the bizarre books he consumed the way normal people consumed Sky News. She didn't know anyone else who read such books – all about drugs, or death, or vanished civilizations, or art history, or cultural theories translated from French or German. His untidy, unhealthy shelves were lined with thick and tenebrous tomes (all hardbacks, which made them somehow even creepier) with titles like *The English Dance of Death, Melmoth the Wanderer, Myths of the Middle Ages, In Praise of Shadows, Remembrance of Things Past, The Golden Bough, Bruges-la-Mort, The Pleasure of Ruins* and *Memoirs of an English Opium-Eater*.

Just looking along the lines of spines made her feel slightly unnerved, as if seeing evidence of an invisible universe running in rivalry with everyone else's. Leafing disdainfully but also slightly fearfully through the books, she found vast blocks of polysyllabic text broken only by illustrations of skulls and saints, strange symbols, disgracefully untidy cemeteries, broken buildings, pagan rites, legendary figures, tyrants of the past, and robots of the future. What was perhaps even more disconcerting was that many of the books bore copious marginalia in Ambrose's showily Gothic hand (he hadn't learned that at school!) - all of which seemed to Fidelma to be nonsensical or wild. It was as if her son had bypassed all rational and respectable tastes, all normal living. She had always seen this as a kind of personal slight. She had once asked Mrs. Gulliver what books her boy Tom read, and had been almost envious to learn that he rarely read anything other than the accountancy press. That must be why Tom was so successful, younger than Ambrose but already a partner at his firm. One tiny part of her was nonetheless defensively proud that Ambrose seemed to have so much more breadth. If only he would stick to nice subjects....

When Ambrose wasn't reading, he was watching subtitled films although (or was it because?) she was bored by them. Or listening to loud, distorted music whose notes appeared to be in the wrong order and whose lyrics were incomprehensible even when they were rendered into English. Which was probably just as well. Then there were computer games, at which he seemed highly skilled.

But what did such aimless intelligence amount to, in this world, where everyone had to pay their way, do the right thing by their parents and by society, keep everything rolling? The world had expectations as well as methods, and it must tame him eventually, although she had failed to do so. She looked forward in vague but persistent hope to a day when she could feel proud of her product - a secure job-niche, him in one of those nice suits from Barry & Knowles, standing up straight for once, with an open smile for once, one day striding straight-backed down the aisle at Saint Aidan's with some nice girl, like that lovely Philomena Cogaidh who had been in his class. Such a sweet girl, too - the old-fashioned, polite kind. Sometimes her vision of this future day was clear in every detail.

But there were as yet no signs of any such outcome, and Ambrose drifted in and especially out of dead-end employments, with ever-longer gaps between them. He lounged across her conscience, a constant worry, a semi-resented reminder of the grossness that had once passed between her and Fergus, a reproach for her lack of success as mother, and as woman.

Ambrose did not talk often, and when he did he usually muttered into his spindly chest. She had once read in a hagiography that Saint Ambrose (whom she sometimes thought of as "the real Ambrose") had been gifted with a honeyed tongue after a swarm of bees had settled on him in his crib, but her Ambrose had not inherited this capability. (To say the least!) Whenever he did vouchsafe an opinion about anything, it would be some bilious, sarcastic comment about religion, politics, popular culture, cherished people – nasty, sneering, snobbish, wounding, uncharitable, illiberal, un-Christian comments. He was the only person she knew who had voted against gay marriage, and this was obviously only done in order to shock her, and register some kind of stupid protest. She hated hearing his views, and recently they had been coursing from him like a river in black spate, carrying rubbish and dirt down from high places. Just a couple of days ago, they had been watching a news item about Gisela Mildew, the much-loved "radicals' radical", who made straight-to-classic speeches about sexual sameness and had devoted her life to making all cultures and countries exactly alike. As she was stepping smilingly up to a Washington podium amidst an ovation to accept another award, long speech clutched in long nails, Fidelma had felt her heart bulge slightly in dutiful solidarity… until Ambrose had said: "For fuck's sake, is that plastic prostitute still alive?" and pressed Off before lurching out of the room to his own, whence a minute later came Slavonic death metal at a very high volume.

Fidelma had been really quite shocked, not so much by the profanity (she was almost used to that from him) as by this reminder of his rejection of mainstream virtue in favour of… in favour of… well, what? His own private morality, he had once called it – so very private, she had retorted with a rare sense of making an adequate riposte, that no-one else in the world would recognize it as being moral. She had almost felt Gisela Mildew must have heard Ambrose's expectoration, and she had felt absurdly embarrassed for him. She had hammered on his locked door for over two minutes, telling him to come out and apologise, but all that had happened was that the "music" had become even louder. She had returned to the living room and sat unseeingly in front of the TV, feeling a little like crying. She didn't know where he got his ideas from. What impelled him to be so *bitter*?

Ambrose had always had everything. Everything. More than she had had. And all she had ever asked in return was a little politeness, a little polish, some reasonableness, some acquiescence in other people's equally valid pleasures. Instead - profanities about humanitarians – no interest in getting a job – an un-male indifference to the Irish football team – no interest in buying himself a Barry & Knowles suits (which were presently on special offer). He had even been known to grunt in contempt at her purchases, as if he knew about fashion! Last week, he had told her that her on-trend new coat made her look fat. Yet she spent three evenings a week soulcercising – and on the occasions she glimpsed her naked form in the bathroom mirror, she could see she had the torso of a thirty-something.

Besides, if society was as contemptible as Ambrose said, why did no-one else seem to see it that way? What about Tom Gulliver, and all the other young people, whose dress sense or language might not be to her taste, but who were otherwise becoming reassuringly like their parents? They were all shaping up for success – perhaps rather too literally in the case of Tom Gulliver, who was even developing his late father's pot-belly.

Of course, she had often said to Ambrose, society wasn't perfect - and in her own way she sought change through her choices as ethical consumer and floating voter. But it had been good enough for Fergus, and of course for Dad. Your grandfather, she had told Ambrose, had never felt the need to rebel, drop out, had never let his dreams take hold – he had been a proper man. She frequently asked Ambrose what gave him the right to believe he was right, and his grandfather had been wrong? What made him so cocksure, so contemptuous of all the little things that had made life pleasant for people? What, after all, had Ambrose done with his comfy life? He had no right to judge anyone. But when challenged, he would just grunt and move away. He had no answers to anything.

Ambrose – so unsuitable a name, and less appropriate almost hourly. He was always so graceless - unhappy. She had hardly ever seen him enjoying himself – and even on those extremely rare occasions, it had been more startling than satisfying. There was a ferocity to his fun, as if something was about to burst through all barriers… as if it was a prelude to some pagan extravagance. He was like a sufferer from borderline personality disorder at times, a wild thing from the deepest woods.

She thought of a time up on the Head, years ago, when he was still very young, when a violent gale had blown up unexpectedly out of a clear day. It seemed almost to have been a signal to him. He had just run away from her nervous hand, her safety, and on and on up towards the ridge, shouting something she couldn't understand… but she didn't really want to think about the way he had looked as he feasted on that wind - or the hatred that had flickered like knives in his eyes as she plucked him by his hand and pulled him back from the brink. She had never taken him there again. It was a Dangerous Place. And his trousers had been filthy!

She fretted on this sorry history tonight, as so often. She was rarely happier than when she was worrying - but it was also partly because even here among all the shining surfaces something of this evening's energy could reach her. There was a hyperboreal hint in the chimney, fingers were feeling her ankles, and to the right of the TV was the grey-black slab of PVC double glazing framing black spear-points of Leylandii swishing in obedience to uncontrollable forces. She thought she heard a door closing upstairs, and she went hopefully out into the yawning hall to see if he had returned. But there was no response to her "Ambrose? Ambrose?" except a thickening of the silence. It was too quiet for comfort. And it was chilly out there, even with all the lights on. She went back into the TV-booming living room, but couldn't relax. She crossed to the window, bony arms folded in front of ungenerous breasts. Beyond the agitated coniferous zone she could just see the stolid shape of the Head, silhouetted at the moment by some strange light effect, and that seemed to satisfy her, because she returned to her seat and the giant screen, which was telling an oddly comforting tale about religious riots in Egypt.

But what brought her troubles to mind more strongly than usual was that evening's awful scene. She had been in such a good mood too, after finding a new dress at half its former price – and she had been determined to broadcast bonhomie even to her ingrate offspring. She had bought a "Luxury Range" curry from the supermarket. She found this curry acceptably mild, and she assumed that Ambrose (with his fondness for foreignness) would appreciate her thoughtfulness. And really it had smelt quite nice as it heated, and she had had a small glass of rosé which had thawed her. As Ambrose came in she had even been singing along to the radio, a song that even Ambrose must surely find catchy. It had been the

UK Christmas number one, and ten million downloaders couldn't be wrong, could they?

"La la la, la la la la la, give your love to the world, la la la, la la la la la, joy is unfurled!" she trilled, as she smiled as kindly as she could at her son – although he didn't obviously deserve any consideration, as he stood there wild-eyed and windswept, his outfit an impractical disgrace, his silly shoes leaving slimy mud on her high-polished floor. But still she persisted, while he peeled off his wretched jacket and hung it so carelessly on the hook that it immediately slid onto the floor, from where she must have picked up his jackets a thousand times… ten thousand times? Twenty? She went over to twitch it up, looking meaningfully at him - but he didn't notice. He slouched to the table to collapse into a chair, and she was still managing to smile. But she stopped when he flicked off the radio right in the middle of a chorus, muttering, "Hate that fucking song."

"I was listening to that! Put it back on, please! And don't swear! How many times must I tell you?" Silence. "Ambrose! Put the radio back on!" No reply. He took out a book – the usual big, hardback kind, some German waffler she supposed – and began to read. Or pretend to read. No-one really read books of that kind, did they? Or if they did, they didn't enjoy them. She bit back words she had been about to utter – but her mood had gone. Tension stirred in the fenugreek-fragrant kitchen - even more than had become customary. The trees in the garden bent almost double in a particularly fierce gust, and seemed to have difficulty straightening again. She shivered as she looked out.

"What's for dinner?" he grunted.

She said nothing this time, but turned the radio back on, just in time for chorus 7, and Ambrose stood up and headed off towards his bedroom – still leaving a trail of mud. He was like some shambling animal, and anger fizzed and flared inside her. "Where do you think you're going?"

"Three guesses!"

The childish reply grated, but she swallowed, and made a supreme attempt.

"OK, Ambrose, the song's finished now – and dinner's ready. I got it specially, you know – it's Luxury Range! Don't let it go to waste!" He seemed to make an effort in his turn, judging by the gurnings that passed across his face as rapidly as any facial expressions could cover the disquieting distance between brow and chin. He turned off the radio, and sat down again, the book pushed to one side.

"What are you reading now?" She narrowly failed to keep acerbity out of her tone.

"You wouldn't understand."

"Now how do you know I wouldn't understand? Have you ever tried to discuss your books with me? I'm not stupid, you know. Go on - try me!"

He sighed heavily and started to explain, but within a few multi-syllabic moments she had indeed lost the track, and this aggravated her. Either she really was stupider than her son – and she had been near the top of most classes at school – or he was confusing her deliberately, to make her look foolish. She knew which explanation she believed. She turned away to cover her annoyance, trying to think of something clever to say, and ladled curry shortly into two of her prized Royal Worcester bowls, a legacy from her parents. He had stopped talking, and for once was looking at her directly as she placed the steaming bowl in front of him. Was he smirking?

"You see?"

"OK, Ambrose – you win! You've had your little laugh at my expense! I hope you feel better for it - that you're pleased with yourself!" Silence fell, full (she was sure) of smirking, while he dipped a spoon carelessly into the curry and stirred it around gloomily. Some of the sauce splashed onto the table, and she stared at it, her hands itching for a damp cloth. He wasn't eating! Her highly regulated jaws touched tensely, like old electric wiring.

"What's wrong with the curry?"

"I've decided to become a vegan. I can't eat this shite!"

A whole new chasm opened up inside her, to unite with thousands of others. But this one felt different somehow - larger, wider, deeper, darker. Some switch clicked inside - this one was overload. Added to all the others it was suddenly too much. Whatever it was about his special surliness, or her tiredness, or her balance of hormones, or the weather - whatever, it felt in that instant like the ultimate ingratitude, the last intolerable example of Ambrose's awfulness – an insult just too far after her thoughtfulness of that evening (and all evenings for twenty-three of the best years of her life).

The exchange exemplified her whole self-sacrificing existence – all his shortcomings as son, and as a (pathetic excuse for a) man. Bitter resentment at the way he had behaved that evening, and always, ignited in her like spillage at a petrol station, and in that unguarded instant her town tones relapsed into the Corconian cadences of childhood. She threw her fork onto the table, which made him start, and actually shouted – so loudly that Sandra Gulliver next door heard her even above the televised snooker -

in that moment of release forgetting all she had ever told him about manners. Veins cabled on Fidelma's slender neck, and her hands gripped the edge of the table until they went beyond white.

"How dare you? How dare you sit there, and say that, to me? Here I am, all day, every day – thinking of you – working for you – buying things for you – paying for you – explaining you – putting up with your rudeness and ignorance! I've had about as much as I can take from you, Ambrose! You are the rudest, most ignorant... most... most useless son anyone could have! I'm ashamed of you! I've always been ashamed of you! You have no idea how to behave – you can't get a job – you don't have any friends – you can't even get a girlfriend! To think of all of the things your Dad and I went through for you! All that dirt, and disgust – all that shame, and pain! And what have I ever got in return? No – shut up, Ambrose! I'll tell you! It's about time you were told! NOTHING – nothing, do you hear? – except rudeness – ignorance – selfishness – weirdness – swearwords – and – and mud all over the floor! And for Christ's sake why can't you even put your coat on the hook properly?"

It was appalling, and she knew it – tasteless, vulgar, undignified, and she knew that too – but she couldn't help herself – especially as she saw that Ambrose was sitting there stunned, for once listening, realizing her frustrations, noticing that she too had needs. But in the same second, she stopped, stunned by the unforgivability of what she had said - and the knowledge that it could never be retracted. And she had seen, too, that his face was wide open in shock and hurt, his chin trembled, and for a couple of seconds a frightened baby seemed to peer out through those large light blue lenses before the security shutters came clanging down, this time with a terrible sense of finality. Closing down... closing down...

She stood aghast at herself as he rose wordlessly, picked up his Royal Worcester bowl and threw it at the wall. Even the sound of crashing china sounded muffled in the sudden silence, and she watched paralysed as he put on his still soaking jacket and padded over to the back door, leaving a new muddy trail.

"Ambrose - wait...!" she managed to croak, but maybe the words never came out, because her throat was constricted, her mouth dry, her lips numb. The heavy door banged to, but that was heard as if underwater... and then her senses came back with a cold surfacing, and hot tears pushed disastrously through her make-up. What had she said, what had she done, she asked herself over and over – Useless... disgust... ashamed... She couldn't, she simply couldn't, have said those words! Could she? She had... Oh my God, Ambrose, I didn't mean it!

She dashed to the door and threw it back, looking for him, to call him back, to beg him to come back, so she could explain, apologise, ask for forgiveness, so they could start again - but all there was outside was wind, and sleet, beating into her face, battling with her for the door, howling up the hallway - and all she saw before she managed to push the door shut again was her usually familiar garden, disturbingly transformed into an older field-self, the prinked lawn whistling and rushing away vertiginously to the black line of watching conifers, behind which was the glow of the town like an inferno.

Ambrose was out there in that - out in that new-old place, somewhere in a suddenly strange town - and her words were out there with him, riding on his shoulders, flaying his sides, and whispering in his ears like a goblin. She pressed her back against the door, and her head and the palms of hot hands, listening to the wind and hating it, staring for long minutes into miserable space...

Now, several hours after, the kitchen cleaned, the broken bowl discarded (not without regrets), the mascara mended, she was in control again. But the long-case clock was telling two in Westminster chimes - three-and-a-half hours past her bedtime. There had been no news from him - although that in itself was normal - but the pubs had been closed for hours. Where could he have gone on such a night - with nowhere to go, no friends, without any food, or even a coat? Where on earth?

DESCENT FROM THE CROSS

Deathly wetness filtered through Ambrose's frame – but he burned with personal fire. The macerating wind – the insistent sleet – the slimy mud – stones – spines and thorns – all of these had scourged his skin, but now he was above these things and everything else, as he lay with his face pushed deeply into a bramble bush. An ugly and unimportant existence had been stripped away, it seemed, left hanging like rags on outstretching branches. He felt peeled, and pure.

His eyes stayed screwed shut, because he knew the second he opened them he would re-enter the world he had so lately left, and so little regretted. And what, in any case, could possibly be more wonderful to see than that which he had just seen? What more glorious? What more terrifying?

Yet again he relived the confused prologue to his prostration – those last few hundred metres of ascent, the most difficult distance he had ever travelled. In his imagination, he wiped again the hail off the frozen muscles of his face, felt the rasping in his throat and the aches in almost every sinew, smelt salt crystals being smashed in the coves below, saw again the swirling orange-brown that made stones assume the shapes of slumbering beasts, and bubbled around the slender shaft of the Cross. He heard again that reckless roaring of the gale with its answer in the pines, and then its deafening cessation – when the fog of his journey had lifted so unexpectedly, and there had been a single heart-stopping last explosive noise as if rocks were being… ripped.

Cerements of cloud had dissolved, and stars invisible for days became brilliantly apparent. Their sharp beauty had impaled him. He had grinned in delight as comets visible only to him raced in with startling news from the Oort Cloud. And all this time the Cross had stood tall above and in front, touching him with its stretching shadow, silently silver and stark, glistening with cold and comet-light – waiting. Waiting. All breath suspended... suspended... suspended... sus...

And then… incredible! A miracle!... the hugest of huge movements, and Something had come…

Bushes trembled, then parted, and a tree tilted to an acute angle. The concrete base of the cross cracked wide, and through the growing gap a crooked crown of vegetation started to lift itself, and as it moved it had seemed to the awed Ambrose that it was... hair. He fell flat forward, pole-axed with dread, but somehow although his face was hidden he could still see – and see much, much more than he had ever seen before.

An apparition rose up, and up, and up, effortlessly, endlessly - with a long slow smoothness, stones and soil tumbling down its flanks as it grew and altered its appearance into Someone Ambrose knew, and feared in every fibre. He felt he had spent his life expecting - and avoiding - this moment.

And still it grew, greater and greater, until it was taller than the Head and had planted itself in the sea. The thing, through which comets could curiously still be seen, started to unite with the sky, and Ambrose saw that two points he had thought planets were actually eyes. And such eyes, brighter than Polaris... orbs that could encompass universes, organs of impossible experience and fathomless futurity. Eyes that constantly changed their size and colour, in which Ambrose could read cosmologies, and tales of vanished civilizations – eyes that slowly turned their deep regard upon him and stripped away all, leaving Ambrose an ecorché, bloody and raw, transfixed on a cruel spike, giddy above a geography of gulfs.

And yet the eyes were also personal. Somewhere in the depths of all that time and space Ambrose saw a certain sorrow, a mercy, almost a fellow-feeling, as if this stupendous star-eyed Person could comprehend how hard it was to be him, loser of losers Ambrose, in his bolloxed Ireland – how hard to be anyone, anywhere, in such a world. Amongst the innumerable items the eyes had seen or were seeing was him, and he was shriven – ashamed of his smallness, his weakness, his transgressions, the things he had not done and would never do, the things he had never known, or even been able to imagine. One tiny part of him resented the intensity of this examination, and jerked reflexively, but he was pinned like a beetle on a museum board – and most of him relished this ray that played on all his secrets, that came to clear the cataracts of his life, disinfect Man's estate. He squirmed and shouted in a sort of ecstasy – he felt a pain that passed physics and lost itself in pleasure...

... an interval...

... while galaxies were generated and eras were extinguished... until through the pain at last had come numbness as all infections were cut away, all bleeding staunched, all hurts made well. And he was clean, clean, clean in a way he had never been clean before, clean like a mineral spring on a new-minted star, clean-ringing as a sounding brass, or a tinkling cymbal. Words and phrases he did not remember having heard ever before came crowding, and he rolled them relishingly on his tongue, as the wonderful eyes held his and comets wheeled in the most translucent of all skies that had ever been, or would be...

His eyes flicked open at last, as the cold infiltrated into him, and the quotidian world insisted on being heard. It was as dank and anti-climactic as he had dreaded. No comets! No stars! No sky! Nothing supernal, no supernature – just nature, and that of the most uncomfortable kind, with its dreary murk through which a dozen Januarys were blowing – melancholy precipitation, unyielding earth, black branches – and, just visible close by, a bare and beaten cross, made of the most ordinary concrete mixed by the most profane labourer. He was squatting, shivering on a dead planet.

And yet now he was more than he had ever been.

So much more that he couldn't begin to comprehend – and the growing knowledge thrilled through and enkindled him until his skin felt like it was steaming. What remained of his clothes clung unpleasantly – they had never been comfortable, and now they were sodden and torn. He might as well not have anything on at all... and the observation became action, as he stood up and cast off the tatters until he stood revealed and relieved. It seemed only appropriate that his contemptible body should be as new and naked as his mind. He threw away with cathartic contempt his jacket, his shirt, trousers, socks and shoes and underwear – it didn't matter that his jacket contained his wallet, and his cards, his Smartphone, the house keys. Who could care about such things in this sudden world? He had been reborn, freed from all burdens, or all except one – and that felt to him more like a joyous responsibility, a great privilege reserved to him, of all the world. He laughed out loud, and stretched his long limbs languidly through the sleet, one after the other, watching as the drips exploded and slimed around his nakedness. He laughed again, and again - then looked down to where the town should have been visible, to find that after all it was. Fog was forsaking the heights at last, and he could see the lighted line of the promenade curving northwards towards the city – the latter an angry orange penumbra basking in its own pollution.

He stood and stared for ages, almost oblivious to the physical world. What did that matter at this stage in history? This was a Moment among Moments. The scheme of his life had been remade in a few seconds. Or hours. Or years. He – he alone, of all the people of the town, all the people of the city, all the peoples of all cities – had seen Beyond. So now he clicked to a different calendar. He had a notion that when he got down to the town everything would have altered – and he would be in a different century, moving with secret knowledge among different, and much finer people.

And so after a time he went down from the heights, angels aiding him. Or so it felt. The stones and spines that had scored him – the springs that had doused him – the mud that had betrayed his feet – the trees that had tried to trip and tangle him in their roots – all now seemed tamed, slicked downhill, and he progressed down the track as painlessly and easily as if in Stephen's Green in summer. He stood on the same stones and they did not cut him, brushed against the same branches and they stroked his cheeks like the woman's hand he had never felt, passed below the same thrashing trees but now they were whispering of boundless Love – and when he got down to Head House, he was lifted over the wall and his unprotected feet landed as lightly on the concrete road as if he had been a kitten.

The roads were carless, still, enchanted all along their length. Nothing moved beneath the streetlights save him - and he was more Spirit than flesh! The villas that had seemed so heartless and cold, domiciles for the dull, now looked like soul shelters – the glowing fanlights a symbol of the divine spark Ambrose now realised resided within each dwelling, and subsisted in all hearts. In one house, ironically named "Mon Repos", the curtains downstairs were open, even though it was almost dawn, and a man sat staring so intently at pornography from Thailand that he didn't see Ambrose standing in the garden, looking in long and lovingly at the seeker so athirst for God's gestalt that it was getting between him and his repose. Ambrose glowed radioactive with warmth, smiled beatifically and lifted his hand in benediction...

It was then the man turned, sixth sense or coincidence, to see in the spilling electric light, immediately outside his window, in his garden, at 6.24 am on a disconsolate morning, a completely naked man with a mud- and blood-smeared face and a manic grin, his hand raised as if to throw a stone. His heart jumped, he shouted "Jesus!" and, recoiling from the vision, he fell backwards over his chair and knocked himself out on the corner of the grate. It was 6.26 when Ambrose left the garden, after first pressing his nose to the glass to stare in the greatest possible satisfaction at the dramatic outcome of his first conversion.

He almost floated over the garden wall with the wonder of it. To think that he (contemptible he, Despicable He) had had such might put into his hands that merely uplifting one of them could overfill a strong man with The Light! What a privilege! What a responsibility! He would need to exercise his new powers wisely – but he had obviously been granted them for some great Purpose, a brilliant and benign Purpose. He almost danced with gratitude. The late-night seeker would be the first of very many who would be put back on the right road – and because specially singled out, specially blessed. He had looked so wonderfully peaceful lying there… When the man awoke at last, Ambrose knew he would feel totally different.

It was just a few unpeopled streets from there to home, but he moved very slowly and sensually, feeling each crack in the paving with his toes, sensing the hum of the universal order below his bare soles, anticipating all the things he would do for all the unknowing seekers. He stood in the middle of one street, with his arms outstretched level with his shoulders, and turned round and round again, then faster, and faster again, and yet faster, until all the houses became one terrace, and all directions the same. It was considerably later when he got to his house, but he still felt dizzy, so he stood for a moment at the end of the driveway looking at the old place with his peeled, pure eyes. The front faced east, and the house looked ordered and attractive in the brilliant but brittle orange of a new day. The Light had come home with him!

The last time he had seen this place, he seemed to remember, there had been some kind of trouble. He seemed even to recall flying from it, running unprepared into a certain winter's night centuries ago. He remembered darkness and doubt, hurt and hatred, some urgent errand - but why and what that errand might have been he could not recall, and did not care. What was certain was that never before had he walked up this driveway with such a sense of direction, such satisfaction. He had come Home, and it felt like the first time. Although his body was drooping with fatigue, his spirits were stratospheric, and he stopped to bow in thanks to the blackbirds heralding his homecoming from all the Earth's trees.

He could not think where his keys had gone, but it didn't matter, because a light was on inside, now pale against the Day. So he banged greatly on the door, the hail of a hero, an exiled king returning to claim his own - and the sudden thumping almost bounced Fidelma off her chair, where she had fallen at last into a troubled doze just a few minutes earlier. After seconds of incomprehension, her dry eyes clicked wide, and she raced down the hall and threw back the door.

No wind now, no sleet; and there on the step stood Ambrose, swaying, black against the dawn – and she cried in relief. But even as the exclamation escaped, she registered that he was naked – smeared with filth, and clearly intoxicated. He beamed with brilliant benevolence, half-turned and waved his arm to indicate the garden, and as the sun made her eyes smart, he was declaiming the wildest nonsense. "Awaken, Fidelma, awaken! Behold - it is the Morning of the World!" Saying which, he slid gently to the ground.

OLD MEDICINES

Fidelma was more perturbed than usual. On a normal day, if any day spent even partly with Ambrose could be called normal, it was rare to see his scowling face before 1pm, and neither shouting nor reason had ever proved effectual in altering his habits. But now, just a few hours after his spectacular reappearance, and despite obvious exhaustion, he was fidgeting and fretful. One of her Valiums had calmed his carphology, but every time she peeked into the room, his head swivelled towards her, his eyes glittered, and he was muttering things. Bizarre things! Crazy things...

She had bent over twice to listen – but this had been a mistake, because on both occasions he had unexpectedly bellowed out the words, to startling effect. But whether shouted or sotto voce, the things he was saying were disjointed, nonsensical things of a kind she had never heard him say before, could never have imagined of him. "Mission" – "renewing" – "healing hands" – "The Light"... All kinds of nonsense, obviously from one of his films. Clearly, whatever drugs had been given him were still working through the tangled forests of his mind. To think he had walked along the road NAKED! She thanked the God in which she did not believe that it had been so early, and a Sunday. She shuddered to imagine how busy Sandra Gulliver's clacking tongue would have been if she'd seen Ambrose in his Adamic state.

Dragging Ambrose's naked form into the house from the doorstep had been a daymare, with the prospect of an early pedestrian happening past at any moment. She was a small woman, and he had seemed remarkably heavy for so skinny a boy. She had almost come several times to frustrated tears as she tugged and tugged and he slid along a lumpen half inch at a time. And where to look? Her pink babe had been implanted into a hirsute and horrid stranger. It was strange she should never have registered this before, because she bought many of his clothes, and carried his measurements on a little card in her purse, between her phone top-up card and her coffee-house loyalty card. Somehow it was only now she finally realized Ambrose had become a man – physically, at least. Her effort was accompanied by an agony of embarrassment – she had not been able to concentrate fully until she had rolled him in a sheet to hide his shame (this also made it easier to slide him along). He had looked so eerie swathed in white – it was too like a shroud, and he had been so dreadfully cold - that even then she had not liked to look at him. And yet as she heaved and pushed, even through tears and his smears she noticed that his face looked calm and clear. As she bent over him, for a moment their pose mirrored a small olive wood Pietà that hung on the wall, brought back from Fátima by Mary.

She had manhandled him finally to the foot of the stairs, and then mercifully he had opened his eyes (she could not help feeling annoyed that he had left it so late). Then he actually smiled. It was a smile she didn't particularly like, remote and impersonal, as if intended for someone behind or above her. But she had not seen him smile for such a long time - and he had known her, because he had murmured, "Bless you, Fidelma…"

He had never blessed anyone before, to her knowledge. Nor had he ever called her by her first name. It added to the sense that it was not really Ambrose, but some stranger who was now struggling to a sitting and then a wobbly standing position in her hallway. But she said nothing, just helped him slowly up the stairs to his room, checking that the sheet was neither impeding his feet nor showing his shame. Pushing him down eventually on his bed, she had laved his face and hands with hot water. She had not wanted to touch any more of his body, although she rued the mud and bloodstains he was depositing on pillows and duvet. She broke open her brand-new first-aid kit and took his temperature. She was surprised to find it normal, and even slightly disappointed, because that would have been a symptom of something. She dabbed his brows with homeopathic ointment, then sat on the edge of the bed and massaged her aching arm and neck muscles while she tried to assimilate the night's events, and wondered what to do. When she thought he was drifting off to sleep, she took a shower to wake herself - but when she looked in again, he had been as he had remained ever since - rocking and muttering, exhausted, novelty-doll-like. She was reminded uncomfortably of Fergus at the end.

Ambrose had disregarded the food she had brought – even though she had avoided meat, after his outburst the previous evening. Even the cappuccinos he had always expected at particular times were ignored, cooling slickly by the side of the bed. She could not help feeling annoyed that she had gone to the trouble of making them, dirtying cups for no reason, but still she said nothing. It was vital not to upset him today, to let him sleep it out. But he was clearly not ready to rest, and several times she had needed to push him back into bed and tuck him in yet again. Every time he tried to rise he seemed stronger, and of course she could not prevent him getting up eventually. It was vexing to the edge of tears, especially after her own lack of sleep, but it could not be helped. She tried reason, but he seemed oblivious – that was like him, anyway. Even when she had finally lost her temper and told him "Snap out of it!" he had just looked through her. She thought for an uncomfortable moment of Mary in her transport, her transparency.

He sat on the bed, wearing pyjamas she had extricated from a long unopened drawer, with his long feet splayed flat, and his head dully down between drawn-up skinny shanks. His voice was unusually clipped and precise, but what it expressed was arrant nonsense. "I must needs take up my bed and walk. I have a Great Work to undertake". He must have been given some very powerful stuff, she thought, wondering again whether she ought to call the doctor. But then what if there were drugs in his blood? That might mean the Gardaí.

She sat across the room from him, below a huge poster advertising a Japanese anime festival, in which a Europeanized hero was firing a ray gun at a mass of monsters. The garish colours clashed repulsively with the wall – but then almost any artwork would have clashed with his purple and black colour scheme.

Ambrose raised his head and surveyed all round, and he did not seem to like what he saw either – because he stood, unsteady still, and crossed to where his mother was seated. Stretching above her, he pulled down the poster with an effort, and cast it into the middle of the floor. He added a similar poster from the opposite wall to the pile, and then a limited edition photographic print of several almost naked women, for which he had paid a very substantial amount for someone who was so rarely in employment.

Fidelma had never approved of these artworks, so was secretly pleased as well as surprised. She looked on in silence; best to let him get it out of his system. She was even more surprised to see him turning his attention to his bookshelves. Soon armfuls of books, many of which she knew had been very expensive, were teetering precariously in the centre of the floor. She interjected gently. "Ambrose – maybe you should leave this until tomorrow?"

"I must needs brook no delay – I will not be able to repose in a bedchamber festooned with such productions." Again the same weirdly precise phraseology and pronunciation, and the archaic expressions. Her lips straightened; he was taking the mickey! But she held her peace, went along with his game.

"Ambrose – seriously now! You're not yourself!"

He dropped more books onto the pile, then turned to face her. "You are correct, woman – I am not myself. And I am surpassing pleased not to be myself! I have become..." He stopped. "Well, that will become clear. All I will vouchsafe at this juncture is to reiterate my late assertion that I will not be able to rest in this room until it no longer contains these... idols."

The last word was filled with extremest contempt, of the kind usually reserved for priests, TDs, Gisela Mildew, and sports fans. He scooped more books from the shelves. The shelves were mostly empty now, and the walls had unfaded purple rectangles to show where pictures had been. She sighed. In certain ways she knew him well. "OK, Ambrose – let's make a deal. If we get these books and other things out of your room, will you go back to bed and rest?"

He nodded, and so in several silent, strenuous journeys they collected the things from the floor and toted them downstairs, stacking them neatly in a corner of the kitchen. "We'll worry about them tomorrow," Fidelma told him firmly, and he nodded again. Then without saying another word, he plodded back up the stairs, and all went quiet. Too quiet?

She peered surreptitiously into his room. The central light was on, but he was at last deeply asleep, still wearing the shoes he had put on to port the stuff downstairs. She took them off and he didn't stir, so she pulled the blankets over him. He looked atrociously vulnerable with just his head sticking out, and she stood looking down at him for a few minutes thoughtfully, then bent down to kiss his forehead – something she hadn't dared to do for about two decades. Even now, it was the pointiest of pecks. Embarrassed by her emotion, she went down to the kitchen.

She considered the large pile of books ruminatively, and picked up one to examine the elegance of its production. *The Anatomy of Melancholy*. What a strange book - paragraph-long sentences, and made up almost completely of lists of disasters. A moan hundreds of pages long, written in an antiquated and affected style. Why had anyone ever wanted to write such a negative book, even in the bad old days? Even more to the point, why would anyone today want to read such a book, when there were so many uplifting books available, and more produced every day? She put it back with its weird fellows.

How strange that a collection so expensive and so laboriously assembled, so frequently and deeply read, so heavily annotated by their owner (a habit that annoyed his mother) had all been discarded in just a few minutes of clarity. This was some new whim, obviously. But what form would it take this time? She had spent so much of her life trying to second-guess his fads. Maybe he would change his mind tomorrow, and put the books back. If he did, she would pretend she hadn't noticed – if he didn't, off they would go to the charity shop. It seemed a moderate approach, and she was pleased by her judiciousness. Now she would go to bed. It had been quite a day – and she had work tomorrow. As she undressed before getting into the bath, she listened hard, but there was a hard silence over the house - a silence that hummed like a pylon.

*

The following morning, he stayed in bed, tired and taciturn - but she preferred that state of mind to that of the day before. He had met her eyes for a few seconds, and then looked down at the floor, saying in answer to her questions that he felt quite well, that he wanted to do some serious thinking, promised that he wouldn't leave the house, and that yes, she ought to go to work, and he would be fine. He had even chewed thoughtfully at some toast she had brought. So she thought she would risk it, but left her work number by the phone, and made him promise to call if he needed anything - which he had agreed to do, slightly testily.

The office took her out of herself, as it always had. There was something about other people's tax problems that she found vastly soothing, as well as fascinating – perhaps especially as she herself did not need tax advice (or even a salary). She had always liked maths - and she felt, too, that she provided a kind of humanitarian service, by allowing people to achieve financial and life goals. The job seemed to provide insights into the very nature of things - the transactions and negotiations that shaped the world - and by expediting these exchanges she felt like an engineer of modernity. She also enjoyed the interchanges with the other staff - delightfully unaware that her nickname was "Fartelma".

As she piloted the Audi homewards through a torrent of traffic, she realized guiltily that she hadn't thought about Ambrose for several hours. She would make up for it by being especially kind and thoughtful. She was looking forward to seeing him in a way she hadn't done for years, anticipating a quiet evening spent watching some nice programme with him while he recouped his strength. She would watch something he wanted to see – it was a night to be more than usually self-sacrificing.

But even before she opened the front door, she could smell the paint. Paint? "Ambrose? Ambrose?" No reply, so she pursued the odour, which became much stronger as she mounted the stairs. The door of Ambrose's room was open and the light on, and there was a brilliant glare. She gasped.

Even on the sunniest of mornings, light venturing into that purple-black gloom was benumbed and beaten down, but now even though it was dark outside, the room dazzled and danced with pure white light, still wet gloss, all bearing the appearances of having been painted in great haste. She looked aghast at all the streaks and drips, and the areas where the purple and black were imperfectly covered. The shelves were still there but gleamingly empty, and all the remaining artworks had disappeared, or been painted over. One of the eyes of a Slovak transvestite musician on a poster had escaped being coated, and looked out even more weirdly than before from a whirlpool of white. The wardrobe and chests were all open, and empty, and they had all been daubed in the same merciless white – as had the bed and even the bedding! Egyptian brushed organic cotton (50 Euros a set)...

"Ambrose? Ambrose? Come here this minute!"

As for the deep carpet, Ambrose clearly had not meant to paint it, but there was so much Cloister Crème adhering to it that he had evidently been unable to avoid walking some of it along the landing and into the bathroom. Here he had also dropped a heavy-laden paintbrush, which he had forgotten to retrieve after over-enthusiastic and badly-aimed urination. (As usual, he had not flushed.) She covered her face, and counted to twenty, a trick she had when under severe stress – but it was no more effective than it ever had been, because when she got to twenty-one the scene had not changed in a single detail. This couldn't be happening! Why oh why had she left him alone? She darted downstairs half-dazedly in search of the culprit, and as she did there was a new smell – one intrinsically sinister. Smoke...

It could have been much worse, she would reflect later, as she lay like a clothes-peg in bed – but at the time it had seemed like the worst thing in the world to see through the open kitchen door Ambrose standing in the bitter back garden using her best spade to stir a huge fire in the barbecue brazier – and he was naked again!

In the red rush and flare, the intensity of his attention, and the white paint that had adhered to large areas of his body, he looked to her horrified gaze like some sort of shaman, brewing up demons millennia ago somewhere very far away from Dublin's dormitory suburbs.

Sandra Gulliver was staring over the garden wall, scandalized, thrilled. The smoke was poisonously plastic, and Fidelma saw he was incinerating his clothes, his books, his DVDs, his CDs. A Siberian draught was passing through the kitchen and through the house, carrying dioxin-stink everywhere and up the stairs where it warred with the paint. Ambrose noticed her open-mouthed observation at last and called out in innocent pleasure – "Behold! The Bonfire of the Vanities! So passeth all flummeries! Soon with God's help we shall light such a fire in this land as will spread through all the kingdoms of the earth!" Faced with this incendiary prospect, all Fidelma could do was stand and cry at the ruin of her evening, and her house.

GETTING BACK TO BASICS

The stairs still smelt of paint, and when Fidelma looked closely at the carpet she could see the spectres of splatters – but the men had done a good job cleaning up the mess and repainting Ambrose's room. The boy – more than ever *boy* after this! – had insisted that his room should be completely white and "contemplative", and Fidelma had agreed readily, in the hope it might settle him to have his room just the way he wanted it. Besides, a bit of sensible spirituality would calm him down. She had cunningly secreted some healing crystals in his room.

Fidelma had taken a few days off work until Ambrose could safely be left alone again. She had told her manager a fib about Ambrose being in a minor car accident, because she did not want to mention certain phrases that were on her mind a lot – "nervous breakdown", "schizophrenia", "mental health issues". While of course her line manager would have been terribly sympathetic, and would *never* have judged, Fidelma had a shrewd foreboding it would not be advantageous to be associated with such phraseology. She had also wanted to ensure that Ambrose was kept away from the men doing the painting work. She had always been slightly ashamed of him - and ashamed by her shame. Now if only she could have back the old Ambrose she thought she could have been content. At least he could have been relied upon to wear clothes when he walked around the house!

To make matters worse, he had not bathed or shaved since that night, and there was a discernible darkening of his usually sallow epidermis. She even thought she could detect a faint fetidness in the air as he approached and after he had passed, as if from an old, damp dog. (They had never kept a dog, partly because Fidelma had such a sensitive nose, but also because she was quietly terrified of them. The thought of their hot and sticky tongues and dirty paws always made her perspire. And cats were little better... all those hairs floating innocently everywhere, their constant licking of their... areas, the way the Gullivers' sneering ginger animal used to dig and defecate amongst Fidelma's equally spaced organic herbs.)

Ambrose now was even more like a half-tamed house animal, or a wood kern - a shambling presence that might at any moment do *anything*....

Those few days at home had not been restful ones. Fidelma had always been a desultory sleeper, but now she found herself patrolling the house at all times, taking in every detail with quick eyes, listening with all her might, resenting having to be awake, having to be there at all, thinking about work piling up in her office. The painters had gone, but Ambrose's indecency could still be visited upon her, as he had started wandering too, his padding tread and her quicker slippered steps often criss-crossing and echoing each other through the expectant rooms and passageways of the smallest hours. On one occasion they had met on the landing at 3.17, but luckily Fidelma had just come out of her bedroom and she was able to dart back in quickly with just the faintest squeak of fright.

Now that she thought about it, perhaps Ambrose had always had body issues. He had always avoided sports gear, as well as the sports themselves. He had never been known to wear shorts – even though she had bought him some lovely designer ones over the years. She sighed at the thought of the money she had wasted trying to make him look normal. (More normal.) But whatever clothes she did prevail upon him to wear – howsoever elegant, howsoever many celebrity endorsers or tiny tailoring details – they just hung from him, like seaweed thrown into a tree.

She had double-locked the front door and hidden the mortice key, and all the window keys, so he couldn't wander casually out into the front garden or the road. He could have climbed out over the back wall had he wanted to, but so far thankfully that apparently hadn't occurred to him. It was a quiet road, not dangerous – but his presence might have endangered public peace of mind, because since he had incendiarized all his clothes he had needed to resort to blankets and sheets as what he now insisted on calling "raiment". These were not entirely satisfactory. She shuddered at a few of the sights she had seen of late.

Fidelma knew Sandra next door was keeping a watch for further excitements, because sometimes if she was out in the garden she would look up quickly at the Gulliver house and see a flicker of movement, where her neighbour had just let fall a curtain or stepped back out of sight. She wondered whether she should go in and have a word – explain that Ambrose had been drugged and was having a few problems, but that he would be fine, and that she (Fidelma) would really appreciate it if she (Sandra) could keep things to herself until he got better, speaking as one mother to another… But she could not pluck up the courage to abase herself to that extent, especially to someone who was not quite - well, someone who had *such* curtains. She also guessed shrewdly that Sandra would probably not be amenable to appeals for motherly solidarity. Her parrot face, her calculating eyes, and her defensively folded plump arms somehow did not convey kindness. In any case, she had probably already told everyone. Fidelma thought of all the times she had been complicit in Sandra's vicious asides about other Tara Road residents, and determined that she would never join in tittle-tattle again. Almost certainly not.

And what if Ambrose didn't get better? She couldn't afford to take too much time off work – well, she could manage, but Dubai would have to wait. In any case, she enjoyed her job, and could she cope with being in Ambrose's company so much? He was even more different now than he had been before. Besides, she had so many other commitments, like night school. It would get so boring just sitting at home, when she could be facilitating Emotional Openness through Oneness.

Ambrose had slept in the front room for a couple of days while the repainting was going on. It had really been more staying than sleeping – for when she had looked in late on the first night, he had been sitting yogically in the middle of the carpet, legs crossed, hands on knees, palms uppermost, staring out of the window down on the electric prospect of the town. He was wearing one of her dressing gowns, but nothing else – and it was much too small, much too pink, and it boasted rather too many images of kittens. It also had a distressing tendency to gape open as he shuffled around the house and out into the back garden to stare at the sky, or the Head, and nod sagely as if agreeing with someone who wasn't there.

The door had squeaked as she had opened it that night, and he must have heard, but he didn't react as she insinuated into the room to peer from the side. His eyes were open, and she could see a tiny version of the town reflected in his pupils, but he didn't look at her. His chest moved slightly; otherwise he was abnormally immobile, scarcely even seeming to blink. She stared into his face until her own eyes ached – but his eyes remained still and full, minuscule mirrors of neon follies.

"Ambrose? Ambrose?" she whispered, and the sibilance seemed to run round the room, chasing into the corners, but he did not register her. What was going on behind those screens? Baffled and hurt, after a few minutes she had sidled off to bed, where she had scarcely more sleep than he did. The next night it had been the same, so when he was able to go back into his room, she had been pleased not to see him emerge again for almost ten hours.

When he did emerge, he looked terribly thin, even by his standards, and his eyes even more protuberant. This was hardly surprising, as he had eaten nothing except dry bread and drunk nothing but water for several days. She was very worried about his stools, and had asked him several times, but he would just smile his new, distant, detestable smile. But at least he looked alert, and when she offered him a cup of tea made the way he preferred it, in his special mug with the skull on it, he looked kindly at her. She liked that look; it promised an easier kind of relationship between them, and when the time was right, and he was better, she would reciprocate appropriately. He stretched out his hand for the mug, looked intently at its decoration, and then shattered her hopes.

"Behold! A memento mori – 'tis meet! Surely this vessel has been given unto me as a sign and a token! Resurrection lieth beyond the Valley of Dry Bones!" The tea steamed as he looked fondly at the skull ornament. He raised the mug to his lips and drank it all down in one go. She winced – it had been very hot. But he did not wince, although his eyes were watering. "And thus I have quaffed of the cup that was proffered – and so I dedicate myself to the Task."

Fidelma unbent into a kitchen chair. Her voice came tired and tiny. "*What* task, Ambrose? Please tell me what you are talking about."

He stared in surprise. "Why, the Task, woman – Task with a capital T - the Great Renewal – the re-dedication of the Land to the Lord! What other task so worthwhile? All else is fiddle-faddle!"

She had heard these words and words like them frequently since Naked Night. "Woman" aggravated her especially - so dismissive, almost contemptuous. She drummed her nails on the table, and noticed that the polish was peeling. She counted to twenty, but as always things looked much the same when she got there.

"Look, Ambrose – this has got to stop! I've been very patient up 'til now – but you have to appreciate that you can't just disappear for a night, come wandering back through the town stark naked and talking like a madman, and then just expect me to understand! What happened that night? Where did you go? Who were you with? And what is this stupid Task, for Heaven's sake?"

She put her hand on his arm angrily, imploringly. Such skinny arms he had – unfit for any task, let alone one with a capital T! She found herself softening. "Please tell me. I want to understand, son – I want to help you." She hadn't called him "son" for nineteen years. But he turned away so her hand fell heavily back to her side, and looked out of the window at the distant Head.

"I cannot vouchsafe…" He stopped, and put his hand to his head. He swayed slightly, looked confused, lost, even frightened. "It hurts sometimes, Mum…"

She felt as if someone had turned on a lukewarm tap in her breast. "Oh, Ambrose, Ambrose! You need rest – a good long rest. Why don't you have something to eat – something small? Then go to the lavatory, and when you've finished there take yourself off to bed. Stay there as long as you like - there's no rush."

"But I have much to accomplish ere rest! Imps will interpose 'twixt me and the domain of Nod!"

She knew about work-anxiety. But of course hers was real work. She conquered another spasm of irritation. He wasn't well, he wasn't well! If only he would eat something, let his body do what it needed to do! What was it Dr. Kumiswaramy was always saying? Ah yes, "Clear colon equals clear cognition". (They were so much wiser in the East.) "Whatever it is you feel you have to do, Ambrose, it can wait another couple of days! Come on now, have something proper to eat, something to clear your system."

She piloted him over to the food cupboard, and opened it to reveal cornucopian contents. She started to pull down a bedazzling array of tins and packets, piling them on the counter. "Now you just put a bit of this into a bowl, with a banana and some soya substitute, and that'll get you going again. Just to make sure, take some of this too. And you should take a couple of these to keep away colds, and a bit of this to give you half your recommended daily intake of riboflavin and magnesium. Then you should take some of these berries. They've done wonders for my stress. And how about some of these? Ooh, and I'd forgotten I had these…"

The counter-top seemed too small for the array of packaging, but she kept pulling down more and more items in her eagerness to fulfil her son's needs. Ambrose picked up a pack of rice and opened it, and she was pleased. Then he filled his mouth with it, dry and uncooked as it was, and she was not pleased any longer. She remained displeased when he spat it out onto the floor.

"Our Mother does not eat such provender!"

"What are you talking about, Ambrose? Of course I eat rice! But you're meant to cook it first! Let me." She was amazed at her kindness and restraint, as she filled a saucepan with water and poured in fresh rice. She would cook him a meal he simply couldn't refuse, and after that maybe he would feel better, calmer, more sensible. No wonder he should be out of sorts with a stomach full of dry white bread, rotting away starchily in there, building up bubbles of wind where there should never be bubbles of any kind.

She took out more ingredients and began chirpily to describe the tasteful and nutritious meal she would cook, and her own description made her hungry. She turned around with a smile, saying, "Oh I forgot you don't eat meat any longer but what we can do instead..." – only to find that Ambrose wasn't there. It seemed he hadn't been there for some minutes because the swing door into the hall had stopped swinging. Her internal tap had been running cooler; now it ceased. She threw down her wooden spoon in exasperation – then she picked it up again and wiped up the tomato stain from the tiles. She needed to retain *control*, for both their sakes – and there was no need for the house to be a mess in any case.

She strained her ears. Nothing. She went into the hall, and she looked up the stairway. The familiar scene felt strangely sentient, as if something had just stopped happening, and would happen again when she wasn't watching - the walls displaying new and interesting angles, their pastel hues new troubling depths of intensity. Brooding... frowning... silence... Wait! What was that noise? She slipped noiselessly up the stairs as the ceiling seemed to arch vigilantly over.

The sound resolved itself into two parts – thudding and then an almost inaudible scrunch. As she came up the stairs, she saw something being thrown onto the landing from Ambrose's room, then the door was closed silently but firmly. She looked down in puzzlement at a drift of purplish fragments and dust – then realized they were the pulverized remains of the healing crystals from his room. But they had been under the bed; he must have been lying on the bare floorboards to spot them. The thudding must have been him stamping on them. The smithereens bothered her – they had been quite expensive, as was only to be expected for an authentic Glastonbury product. And what now would contain or mitigate all the negative energy flying around the house? Experts had proved that people couldn't sleep properly if they didn't have enough ions. They needed all the ions they could get in that house, with its north-facing bedrooms. (Or was it south?)

Ambrose's door jerked open, and he stepped out onto the landing and headed purposefully towards the bathroom without looking at her. As he stalked down the corridor she saw beads of blood on his heels where he had been cut by the crystal glass. The blood clashed appallingly with the pink of his (her) dressing gown. There were sounds from the bathroom – heavy movements, grunts, muttering, a hawk of spit, liquid spattering onto lino – and he came back and walked right by her again. The just-cleaned carpet now had tiny spots of blood and trampled-in purplish dust – and going into the bathroom she saw what she had expected to see. With a sigh, and a gag of nausea, she started to mop around the base of the bowl. But – she looked into the bowl to confirm her nose's testimony– at least he'd been!

LEVEL 3

He had been sleeping better, and Fidelma congratulated herself on having managed to conceal a Native American dream-catcher under his mattress. They so often gave results! He was also eating regularly, if abstemiously – very regularly, because he would materialize in the kitchen at exactly the same times each day. Exactly - which was extraordinary when she thought about it, as there was no clock in his room, and he never wore a watch. Yet there he would be, as precise as she, the two of them alike in that at least. The petite, precise, perfectly turned out woman stared quietly appalled across the table at a shambling beast wearing an array of items - some his, some hers, and sometimes even items of soft furnishings, like a towel around his waist, or a curtain draped diagonally over one shoulder, toga-like. Her Brown Thomas sillage warred with his silage undertones. Their meals sometimes seemed like a meeting of two stages of evolution; she smiled thinly at her own wit, and wished she had someone to share it with.

Not only was there no clock in his room, there was nothing in it at all - except the bed with its white bedding below the window with the always drawn blinds, and, as of yesterday, grass strewn all over the floor. This latter refinement had come about in the surreal fashion that was now becoming commonplace in 32 Tara Road. The previous morning, while chomping morosely on a hunk of dry bread, he had fixed her severely with his left eye and blurted, "Woman, like the Galilean I must needs have rushes 'twixt foot and floor, to confound the animalcules!"

It had taken several minutes to understand what he wanted, but when she did she had thought it best to humour him. Not only was this the best thing to do from a mental health point of view, according to just about every expert - but she worried what he might do if she thwarted him. The fixity of his face was at times deeply unnerving... his eyes shining, but hard and dead like pebbles on a beach.

Finding rushes presented quite a challenge. The grass in the garden had never dared to grow long enough under her absolutist eye - and there were no thatchers in the phone book. Why would there have been, she asked herself almost angrily. This wasn't Connemara! Eventually, she had bought some guinea pig bedding from the pet shop, and taken it out of its polythene packaging. She had been correct in her surmise that Ambrose, who had never evinced any interest in natural history, would probably not know the difference between rushes and Mr. Snuffly's Snuggle-Up. He had said nothing, but his eyes seemed momentarily softer, and he cast it onto the floorboards, and started to walk up and down on it with increasing speed, mouthing inaudible words. She shook her head and closed the door, just as he seemed to be about to break into a run. He slowed down gradually to a more contemplative pace - a literally ponderous padding that he kept up for ages, as his words started to become audible, almost like a chant - but still they made no sense - "Salmay, Dalmay, Adonai, Sator, Rotas, Ratapan, Shooby-Doo" - at least that was it sounded like, as she pressed anxious ears to his door.

It bothered her, having that grass there. When Ambrose had thrown it down, she had noted a cloud of dust that hung in the air for a few moments before dispersing - into the bedding, the blinds, crevices behind the skirting boards, even the paintwork, there to lie and grow and attract more, almost certainly to give rise to respiratory and hypoallergenic illnesses. She was sure it was full of insects too – despite Ambrose's assertion it would combat animalcules, and even Mr. Snuffly's assurances as emblazoned on the packaging. She had accordingly hidden insecticide in her bedroom, and whenever he left his room she would charge upstairs and dash around his room spraying the floor. Then she would race back downstairs, and sit at the kitchen table as if she had been there for hours, humming loudly if Ambrose was passing through. Another small skirmish in the never-ending war against infection!

He had also stipulated certain "foodstuffs" – chiefly dates, figs, unleavened bread, extra virgin olive oil. She had dutifully searched them out, and been surprised by their price - ironic that such ascetic food had such an epicurean price tag. She watched him sidelong as he smeared bagels with olive oil and chewed them with a pained expression. It was clear he wasn't enjoying the taste. But she said nothing, just observed him closely. At least the diet would keep him regular. (She was able to monitor his outcomes closely, because he still seemed unable to master the flush lever.)

Mother and son would sit at opposite ends of the table – him always at the end from which he could see the Head. She had soon noticed that his eyes kept flicking up there, and before long, she guessed where he had gone on the fateful night. After having watched him carefully for the length of several meals, she ventured to ask. "Is that where you went that night, Ambrose? Up there?" She indicated with her head.

He looked her gravely in the face, and swallowed a large chunk of bagel with a grimace before replying. "'Twas upon the Mount of Pines, aye."

She was becoming inured to the archaisms, and pushed her advantage. "And who were you with?" But he had subsided back into silence – a silence at odds with such lustrous eyes, which clearly had a great ferment going on behind them. Two minds were fighting in his face. His hands were trembling slightly. The combination reminded her uneasily of fanatics in TV dramas, like that award-winning one she had watched the other night, with that English actor who had been in that police drama. She chewed a fingernail – a childhood habit very recently resumed – while she tried to remember the actor's name. She almost forgot she had asked Ambrose a question, so nearly fell off her chair when he suddenly thrust back his chair with such force that it fell over and went skittering across the tiles. He stood staring eagerly out, his jawline ferro-firm, his eyes far-focused. "I was with…HIM!"

The last word was bellowed, and it even made Sandra Gulliver, sitting with her head always tilted hopefully towards the adjoining wall, start in her seat.

"Good heavens, Ambrose! Don't do that! You'll be the death of me! Who were you with? What was his name?" Fidelma wondered for a moment whether maybe Sandra had been right, and he had been on some assignation of the kind that were becoming almost fashionable. There was one of their bars in the town now, and she wrinkled her nose before hastily feeling ashamed of her distaste. But such ideas vanished as she looked up into his face, because it bore an expression that was both otherworldly and infinitely kind. There was nothing mundane, nothing carnal, in that look. In that moment, Ambrose looked decades older – ineffably experienced. He had an almost monumental quality, a distant grandeur and almost a beauty she had never seen before. She shook her head in pleased disbelief - and then he spoke, and she fell back to earth.

"DEATH, yes –" He rolled the word around, as if tasting a delicacy for the first time. "Yes, Death. That will be your lot – and sooner than thou knowest. That is Man's estate, and Woman that was taken from Man's ribcage must needs share in his doom. We all must pass away beyond the Elysian Fields. Yet I say unto ye that it is a joyous fate – a joyous fate.

Joyous, I say? Yeah, joyous – because those who die in grace will pass into heavens that are more than good! Good, you say? Good heavens only? In such judgement you err egregiously."

His egregious auditor opened and closed her mouth. When Ambrose resumed, his voice was slower, deeper, almost rumbling, stones rolling in a rising river. "And yet... and yet... I descry in thee a childish yearning for the Truth that will stand thee in good stead at the weighing of all worths. But those heavens, those celestial firmaments to which your unworthy self alludes, those are more than good! They are great – nay, they are Godly! They are the boundless mansions of the Divine Architect, and they are richly appointed – of marbles and obsidian and jasper and coral and fine stuffs are they made. And chalcedony – and frankincense and myrrh... They stand in illimitable olive groves extending even unto the universe's uttermost edge. Cherubim and seraphim stand there on guard with the flaming sword that faces in all directions – and henceforth at the uttermost end will ensue the Host that will return the right and just to... their right and just places... and banish the Angel of Light, the Dark Lord, to Level 3..."

He stopped, swayed, and sat, his sweating face in his hands. She rushed round the table and touched him on his bare shoulder. His skin was clammy and hot. He was whispering – "Beelzebub! Sauron!"

Fidelma couldn't place Sauron. Old Testament, obviously. It looked like this religious fixation wasn't going to go away soon. If it was religious – she had never played a computer game but knew Level 3 was a gaming term. It had been five days now, and his crazes normally only lasted a day or two.

There had been a time when she might have welcomed religiosity in him – it would at least have been categorisable. But this religion seemed positively dangerous in its ecstasy and obscurity. It was an extreme version of a socially acceptable eccentricity – like choosing to have pneumonia rather than a cold. How like Ambrose to be excessive! She wondered what to do. This new force needed to be tamed somehow, driven into channels rather than being allowed to foam madly about the land. Or - ugh! - about his mouth... there was drool at the corners of his lips, as he hunched at the table with his hands screwed into his eyes. She dabbed at the acrid bubbles and strings with kitchen towel, feeling slightly sick. Thank goodness for cleaning fluids!

Ground rules. Guidelines. Life-key words. Those were what he needed - what everyone needed. Religion always had to be organised, in case people took it too seriously. She would buy him a Bible, so that at the very least he would be exposed to more sensible, modern Christianity. Or, even better – she gasped at the serendipity – there was that new book by "Daddy Jimmy", the Irish Church's "Apostle to Youth" and a prolific author who was always at odds with the stuffy old hierarchy. Everyone was talking about it, and she had read a review in some unexpected journal. She Googled her mind for the title, then recalled it with a smile. How could she have forgotten? It was almost too clever: *Wicked Faith – RC 4 the 21 C*. It was selling amazingly well for a book by a Churchman. But it was admittedly a controversial book, and perhaps it needed to be balanced out by something more orthodox.

She had another inspired thought. She would get Mary to come and see him. Apart from being blood, she was as rooted and sensible as could be hoped for from someone who could believe in the possibility of Immaculate Conception. Mary's faith had almost always been of the reassuringly unintellectual kind - characterized by decorum rather than demonstrations. Grace before meals, silent prayers, good works, money for the black babies, macramé. Dad's kind of religion – Granny's kind of religion – and probably Great-Granny's too, going all the way back into the hoary prehistory of the 19th century. Fidelma saw with her decorator's eye a mélange of Ave Maria plus antimacassars, ivory and rosewood rosaries, Padre Pio prints in dark oak frames, stuffed songbirds under domes. Mary typified this old mainstream, this almost extinct establishment. She would be the ideal antidote to "Daddy Jimmy's" unorthodoxy.

All this zipped through her mind as she dabbed at Ambrose's drool, and then helped him up the stairs to his "cell". She wished he wouldn't use that word. He might use it one day when others were present, people who wouldn't understand, might think the worst of her. He collapsed on his bed, and she forced him to swallow some herbal remedy headache pills. Then she had some. They were very good tablets, except that they sometimes took several hours to have any effect. But Ambrose's snores at length became steadier, and so she crept out and drove down to the town.

She passed the Victorian villas that had given Ambrose so much food for thought; she had always seen them as eminently covetable. They were the kinds of houses that could make a person overlook other problems.

A Modern Journey

Their generous proportions and specifications reflected the expansive times in which they were upraised to house Dublin's newly prosperous. In one of these, there would be real scope for her furnishing talents. And such gardens... she saw them full of flourishing fuchsias and perfect grass, and heard passers-by making approbatory remarks about their owner's hard work and good taste.

She bustled into the shops looking for clothes for Ambrose – all white, as he had demanded. These were more difficult to get than she had imagined, so eventually she had recourse to the sports shop. Even there, the clothes all seemed to have logos of teams, but she did the best she could. She itched to buy him other clothes, expensive ones to demonstrate her love at this difficult time. There were so many lovely things, but seeing them just made her sad, because neither the old nor the new Ambrose would ever have appreciated them. Her hands moved among the clothes caressingly, and she quit the shop with considerable reluctance.

Town Tomes was the last surviving bookshop in town. She hadn't been in here since her Christmas visit, an annual ordeal when she would stare slightly helplessly at all the serried softbacks, hoping that the title or front cover illustration of one would suggest Ambrose might find it interesting. There were so many books in the world, but then that was a good thing, because everyone had a book in them, didn't they? (She would write hers one day.) But when it came to Ambrose, she had made quite a few bad choices over the years, and he had always told her. She had once bought what had looked like a highbrow book called *The History of Western Art* – but her eyes had unaccountably skipped over the words in smaller font – *Told For The Very Young*. Then there had been the time she had bought a black-bound book decorated with silver skulls at the time he had been reading about Aleister Crowley – only to find that it was a bestselling vampire novel for teenage girls. She had found that book on top of (not even in!) the dustbin that same Christmas Day – one of several Christmas Days when he had not bothered to buy a present for her. Although nothing was arguably better than his usual offering – cheap jewellery bought just before closing time on Christmas Eve from the ultra-downmarket jeweller in the High Street, often still with its price tag attached.

But she felt empowered today, because she knew exactly what she wanted, how to navigate in that sea of knowledge. She went to the Paranormal & Religions section - Korans, Kabbalas, Nostradamus, Old Moore's Almanac, yogic flying, astrology, leylines, Tarot, ear candling, colonic cleanliness (she had that one), and there right at the end was *Wicked Faith* – everything spiritual one could possibly need. The front cover was very clever - a medieval image of Jesus onto whom someone had Photoshopped low-slung trousers, a puffa jacket and a One Direction haircut. If that didn't get the youngsters crowding into church, nothing would!

As she drove the few miles to Oldtown and Mary's convent, she wondered how she should broach the subject. Mary hadn't seen Ambrose for years – and she hadn't even asked about him the last time the sisters had met. Aunt and nephew had never had anything in common – although there had never been any unpleasantness between them, just long silences over what should have been convivial visits, with Ambrose scowling at something only he could see, and Mary looking imploringly at her irritated sister. Why should Mary help Ambrose, really? He had never done anything to deserve her consideration. But then Mary really had no choice. If she wouldn't help for Fidelma's sake, she had to for God's. Otherwise what kind of a nun would she be? Fidelma thought of some of the nuns who had taught them at school, and felt doubtful. Yet compulsory kindness was supposed to be part of the deal.

The House of the Maids of the Holy Name still dominated its little hill, although its elegant isolation had been compromised in the Celtic Tiger years by huge executive houses which had marched right up to the cod-medieval gates and high wall while the nuns were distracted by Heaven. But still the complex was an impressive sight as Fidelma's car nosed between the tall iron gates – a substantial granite-faced box seen between coeval cedars across an immaculate lawn. It combined post-Georgian rectangularity with 'Gothick' furbelows, and was wrapped around a medieval-style cloister modelled on a Tuscan example.

It had been built in the 1850s in a defensive flush by an Old Money spinster who had been on a Grand Tour of Catholic Europe, and witnessed the Godless Year of Revolutions. She had never known that her Italian architect, whom she had chosen chiefly because he had worked for the King of Naples, had been a member of a radical political society (which was why he had been living in penury in Dublin). Even worse than this - he had incorporated into his design for Oldtown numerous Masonic in-jokes and symbols. His efforts had however been wasted, because nobody had noticed – and in one of history's myriad missed ironies his subversive buildings had gained a reputation for orthodox respectability, where middle and upper class girls with vocations could safely be sequestered until Jesus came at last to claim them. It had ever since been a contemplative island in a stormy sea, although these days its inhabitants were fewer in number and older in body than ever before. Mary was its youngest inhabitant by two decades. On the rare occasions the habited residents (theirs was one of only two orders that still wore habits) went out into the world, they were objects of pity or condescending curiosity.

The convent possessed impressive views over the Bay, the Head and the Wicklow mountains – not that the rustling, infrequent inhabitants seemed to notice. Fidelma had once commented on the beauty of the prospects as she and Mary walked in the gardens, and had felt chastened when Mary had said gently, "I don't really think about such things now. We are supposed to think about things a lot further away!" If someone who could say such things – and mean them – couldn't understand brain-fever, who could? The more Fidelma thought about it, the more she congratulated herself on co-opting Mary, whose religion could for once be of some practical use.

Still she felt awkward as she sat fidgeting in the waiting-room, her eyes roaming restlessly between the crucifix that was the sole ornament on the white walls (she was reminded of Ambrose's room), the door through which she had entered from the outside world, the door through which her sister would enter, and the small arched windows through which she could see a small segment of February. She ought to have visited Mary ages ago. It was too obvious that she was only here because she wanted something. She was still fidgeting and fretting when Mary entered, moving across the flagstones with calm economy.

Fidelma could not help thinking that Mary had let herself go even further. She seemed to have become smaller and even slighter, her hair greyer, her hands veinier, the little that could be seen of her legs below the grey habit even bonier. Yet the skin of her face looked unlined and shiny, as if from a lifetime of calming thoughts and regular moisturisation. Her eyes were clear, her smile childlike. She took Fidelma's hands and kissed her lightly on the cheek. Fidelma was surprised and touched, and her reserve melted - too quickly, because she found that she was simultaneously explaining and trying not to cry. She had had no one else to tell, and so now the dammed-up words tumbled out, and as they tumbled she knew how foolish they sounded.

Yet Mary didn't laugh or look impatient – she just sat quietly opposite, backlit by clean hill-light, listening hard, her brown eyes full of concern as the jumbled narration went on. And when Fidelma at last faltered to a halt, Mary took her hands again, assured her she understood, and not to worry. It was almost certainly just a phase, because Ambrose wasn't – if you don't mind my saying, Fi – an obviously religious person. There were, she went on gently, as you know Biblical precedents for sudden conversions, and usually they were signs of great grace. But somehow - how can I put this? - that didn't seem likely to be the case this time. Fidelma, half-laughing, dabbed her eyes and had to agree. Although God does move in mysterious ways, and you could never really be sure... Mary shook her head in doubt. One morning soon, she told her sister, Ambrose would probably just wake up and it would all be over. He would be back to normal, the same...err, *interesting* young man she remembered so well. But if it would make Fi feel better, if there was even a remote possibility that she might do some good - of course she would come.

They made an appointment for two days hence, which was the only day during the week that the nuns were allowed to leave the convent for a few hours to attend to profane business. Mary had not availed of this liberty for several years. "Somehow, I don't really miss it," she explained apologetically. "Oh, I hope you don't mind my calling it profane?" Fidelma thought of some of Ambrose's outbursts, and assured her that the word was not out of place. They went out companionably into the gardens, along corridors that smelt of stone-damp and shone with wax, and through cloisters lined with marble tablets to ex-sisters in receipt of their rewards. A fountain spumed gently all to itself; starlings strutted in weed-free, box-edged flowerbeds that in summer would be geometric blocks of lavender and lupin. As they walked and talked, the sisters would occasionally steal curious glances at the Head with its just visible Cross.

Forty minutes later, Fidelma was back in reality, coasting gently down the hill past all the brick boxes where businessmen lived today's version of the Good Life, cheek by habit with an older model - cars rather than cloisters, barbecues opposed to breviaries. She felt much happier. Crying had drained her choked cistern, and now she had a plan of action, and resources to carry out the plan. She also had an ally, and a confidant. It would be highly salutary for Ambrose to be quizzed by someone who would know what he was talking about. It would hopefully shame him into behaving a little more sensibly.

It would also, she reflected, do Mary no harm to be out of that frigid prison for a few hours. Maybe they could even get in some shopping; Mary's tights were such a sight! Surely it couldn't be against the rules for her to wear comfortable clothes. It would do Catholicism a world of good if some of its representatives were seen once in a while wearing a decent bit of fabric. After all, they needed to attract a younger crowd. So she would be doing two kindnesses in one. Maybe she wasn't such a failure at all. She found something up-tempo on the radio.

SISTERLY FEELING

Fidelma felt as if her intestines were knotted, her tissues befouled with slime. She had always had a certain claustrophobia about her colon, an idea that if it wasn't really clean she could not function at full capacity. It made sense, after all, that anybody, any body, would function better if purged of fats, residues and what Dr. Kumiswaramy so wittily called "badteria". (She had once seen a picture of a huge ball of fat that had been collected in London's sewers, and sometimes in her dreams it would chase her.)

Badteria - so clever! Thank goodness for Dr. K., the chubby and cheerful New Irishman. She couldn't care less what people whispered about him. He was a bold and original thinker, and the bold and original were always resented. They needed support from people like Fidelma - people who could see beyond the shibboleths. His Goatstown clinic had almost a whole wall-full of degrees from Indian universities, visually attractive as well as authoritative. He had no fewer than three doctorates in aromatherapy, for a start. Those who didn't like him were just afraid of change and difference, or maybe they were racist - probably unknowingly, she conceded charitably.

At any rate, they were doing the bidding of Big Pharma - and if there was anything Fidelma hated it was Big Pharma. Apart from racism, of course. And sexism. And inequality. There were so many things wrong with things. Sometimes you just had to forget them, and have a bit of pampering. Dr. K.'s unique combination therapy - Ayurvedic texts, herbal remedies, aural inspection, facial freshening and internal irrigation - had always worked for her. The whole experience was wonderfully pleasurable... there were even dizzying moments, after drinking his tonic and during the highest-pressure hosings, when she had felt out-of-the-body ecstatic, when all she could see was his smiling face close to hers, and her body felt as if she was being stroked all over by knowing hands. It was so much more pleasurable than going to boring old Dr. Benson, who only had two degrees on the wall of his surgery, and those from stuffy old colleges. They were so much more authentic in the East; some day she would travel there, and learn how to be a better person.

As she thought, she rubbed some of Dr. K's special salve into her cheeks, the ingredients of which he kept a closely guarded secret. She had asked what went into it, but all he would say, with his brilliant smile (such lovely teeth - so unlike Ambrose's), was that the ingredients were traditional, and infinitely renewable. Its smell took some getting used to, but after several months her crows' feet were definitely smoothing out. The prospect of seeing her friend – because he was more than just a professional – cheered her greatly. And she needed cheering, because for the last two days - ever since the moment her car had pulled up in the driveway after her visit to Mary - she felt she had been under sustained bombardment.

The first sign of trouble had been to find nailed to the front door – *nailed*, to her lovely polyvinyl door - a pathetic bundle of dyed chicken's feathers and wire. It was, she realised immediately, the dream-catcher from under Ambrose's mattress. And below it was a piece of paper, messily torn from the visitors' book on the hall table, and hastily written diagonally across it a single, senseless word – "HEXHAG". What did that mean? And what did he have against the dream-catcher, anyway? It was at worst harmless fun - and it might actually have been helping him.

She felt slightly like swearing, but of course she did not. She didn't ever swear. How could Ambrose have done this? The front door was the mouth of the house's face and it ought to be kept tidy and clean at all costs – like teeth, even and clean, light in colour. (Unlike Ambrose's.) A clean front door signified a clean house, a clean house good vibrations, good vibrations a better chakra. (Curtains were vitally important, too - a house's eyebrows, and she was relieved to see that they at least were as they should be – newly dry-cleaned, opened equally so the same amount of material showed on either side.) How many times had she explained her ideas to Ambrose? He knew what order meant to her. And yet he could do such a thing! It showed how sick he was.

She almost fell down in fright to find Ambrose sitting on the lowermost step of the staircase. He was regarding her with great and inexplicable sternness. The effect was less impressive than it might have been because he was wrapped in a lime green candlewick bedspread, and wearing just one boot. The other foot was bare – and filthy – although it wasn't as dirty as the bits of his face still visible behind his un-designer stubble. But still he was a disconcerting presence.

"So you have come, witch!" he said. "I wonder you dared! I have been anticipating your advent these several hours. Doubtless you have returned to determine the efficacy of your entrancements and unguents. But I have foiled your machinations... see!" He pointed to the ruin of the dream-catcher. "Behold! Thy alchemy has no jurisdiction here."

He looked with passionate intensity at the corner of the ceiling, as if through force of staring he could penetrate all veils, and shook a fist at the innocent angle. "Mephistopheles, thy leechcraft will avail thee nothing! Nay, Sir Demon, send as many witches as thou wilt! All thy trickery of feather and flex, thy coloured glass, thy sweet foodstuffs and spirituous liquors – I scorn them, and thee!" He snapped the fingers of both hands at the corner of the hallway violently and repeatedly, and laughed infinite repudiation – while Fidelma stood in the bone-freezing breeze from outside, still holding the bags containing his new clothes and his copy of *Wicked Faith*.

Then he turned, his face calm, and asked - "Those receptacles bear tributes?" Before she could reply, he had taken them gently and was halfway up the stairs. She dazedly watched his shuffling ascent, imperilled by the dangling laces from his boot, then went numbly into the kitchen – so numbly that even when she found that he had smashed a bottle of gin on the floor and thrown a bag of sugar into the resultant puddle, she did not feel anything, or do anything except mechanically pick up the shards and mop up the mess.

She heard the front door bang as she was finishing, but even the knowledge that he had gone out for the first time since his attack – that he was let loose upon the town – failed to motivate her into action. Instead, she stood for a moment and counted to twenty, then mixed a stiff G&T, and took the dictionary from the shelf. "Hexhag" wasn't in it, and that somehow made the word worse. It had an ugly and aggressive sound, like someone clearing their throat before spitting. Not content with other people's rubbish, Ambrose was making up his own.

She had just finished watching a landmark documentary about sexism in the insurance industry, feeling she had absorbed worryingly little, when he returned. She was feeling slightly tipsy after several more gins, so listened at first abstractly as the front door was thrown back with a crash – although she had rueful visions of hall paintwork. She would probably have stayed there, had she not recognized the sound of dragging. Something heavy. She had a vision of the deep pile carpet with a dirty groove along its oatmeal length, and bustled fearfully out to observe.

Ambrose was part way up the stairs (fully dressed, thank God!) with his back to her, and he was pulling at something very large. But before she registered what he was manhandling, she stared at the crown of his head, where there was a perfectly round bald patch which had not been there that morning. His whole hairstyle was different. He turned his head as he hauled the object up another step, and she saw the full effect. Ambrose's hair was normally a little untidy – there wasn't much that could be done with it – but at least it did not look all that abnormal. Now, however, it fell neatly around the crown of his head in a pudding-bowl style. The effect was not a good one. With his long face, bulging eyes and pallid coloration, it made him look like some human-reptile homunculus. The effect was made even more unfortunate because he had had the crown of his head shaved too. It reminded her immediately of a medieval docudrama she had seen a few weeks ago. It was supposed to be a monkish cut. He couldn't have *paid* someone to do that - could he?

Then she noticed his eye was puffed up and his nose had been bleeding. She rushed up the stairs towards him, but the thing he was dragging stood between them. "Ambrose! What have you done to your face?"

"O, it is as nothing. I have been in the marketplace, and was beset by baseborn churls."

It was only as she was trying to decode this that she registered what he was hauling up the stairs. It was a huge plaster nightmare that had been blocking the window of a local charity shop for months – a chipped and flaked tableau of the Crucifixion, five feet high and almost as wide, with one of the Saviour's hands missing and the right-hand mourner lacking one sandaled foot. Whatever individuation there may once have been in Jesus' face had been largely effaced by time – including very recent time, because His nose reposed in the middle of the hallway, knocked off as Ambrose had pulled the thing through the narrow doorway. She stared at the detached proboscis for a surreal second before she asked.

"Beset? By who?"

"By whom, thou meanest! But stay!" He smiled with maddening kindness. "How couldst such as thou know such things, o ye of small orthography? Mine besetters were demons, howsoever humanoid in their outward semblance."

Fidelma didn't notice the slur on her grammatical abilities straight away.

"Demons? Don't be ridiculous! They were people, Ambrose – people! But why? ... What did you say to them?"

He looked at her with gentle remonstrance.

"Thou didst always blame me for all that befell! But I forgive you your trespasses, as you shall forgive those who trespass against you - and lead us not into temptation, and deliver us from evil, and give unto us our daily sliced loaf... and if thou wilt but desist from interrupting, I will continue mine narrative. Yea, I spake unto the varlets. I vouchsafed Yahweh's message of hope, but they were mired in ignorance and sin. The Slough of Despond, I warrant! At first, they didst but scorn and mock me; latterly, they waxed full wroth, and were moved even to violence."

"But what did you say, Ambrose? It must have been something you said that annoyed them. People don't just attack strangers, do they?"

He managed to look simultaneously impatient, indignant and pitying. "I repeat - it was but Yahweh's message of hope that I broadcast. Oftentimes, dear lady. the invalid hateth the apothecary, the valetudinarian his leech. I quoteth but the Scriptures – and the Apocrypha – and the Septuagint - and then, gramercy..." he simpered, "...some of mine own texts. But it happed that these good seeds fell atop stony ground, and fell afoul of the slugs of Satan, the molluscs of Mephistopheles, the gastropods of...."

Fidelma felt a headache was imminent, and put up a hand to stay the torrent.

"Yes, yes, but there must have been some reason..."

"I merely bore witness, as I have previously deposed. I told them of Yahweh's infinite goodness and pity... and they jeereth. There was much shouting and commotion, yet I told them that even such as they might be saved. I told them that if their burdens were heavy they could pluck off." He stopped, plainly nonplussed. "'Twas this that angered them unaccountably – they became as wild menne, and set upon my unworthy personage with the flails of their fists and scourged me with their sandals, and all the while they shouteth foulness to the amaze of the populace."

Fidelma put up her hand. "Oh, Ambrose, Ambrose – don't you see? They thought you were saying...that you were saying..." She *did* have a headache now, and then she noticed that the Saviour's other hand had fallen off. It was too much, so she retreated, stopping only to shut the door, and place the Holy nose on the hall table.

*

Later, after a long hot bath, headache in abeyance, she knocked on the door of his room. "I bid thee enter, save you be a demon!"

She entered, to be confronted by the gigantic plaster tableau propped against the wall. It had lost one or two more details somewhere between the fourth step of the stairs and his room, and even the most Biblically literate might have had trouble working out exactly what was being represented. "Of course I'm not a demon, Ambrose! Don't be ridiculous! It's me, Ambrose... your mother, remember? De-mum, you might say!" She thought this excellently funny, and worthy of at least a small smile - but he didn't react, except to send his eyes scurrying once more from floor to ceiling and back again. And back again - and back again. She had to stop looking at his eyes - they made her dizzy.

"Ambrose, I wondered if you had read any of the book I bought today. I got it because I thought you might find it... um, interesting." She had almost said "helpful". *Wicked Faith* was lying open and face down on the floor. He nodded towards it. "Yonder oxymoronically-entitled tome? I have perused some few of its leaves – but truly it seemeth a contemptible manuscript, a tinkling bell when great brazen instruments are needed to give utterance to its import. Truly, this 'Daddy Jimmy' seemeth a pantaloon."

"That's very harsh, Ambrose. And religious people aren't supposed to judge, are they? This book is very popular, and is selling like hot cakes. Look, it has a Foreword by the Pope - and Gisela Mildew likes it. Something they can agree on must be good!"

"If we who know the truth cannot judge, whom can? But in truth, I was waxing charitable. A part-cooked comestible would contain infinitely greater goodness than said tract. Hast heard the Parable of the Pie?" Fidelma shook her head warily, guessing that even if she said she had heard it he was going to relate it anyway. Ambrose looked proud. "'Tis of mine own devising, albeit angelically intuited. Envisage this happenstance - a man of great heart but also belly-hunger. Envisage also a man of much heart-hunger but plenteous belly. To whom wouldst first givest a sweetmeat?"

Fidelma felt her head spinning with the nonsense of it, but she gamely tried to go along. "Em... to the man with belly-hunger?"

Ambrose chortled delightedly, and kept chortling for an inordinate time, holding his sides and stomach as if they ached. Fidelma stared at him in growing unease, as his body kept jerking with laughs which started to become coughs. Eventually he replied, although his words kept getting interrupted by retreating chortles.

"Nay – thrice nay! He he he! The answer to this riddle is this: thou wouldst give unto whichsoever hath the greater hunger!"

To Fidelma's un-theologically trained ears, the parable left something to be desired. But it was clearly futile to try to unpick it. She sought to turn the conversation into profitable channels. "But what is it you dislike about *Wicked Faith*?"

"Pshaw, 'tis but the witterings of a wyvern, the balderdash of a basilisk-eyed loon!"

Determined, she picked up the book and opened at random. "How can you say that, Ambrose? All the people buying this book can't be wrong! Listen to this - just listen for a second: 'Faith is cool, and we need to be 100% open about it, whatever our personal bags. It's great that 'faith' and 'face' sound so alike, because we should wear our faiths in our faces, and face our faiths.' Don't you agree with that? You wear your faith in your face." (At least, the bit I can see behind that stubble, she thought, daydreaming of a sane son, a sharp razor, soap and hot water.)

But all he said was "Pshaw!"

But she was dogged in her way. "Well what about this then? 'Each of us, in our private lives, can put the 'I Can' into Vat-I-CAN. At the end of the day, everyone is cool, everything is valid, and good is wicked (if I may be permitted to utilise the lingo of the streets).' Now isn't that a beautiful thought, Ambrose?"

"Pshaw!"

She tried again hurriedly, trying to stave off the unreasoning fury caused by that word. "Or how about this – 'God and good are only divided by an O. And what is O? Zero! This means there is no difference between God (or gods) and good (or goods).' How about that? I bet you can't fault *that* thinking!"

This seemed indeed to have struck home, and she wasn't surprised. It really was very clever stuff; maybe she ought to read the book herself. He sat shaking his head in thought for almost two minutes before he replied in a sonorous tone. "Verily, I had not surmised that such sentiments subsisted. I prithee, lend me yon writings that I may visit upon them their desserts."

Smiling inwardly, she handed him the book. She was preparing to leave the field quietly, to allow him to digest it in peace, when he started ripping out pages with manic energy. They fluttered down into a small pile on the floor at his feet, and he looked down on the feuilletons with gloomy pleasure.

"Thus I obey His bidding – to rend Pharisaical writings from each the other, thence to consign them to their lawful element." He stooped and set them alight with a cigarette lighter (where had he got that? He *did* smoke!). The smell of burning paper mingled with kindling Snuffly bedding, and tiny flames licked dangerously near Ambrose's naked foot. Fidelma dashed over to stamp it out, but she was too late to prevent a six-inch square burn mark on the floorboards that she feared (correctly) could never be polished out. She snatched the lighter from Ambrose's hand, and he didn't notice – he just stood looking down at the fluffy ashes and the scorch-mark, and now he was praying! She shouted, called him a fool, demanded to know how he dared, and added that she hoped he was smoking responsibly… but he was heedless, semi-smiling, murmuring all the while in a blend of Latin and High Elvish.

*

That day had become a different day at last, but Ambrose stayed mostly in his room. Yet he was omnipresent. Whenever she swished past his door on some real or contrived errand, she could hear him intoning, but what he was saying she couldn't understand, however long she held her ear against the door. She almost fell into the room once, when the door suddenly opened as he emerged en route to the lavatory. He looked blankly at her as she staggered, but just kept intoning as he progressed along the landing. She could recognize fragments of what he said, but even these made no sense – Thessalonians, transubstantiation, Triune essence, the Force, the Black Rabbit of Fu Inlé – and then he had locked himself into the bathroom, whence issued an interminable series of hymns imperfectly known and inexpertly sung, but delivered with gusto.

At mealtimes he would loom up silently in the kitchen like a demiurge, suddenly at her shoulder, on one occasion making her drop the casserole dish she had just taken out of the oven, to the detriment of both the contents and their container. He had looked down disappointedly on the mess, and then keenly into her face as she stooped to deal with it. He was making faint fizzing noises, and wagging his finger! "Tsk, tsk - a cleanly abode is His delight, dame of the house. Truly 'tis said that it is easier for a rich man to enter Nirvana than a slattern." He took a pack of bagels from the cupboard and crammed a whole one – dry and unbuttered – into his toad-wide mouth, before leaving the kitchen with the rest of the pack.

Suddenly incandescent, she threw her oven gloves at the swinging door, and then was even more enraged when they flopped to the floor and became smeared with stew. She yanked open the door, and shouted after his shambling rear elevation – "You come back here and clean this up this instant!" (Sandra Gulliver, who had her pixie-pointy ear pressed against the base of a wine-glass which was in turn pressed against the partition wall, made an O with her mouth, and wished, not for the first time in her life, that she had X-ray eyes.) "This instant" became another instant, and yet another, and still Ambrose shuffled on up, chewing, while Fidelma shouted until her brow beaded with sweat. Then she bent to clean up, only for the still-swinging door to connect itself vigorously with her bowed head. Then the doorbell rang.

Fidelma opened the door, florid-faced, still rubbing her occiput, stew splashed on her trouser-suit. She had almost forgotten Mary's visit, but now she saw her sister's smiling face with a rush of relief.

"Thank God you're here, Mary!" Mary's smile became even broader at this unusually pious greeting, and the vigilant Sandra jotted down the identity of the caller, and the time.

Fidelma made de-caffeinated tea, and came back into the living room to find Mary looking pointedly at an almost empty gin bottle in the drinks cabinet. Fidelma closed the cabinet in embarrassment, but also defiance. Mary had no right to make value judgments. She explained what had taken place over the last two days, while Mary tried to drink the tea. They always had very strong tea at the convent; it was one of the compensations.

Mary liked to be charitable, but she couldn't help thinking that her sister was not a good advertisement for decaffeinated tea. But then even as a young girl Fidelma had always looked harried – as if a pursuer was always just behind. Fidelma went to fetch Ambrose, while Mary fidgeted in a fatly cushioned chair, and looked around the room. So many fripperies. Such undeserved luxury...

She stood instinctively as her nephew entered. It was polite, of course – and suitably humble for a Maid of the Holy Name. And after all the things she had heard from Fidelma, it also seemed prudent – just in case the poor disturbed literally made an exhibition of himself. He might come in... naked! Where would she look? Where could she escape to? Ever resourceful, she had already picked out a sofa throw that could be used to swaddle him in a split second.

And then...then there was also the Possibility. The one that could never really be ruled out if you had any religion at all. Although she felt genuinely sorry for Fidelma, this was the real reason she was here - the infinitesimal off-chance, the remotest of remote possibilities that there was something more to this fit than Ambrosian attention-seeking. Sometimes, she had discovered, the world really did move in mysterious ways. Magical ways...

Maybe – just maybe, although almost certainly not – there was something Special about Ambrose, and her odd-looking nephew might really have been touched by Grace. It was extremely unlikely, obviously... virtually impossible. All the odds were against it. All her experience was against it. All her reading was against it. That sort of thing had been denied to the world in recent times. And yet... such things had happened to other families, other outsiders, other sinners, in other times. It was, after all, theoretically possible that a Divine Finger (looking rather like that depicted by Michelangelo in the Sistine Chapel) had actually extended out from an Unimaginable Place to point into Ambrose's tiny heart and illuminate it unaccountably with the Light of the World. Maybe, maybe, maybe, there was room for miracles even in this era, although she had long ago suspected she would never witness one. Such things as miracles, Sister Eugenia had confided quaveringly just a few days before, seem to have belonged to the dawn of the world. But just maybe, Eugenia had been too despairing - hardly surprising, for someone who had taken the veil almost sixty years previously, just as society was changing into jeans. Maybe they had all been despairing, too impatient. Against all reason, a tiny taper of hope had ignited itself in her vaulted shadows.

If such as Saul could be saved, who could say what could happen, if God willed it? Some of the saints had led the most appalling existences before they had been Touched. Some day, after all, He would come again as had been Promised, and he would send people to prepare his way. If someone as improbable as Ambrose were to have been selected as a Vessel from among all the billions of possible vessels, it would, if anything, add credibility to that Promise. If such as he could be saved, and turned to great purposes, there could still be Hope, even now, even in this heart withering through waiting...

Ambrose had always made her nervous - one of the reasons she had sought to discourage Fidelma's visits in recent years. He always seemed to be on the verge of something unpredictable, perhaps even unspeakable. But today it was a different order of nervousness, as if just maybe her eternity depended on how she reacted during the next few minutes. Was it remotely credible that someone as un-special as her could be caught up in one of the Great Stories? Yet fishermen and prostitutes had been, so why not her? She had after all led a good life, a self-denying life. And oh how she had always longed for a grand narrative, to make her self-sacrifice worthwhile, to put the dirt of the world in its proper place, to rise above the claustrophobia! Now maybe – maybe – maybe - it might be. O, it should be, it should be, Lord… She shivered, as she always shivered when her ever narrower knees touched the white marble pavement of the convent chapel.

Then he came through the door, and her first emotion was acrid disappointment. Try as she might to pierce appearances, he just did not look like a divinely-selected Messenger. Would a Christian Hermes have had quite so much caked dirt on his naked hands and feet – dirt all the more obvious when contrasted with his white "Harlem Globetrotters" (whatever did that mean?) tracksuit? Would he have been quite so – redolent? (She had sensed his proximity even before he had entered.) Would his hair have flopped around his face in quite such a comical fashion?

She chided herself. Such pettiness! What were externalities in comparison with the Inner Life? To think only of surfaces was to be like poor Fi. It had been precisely because Mary had seen what lay beneath skins that she had joined the Sisterhood. There were insights to be gleaned up on Oldtown's cold hill - the hill that caught the world's winds. In any case, from the moment she looked into Ambrose's upraised eyes she saw that in them, indeed, there burned a fire that darted blue towards her and licked her all over with pale tongues. It may not be a pure impulse, she reflected wonderingly – but by God there was something in him that had never been there before, or that had been heavily hooded – cowled as her sisterhood had once been cowled, to keep their essence inviolate in a soiled world. So many modern eyes were lit only by calculation. Here were eyes that blazed with something else, something she didn't think she had ever seen before in anyone. "Hello, Ambrose." she said, with a slight thrill. "How are you?" Fidelma cocked her head at something she sensed below the question.

"Good morrow, Sister of the Perpetual Chastity. I prithee, sit." He waved his hand expansively towards Fidelma's new suite. His aunt sat down again without thought of disobeying, slightly open-mouthed, impressed (even though Fidelma had forewarned her) by the new timbre in his voice, his confident projection, his aura of ownership. Fidelma looked on unsurely, a once-perfect fingernail in her still-perfect lips. "I am irradiant, I thank thee. Yet what does it profit a man to be healthy, hath he not the benison of belief?"

Mary wasn't prepared to launch straight into deep theology. She had expected less dangerous discussions first. She replied cautiously. "Belief is indeed a great blessing, Ambrose – and one that's denied to many of our brothers and sisters."

There was an edge to that "sisters", Fidelma couldn't help thinking – and she felt as if she were being shut out of a conspiracy taking place in her own living room. Although her sister and son sat almost motionless opposite each other, they somehow gave an impression of circling around each other. Wary as they were, they seemed to have something in common, flicking between them like electricity, a power-source Fidelma could not plug into.

"But how can one be certain, Ambrose, that one has the right kind of belief – that the belief comes from God, and not... the Devil?" Mary hadn't used, or even heard, the last word in years, and it came rather unnaturally.

Ambrose smiled a smile of unbounded patience – a saintlike smile. "Oh, Sister, that even such as thou shouldst doubt! Thomasina, I dub thee – patroness of the unsure, abbess of the Abyss! Truly, I am sent thither in time."

"In time for what? And who sent you, Ambrose?"

He smiled in complete certainty of being believed. "A Great Personage hath selected thy unworthy servant – but thou knowest this! Aye, Sister Mary, I divine thy thoughts – bestirred though they be by doubts. Unburden thyself! Here is a haven! Your doubts discard - your fears pluck off!"

Fidelma broke in - "I've told you not to use that expression, Ambrose! It sounds like... well it's not nice! Remember what happened last time!" But she might as well not have spoken for all the notice the others took.

"What happened up on the Head, Ambrose?" What Mary really wanted to ask was what happened in your head - what was happening in there now? What was this ferment, this pain? He looked away, out through the window towards the Head. Hiding a smile? But when he turned again, his glassy gaze was guileless.

"I saw... Something... and I awoke from dream-shadows. This Someone spake unto me – 'Avaunt thee, dream-shadows! Go thither, ancient Night-Mares!' And lo, the Night-Mares didst depart – although even now betimes I hearken to their fading hoof-beats in the watches of the night, drumming ever fainter through the wilderness. Drum... terrum... terrum... par uppa pum pum!" He drummed his fingers gently, hypnotically, on the padded arm of the chair. The sisters stared at them, and at his transmogrified face.

"I knew what this betokened, so quit the husk, and awoke into a Higher State. I was furthermore charged with a Great Task by One whom thou knowest."

There was a resonance to his words that made Mary tingle faintly. A decades-dormant part of her psyche was stirring. She fought the impulse; this was much too important to make mistakes, to see something because she so wished to see it. She was practical, was she not, her faith rooted in reason. All the odds were against Ambrose being the genuine article. "But Ambrose, how do you know what you saw up there on the Head was real? Your mother tells me you had been drinking."

His eyes were full of pity, and she shrank inside herself. In the distant background, Fidelma snorted. "Of course it wasn't real!"

Ambrose made no sign of having heard this, but held his aunt's eyes.

"I know, Sister Mary," he answered softly. "Oh, I know..." His voice reverberated, while his aunt stared. Had someone else come in? It felt different in the room somehow, as if they were being observed. Mary looked anxiously, instinctively around, but there were still just the three of them present - two middle-aged women, and one young man who appeared almost to be giving off his own light.

It took an effort for Mary to break that significant silence. "But Ambrose, your mother tells me you walked through the town without any clothes on. A divine messenger could surely never appear in that disgusting state!"

That'll fox him, Fidelma thought. But only for a second, because Ambrose was ready with an unexpectedly learned riposte. "Hast not heardst, Sister, of Saint Joseph of Copertino, the Flying Friar who stoodst naked to the four winds before the Cross and crieth, 'Here I am, Lord, deprived of everything!' His worldly foes allegeth that he be deprived of his wits too. But who now looketh more foolish? The sweet saint of Assisi likewise stripped to his skin in the Presence. Raiment is superficial, superfluous, a mere superstition, a carapace I can doff and don as required, but which He seeth through. I snap my fingers thus – and thus - and thus. I wear these vain habiliments, these rags…" He touched the white tracksuit as if fearing contamination, while Fidelma glared. Those "rags" had cost eighty Euros!

"…because I must needs move through the mundane world, and would not wish to render more unto Caesar than he wanteth to witnesseth. Yet why shouldst be offended? Mine naked flesh is but epidermis, and what after all doth the skin signify? It is what is below that signifieth. Thou knowest this - behind thy visage, I descry an understanding of the extreme thinness of all flesh. I see in thy haunted eyes a vision of skulls, row upon row, receding into shadows."

Mary had not expected to be outdone in hagiographical knowledge by her atheist nephew - her *former* atheist nephew. She had never heard of St. Joseph's levitations, nor Francis' love of nakedness. Could Ambrose have invented both stories? But he seemed utterly sincere. Besides, could he, or would he, have coupled lies with such remarkable insights into mortality? He stepped forward now to her chair, stooped, and cupped her face unexpectedly in wonderfully warm hands, and gazed into her. He had not touched her since he had been a baby. No one had ever touched her so caressingly - no one had touched her face since Daddy died. And how many times had even Daddy touched her so tenderly, looked right into her so long and lovingly? She had not realized how much she had missed the physicality of the world, the simple satisfaction of skin against skin. She wanted to close her eyes against the intrusion, but could not, and even Fidelma's glare from over Ambrose's shoulder could not break the spell. A tic flitted across his face like a breeze across water, and he shivered into speech, downloading words from some other dimension.

"I see a little girl running across a field in time and space, and in your arms are flowers of the field. I see a spirit that yearns for escape. But on your heart there lies a darkness - a knowledge that sunlight is as dust and ashes, that the world counts for nothing, and there is only one lasting Love. I see in thy eyes a secret sadness that all which looks so brilliant is under sentence - I see you holding keys to a kingdom under the earth... I see a stone bearing thy name and times. All this is known to me, and to thee - and to no other."

He dropped his hands to his side and stood, slightly swaying, while Mary put up a hand to touch one side of her face, as if to transfer all his warmth to herself. His eyes focused, but hers did not for a lifelong moment, while Fidelma exhaled.

"Well, that's a turn-up for the books..."

Mary did not know what to do, or say, or even think. All she did know was that something remarkable seemed to be taking place, something seemed to have landed from some better planet - and that it needed someone of much deeper spiritual knowledge to untangle it, separate the sense from the nonsense (if it wasn't all nonsense), the Truth from the Error. She also knew that she needed, desperately needed, to know more, to bathe again in the blessing of his baritone. When she answered, her own voice was at first slightly choked. Her Corconian tones gave her an air of deep sincerity. "Can you tell us exactly what happened, Ambrose, please – from the moment you left the house that night? As much as you remember. It would help us to understand. You must see, Ambrose, that this is difficult for, for most people. It's not that people want to disbelieve. Our mother, you know" - she indicated Fidelma and herself - "was a firm believer in The Mysteries. it's just that the world has changed since, since – and the last time was so very, very long ago. We have waited too long, and we are very tired – terribly tired."

Fidelma stared at her sister. Maybe getting her involved hadn't been a good idea after all. And why on earth had she mentioned mother? She had never told Ambrose about that. Rather than reasoning him out, Mary might actually be reinforcing Ambrose in his notions. But maybe she was right that they needed to unravel that night before they could start to ravel back reality.

The so-different, so-similar sisters listened with doubt, then fascination, as Ambrose started to speak, clearly, with fewer archaisms than had become usual - about his flight, his feelings, and what had happened, by himself on the howling hill. The short afternoon started to unite itself with millions of predecessors, the hard lines of the furniture began to dematerialize into dusk, and the actual bled into the uncertain.

ANGEL IN BEIGE

Ambrose and Tom Gulliver had started at the same secondary school on the same day. On that day they had both left at 8.15, both wearing identical uniforms, both carrying new satchels, and both had been watched down their respective driveways by their respective mothers respectively wondering where all the years had gone. But by that afternoon, their routines had already diverged. Tom ambled immaculately back up his driveway at 4.15, the time he had been expected - while Ambrose drifted back to his house almost two hours afterwards, his uniform wrinkled and torn, and one side of his face purple where he had been punched. For the remainder of their schooldays, they had continued to leave their houses at more or less the same time, but they never travelled together to school, nor did they associate whilst there (in the last two years, Ambrose had often absented himself entirely), nor did they come back in tandem to Tara Road.

Tom passed on most of the anecdotes about Ambrose - and there were many - to his mother, who acted appalled but was privately delighted to hear of Ambrose's eccentricities, wrong answers in class, being made to look foolish, being picked on by bullies, arguments with staff, experiments with alcohol and (it was rumoured) cannabis and magic mushrooms, and eventual truancy. But Tom was not malicious, and he suppressed some of the worst stories, because he felt sorry for Ambrose, and sometimes even felt ashamed when he saw him being picked on, and did nothing to help. Not that there was much he could have done - he was not physically powerful, and no one really paid any attention to him.

Ambrose, on the other hand, had always been un-ignorable. Tom was not the only one who felt strange respect for the way Ambrose refused to compromise - whatever was said about him, or done to him, he just stood back up and went on being himself. Tom could never have emulated him. Quite apart from lacking the courage, Tom didn't really know what he stood for in any case. He was also aware that Ambrose possessed a special kind of intelligence that on very rare occasions would stab out of him like a floodlight beam, briefly blinding his classmates and even the teachers. There had been an English teacher who had stood in for a term to cover for a sick staff member - a long-haired, dreamy-eyed man who wore 1960s-style velvet jackets - and he had zeroed in on Ambrose right from the start, seeing in the humped shape at the back things no other teacher had ever noticed. He and Ambrose seemed to have read the same books, to admire the same artists, to listen to the same music, and find the same things amusing. Not funny - Ambrose had never been known to laugh - but under the temporary teacher's tutelage sometimes he had come close. For that term, in those classes, the teacher and Ambrose had telegraphed rapid in-references and superior culture to each other far over the heads of the bored and resentful mass - and Tom was not the only member of that mass who had marvelled, then briefly pitied, when that term ended and the usual teacher returned, and Ambrose reverted overnight to taciturn type.

So he had felt genuinely sympathetic when he had heard about Ambrose's misadventures, and kept a well-disposed eye on the house as he went to and from work. His interest was in any case kept permanently piqued by his mother, who would regale him with the day's snippets as soon as he got home - the naked bonfire, the shouts, the banging doors, the hammering, the lights clicking on and off at all hours of the day and night, the white clothes, the monkish grooming, the importation of the huge Crucifixion, and most recently Mary's visit. He disliked his mother's malice, but he couldn't help finding it all vicariously fascinating. It was as if Ambrose existed for the purpose of showing what possibilities there were in the world - and what pitfalls. He was a walking cautionary tale. But whenever Tom expressed any sympathy whatever for Ambrose, his mother would make impatient noises, and remind him that she had always said Ambrose was a bad lot, and would come to a bad end.

"It's his mother I feel sorry for!", she always ended piously, and mendaciously.

On the morning after Mary's visit, as Tom was plodding down the driveway, his suit feeling even tighter than usual, his briefcase heavy with sandwiches and chocolate, his face brilliant with anti-eczema soap, he was pleased to observe that a peculiar black object was keeping pace in the adjoining driveway, just visible over the privet. "Catalogue!" he called genially. "Long time no see!"

The peculiar black object said nothing for a moment, just kept moving in time with Tom. Then it spoke, but thoughtfully, only to itself - "Hmmm, the hedge hath spoken! Mayhap Jack-in-the-Green or Old Man Willow hath tidings to impart! What ails you, sprites of the verge?" There followed incomprehensible mutterings, and the hedge started to shake violently. "Speak! Speak, O foliage!"

Tom called, "Ha, ha - stop taking the piss, Ambrose! It's me! Tom! Tom Gulliver!"

At that moment, the driveways ended at the road, and the two met face-to-face. Tom started in dismay and concern at the gargoyle that confronted him. Ambrose had always been painfully tall and skinny, and now these qualities had been accentuated by recent abstemiousness. His new and mangy-looking beard did nothing to mask the concave cheeks, and the skin that just managed to contain his skeleton was stained with old and new experience. His mother had told Tom about Ambrose's coiffure, but nothing had prepared him for the actuality. How was such hair possible, even with loving-cup ears to act as heraldic supporters? Yet all in that bombsite of a face was subordinate to the boggling blue eyes that seemed at once so insightful and so innocent; they lighted on Tom now like the appraisal of a kindly philosopher.

It was only after a few seconds that Tom remarked Ambrose's attire - completely white, or what had until recently been white - a sweatshirt and jogging bottoms clearly intended for a stockier man. His feet were bare - in February! - and by now had assumed pavement hue – the camouflage aided by the occasional piece of paper or cigarette butt that would briefly cling to his calloused sole and cracked heel. He carried a lunch-box containing pulses, and a tall wooden staff he had fashioned for himself from another neighbour's recently-planted cedar sapling (the tree subsequently deceased, the neighbour incensed). A baked-bean tin, still with its label, had been attached to his belt as a begging-cup, something he felt a holy mendicant ought to possess. But no one ever put in any money, as he never remembered to mention it.

Tom's kindly heart expanded. That even Ambrose should have ended up like this! He didn't know what to say, but luckily Ambrose pre-empted him. " 'Tis you, brother Gulliver! Whither away, fellow sojourner?"

"Eh? Oh - to work! It's that time, you know! Needs must, and all that!"

"Thou labourest in yonder lingam, methinks." Ambrose gestured vaguely towards the silhouette of Tom's office block. "Verily, 'tis a plutocratic phallus! 'Needs must', thou sayeth? There, brother, I apprehend thee - for we (thou and I) knowest (do we not?) who driveth that chariot! 'Tis all in here - in the brain-pan!" He pushed his face close to Tom's to tap him on the temple, and Tom noticed a rank smell, saw tiny pustules on his face. He tried not to blench, but he couldn't help averting his head to avoid the dead vegetation of Ambrose's exhalations. Ambrose did not seem to have noticed.

"I - anyway - where are you off to?"

"I must needs visit yonder Sodom to broadcast my informations to its denizens. The people wallow in feculence, brother!"

"Oh? Really? Well, I... that is... well, well, well!" Tom wasn't quite sure what feculence meant.

"Thou dost not apprehend, plainly! Come, brother - my way and thine lie together for some distance. Let us walk and discourse together!" He put his arm through Tom's, and started to tow him along. He was unexpectedly strong, and Tom had been taken unawares, so he found himself being pulled along at an uncomfortable speed.

"Whoa, Ambrose! What are you doing? Stop!" Ambrose obliged, and rolled slightly reproachful eyes at him. Tom coughed, and straightened his tie, although it was already straight.

"You mustn't do that sort of thing, Ambrose! People might get the wrong impression!"

"You allude to the Turin cloth?"

"What are you talking about, Ambrose?" Tom felt he had walked through a familiar doorway to find himself standing in empty air; it was much too early for surrealism. It would always be too early, so far as he was concerned.

"Art not ready for this Level?"

"Eh, no - that's right, Ambrose. Exactly! Shall we walk? I need to get to work, and you need to... well, you need to get on, too."

"You have the right of it!"

They walked side by side in silence. Ambrose's threat of "discourse" seemed to have been forgotten, and Tom was pleased at first. But after two minutes without speech - although Ambrose's mouth was always shaping words - Tom felt he had to break the silence. He cleared his throat. "How are you, Ambrose? How are you feeling?"

Ambrose slid him a glance - sly? - then looked away again. "My feet are more lightly attached by the moment."

Tom looked down reflexively at his companion's feet, but they looked as normal as filthy, naked, long-nailed feet could look on that frigid kerb.

"How do you mean... exactly?" he enquired warily.

Ambrose stared, as if amazed by his ignorance. "My feet press less heavy on the earth day by day! I feel myself becoming ethereal, legend. I gad with giddiness!"

"Em, I don't want to offend you, or anything, but maybe if you ate more? Here!" With a pleasantly purgative sensation, Tom made a great sacrifice. "Why don't you have one of my sandwiches? This one's peanut butter and jam. I've got four more."

Ambrose peered at the foil-wrapped wodge, then pushed it away gently. "I thank thee, but thou needst this to fill out thy concavities - although in troth these are already outnumbered by convexities!"

Tom flushed. "I was only trying to help!"

Ambrose put his hand on Tom's shoulder, and left it there. It seemed to Tom almost to tingle. "I am cognizant of this, brother Gulliver. I intended no offence, but all earthly considerations fade when one stands, as I stand, on the edge of a precipice looking down on an untraversed country. Soon I will be wafted thither to that fair territory. Foodstuffs, then, and sweetmeats - possets, sherbets, coconut lumps and such - seem gross, a barricade, a blockage against light and lightness. I dine principally on dreams."

His hand was taken away, and the tingle turned off. His voice was softly proud, reminiscent - his face numinous behind the dirt. Mad, mad - but for a few seconds Tom wished he could see things like that. He pushed the rejected sandwich back into his briefcase with a sense of disgust at his own appetites. He envied Ambrose's emaciation. He noticed how everyone they encountered paid no attention to him at all, but stared at Ambrose, and kept staring at him. It had always been that way. After a minute, he asked, "Do you ever think of school, Ambrose?"

The other darted an unexpectedly sharp look at him, and took about thirty seconds to answer. "I have drawn a curtain across those windows. That prospect never pleased..."

"Me too - I mean it never pleased me either. Even though no one ever paid much attention to me. I never even had a nickname!" Tom's voice quavered infinitesimally. "At least people paid attention to you! But I know you had a bad time. Even some of the girls used to have a go at you. Do you remember that bitch Philomena Cogaidh? There were times when... well, there were times when I wanted to help, but of course I never did. And maybe no one would have paid attention anyway. I... anyway, I wanted to say sorry! Perhaps if some of us had helped, maybe all this wouldn't have happened."

"All this what?"

"You know - all this!" Tom's hand waved vaguely down Ambrose's length. "Maybe with encouragement and support you might have done something... well, something more useful! A bit less unusual... Do you remember Mr. Carroll?" That was the temporary teacher with whom Ambrose had had a rapport. "If he had been there for a bit longer, or there had been more like him, who knows what might have happened? You know, to pick up the kids who fell between the cracks. Maybe you could have been - oh, I dunno, a writer, maybe, or..."

"Those curtains are closed! I beg you not to disarrange them!" Ambrose had raised his voice only very slightly, but there was steel in it (maybe a touch of fear also).

Tom was surprised, and slightly offended. "I'm sorry - again, I was only trying to help! Give over, Ambrose!"

"Pax, mon frère! I turn the other cheek thus," and Ambrose literally turned his head away from Tom, so that he was staring into the downstairs window of a house from which an elderly man happened to be peering out at a world whose moral tone horrified him daily. The man's disapproval deepened as he met Ambrose's eyes, and he yanked curtains across. Ambrose made a moue - "Behold, yonder scrimshanker closeth his curtainth - curtains - in the fathe - face - of that which displeaseth. 'Tis the past I loatheth! As for him, who knoweth what dæmons wander through his night-hours?"

"You don't think much of the present either, do you? You never have, as I recall! I remember you joking with Mr. Carroll about..." then he stopped. Ambrose held his gaze gravely until Tom had to look down and away.

"The present is o'ershadowed by past and future. There is but one hope - and that I bear in my bosom, like a torchière of Truth. Today I will impart this truth in the public square."

"Run it up the flagpole and see who salutes, eh? Good luck! My day'll be a bit different! I need to deal with a corporate tax problem for a shell company based in the Caymans who want to do business in Ireland via a Luxembourg subsidiary. It's quite a complicated case. And then I need to go and see a client in the service sector, and what with the recession, and the overheads, and all the key indicators way down, things are looking a bit dicey for him. He's over-extended, he has creditors breathing down his neck, and it's up to me to..." He was boring himself, and petered out.

Ambrose laughed, a thing that Tom had never heard him do before. Then he did it again! "We all sense hot breath on our napes - whether prickings of conscience, avenging angels, e'en dæmons! But there is only one Overhead!" He put both arms over his head so the palms of his hands touched, and then parted and spread them slowly wide, encompassing the firmament with a curiously impressive gesture. It had a bigness and generosity about it, as if he were making some great gift - of the universe, to the universe. Thus they came to the junction where their paths diverged - Tom to his office, and Ambrose to the market square. Tom stood and looked after Ambrose for a moment, as he stalked on amid nudges and turned heads - a stripe of off-white receding but somehow never shrinking. Tom walked thoughtfully towards work.

*

Fidelma always tried to avoid town whenever she knew Ambrose would be there. She hated seeing him being laughed at and humiliated - he may not have minded, or even noticed, but for her it was a deeply personal disgrace. But today she had needed to collect something early, and so just a few minutes after he had parted company from Tom Gulliver, she spotted him across the street, striding along oblivious to all the grinners, even the two small boys behind who were poking him with a stick. She was shamefully torn between intervening and ducking diplomatically into a shop, but as she dithered, an elderly woman, who looked noticeably elegant even from across the road, said something to the boys and sent them away. Ambrose was oblivious to this Samaritan too, but just strode on self-mesmerised, wrapped in mysteries.

Fidelma crossed over. "Excuse me – I'm sorry to bother you, but I just wanted to thank you for being so kind just now. I was just about to come over, but you beat me to it! You see – that poor boy is my son, and he's not, well, he's not quite right at the moment. He didn't see what you had done, or I'm sure he would have thanked you himself." She wasn't sure of this at all, so she changed the subject. "I don't think we have met, but your face is very familiar. I must have seen you around town. My name is Fidelma Sheehy-O'Connor, and that was my son Ambrose. We live in Tara Road."

The elderly woman proffered a hand to shake, an unexpected gesture. Fidelma noticed how exquisitely tailored she was in subtle tweeds and understated jewellery, country gentlewoman as interpreted by Bond Street. Her voice was soft and mellow, but hinted at firmness. "How very nice to meet you. My name is Letitia Shaughnessy-Don. I live at Head House."

Letitia Shaughnessy-Don! Fidelma's heart dilated. How had she not recognized her? Head House was the grandest dwelling in the town by lightyears, elevated above all others geographically as well as socially, a vision of Georgian grace built by an Ascendancy family that 150 years later had found it expedient to ship out shortly after the Black and Tans. And this, then, was the world-famous socialite, last of an old Catholic family who had taken back the house in 1922 "after a brief interregnum", as the then Shaughnessy-Don (Letitia's grandfather) had put it in humorous allusion to their 1594 expulsion from the estate.

Head House existed in its own imaginative sphere, a rumour of distinction that cast glamour on the town, even without any of the townspeople ever being invited through its gates. It was however possible to obtain glimpses from certain angles high on the Head – chimneys, a segment of the south elevation, a Venetian window, the angle of an orangery, a glittering lake in the grounds – all seen from far away through a cordon arboréale of specimen trees of species that didn't grow anywhere else hereabouts, possibly nowhere else in Ireland.

The Shaughnessy-Dons had likewise always existed on a rarefied plane, existing chiefly in social columns and in the pages of journals to do with horse-racing, hunting and Old Masters. Although the distance between their houses was little more than a mile, Fidelma had never met anyone who knew Letitia or who had ever been to Head House. She didn't even know anyone who knew anyone who knew Letitia. But still she felt she should have recognized her immediately - although one simply didn't expect to find Letitia Shaughnessy-Don just walking down the High Street. It seemed ridiculous to associate such people with shopping – to think of the Shaughnessy-Dons buying sausages!

She recalled reading that Letitia Shaughnessy-Don's husband and their only child had been killed a long time ago in a car accident. Clearly she could not refer to that. Unfortunately, she could think of nothing else to say, but just stood there going pinker. What to say to someone who knew everyone, had been everywhere?

Her new acquaintance rescued the situation. "If you're not too busy, Fidelma – I may call you Fidelma, I hope? – why don't we go and have tea? I hope it doesn't seem impertinent, but I would very much like to hear your son's story. That is, if you don't mind?"

Fidelma did not mind. In fact, she couldn't believe her luck at thus happening upon one of the most famous and fascinating women in Europe. Her heart bounding, she followed Letitia dazedly up the steps of the Grand Hotel, the town's oldest and most expensive establishment. (She'd called her Fidelma!) The maitre'd – the town had just one, all of Ireland only two – bustled up effusively, and ushered the "ladies" (a word which had much more resonance when one was in such company) to the best table, where passers-by who gazed in between the wisteria trunks could see that whatever else had altered for the worse, Shaughnessy-Dons still chose the Grand.

Fidelma felt appallingly out of her depth in this antique milieu. She had never come in before, and yet she had passed it hundreds, perhaps thousands of times. There had never been anyone else to go with, and she had never dared to go in alone. The wonderfully-comfortable chintz-covered armchairs – the equestrian studies – the lamp-toting cherubim – the fragrant turf fire in the inglenook – the jasmine tea – the most delicate pastries ever confected… there was joy as well as unease in the moment. She had arrived, at least provisionally, and she tried to persuade herself she deserved to be here. To show her new friend how accustomed she was to such surroundings, she started to talk, at first with precision and reserve. But as the tea warmed her, the front of her dress became slightly spangled with icing-sugar, and her enviable interlocutor nodded so smilingly, her talking became a kind of confession. Her new friend sat poised across the walnut table, impeccable, at ease beyond emulation, and her grey eyes didn't miss a thing.

*

Rain splattered soundlessly on the glass sides of the Financial Services Center (the American orthography reflecting the owners' aspirations) – erected contrary to planning guidelines, reputedly thanks to bribes, and hated for its long frigid shadows by day and fluorescence at night. It was unnaturally warm on the fifteenth floor, and Tom tried to concentrate on the strings of numbers that were passing across his screen, striving to speed up flows as his own arteries clogged. But he kept wondering how Ambrose was doing.

That visionary (who was not thinking of Tom) was in fact having little luck getting anyone to stop and listen. But he was indefatigable, and all passers-by were asked, "Hast heard the News?" Most sidestepped him completely. Some were polite enough to mutter, "Not today, thank you." A rude few laughed scornfully. One man with a bibulous neb was angrily uncomprehending – "What the feck are you talking about?" A young man trying to impress his girlfriend waxed sarcastic – "Oh do tell! I'm sure someone who looks as successful as you do must have some invaluable insights!" Lads dressed for football came along, and their captain joked, "Look lads, it's feckin' Jesus!"

It would have dispirited a lesser man. But Ambrose's assiduity was rewarded, just as the rain stopped and the sun opened one lazy eye to see what was going on in its system.

"Hast heard the News?" he enquired of a young woman carrying several parcels. She was, to all appearances, conventional - neatly if cheaply dressed, brisk in her movements, her face impassive - but her reaction was anything but conventional. Something about the question, or her state of mind, or simply his appearance, made her think of things she would have much preferred not to think about. She stopped dead, panic-stricken eyes trained on him, lifted her hands to her head, cascading parcels that chinged of shattering glass, and started to scream. Real screams - appalling, all-alerting, soprano screams upon seeing his eagerly ugly face so suddenly and so close, his frame so lanky and unhygienic, like an ancient nightmare released into the daytime community. Shattered parcels around her, she stood in the middle of the busy street with her hands over her ears, shrieking and shrieking as if her small frame contained a consignment of klaxons. Ambrose thrilled to his marrow; it was the first case of demonic possession he had seen. Luckily, he knew what to do.

He clutched her arms firmly to stop her twisting away and fixed her eyes sternly, and she started immediately to subside. His eyes looked to her like mountain lakes, and she fell willingly into them, hoping to drown. Her face contorted, she started to laugh through smears of tears - then stopped, and began to suck her thumb.

"Unhappy woman, who hath ensorcelled thee?" Ambrose shouted in her face. She just kept sucking her thumb, looking at him with little girl acceptance. An anxious-eager crowd had coalesced. "I am apprised of her diabolic burden," he explained. "It's in The Book!" He held up a large Morocco-bound missal as proof, then turned back to the thumb-sucker. Men in the crowd looked uneasily at each other, and wondered whether to intervene.

"Bewray thy persecutor, maid, and I shall avaunt the hex. Whither shall I project the sprites? Into yonder capacious vessel?"

He pointed at an obese onlooker, who purpled and went up to the unperturbed Ambrose, spraying tiny globules of spittle into his face. Ambrose did not flinch - in fact, he did not even seem to notice.

"What? What did you say? What did he say?" He turned away from Ambrose to appeal to the onlookers, only to see that they were either trying not to laugh, or grinning openly. He spun back towards Ambrose, but Ambrose was paying him no attention, instead placing a hand on either side of the girl's head. The fat man and everyone else gawped as Ambrose spoke clearly and authoritatively, in a kind of tone none had ever heard. They liked hearing it - and what it was saying somehow didn't seem to matter much.

"I addresseth the occupants of thy occiput. I have come to expel thee from these purlieus. Depart this brain-pan, I command thee! I sayeth, departeth!" He gripped fiercely onto her head as if he was expecting it to revolve (he was), and the girl went white before slumping. The crowd gaped and inhaled sharply, and the quicker-witted moved to assist. But Ambrose raised a hand, and everyone stopped, and some would later swear they had seen on his upraised palm certain significant marks. "Lo! Lo!" His voice boomed out, over the traffic. People even on the far side of the busy road looked over. "I have banished them from hither to thither. In this gargantuan bottle they must eftsoons languish."

He pointed again at the fizzing fat man. Even as Ambrose was unhanding the woman, and saying "My work here is done…" the incensed man raised a surprisingly tiny right shoe and kicked Ambrose in the testicles with all the authority of twenty stone. His voice rose as Ambrose folded, and all the male onlookers winced.

"You bastard! I'm big-boned! I can't help it! My calorie intake is normal for someone of my demographic!" Tears oiled out as he stood panting in all his upholstery. "I'm on… special medicine…"

He realized that he had just assaulted someone, and he pushed off as quickly as he could through the crowd that was luckily focused anxiously on Ambrose. Someone was calling for Gardaí and an ambulance, but a stentorian voice arrested them all, coming from pavement level. "Stay! Stay thy digits! See, I rise, like as to Lazarus! I feel no pain in my stones. I rise! I am impervious, and whole. See, I dance and sing!"

Ambrose sprang up, and his face was ecstatic. He threw his arms around a recoiling elderly man, then danced a waltz with his wife, the effect of which was marred when his feet interfered with hers, and he and she crashed to the ground. But he sprang up again in a trice, crying "Lord of the Dance!" and whirled laughingly around the other onlookers, making some recoil as he thrust his frantic face within an inch of theirs, before dancing out of the circle and catapulting over a fence into a nearby building site. Everyone was captivated, and it was only his dance partner's husband who heard her say, through gritted dentures, "I think… he's broken my leg…"

"Lo! Lo, I quoth! Pain hath no dominion – there shall be no pain whither we goest!" The voice was resounding, huge, comforting. Ambrose was standing on the first floor scaffolding of a kebab shop undergoing refurbishment, and the crowd had swelled to several hundreds. He had picked up an electric drill, and now placed the tip of the bit against his forearm. He stood motionless, and stared at it – and everyone at him and it, as time froze. Even the workman whose drill it was, and who had been hastening back along the planks to snatch it back, seemed static, mid-stride with his mouth slackly open as if it had always been slackly open, one hand raised in futile warning.

The world had stopped moving but for Ambrose, stopped breathing but for Ambrose, and everyone imagined they could see veins pulsating in his arm as he placed pressure against them with the diamond-tip. He smiled a secret smile to himself, then turned the same towards them, before he pressed "On". As the drill buzzed into life, some turned away, some could look nowhere but at the whirring metal – but most were staring at his transported face as the drill bit bored through his left forearm and a stream of blood and gristle started to spill steadily onto the scaffolding. They had never seen anyone look so happy.

TRANSFUSION

Within an hour, #maddrillman was trending on Twitter. Jerky phone footage showed Ambrose with his face and clothes smeared with his own effusions, descending from the scaffolding, thrusting aside hands of help, pulling away from police, walking away from the ambulance and out into the crowd – still smiling that secret smile, extending all-embracing hands and arms, while paramedics came pushing behind, trying to grab his wounded arm to staunch his flow. They could not reach him, or if they did they seemed unable to keep hold, as if they were clutching at clouds. "Away, myrmidons..." he murmured.

Gore oozed out of him as he came among the press of people, who recoiled but could not tear themselves away from the horrible-wonderful sight. He was speaking, but what he was saying no one could hear, and even if they had heard, it would probably have made no sense. It was enough for that crowd that here among them was a man who had pierced his flesh and felt no pain, and whose face was beaming bonhomie and secret knowledge even as his life-force spattered onto the road. Certain hearts expanded and were lost; certain minds spread-eagled themselves; some hands stretched to touch…

… but he was gone, gone as if he had never walked among them, whisked away by medics, bundled with rough kindness into an ambulance – a last view of him before the doors closed as he towered in smeary splendour over the short attendant, who looked almost as if he were bowing. The ambulance pulled away and most of the crowd broke away like birds hearing a gun, just a few standing wistfully for a few moments before moving away slowly.

*

Ambrose was treated at the town's hospital, a process he underwent without complaint. On the contrary, he bestowed blessings and tried to pat the staff gratefully on their heads as they bent over his wound. He swallowed a sedative, although it seemed to have no effect, and underwent a tetanus jab without flinching. Fully alert and sitting up, for a long time he refused to divulge his full name and address, to the exasperation of the irritable, unfit Garda detailed to elicit that information.

"What is in a name? Ambrose by any other name would smell as sweet. Hee hee!" He found this equally funny each time he said it.

The Guard, Rogers by name, rancorous by nature, disappointed by experience, did not find it funny even the first time. Nor did he find it amusing to hear Ambrose parry his next enquiry with "My abode? What of it? My address is not of this world..."

Eventually, Ambrose imparted his details, but not until he had told Rogers the histories of St. Simon Stylites and other self-mortifiers, ignoring broad hints that this information was not required.

It was only after the exasperated man had said, "Would sir mind shutting the fuck up?" that Ambrose had at last desisted. But still he sat there gazing benignly at the officer, to his great confusion and even greater annoyance. Rogers tried to ignore him, but every time he looked up, his charge was smiling lovingly at him, and once he said, "I divine thy inmost fears, O beadle..." The by now highly agitated officer avoided further divination by turning his back. Ambrose raised his hand to bless the burly rear elevation, and sank back into the crisp bedding with a sigh of satisfaction. Rogers, who had seen this reflected in a glass partition, balled his fists.

He was relieved when at last a sister entered, and after a cursory examination of the wound, re-bandaged it, and said Ambrose could be discharged. But he still had the duty of ensuring Ambrose was decently dressed in spare hospital clothes – a process he resisted, and which was only achieved after twenty minutes, and with the assistance of a chunky porter. Then both escorted him, all three red and hot, down towards the lobby.

After the excitement of being dressed, Ambrose had stalked co-operatively between them, and they had started to breathe properly again. But as they turned a corner, he unexpectedly broke away and crashed through the double doors into the Neo-Natal Unit. There was a pandemonium - "Hey! Hey!", "Press the bell! Press the bell!" - screams, and breaking crockery.

A clear voice rose briefly above feminine hubbub – "I bring you news of a birth the likes of which shall astonish the earth... A little child shall lead them!". His swearing escort caught and brought him to the waxed floor, Guard Rogers taking the opportunity to elbow his charge in the face – a proceeding which gave him much unofficial pleasure (the possibility of such moments was one of the main reasons he had joined the force). Ambrose went limp, although not unconscious, and they had to drag him between them into a spare office, with his feet trailing along the tiles and a face once again bloodied - yet still glowing with almost intolerable goodwill.

Here he was checked over again by the square and (very) senior sister who had discharged him half an hour previously, who told the porter he was a clumsy eejit and he would hear more about this disgraceful incident, and Guard Rogers that he was incompetent, and she would complain to his superiors. She and a junior nurse then cleaned Ambrose's face and bathed his (luckily unbroken) nose in iodine, before she discharged him again. All this time, Ambrose fixed upon her a look of ineffable kindness. "Maiden of the medicaments – I forgive thee! Thou knowest not what you do!"

She snorted, and spoke through even tighter than usual lips. "Oh, I know what I'm doing all right! Don't you worry about that! Now get him out of here!"

"Farewell, lovely maid…" were the last words she heard as he disappeared into the service lift, by means of which he could be dragged discreetly (and ungently) to the lobby, and the Garda car. The porter clapped the officer sympathetically on the shoulder as they parted company. (The senior sister was uncharacteristically quiet for the rest of her stint; no-one had ever called her lovely before - and she really was a maid.)

Ambrose enjoyed the journey in the car, repeatedly opening the window with the electric button so he could peer out, admitting a gelid blast and a rush of rain each time, much to the displeasure of both Guard Rogers, beside him in the back, and the officer driving. When they halted at one traffic light, he whirred the window open again, and extended a long arm to knock on the window of the car in the next lane. The other car's window was wound down hastily, once the driver saw it was a Garda car.

"Good morrow, fellow pilgrim!" Ambrose was saying, and then Rogers managed to gain control of the electric button and close the window again. Ambrose didn't seem to mind this unceremonious cessation of the conversation. His face was rapt in childish contemplation of the lights of the town, and the swish and rush of the motorway traffic. "Behold Gomorrah! Behold Sodom! Behold Babylon, Nineveh and Ur! Behold

Babel! We have medicined Babylon, and she is not to be cured. Let us therefore leave her!"

"Can't you behold his fuckin' hands, John? Stop him opening that window, for Christ's sake!" the driver demanded.

Ambrose leaned forward and hissed almost in the driver's ear, startling him so the car swerved into the adjacent lane, which elicited a blare of car horns.

"Aye, beadle, for Christ's sake – all is for Him. All!"

"God, that was close! Can't you keep him still?"

Ambrose sat back, pleased at this theological turn. "Aye, God is close… thou art wise, charioteer." There was a pause of perhaps ten seconds, before Ambrose held up a hand impressively, as he did so emitting in a distressing treble the words, "Amazing Grace, how sweet the sound…" The others jumped in fright, and the car swerved again.

Rogers had an idea. "Ambrose – I've just had a message from the Big Fella. He says you're to keep quiet, and do what you're told."

Ambrose's head swivelled towards him in the dark interior, and by the flicking motorway lights, he looked thunderstruck. He leant over and looked keenly into the policeman's face from a few inches away; Rogers blanched and leant backwards. "Thou too hast heard? I have misjudged thee, and entreat your exculpation."

"Granted! Now can't you shut up – and keep that window closed? It's what God wants, remember!" He winked at the driver in the rear-view mirror, and both men unbent slightly, while Ambrose looked thoughtful. His lips moved, but neither could hear what he said – and neither wanted to. But his face was oddly interesting in repose, and Rogers watched him surreptitiously. The streetlights striped across his face as they progressed, and in their intermittent illumination, Ambrose's ears seemed less prominent, his hair less porcupine-like, his physiognomy less piscine. His eyes remained large, and lustrous, and under their influence even these men were silenced. They had never encountered anyone like him, and he made them very uncomfortable. It was therefore a relief to both when the car at last pulled into Tara Road.

Rogers' voice was rich with envy as they pulled up outside Ambrose's house. Fidelma's car gleamed even in the dark, and the policeman looked at it, and the house, and suddenly he was reminded how he hated all the comfortable people. He tried to mask his bile in sarcasm. "A nice road this, Ambrose – very nice. Now what makes a well brought-up lad like you want to leave your nice house on a nice road like this? Can I make a suggestion to Your Eminence?"

"Assuredly." Ambrose looked into him.

The Guard was unexpectedly disconcerted. However ludicrous this lad, he had gravity. He wriggled inside. "Tell you what - why don't you organize your religion over the internet instead of out there on the street, causing a public nuisance, and getting yourself hurt?"

"That is sooth! Mayhap our pilgrimages crossed today for just such a communication of import. Mayhap by means of this device The Word can be more widely spake! The internet... I thank thee, O officer! Here is my token on't!" He leaned over and kissed the other on the forehead. Before the stunned man could react, Ambrose spoke again. "Nay thank me not! 'Tis but thy due, worthy public servant! And now – exeunt!" He opened the door and got out smartly, while Rogers sat open-mouthed. Suppressing his anger, he got out his side and followed Ambrose up the drive, slamming the door to shut off the driver's guffaws. A woman was looking out of an upstairs window in the house next door.

Ambrose had vanished by the time the policeman came to the front door. He looked around in worried annoyance, and then saw him, kneeling behind an ugly tree, staring skywards, and muttering something. He snorted and rang the bell, then turned to keep an eye on his charge, in case he decided to bolt. Silhouetted becomingly by light behind, Fidelma put a hand to her lovely mouth. "Omigod! What's happened?"

"Good evening. Are you Mrs. Sheehy-O'Connor? Mrs. Fidelma Sheehy-O'Connor? I'm Garda Rogers. I've brought your son home. There's been an incident."

Her eyes followed his hand, and he noticed them widen as she spotted Ambrose, on soiled knees behind a laburnum. He was wringing his hands, and swaying. "What's happened? What's he done now?"

"You mean you haven't heard? You haven't seen maddrillman on Twitter?"

"*Drill man?*"

"May I come in?" He had heard rustling coming from next door - the dividing hedge was just a few feet away - and knew they were being listened to. Probably the same woman who had been looking out of the window next door. He jerked his thumb several times meaningfully in the direction of the sound and winked significantly at Fidelma. She realized what he was signifying, and stood aside to let him enter, before stepping into the garden and guiding Ambrose in gently. It was only then she noticed the surgical dressing, and she looked horrified.

"It's all right now, Mrs. Sheehy-O'Connor. But I'm afraid your son has been a bit of a botheration..."

Ambrose stayed in the room, looking interestedly at the wall, while the policeman placed more than adequate buttocks on the edge of a chair he could never afford to own, and explained the events of that day. Fidelma sat with her hand shading her eyes, as if the images he conjured were too brilliant to view. Then, just as he finished his account, Ambrose exhaled loudly and they both looked at him. His fingers were fluttering on outstretched hands, as if he were typing. He smiled gnomically, spoke a single senseless word - "Ambrosenet!" - and left the room.

MESSAGES RECEIVED

Ambrose came back downstairs a few minutes after the policeman had departed in a flurry of warnings and advice. He found his mother sitting where he had left her, holding a half-empty glass while she tapped her fingernails on it. She looked up as he entered, and shook her head. "Ambrose, Ambrose... What am I going to do with you?"

Ambrose didn't reply immediately, but stood there uncertainly, his eyes rolling. But when he did speak, she detected a flicker of normalcy. She was even more heartened by almost unprecedented politeness. "Where did you put my computer, please?" Please! The word warmed her, very slightly, like a log fire seen through a window.

When they had cleared his room, she had put his Apple (a birthday present of the previous year, which he had greeted with his usual grunt - although he had used it constantly ever since) into one of the spare bedrooms. Now she preceded him upstairs, daring to hope that maybe the physical trauma of that afternoon had somehow jolted something back into its place. At least, more into place. Last year, he had been writing some kind of book, locking himself away in his room with the computer for whole days, accompanied only by a death metal soundtrack. Maybe now he would re-discover it. At the very least, if he was in his room she would know where he was.

She carried the machine into his room, then, after a struggle, restored the computer desk to its former place. She would not allow him to help, with his hurt arm. It did annoy her that he hadn't even offered to, but then the old Ambrose wouldn't have offered either. She left him connecting up and typing in passwords (he could remember those - even if he couldn't remember to say 'Thank you'!), and descended again into the sitting room, where she felt she deserved another gin.

Delightful peace ensued. There was more on the following day, yet more on the next, and she started to uncoil. She even ceased her insecticide-spraying operations so that she wouldn't interrupt the magic charm. He emerged at meal times and to visit the lavatory, but was otherwise ensconced in his room. She could almost have been by herself in the house, and she could go out and leave him alone while she went to the shops, almost certain he would not get into trouble. It was quite like old times, when Ambrose would be in his room and Fergus away on business - just her, and a house to cleanse and re-cleanse. It gratified her to think that Sandra must be deeply disappointed by the sudden quietude.

Blessed peace... such peace... such a great deal of peace... It almost felt like too much. What was he doing in there? Hadn't things suddenly become - a perverse thought, she realized - a bit boring? She moved constantly through the house, her fingers itching for something to do, but all rooms yawned back immaculate. She found herself re-making beds that were never slept in, opening drawers whose contents she knew to the last item, relieved to find rain-stains on the window that she could wipe away. Westminster chimes rang out on quartz cue, and they sounded like they were ringing out over some abandoned city. She turned on radios and televisions, but the relentlessly cheerful voices only emphasized the dearth of actual cheer. She almost ran to the phone on the rare occasions it rang, and almost bought another conservatory.

She was eating breakfast at 6am on the fourth day, when a proud face peeped around the swing door. She spilled tea; his bare feet had made no sound. "'Tis done!" His head disappeared.

"What? What's that, Ambrose? What's done?"

He looked around the door again, smiling archly, and crooked a beckoning finger. She bolted her toast and followed him to his room. She was distressed (although not shocked) to see how untidy it was. The guinea-pig bedding was discoloured and thin, and there were crunchy things on the floor. She didn't want to know what they were. The plaster monstrosity against the wall appeared to have shed yet more defining details. The white paintwork, done so recently, seemed to be yellowing already. There was a background aroma, a compound of sandalwood incense and sweat - a smell that reminded her uneasily of the floral-feculent bouquet of Fergus's ward. Ambrose pressed a button, and stood back so she could see the screen. His voice sang achievement. "Behold - Ambrosenet!"

An image of Ambrose's face loomed up out of blackness, growing until it took up all the visible area. The camera kept zooming in, slightly unsteadily, and the face grew disquietingly huge. Closer in and closer yet, until it was possible to pick out pimples and pocks - closer still, until all that could be seen was part of a nostril, with a glint of mucus, and his mouth surrounded by super-magnified ragged beard. The lips parted to reveal a crooked yellowish range of teeth, which strongly suggested halitosis. The mouth moved, and "AT LAST!" boomed out so unexpectedly that even Ambrose jumped. He adjusted the volume in time for the next words. The words also appeared on screen, white against the darkness of Ambrose's gullet. A tiny red dot bounced onto each word as it was uttered.

"The Answer to"
new screen -
"the Question you have"
new screen -
"always wanted to know the answer"
new screen -
"to".

The huge mouth smiled, to frankly sinister effect. "AMBROSENET" it thundered, and Ambrose needed to turn down the volume again. Then he needed to turn it up again, because his voice when it resumed was whispering - and what it was whispering was so complicated that Fidelma had lost the thread within forty-four seconds. Even with the volume at full, Fidelma could not make out much, so she looked worriedly at the words emerging from the giant gullet, although sometimes she could not see the bouncing red dot against the lurid tonsillar background.

"Jesus - John the Baptist - Ezekiel - Revelations - The Beast - Meggido - Merovingians - John Dee - Nostradamus - Rosicrucians - Eric von Daniken - Great Pyramid - the Brazen Head of Prophecy - Year of the Rat - 137 - world peace - solar system - Darth Vader..."

Where did he get all this from? How could he keep it all in his head - let alone connect it together? And why couldn't she understand it? Although she had heard many of the words, and had even watched documentaries about some of them, put together it sounded frankly meaningless. Yet she was as intelligent as anyone else. And yet there was obviously something in it, because people were always writing best-selling books along these lines. Perhaps this was what his book was about; perhaps he was even writing a best-seller!

"Knights Templar - Da Vinci - Celtic Church - Mary Magdalene - Pope Joan - Aix-en-Provence - Eye of Horus - Rosslyn Chapel - Banco Ambrosiano - Temple of Solomon - sacred geometry - Federal Reserve - ornithopters - faked moon landings - Roswell Incident - Parable of the

Pie..." He smiled beatifically at his mother and held up a hand, clicking the mouse expertly with the other. "See? The Message is already as yeast in the world of Men - see my silent army, no longer silent!"

There were hundreds of messages in his inbox. She skim-read some as he clicked down the list, opening and closing them too quickly. Some were spam - porn, opportunities to avail of monies left by careless diplomats in Ivory Coast bank accounts, an ad for electric drills. A few were malicious, like the one that started "U mad fucken moron why dont u shut the fuck up..." Another showed St. Ambrose's preserved body in Milan, and the caption, "Wish you were here!"

But there were many others asking questions in apparent seriousness. Questions like (if she had read it correctly) "What do you think of Schickelgruber's claims that the 'neolithic' skeletons of Saint Etienne were extraterrestrial in origin? It is surely significant that the so-called 'skeletons' have disappeared." There was an invitation to speak at a conference. A journal sought an interview. She had never heard of the journal - still, her son was going to be interviewed, as if he was important! There was even praise - "At last, the truth emerges" - "Brilliant blog!" - "Fraternal greetings"- "breaking through the MSM". There was even one with the subject line "Our saviour!" Reading these made her well up slightly. It was the very first time, so far as she knew, that anyone had ever praised Ambrose. OK, some of the senders obviously had issues - even so... People were asking him to predict their futures, and one thanked him for money apparently won through his advice. "What's this?" enquired Fidelma jocularly, pointing at the message. "Didn't you get some for us?"

He batted away the query with "Pshaw!" Most unexpectedly, there were requests from women who wanted to meet him. Fidelma wasn't sure she quite liked the sound of the Chair of the Sexual Healers of Wessex - whom she imagined (correctly) as a plump spinster with facial warts, and a smell like foxes. Still, they were offers... She thought it heartening that Ambrose's religion seemed to be so inclusive. Fidelma swallowed and put her prejudices consciously aside; corresponding even with people like these was surely preferable to lonely looniness. There would surely be some normal people among his new correspondents, who could steer Ambrose in wiser directions.

And if he did write some kind of book... perhaps there was an outlet for his gifts and odd knowledge after all. She stood beside him, peering down on his shaven crown, remembering the bizarre baby he'd been. He had clearly forgotten she was there, absorbed completely in the scrolling words, his hands moving expertly, his tongue protruding as it always had when he was concentrating. It made him look absurdly innocent, and she felt a gush of affection. She wanted to touch him, and her hand twitched in his direction... but instead, she stole out of the room.

Two more quiet days. Whenever Fidelma looked in, Ambrose was immersed, and rarely even noticed her irruption. It was really quite restful, or it would have been restful, if Fidelma had been the type of person who could rest. She wondered what on earth he was cooking up. But an especially enjoyable session with Dr. Kumiswaramy had almost dispelled her tension, especially as she had confided her problems to him, and he had responded with his usual wisdom and warmth. He had suggested that perhaps Ambrose had a dangerous build-up of intestinal bacteria, and although he usually only treated women, he had offered a 50% discount on his usual fees for Ambrose, as Fidelma was such "a dear friend". She had welled up - it was at times of stress you found out who your real friends were!

Then the truce was broken.

*

She had been polishing some already gleaming copper items - admiring their warmth, and the way that the room was reflected distortedly in the curved surfaces, when the doorbell rang. On the CCTV she saw a clean and smiling couple, smartly dressed, standing on the cold step, carrying publications of some kind. It was a sigh-making sight - the toothpastiness of their grins, the cut of their coats, the ominous armful of 'literature' betokened superstition sales executives. But if she didn't answer the door, they would ring again, and arouse Ambrose. And they would just come back and annoy her on some other occasion when she might be even busier. So she opened it, intending to give them a curtly polite refusal.

"Good evening!" the man said with billion-watt energy, clearly merely the opening salvo in a bombardment of Great Tidings. They shone with frost and foolishness. "We're Jehovah's Witnesses, and we are here to..."

Fidelma was just about to mutter something about not being interested and close the door, when it was flung back against the wall with a crash and Ambrose rose up behind her, bulbous and sharp-armed like a giant mantis.

"Enter, I bid thee! Enter - serendipitous strangers! Thou art twice - nay, thrice welcome!"

The callers looked at each other in startled pleasure at this peculiar but rapturous reception, and came in before Fidelma had time to close her mouth. As they stood expectantly in the hallway, Ambrose bent and peered sharply into their faces from just a few inches, and they could not help blinking and pulling back slightly. Fidelma wasn't surprised; she could smell his breath from where she was. "Well, thank you so much for letting us reach out to you today..." the man began, with a hint of nervousness, but Ambrose cut him off.

"Thou art witnesses? Well met, well met! We are then comrades!" He threw his arms around them, first the man and then the woman, kissing both of them glutinously on their brows. Strings of saliva stayed behind. The woman looked very thoughtful as her face re-emerged from his oxter. He then started to half push, half-pull them up the stairs, and both half-turned to look almost beseechingly at Fidelma as they went out of sight around the corner of the landing.

"What? Are you already a Witness?", the man was saying in surprise.

Ambrose's answer reverberated down the stairwell. "Yea, brother and sister - but unhappily I have seen Him but once. So I have many questions for you - many indeed! Come, come! My cell will be our moot-chamber. We will not be disturbed there for many hours. But first I must entreat you to delineate the details of thy dalliance with the Deity. How was He habited? How garlanded? Speak to the purpose!"

"What? I beg your pardon..."

"Hast not ears to hear, jackanapes? Thou sayest thou saw! I repeat - how was He garbed? How garlanded? Art not an angelic intelligencer?"

The voices were suddenly cut off, as Ambrose's door was banged shut. Fidelma had still not closed the front door. Ambrose had sounded *angry*. She started to move hastily up the stairs, but before she had got halfway Ambrose's door had opened again, the couple were out on the landing and the man was shouting. "Keep away, I'm warning you - keep away! You're fucking mad!" The two came running recklessly down the stairs, empty-handed and frightened, and as they passed the gaping Fidelma, the man repeated, "He's fucking mad!"

Ambrose came loping behind, his arms full of their journals, and pursued them down the stairs and out into the drive, strewing magazines everywhere and shouting. "Thou art no Witnesses, but Witlesses! Liars! Lollygaggers! Jobernols! Lackapates! Pilates!" Then they had gone, and a moment afterwards Ambrose loped back up the drive. "The energumens have been exorcised! It is a signal victory. I wager they will not return!"

"No, Ambrose, they probably won't..." Fidelma did not feel sorry for the Jehovah's Witnesses, but Ambrose's aggressiveness had alarmed her. She well knew what wildness was in him. What would have happened, she wondered, if he had caught the fleeing couple? There had been such a look on his face...

She was still pondering on the incident in the evening when the front door came alive again. It was 9.03, just as her internal clock had warned her to prepare for bed. She would have sworn, had she not known that swearing solved nothing. On the contrary, it knotted up karma and impeded blood flow.

She had planned her night in soothing detail. Vitamins. Ironing. Flossing. Facemask. Examination for lumps. Bath by the light of scented candles. Ten pages of current book. Lights off at 10.20. She hated anything that interrupted even such small plans. And tonight she badly needed her-time. She was also slightly afraid, because a few weeks ago the local papers had mentioned a wave of distraction burglaries, whereby people were kept talking at the front door while accomplices crept in at the back. This was why she had finally had the CCTV installed.

She saw in the uncertain colours the unexpected sight of a woman and young girl - the woman mid-thirties, the child perhaps seven. That the visitors were female was not necessarily reassuring. Fidelma knew it was wrong to judge by appearances, but there was something about these two that troubled her. The woman was large, and blowsy, raven locks striped with lavishly applied peroxide. Her features seemed irregular and intrinsically ill-tempered. The overall effect was of someone onto whom a fridge had been dropped, and who had then eaten all of its contents. Her clothes even in this light were obviously designer knock-offs. The girl - certainly her daughter - was dressed like a tart, and when her eyes flicked across the camera's field of vision they seemed to Fidelma to contain a kind of calculation highly inappropriate in a child of her age. The ugly, unjust word broke into Fidelma's consciousness – tinkers! Sometimes she hated her instincts!

She scanned the CCTV screens covering the back of the house in case father/husband/brother/cousin was trying to prise open a window. But there was nothing moving on those screens, as she stood with her fingernails tensely tapping the phone handset that would either blank or acknowledge the visitors. The buzzer went again. Fidelma stared indecisively at the callers, both of whom were looking straight into the camera now, making her squirm even though she knew they couldn't see her. As she stood irresolute, willing them to go away, Ambrose came, cat-like, and without looking at her or speaking, opened the door. The pair rushed in eagerly. They were *tinkers*, and Fidelma could have wept at their clothes and the woman's badger hair. But they paid her no attention.

"It's you! It's really you!" the woman exclaimed, staring at Ambrose. "Look, Mollie! It's him - the Drill Man!"

Ambrose stood lofty, quiescent, waiting, smiling slightly. The woman gabbled on, sometimes breaking into Irish or gammon, while the girl stared shyly, and sometimes sucked her thumb. "... hope you don't mind our coming, sir. Begging your pardon, but we had to. We saw... you know... we saw... you, and the drill, and the no-pain. It was on the computer. And then we found your website. And I says to Mikey - that's my husband - that's who Mollie needs! A *dochtuir, asarlaí*, a wise man, Yer Man who can control pain. A man who can take on pain - other peoples' pain - a Country Man who can heal. This is Mollie, sir... Say hello to the gentleman, Mollie!"

She pushed the girl forward, much against her will, and Fidelma saw that she was, if anything, even more dishevelled than she had appeared on camera. Her left foot lagged clumsily behind the right. The woman prattled on, and Fidelma relaxed at her obvious sincerity. Not burglars, after all! And she had called Ambrose 'sir'! She had practically curtsied! But how could she get rid of them now? How could Ambrose have opened the door? There was more rural rattling - "...began last year, when she had some pains in her leg, d'you see, and they've been getting worse ever since, and now the doctor sez there's nothing to be done and the leg will have to come off, and..." Fidelma realized the woman's attention had switched to her. " ...this kind lady will understand, I'm sure, being a mother and all, God bless, you're a lucky lady, and such a lovely, kind face and all... And your name's Sheehy-O'Connor, isn't it? I wonder if we're related at all? Lots of our folk are O'Connors. Who was your father? What was his trade?"

Fidelma instinctively drew herself up at this suggestion, but she tried to keep her voice frost-free, and even to smile. Yet she spoke too quickly, and even as she spoke, she knew how it must sound. "Oh I doubt we're related!

I doubt it *very* much! My father was from Cork; I don't remember ever seeing any of you people down there! Besides, he was too... too..."

The woman eyed her up and down, her eyes two lime-drops of ancient resentment in a face both atrociously weathered and worryingly wide. "*You people*, is it? Oh, I know what you mean, right enough! Sorry if the blood of the High Kings isn't good enough for you! But anyways..." She turned her back superbly, and looked solely at Ambrose, ignoring Fidelma's panicky attempts to explain. "As you can see, sir - here she is... my little girl... apple of my eye, and her Da's... breaking his heart... breaking my heart... can't you take it away, sir? Please!" She stopped speaking at last, but now she was crying, salt flowing without sound, seeping like sap from a pine, while her daughter was looking expectant, dumbstruck, hope and fear following each other across her sallow face, her pathetic frame quivering.

Ambrose had gone down on both knees in front of Mollie. In front of a girl like that... Fidelma couldn't believe what she was seeing. Even kneeling, he was the same height as Mollie, and his eyes held hers in a forcefield. As they locked on, Fidelma saw a vast tremble pass through the girl as if an unexpected gale had sprung up from somewhere far away and extremely cold. Something keened through the hallway, the house, the world. "Ultima Thule - Asgard... Ultima Thule!" whispered Ambrose in a kind of moan.

The woman was muttering, her hands clasped in prayer, but to Fidelma it was pagan gibberish - "Our gathra, who cradgies in the manyak-norch, We turry kerrath about your moniker, Let's turry to the norch where your jeel cradgies, And let your jeel shans get greydied nosher same as it is where you cradgie. Bug us eynik to lush this thullis, And turri us you're nijesh sharrig for the gammy eyniks we greydied Just like we ain't sharrig at the gammi needies that greydi the same to us. Nijesh let us soonie eyniks that'll make us greydi gammy eyniks, But solk us away from the taddy..."

Ambrose placed his hands around the girl's left knee, long fingers interlinking about the joint, and Mollie trembled even more, as if at any moment she would fall, the house and street shake themselves to pieces. And he was speaking, not whispering now, and although no one could quite make out what the words were, it was sonorous and deep and reassuring, a voice that came through from somewhere else. As the words streamed out like light, Mollie put her right hand to her mouth and emitted a series of small shouts - "Oh... oh... oh..." - while her mother stared at

Ambrose with all her strength, her face intense, her melded hands shaking with sincerity. Fidelma too was mesmerized, staring at Ambrose's alien face, his slender hands encircling the skinny knee, the girl's dirty lower leg on which veins had raised themselves as if to meet Ambrose's touch. And the girl shook until her teeth were sore, and her eyes opened and opened and opened - then with a climactic "Oooh!" she gave one final convulsion, her gaze breaking to the floor, her chin dropping onto her neck, her body a boned fish, a small quantity of vomit dribbling disgustingly down her cheap coat. A reflex reflux, noted medically minded Fidelma with an un-medical shudder, thinking ruefully about the carpet, as Ambrose stopped chanting and Mollie's mother burst into wild applause.

L-DAY

When Fidelma had parted company with Letitia Shaughnessy-Don outside the Grand Hotel six days previously, she had somehow - what *had* she been thinking? - invited her to Tara Road to meet Ambrose. Letitia Shaughnessy-Don. To Tara Road. To meet Ambrose! And Letitia had accepted...

Now, in under twenty-four hours, she would be hosting one of the Shaughnessy-Dons in her house. Horror at what she had done in an excess of snobbish joy made her stand still in the street - where she might have stood for several minutes had not a woman pushing a pram emitted a testy "Excuse me!"

Letitia Shaughnessy-Don. Tara Road. And Ambrose. It felt almost like lèse-majesté to expect such a woman to come to such a house to meet such a boy! He might be rude. He might be nude...

What was almost as worrying was the possibility that she herself might commit some terrible faux-pas. Her new friend floated in such rarefied air that just about everyone else in town must seem... common. Including herself. There - it was out! For someone used to Monte Carlo, or the Upper East Side, or Chelsea - Fidelma even remembered seeing a picture of Letitia with the Queen - the town must seem appallingly provincial.

How strange to think that when Fidelma had moved here from Cork, it had seemed the epitome of chic modernity. It had taken twenty-five years for her to grow a carapace of social confidence - and now this reckless invitation had whisked it away, leaving her appallingly exposed. What had she been thinking? She moved slowly through the crowd, thinking of how each room in the house would appear to someone who lived among antique glamour. Seen in that light, even the exterior and the garden were problematic. She guessed Head House did not have PVC windows. Nor, probably, concrete frogs, or koi. And were Leylandii quite the thing? She could not have felt less adequate had she been about to host a State banquet.

There was, however, one consideration that buoyed her up - that Sandra would be madly envious. It would be the ultimate cachet. Fidelma daydreamed of saying apparently casually, "As Letitia was saying to me just the other day..." while her neighbour boiled. But there was someone else speaking to her - strikingly pretty, early 20s, fashionable. It was that girl Philomena - who had been at school with Ambrose, and whom Fidelma had ludicrously fantasized would make Ambrose an ideal wife.

"Excuse me - you are Mrs. Sheehy-O'Connor? Ambrose's mother?"

"Why yes - for my sins! It's Philomena, isn't it?"

The girl nodded; she looked strained. "How is he, please? We all saw - you know - the footage on the web, and we were very worried."

"Thanks for asking, Philomena. You're very kind! He's doing quite well now, although I'm afraid he isn't yet back to normal. Physically, he's fine. His personal issues may take a while to sort themselves out. But I'm sure it won't be long now."

Philomena nodded again, and reddened. "Oh that's good! Thank you. Please tell him we were all asking for him."

"All? Who?"

"Oh, you know, everyone in school - who was in school, I should say. Anyway, I must be going. Thank you, and I hope he gets well soon. Goodbye." She smiled, and threaded quickly away through the shoppers as Fidelma stared after her shapely rear elevation. It was the first time she could recall anyone had asked after Ambrose - and that it should have been this girl, of all possible enquirers!

When she got to the corner of Tara Road, there was even more to think about. There was someone waiting outside the gate. Two someones - and not the sort of someones she would hope to find waiting outside her gate, waving enthusiastically as they saw her turn the corner. With a suppressed groan, she recognized Mollie and her mother. She hoped Sandra wasn't monitoring the road - but as she darted a glance towards chez Gulliver, she saw the upstairs curtain flicking. Her unwelcome visitors were clad in identical garments, even down to the lucky heather in tin foil pinned to their tawdry fronts. She inhaled deeply through slightly flared nostrils, as Mollie's mother hailed her. "Is it yourself? That's grand! Is his honour in?"

"I'm sorry?"

"His honour - the big fella himself?"

"Do you mean my son, Mr.... I mean, Ambrose?"

The woman looked at her, wonderingly but also defensively, clearly piqued by the suggestion of ice. "Who else would I be meaning? Is he in, or isn't he, Missus?"

"Em, no, I think he is probably down in the town. He tends to spend the day down there... you know, talking to people."

"Preaching, you mean!" The woman's smile broadened again, and she went on with renewed good humour. "Ah sure he's a quare one, right enough - a quare one indeed! And he looks it too! But let me tell you this, Missus - HE'S GOT IT!"

She looked eagerly at Fidelma, clearly hoping for answering enthusiasm. Fidelma scrabbled for meaning. What on earth was she saying? What had Ambrose got? All she could think of, and she hated herself for thinking it, was that he had contracted some disease - perhaps from this very pair. She spread beautifully gloved hands helplessly - also to ward off putative pestilence. "I'm sorry...?"

The woman looked at her with surprise and scorn. "It! The Touch! The hands that cure - the wise man hands! The Medicine Hand! See..." She pushed Mollie forward roughly, and Fidelma noticed wonderingly that the girl's left foot was no longer dragging, and her face looked marginally less pinched. The woman's voice was triumphant, slightly awed. "Her leg, d'ye see? It's better! It's well - it's whole! The doctor says so this very morning - and he doesn't know how! But we do - Missus, your mad *buachaill's* cured Mollie!"

*

It was three o'clock on L-Day. Fidelma felt as if she had been stretched over a frame, and scraped with oyster shells. Every part of her throbbed with tired tension. She could not get rid of the smell of bleach from her hands, even though she had worn gloves during a marathon of cleaning that had only finished at two am, and resumed at six, after four hours of muttering and tossing. The house also smelt slightly of paint, because she had thought the hall wall looked grubby, and there had been just enough of that colour left in the garage. But the house was at least free from dirt, and her guest would hopefully notice. The place did look good, she felt, even though she would have preferred it if there had been less chrome and more chronology about the furniture - and an Old Master on the dining room wall instead of the sub-sub-Picasso etchings she had borne back in misplaced triumph from the local art fair.

Fidelma had decided she would not tell Ambrose about Mollie. It would just encourage him, especially after Mary's deeply unhelpful intervention. She had enough to contend with without Ambrose getting it into his poor noggin that he possessed some kind of miraculous Power. There was quite enough nonsense in there already. She had only encountered him once in the last twenty-four hours anyway, when their paths had intersected on the landing at about midnight - she with her hair tied up and her face flushed, carrying a heavy bucket of equipment - him sporting another white tracksuit and a white-tipped brace of facial carbuncles, fondling a large ebony rosary she had never seen before. Another charity shop find, obviously. A faint hope that he might help had fluttered into life when he lifted an imperious hand to arrest her progress. "Halt! You are heavy-laden, woman of the house. Seekest succour?"

"Ooh, you are kind! Would you like to take this cloth and cream cleanser and clean out the third bathroom? It hasn't been cleaned since last Saturday, and needs a good hard scrub! And after that..."

But he had wagged a digit, and laughed in gentle mockery. "Nay - the succour of which I speak is unearthly in origin! Forsake thy - brushes - and cream cleanser - thy bleaches and powders - thy unguents and potions!" As he enumerated the items, he had reached into her bucket and thrown them in all directions. "Abandon thy outward semblances, and consider the spiritual germs that multiply in thy nooks! Pray for guidance. Art READY, pilgrim?" She winced at the volume of "READY" and jerked the bucket away, but he had already taken hold of the special brush for cleaning the Venetian blinds. For a moment, they had pulled at opposite ends of the implement before she needed to let go. He had then tossed it contemptuously down the stairwell. "There let thy tools lie till Doomsday - which may be nigher than thou thinkst! Think on't!"

He had floated onwards in a cloud of benignity, the beads of his rosary clacking together in the most aggravating way imaginable. She had darted his back a look that might have disconcerted even him had he seen it, before dashing down the stairwell to pick up the tools - surprising herself with the forcefulness of her vocabulary. But she soon scrubbed away the interruption, caught up despite all her worries in a reverie of hygiene, reassuring rituals - scrubbing the scrubbed, straightening the straight, dusting the dust-free, disinfecting the uninfected.

But now she flagged as she watched the impossibly elegant figure approach up the driveway. A shark-handsome grey Mercedes was pulling away smoothly along the road. The awfulness of Ambrose rose up to crush her hopes, and it was with a blend of trepidation and resignation that she opened the door to social failure. Her smile of welcome was too thin, her face too haggard, her house too clean, and her guest too beautifully clad -

but it was too late to do anything except trust to Fate. Her hands (bleach-smelling!) trembled slightly as she poured out the single estate Darjeeling that had been the most expensive tea in the supermarket.

But Letitia was charmingly natural, and if she felt contempt for the fixtures and fittings, she gave no sign. She commented instead on Fidelma's "lovely" house, the "superb" view of the Head, the "interesting" artworks. She sat on the leather suite as though it had not been made in China, sipped the single estate, and animadverted on the weather and the news, as all acquaintances ought. Fidelma was surprised to find her voicing some very old-fashioned opinions. Had such opinions come from any other source, Fidelma might have challenged them out of a vague sense of duty to the future. But, overawed, she nodded along, both dreading and looking forward to the end of the ordeal.

It was difficult to know what to talk about, so she eventually blurted out the story of the visits from Mollie and her mother. Her guest seemed genuinely interested, and not at all repulsed. After this subject had run its course, Letitia seemed to raise an eyebrow, although in fact she had done nothing of the kind - and Fidelma knew it was time to introduce Ambrose into the equation.

He came in like a Sasquatch, as filthy as she had feared, as aromatic, as unimpressed as his mother had been overwhelmed. But Letitia looked straight up into his face, and smiled warmly. "Hello, Ambrose. I'm Letitia. Won't you come and sit down beside me?"

He grunted, but did, to Fidelma's great surprise. He sat stiffly upright, staring straight ahead, hands on his knees, while Letitia assessed him with a hint of humour, but also deep interest. The contrast between effortlessly elegant lady and hirsute visionary was surreal, and Fidelma was reminded of a photo she had once seen - Rasputin surrounded by Romanov women. (The Ape of God, one of the nuns had called Rasputin - a nickname that could easily be applied to Ambrose, except that apes did not have such long necks.)

Letitia spoke with animation. "I live up at Head House, Ambrose. I believe you saw something special up on the Head."

"Yes. At the Cross." His eyes augured her. Letitia was the only person, Fidelma reflected, who seemed able to meet his gaze these days. There was an deep assurance about Letitia, Fidelma thought - a sense of entitlement. She had the confidence just to be herself. But now she sounded ruminative, as if powerful emotions were at work behind her serene facade.

"The Head is a special place, Ambrose. There's no denying that. Something about its size, and its position, I suppose. It's always been special to me, anyway. It's practically part of the garden. I see it first thing every morning, and last thing every night - and I sometimes go up there on winter nights, when the moon is full and the whole world looks like a painting by Palmer." She stirred her tea absently. The tiny metallic clink of spoon against china told Fidelma about salons she would never see.

"I spent a lot of time up there when I was a girl, Ambrose. Whole days walking the cliffs, watching the cormorants, befriending the ponies, exploring all the secret tracks. There used to be wild goats - so impressive, looking at you with those oval eyes, like old Pan himself! I remember one day going in under the gorse - that fabulous smell! - and finding a dried-up bog, with a cow's skull and the remains of its hide. The poor thing had obviously got trapped. I felt I'd stumbled on a pagan shrine! There are some parts I don't care to visit - old pines up to their knees in dead needles - patches of hemlock and nightshade where you feel eyes fixed on you! A girl went missing up there in the Forties, and people say they have seen her - but when they turn the corner she's gone. Oh, it's easy to laugh sitting in this lovely room" - she inclined her head graciously, and slightly apologetically, towards Fidelma - "but when you're there, it's a different matter altogether! There are ruined houses too, and odd bits of wall running up to cliffs, all strangled in bramble. Then there's a spring that was sacred in the old days. The most delicious water, by the way! It's the kind of place where there's every kind of memory. It's a place wonderful things really might happen. I love it!" She touched her tweed-guarded heart, and sipped tea, her eyes for a few moments astoundingly youthful.

Fidelma was surprised Ambrose had not fidgeted or interrupted, as he would surely have done had she (or, probably, anyone else) made such a long speech. She interrupted, slightly jealously. "Yes, it's a nice place, right enough. Good views. But it's not very accessible, is it? Some of those footpaths are a disgrace! Can I help you to some more tea?"

"Hmmm? Oh, no - no, thank you. It's delicious, though." Fidelma could see Letitia's cup was half-full, and wondered if she had misjudged the beverage. She didn't like it herself. She usually drank herbal teas. Quite apart from the caffeine, it was so important not to fur the tongue.

Letitia had resumed her unexpected antiquarianism. "In the Middle Ages, people would walk there from all over Ireland, and even further, to put flowers on St Alba's grave. They used to hold Masses up there in the

Penal days. They could see if the soldiers were coming." Ambrose was following closely, but Fidelma was losing interest. She wondered casually how many calories were in each of those biscuits.

"In the Sixties, Father Reilly asked my father about placing the Cross on the Head, close to Alba's Cell. Daddy wasn't devout - but he gave the land and some of the money anyway. He never saw the Cross of course, because he died a few months afterwards, but I always think of him when I see it. When the Cross was unveiled, I was there. There was a newspaper photograph of the unveiling, and there I am in the front row, wearing the most frightful hat! Almost all those people must be dead now, I suppose."

She smiled faintly, and stood, her knees making the tiniest and genteelest click, and went over to the window, gazing at the Head. "Boring memories of an old woman! And there's no reason at all why you, Ambrose, or anyone, should be remotely interested in them... except that they may give you an idea why I am so interested in talking to a young man for whom the Head also has huge significance."

Ambrose's voice, when it came after this long and mellifluous speech, was harshly jarring. But as with Mary, he and Letitia seemed to understand each other on some level beyond Fidelma's comprehension. As before, she felt excluded, insulted by omission. "Thy recollections, Letitia, are the stuff of life. But what is of more consequence is thy susceptibility. Thou knowest there is Another Side. Thou realizest that place is a portal. The earth's skin is thin there."

"That's always been my feeling! 'The earth's skin is thin there'. I shall always remember that phrase. Thank you, Ambrose. But please tell me what you saw!"

He was about to speak, when Fidelma said "Oh, God..." Socialite and son followed her gaze.

An unprecedented procession was wending its way up the driveway. It was led by - Fidelma put her face in her hands - the girl Mollie, her mother, and a man with a detonation of blond frizzy hair, whose acrylic ensemble had first challenged sensibilities around 1973. Bell-bottom trousers flapped around distressingly bony ankles, and highlighted scuffed brogues. Several others were following in his noteworthy wake, many broad in the beam, and the broader they were, the more likely to be sporting clothing that clung where clothes should not. Fidelma couldn't imagine how they had all fitted into the rusty white van emblazoned "Mikey Walsh - Driveway's, House Clearence's, Waiste Disposal" parked at the end of her drive. That such people should arrive at all was upsetting; that they should arrive in such numbers was frightening; that they should come *now*!

"It's those tin... those members of the Travelling Community! I can't apologise enough... I'll get rid of them, somehow."

But Letitia was standing beside her, smiling delightedly. "It's up to you, of course, Fidelma, but they have obviously come to thank Ambrose for healing their daughter. It would seem strange and ungracious if you were to turn them away. I really think you should let them in!"

What could Fidelma do but open the door and smile as widely as she could? Her sitting room became thronged with the sort of people whom she would never have expected to see in her sitting room, or the sitting rooms of anyone she knew.

All revolved around Ambrose, his wing-nut head and bony shoulder-blades above a hubbub of round-headed, broad-bodied, ebullient visitors wearing clashing colours. The table was piled high with thank you cards, bottles of cava and whisky, crates of beer, boxes of chocolates, bunches of flowers. Blond-frizzed Mikey had even pressed an envelope firmly into Fidelma's hand as he came in "Just to say thanks for what the *buachaill* did!" and she had opened it to see a substantial wedge of money. She retained just enough wit to push it back firmly into his hands, and resist further efforts to press it upon her. Another man looked over her furniture with a businesslike shake of the head, and offered to replace the lot with Polish imports for just 5,000 Euros. But she wasn't listening. She had just realised that people had come to see Ambrose. Not only that, but to admire him! Almost to adore...

Hard hands were pumping his and resting caressingly on his shoulders, eyes were eating him, lips were brushing his cheek, and one woman even kissed his healing hands in neo-feudal fealty. As if all this was not strange enough, Letitia Shaughnessy-Don knew these people, and they her. She addressed them by their names - Mikey, Mairéad, Mollie, P.J., Brenda - and they replied in tones of warmest respect. One of the women came close to curtseying. "To be sure, 'tis yerself, Mrs. Shaughnessy-Don, and I hope I find you well this fine day... might a knowed we'd find your honour here with the Wonderman... he's a phenomenon, no mistake... hasn't happened in years... a rare fella, right enough... everyone's talking about him..."

Wonderman! Letitia Shaughnessy-Don a friend to tinkers! Fidelma's constructs collapsed, and she stood there mechanically shaking hands and blankly smiling at a succession of strangers congratulating her for

Ambrose! It was too amazing to take it in, but it touched her deeply, and she stood on the edge of the emotional circle, anxious amongst their egalitarian ease, almost crying amidst their laughter.

THE AMBROSE EFFECT

The media brooded on epochal matters. There was a clash of divas on *Price of a Song*. A courageous gay celebrity was splitting courageously from his husband because the latter had courageously expressed the wish to convert, or convert back, to female or male. And there was a World Cup demi-semi-final of a sport, from which the Irish team had been expelled in the first round. But they soon noticed that something truly extraordinary was occurring in one of Ireland's stolidest suburbs, a place where nothing interesting was thought to have happened before.

There was, first, the obligatory Twitter flutter - a peculiar-looking man (a gift to caricaturists) drilling through his own ulna for some reason known only to himself. There were all kinds of associated stories racing around the town and the web, rumours and half-jokes, all growing in the retelling - things seen on a hill, magical healings, minds read, noises heard, objects moving in empty rooms, the future foretold (accurately). There was a piquancy about the idea of a boring 'burb waking to find that one of its cosseted sons had become a locus of medieval-style unreason - someone whom the ill-educated and superstitious were flocking to see, and whose garden shrubs suddenly sprouted votive offerings - knotted rags and plastic bags, tiny fluffy animals of indeterminate taxonomy, base metal lucky charms and dangling crucifixes. As if all this were not enough, there was the involvement of a top-drawer celebrity. Top top-drawer!

It was generally acknowledged that Letitia Shaughnessy-Don was the nearest thing to Grace Kelly today's Ireland could afford - an always camera-ready exemplar of elegance and ease, equally at home wherever she went, an admirable/envied ambassador for all things Hibernian. Normally a reserved interviewee, this Irish Icon (as she was invariably called) had told a startled fashion magazine interviewer about "an absolutely fascinating young man who really seems to have something of the visionary about him". She had gone on to tell the story of Mollie's healing, and that the little girl was a Traveller sank barbs into sensitive social consciences. The resultant article was the first interesting one the fashion magazine had published in its thirty-five years, and it raced around the world and all the way back to Tara Road.

And here the media eye rested for a time, journalists milling night and day outside the house where Ambrose laid his puzzled head. All hoped to be the first to secure an interview with the madman-mage. But the door was shut to journalists, and they were forced to content themselves with shots of parts of Fidelma as she drove out of the gates en route to the shops, or ducked in and out of the car carrying bags of groceries - then even these stopped, as she cancelled appointments and opted for home delivery. By way of compensation, the Irish Icon was now frequently to be seen in these unlikely surroundings, as she came and went from the house (the door was opened to her). Each time the press pack saw her Mercedes nearing, it pressed forward in rapacious reverence, and they were never disappointed, as she insinuated neatly between them, strewing words as sweet and insubstantial as almond-blossom, affording glimpses of that famous profile, that hair, those clothes. The *Town Clarion* cleared that week's exclusive about dog poo bins to run a front page story headlined "Ambrose 'perfectly charming' says Irish Icon" - which led to that journal's best ever week's sales.

For Tara Road residents, Letitia's visitations were in welcome contrast to other devotees who were, as one journalist remarked cattily, "more Old Mother Kelly than Grace" (a remark which earned her a reprimand for racism from the Gardaí). Letitia's chauffeur-guided car seemed all the more chariot-like when seen against this background of white vans and people-carriers. Her coiffure and couture, her gull-grey gaze, the glamour of her house, her alertness and wit shed credibility on Ambrose and his asseverations. Ambrose's devotees and Letitia's paparazzi were embarrassing inconveniences for local people, but they were somehow outweighed by the lustre Letitia bestowed on everything in her proximity. It was reported that houses in Tara Road and intersecting avenues had increased in value overnight because of this "Ambrose effect". Ambrose was for the first time regarded with indulgence by the people in those roads - he was still a loony, but now he was a lucrative one. Tara Roaders who had shaken their heads at Ambrose's awfulness, and some of whom had even reported him for simply loitering near their gates, now told journalists that although he was undoubtedly strange, they at least had always liked him. On her rare dashes to the shops, Fidelma became engaged in conversations with people whose faces she had known for years, but to whom she had never spoken. One sympathetic elderly woman took her hand in the supermarket, and squeezed it slightly, and called her "a lady of sorrows" - and the homely phrase almost made Fidelma cry in the middle of the Frozen Vegetables aisle.

She saw Ambrose on journal covers, and heard his name on the airwaves, and blood would beat in her face. Whenever reporters came near, she would dash into shops, or slam the car door, or mutter "Nothing to say, nothing to say" as she pushed past them, head down, crimson beneath her foundation. If only Letitia hadn't got involved, she thought. Ambrose may have started the stupid thing, but he wasn't driving it now. All he did was sit in his room, adding yet more dangerous nonsense to the internet, as if there wasn't enough out there already. He seemed wholly ignorant of the furore. When she tried to talk about it, he just stared at her, chewing with his mouth open, and then turned the subject back to his researches - which in recent days had included the Chinese animal calendar, Zoroastrian fire dancing, and the evergreen Homoousian controversy.

All this time, Sandra Gulliver had been almost ill with envy, all the more intolerable after her initial glee at Ambrose's illness, and in getting one over "that snobby cow next door". Seeing Letitia darting so frequently and familiarly up Fidelma's drive almost brought Sandra out in spots. Even Tom felt her tongue-lash in those days, as he sat in the evenings eating crustless peanut-butter sandwiches at the dining room table, while his mother almost foamed about "some people having all the luck" and "that bitch next door". If only Letitia would come up her drive, she fumed, just once - is that too much to ask? When Tom interjected that he couldn't see what all the fuss was about, she turned on him savagely, saying that of course he wouldn't understand, just like your father! She made savage notes in her journal, and kept breaking the pencil point.

But then it was announced that Ambrose was to be a guest on Liam Larrikin's notorious daytime show - and suddenly she felt a great deal better. She added jam to Tom's sandwiches, and daydreamed of the Sheehy-O'Connors' downfall.

*

Lunch On Liam, slyly abbreviated to L.O.L., was a hugely popular programme whose strapline declared it was dedicated to "Highlighting Modern Ireland". This particular model of Ireland consisted of absent/alcoholic/benefit-receiving/criminal/eccentric/exploitative/homophobic/junkie/love-rat/racist/religious/sexist/violent men who were locked in constant war against women, children and minorities - out there in Ireland's wild hinterland, its houses of hate and streets of shame. There was a Dublin witticism that the strapline should have been "Highlighting Lowlifes".

Liam Larrikin grilled his 'guests' until they were very, very well-done - part-barbecuer, part-inquisitor, part-shocked liberal who sometimes even started his broadsides with a thundering "J'accuse..." (The same Dublin wits had dubbed him "Jackass".) There was a heart-warming side to the show too, as estranged couples were re-united (although who knew for how long?) under the regard of a studio audience whose passionate commitment would have done credit to the Constantinople Hippodrome. And every so often, Liam genially quizzed officially lovable guests (Gisela Mildew had been on twice). But it was clear to Sandra, and everyone else, that Ambrose was being set up for a fall at Liam's fat and freckled hands. Everyone except Ambrose - and Fidelma, who did not know about his invitation. There was a reason guests were nicknamed "Liam's Lambs".

The studio audience whooped and clapped as the lights came up to reveal the celebrated set - a table laden with real food, and a filmed backdrop of a real restaurant. And there in his usual place at the head of the table loomed mine host - a man made on a bountiful scale, a ginger-going-grey giant with brown eyes shoved far into the cheese-toastie fatness of his face, spraying folksy concern indiscriminately over the studio and home audiences. Among the latter today was Fidelma, still off work, who was at that moment sitting down in front of the screen with a delicious mug of anti-oxidant beverage. Liam's bulgy rangefinders swept calculatingly over the serried seats and then froze on the cameras, from which he fed so greedily. (He never touched the studio food, saving his gorging for long nights in his home cinema.)

Viewers of this consummate professional would never have guessed that he had a secret - a serious secret. One part of Liam Larrikin feared the cameras as much as the most lary of his Lambs. Even now, after all those years recording some of the country's most watched TV, a tapeworm of trouble deep in his intestines twitched whenever the cameras' glazed gaze whirred round to him. Why this should have been, Liam scarcely acknowledged even to himself, even in the most sleepless small hours, when all the house felt like it was hunching over him. There were files in his hippocampus he would never open, but could not quite expunge - memories that padded like terrible animals around the perimeter of his mind, trying to burst back into his life, as once they had mauled his childish alter ego as he lay in that high-ceilinged institution, hoping the door would not click evilly open, the sainted men come in again...

Those bastards were dead, that Home closed, and there was no-one now - Liam was almost certain - who knew what they had made him do. Nor what illegal hungers they had awakened in him by their example. He begged often of the God in which he could not believe - for it had been their God - that no-one would ever discover there was dirt at his heart.

He had been wonderfully successful in his career, through his own talent, but also partly thanks to constant monitoring, from Googling his own name in association with certain shameful search-terms to - on two occasions - employing excellent lawyers. He was privately proud of his focus and skill - and nobody viewing him in action on a typical day could possibly have guessed at the burdens he bore from a ruined boyhood, as he gored 'guests' or schmoozed with the celebrated, all in a trademark mid-Atlantic mid-English that somehow managed to be wholly Irish.

But today was not turning out typical. Behind his flabby exterior, Liam was taut with worry. He had heard that a TV crew had been sniffing around, seeking old acquaintances, asking odd questions. Even as he prepared himself for the day's filming, he was gnawing the inside of his cheek, chewing over his conscience, checking for gaps in his armature.

Week after week, Fidelma was drawn against her finer instincts to the dysfunctional display, for the same reason as many others - because it helped her to know that there were very many people who were stupider, uglier, unluckier, poorer or sicker than she would ever be. So she knew the merciless format well, and had gazed in delighted horror into the behavioural bear-pit from which only Liam ever emerged unbloodied. She sat forward in her chair, ready to lose herself in others' awfulness, forget for a while the unanswered question that lolled unhygienically upstairs.

In his slightly slurring slightly American voice, Liam introduced the first Lamb of this Lunch. A hulking, tattooed, ear-ringed, partner-beater who said he still loved his partner (notwithstanding having hospitalized her) dropped bristlingly into a chair opposite Liam, fixing the camera with a look of alertness, yet also unintelligence. And there - amazingly - he stayed sitting, as Liam browbeat and filleted him with fantastic skill and speed. Fidelma marvelled, as everyone always did, at Liam's unscrupulous expertise, as the man broke - disintegrating into self-justification, self-doubt, then self-hatred, before finally breaking into tears appalling to see

A Modern Journey

on such a countenance. It looked as if a tree was melting, and the spectacle was deeply troubling to at least some of the watchers - although the studio audience seemed to have no such reservations, clapping at every new twist of Liam's bayonet. Then they broke into a cacophony of abuse, advice and bawling as the beaten partner was wheeled in, to declare, first, that she hated him - secondly that she still loved him, although she could never trust him again - thirdly that she would give it one more go for the sake of "the little wans". Tears, kisses, and a sneering kind of applause from the studio audience, as the newly washed souls slouched and waddled out, consigned to contempt, their names already forgotten. Fidelma shook her head in wonder at the state of some people, and filled up her mug with more anti-oxidant. And then she spilled it.

Liam had turned to the autocue, and avuncular approbation was superseded by the superb scornfulness that was his trademark - "And now, ladies and gennelmen, for my nex' gues'. You'll prob'ly have read over the last few days extrornery stories about a young guy who not only makes amazin' claims, but does amazin' things - to himself! Among his amazin' claims, one stan's out - that he's here on a mission from God. And among the amazing things he does, one stan's out too - he makes holes in his arms using a thing like THIS!"

He brandished a drill, holding it up to each camera in turn, and the audience oohed. He pressed the button and it buzzed into life. Then he made a circling motion with the drill beside his temple, and pulled a faux-foolish face. The audience rocked in delight. Fidelma sat stupefied, uncharacteristically oblivious to the puddle of healthful beverage that had plashed onto the laminate and was now winding towards the hall.

"Ladies and gennelmen, what can I say? He's prob'ly the bigges' gues' we've ever had, with the most influential friends. Meantersay, you don' get bigger than God! But is he here with a special message from the Head Honcho - or is he just an eejit? Let's ask the man himself! Here He is - the Mad Drill Messiah, ladies and gennelmen, please welcome AMBROSE SHEEHY-O'CONNOR!" He came fatly to his feet as Ambrose padded out into the lights, while the audience vibrated, and Fidelma felt as if the sitting-room wall had fallen on her. Sandra Gulliver chortled and raised two fingers at that same wall, then sat forward, not wanting to miss a second of the evisceration.

Ambrose's appearance was, as usual, unprepossessing. He was wearing one of his once-white tracksuits, which despite Fidelma's frequent launderings had already gone greyish and bobbled with nylon nodules. Whilst waiting in the Green Room, he had become disenchanted with his well-worn running shoes, and so had left them there, his bare feet adding to the delight of the audience, if not the other guests in the Green Room, who edged away from the abandoned footgear.

"A hundred thousand welcomes to L.O.L., Ambrose! *Céad míle fáilte*, my friend! Siddown, siddown! Make yourself at home!"

Fidelma stared at Liam's uncooked pudding face, and hated in a way she had never hated anyone or anything before. She thought she would not be able to watch. (But she had to.) She wanted to rush to Ambrose's room to check whether he was there, because he must be. (But she knew he wasn't.) She wanted to throw up. She had the stupid fleeting fancy that if she didn't watch she could make it stop. She reached for the remote, but her finger failed to press the red button. She wasn't able to; she was clamped to the chair, and she would have to see it - and him - through. The spilled anti-oxidant made it to the hall, then ran out of oxidants to anti.

Just a few streets away, in a house like Fidelma's in size and non-style, and just as silent, Philomena was watching too. Her feelings were more complicated. She had been following her former schoolmate's career since the self-drilling footage - at first with idle malice, then pity and mild curiosity, now some other emotion. She and her friends would text each other - "did you SEE the state of him?". "LOL", "What is he like?" The others had moved onto other subjects, but Philomena unexpectedly found herself unable to switch off from his story. The sight of the drill eating through his arm had given her a nauseous thrill, combined with the image of his exalted face. Who else among her acquaintance would have done anything so - stylish?

She was not remotely religious, but nevertheless she found his stoicism oddly enticing, and some of his reported exploits impossible to explain. That little tinker girl healed - science couldn't explain *that*. And people were saying he was able to see things that hadn't happened yet - there were loads of stories like that circulating. His fans were admittedly not generally the kind of fans someone could exactly be proud of. But it was something to be loved, even by people like that.

And then there was Letitia Shaughnessy-Don - who outweighed all other disadvantages. Someone so sophisticated could surely not have been taken in by a charlatan. To have sparked the interest of Letitia Shaughnessy-Don was to have done something with one's life, to be someone. Most of her other ex-schoolmates were now working in offices, or shops - shops like the shoe emporium in which she spent her resentful weekdays, chewing gum, disliking the customers and irritating the manager. Ambrose offered escape and gave a colour to life, filled an imaginative gap she had not realised existed.

The physical differences between Ambrose and Liam came close to comical. Ambrose sat tall, as unrelenting as a telephone pole, an impression aided by his semi-conductor ears - while his host's body cascaded lumpily in many directions, his huge head dispensing entirely with the customary neck - extreme stiffness meeting (apparent) softness.

"Greatuh have yuh here, Ambrose! I can call you Ambrose, right? It's not, like, Yer Reverence or Yer Holiness or sumthin'?" He looked slyly at the audience for approval (which came).

Ambrose inclined his head - regally, Philomena thought, the unusual word popping into her head from some childish tale. "Ambrose is what I was denominated by my mother, and therefore it is meet thou shouldst so address me. I lay no claim to temporal titles. The things of the earth are earthy." Liam couldn't deny this logic, but he winked at the camera as if he had scored an important point. "Great, great! OK - so let's geddown to brass tacks. First of all, recognize this liddle fella?" He waved the drill under Ambrose's nose, who looked perplexed, as if it reminded him of something he couldn't quite remember. The audience tittered.

"Truly, it resembleth an electric drill, Mr. Lambkin - to wit, a cordless Akanawa XD15 with reverse action. But I cannot comprehend the significance of thy question. Art quite well?"

A tiny bonfire flared up in the Larrikin eyes. It was not unknown for guests to try and score off him, but not normally guests of this calibre, and rarely so early in an interview. He bridled at the lack of respect. He leaned forward, and tapped Ambrose on the knee. "Yeh, Ambrose. Oh, and it's Larrikin. L-A-R-R-I-K-I-N. Goddit? Anyway, as I was sayin' this baby's a 'lectric drill, and the reason you recognized i' is 'coz you used one jus' like it to drill a hole in your arm. Your own arm! I'm quite well - but the question we'd like to know is are you? In the head? Eh, eh?" He threw himself back triumphantly in his complaining chair, his arrow fired, its target found.

Yet the target did not react. Liam was disconcerted; there was something unusual about this guy, even a bit creepy maybe. He remembered his breezy comments at the planning meeting - "Sure, sure, let's get the dork!"

120

- and half-wished he could rewind time. (This was a recurring fantasy; his dreams were almost always reproaches.)

"I am grateful for thy solicitude; I find myself in rude health."

"Rude health, eh? Eh? That seems to be a very 'ppropriate word, Ambrose! Very - 'coz a liddle birdie tells me that you have been wanderin' abou' butt-nekkid!" Oohs and laughs passed through the audience. "What do you say to that, Ambrose? And as for 'solicitude', who was doing the soliciting, we'd like to know! Am I right, or am I right?" The appealed-to audience rippled with appreciation; some were already in hysterics. He was right!

'My habiliments, Mr. Lardkin, are immaterial. Literally immaterial, you might say..." Ambrose paused, a semi-smile sporting on his lips. But Liam failed to respond, because he had never heard the word 'habiliments'. So after several pregnant seconds, Ambrose resumed. "What is material is this, Mr. Larrikin... thou art playing with Peril!"

Ambrose pointed an accusing finger at him, and his eyes had gone hard and sharp - adamant and unforgiving, stones under frost. Liam, perspiring as ever under the lights, shifting in his seat, forced a smile. But he had never seen such remorselessness - no finger quite so flinty.

"You are in danger, Larrikin. Yea, I say, danger - of the gravest kind. All is known. Apollyon comes towards you across the field, trailing judgement! Soon, all will be revealed! All!"

Liam had received threats before, and although he laughed them off in public, they peopled his evenings. His house high on Howth was shielded by fences and cameras, and there were panic buttons beside each of the fridges. This wasn't a threat exactly, but in some ways it seemed worse.

For one thing, it was from someone middle-class, and in Liam's experience middle-class people rarely made idle threats. But what was really unnerving was his sudden feeling that the loony knew something. There was a supreme confidence in Ambrose's manner, a gravitas that belied his oddity - as if he were downloading energy from some far-off source. With his vaguely monastic appearance, his passionate intensity, his expansive vocabulary, Ambrose evoked innumerable horror flicks watched during long nights in the company of low-cal cola. "He's a fucking psycho!" Liam thought – "the sort who listens to classical music!" He wondered how far away the security guards were.

"Wh...what are you saying?" Liam didn't ask what was known, or would be revealed - because in a remote compartment of his mind he knew. He felt a rush of apprehension, suppressed angrily. How could this wild-eyed waster know anything? He forced himself to speak. "Ah ha ha, Ambrose, you won't get away with..." But Ambrose stomped on, oblivious to the rules of this game. trampling down all obstacles. His voice bounced and boomed back from the plastic and plywood of the set, arousing echoes Liam had never noticed.

"It is not thou alone who teeters on the brink - but also these auditors. Thou all - " he turned to the audience, his face full of contempt, and pointed at random members - "standeth in need of succour". He turned back to Liam, "Yet I say thou art the chief transgressor, with thine illicit appetites." Ambrose stabbed the fearful finger at his host, and Liam leapt inside. Stupid, baseless, he scolded himself - calm down! I must be overworked, he thought. But just for a moment it had felt as though...as though... He ran a huge hand over his huger face, and sought to recover the initiative.

"Oh, I geddit! You mean moral peril! I thought you meant something real. Thank Gawd!" He mock-mopped his brows and winked at his fans, many of whom winked back. They preferred judging to being judged. Liam would get the eejit on the rack any second now, and they yearned to see the upstart's entrails.

But try as Liam might to retake the initiative, Ambrose just kept on talking, droning on in a strangely magnetic way, looking through Liam and into the guts of the audience, then past them into space, his voice clear and stentorian in a studio unaccustomed to seriousness or articulacy. The audience stirred uneasily; respectable women smiled at those beside them, but couldn't quite meet their eyes. "Thy sins have found you out! Thy decadence - avarice - selfishness - cheapness - carnal passions - fear - tawdry taste - boundless ignorance..."

Liam had never come across a guest who insulted rather than tried to ingratiate himself with him and the audience. He didn't like that. At all. And the audience hadn't come here to be called names - that was what the loony was for. The loony now taking over his show. But what he liked least of all was that the weirdo had - accidentally, of course! - struck much too close to the mark. It must have been an accident! Mustn't it? Of course it was! And yet somehow danger had come into the studio, was gathering in the gloom behind the cameras. Time to take a hand, Liamo... "Hey, hey, let's keep this polite now, guys! Ambrose - AMBROSE! AMBROSE!"

He shouted, for the first time in L.O.L.'s history, and all eyes were again on him - the audience greatly surprised at his losing his cool - and, even more, his asking for politeness. Ambrose's eyes zeroed back in from whatever they had been viewing, and fixed him with Puritan flintiness. Liam swallowed. Fidelma looked above nibbled nails. "O.K., O.K., but I'll tell you what worries a hell of a lot of people about you. J'accuse... On yer site you have said - and I quote - these are not my words, ladies and gennelemen - 'There is only one true faith. Those who aver otherwise lieth!'" The audience groaned and hissed outrage. How could he? How dared he? Who was he to judge? Strike him down, Liam!

"Or how about this - again, ladies and gennelemen, these are not my words - J'accuse, Ambrose O'Connor - 'Carnal knowledge' - that means sex, ladies and gennelemen - 'carnal knowledge is justified only to a man and a woman'. So whatcher sayin' is that, say, Islam is somehow not OK? And that gays/LGBT/trigender/transqueer/cis✽males are inferior? And a little bird even told me you voted against equal marriage. Like, hey, this is the 21st century! Wake up and smell the coffee! Think outside the box going forward! At the end of the day, Ambrose, is that really what you wanna say to us today - to the whole freakin' century?"

He threw himself back in his chair, which sighed under the onslaught. Some in the audience were shouting angrily at these heresies, but Ambrose just peered mildly at his host. "I acknowledge not thy false religions, nor thy... BLTs. Where findest these in Scripture?"

"Well of course they aren't in the freakin' Bible - because the freakin' Bible's ancient! Like, hello? 2,000 years! Hello? So whatcher saying is that we're all, like, damned or somethin' - unless we get with your programme. Eh? But why should we believe you, Ambrose? Why you and not the Pope - or the High Priest of Cant'bury - or the Dalley Lama - or the Prophet Mohammed (praise be his name!) - or Gisela Mildew? What makes you special? What makes you Jesus - and not just some jerk?"

Ambrose's voice rose up in reply, deeper and creepier than any other voice Liam had ever heard. Ambrose's deadpan expression added to the menace that was massing behind all cameras, whispering and wreathing around the cabling, throwing tentacles around the shoulders of the audience. The audience was turning - turning - the studio darkening, thickening with things and hints of things Liam didn't want to think about then, or at any time. The direful digit came up again, and pointed into his face from just a few feet away. Liam gazed at it and gulped again, as if it had been a tarantula.

"I am no Jesu - but I acknowledge and honour Authority. Thou, however, Jackass, knoweth nothing, but mocketh much. Aye, and I know, too, what stirs in thy shadows. Thy private thoughts and deeds are open to mine eyes, and soon all the world must know!"

"Er, you do...? But you couldn't! I mean, what are you talkin' about?" Liam tried to laugh, shrugged huge shoulders, opened huge legs, leaned forward, tried to beat down bubbling panic. But those eyes! How they lasered him, cutting through defences, lopping limbs, draining all resistance! He crimsoned, and had to swallow several times, and felt more than usually wedged into his chair.

"I see in thy orbs a hurt child - an injured innocent, asking justice of Heaven. I ask thee, Larrikin - what dost thou honour? Thy God? Thou knowest none! Thy parents - if thou knowest them? They must bemoan their bastard by-blow! Thy own person? Who could esteem such a lard-lump - such a mannequin - such a thing of secret, goatish sins?"

Liam sat trapped, poleaxed - anger, amazement and fear all the more disabling for having been so long held down. He knew. The fucking weirdo *knew*! But…but how? Who had told? When? Treason! Disaster! His candied-peel eyes were wide open in horrified incomprehension. His rasher of a lower lip hung pendant, while droplets of discomfort welled in his armpits and shone on his temples. The lights seemed to have been turned up way too high, and his throat was choked with catarrh. Timpani thumped louder and louder. He knew! How? Who? It had been thirty years! And never a breath of it. Not a hint, not a trace - no danger… and every day he had thought himself one day safer and further away....

But now it had come. The Day. The day he had always guessed would come in the end. He had been found out! The jug-eared Jesus had come on for the sole purpose of ambushing him. Who had put him up to it? He thought he could guess... you treacherous bastard, he yelled inside, just you fucking wait! Treason! Disaster! DISASTER!... The Day had come, and it was over. All of a sudden he fell forward in his chair, his head hitting the table, congealing in on himself like butter in a frying pan. The audience gasped, and some stood to see better, and he raised his massive head with an effort and stared around in mortal panic, imploring help, fixing all details, locking his empire in memory as his grip on it slipped and was lost.

The studio moved all round him, and sounds came and went in long waves - things done, things not done, things he could have done, things he should have done... Who was the traitor? Mouth ajar, migraine discs whizzing off their axles, he was aware that one half of the audience was still looking to him for a lead, while the other had already realized that while they were watching somehow everything had changed - that the mad drill guy had somehow hit on something stupendous. Something awful. Something horrible, about this mountain of a man whom they had thought they trusted, almost loved....

Turning his head with a great effort, Liam could see his producer, signalling frantically... do something, say something, do something, say something... But he could not. He could not. It's too late! he wanted to say. He made a supreme rally, but his ghastly guest was still there and huger and louder than ever, Vengeance, Nemesis, a man more hideous than anyone else, a pale phenomenon bringing messages from an appalling past. All that came was confusion. "What the [bleeped by technicians]... Who... But how...[bleeped by technicians] [Bleep] [Bleep]...You're bluffing!...You can't prove... Christ..."

Ambrose, his arm steady as a crane jib, was rolling on, and although what he said was plainly insane it didn't matter because the damage had already been done, and everything was over, over, over... "...prancing popinjay, scrimshanking ninnyhammer, jelly jobernol, mincing molly-boy, Pantagruel, gizzard-grumbler, sham legger, shallow-pated bawd, dommerer, dog buffer, domine do little, private pervert..."

Liam folded for the last time. Consantia had forgotten to gnaw her nails. Sandra somehow ground her teeth although her mouth was hanging open. Philomena laughed, and cried, and laughed again.

HIBERNIAN HALF-LIGHT

Monsignor Jameson's city centre office occupied most of the first floor in an imposing, hideous Victorian building that had once been a Church of Ireland diocesan office. A wintry humorist, he appreciated the historical irony of the dispossessors being themselves dispossessed. Yet he was acutely aware that his own Church was being dispossessed in its turn.

The Enemy now was indifference - a deadlier enemy by far than any Protestants, because it was a by-product of modernity, and to be against modernity meant being against humanity. As a young would-be Counter-Reformationist, he had rushed recklessly into print, in polemics advocating an especially rigorous brand of conservatism. This had earned him a friendly warning from the Cardinal, and taught him to be circumspect. Yet still he watched and regretted the waning of the world's faith, and his own.

He lived when he could in the past - architecture, ceremonial, hierarchy history and heraldry - and prided himself on retaining his lifelong lean physique despite the excellent meals and port that he felt were due to a senior cleric, spiritual successor to the great Prince-Bishops. He had been nicknamed "Wolf" by fellow seminarians, and he was tall and rangy even now. At seminary he had domineered in class and on the sports field, rejoicing in the tangles of doctrine as much as in the firm planting of his feet on the muddy pitch, the power in his thighs, and the satisfying soft noise as someone else's nasal cartilage collided with his thrust-forward palm. The Jamesons had always been fighters; an ancestor had been killed at the Boyne, and others doubtless would have been, had they not stopped off on their way to that rendezvous to do some private pillage. As for him, seven decades had given their gifts and exacted their payments, and his features had become ever more cruelly lupine. Even in decline he was recognizable as a predator rather than a herbivore in the struggle for souls.

In recent years, that struggle he had so relished seemed to have ceased, and he felt at times like a soldier demobbed from a defeated army, ill-equipped for everything except war, loyal to something that no longer existed. For years, he had watched in cold anger as his church liberalised and all the old solemnity was thrown overboard - with nothing equally grand taking its place. The Prince-Bishops of old Europe had transmuted into politicians, and not successful ones. He found himself hating what the Church had become, and he fretted about the future not just of Irish Catholicism, but Catholicism globally. It seemed that all that was magical was being sucked out of life, all the Gothic cobwebs being vacuumed up by the machine of modernity. When he went to Mass, the congregations seemed fewer, greyer of follicle and more déclassé than the week before, and what young people there were seemed listless. He fought the feeling minute by minute - but try as he might he felt himself drying up, and spent more and more time wandering through texts, picking up pieces of the past and putting them down again with a sigh, wondering if he had done enough to help conserve it - and whether it was it worth all the effort any more. What had he achieved in all those years of witness and self-denial? The Church was in much worse condition now than when he had started.

Just that morning, because of the sickness of the usual priest, he had agreed at the last minute to officiate at Mass in a nearby church, a 1960s abomination in concrete, steel and asbestos, of the kind seemingly designed to deter the aesthetically alert from religion. He hadn't officiated for almost twenty years. He had been pleasantly surprised to see several younger people in attendance below the grey dome that bounced his words around for so long that almost none of them were distinguishable by the time they rained down on the congregation. But two of these appeared to spend the whole Mass doing something with mobile phones. He dashed to the door at the end. "Good morning," he said to the startled two, in his rich bass, still faintly inflected with Dublin 4 despite all his years abroad. "I hope you enjoyed the Mass."

"Eh? Oh, yes – yes, thank you, Father."

"Monsignor. May I say it is truly gratifying to have such super-intelligent people in attendance?"

"Oh? Erm, thank you, Monsignor!" Their voices were naturally high-pitched, and they also rose aggravatingly at the end of each sentence.

"I'm not just being polite! There are very few who could simultaneously absorb the timeless wisdom of St. Paul of Tarsus while sending text messages to all their friends. Or were you perhaps exchanging some highly important sports results? Or some pop news, perhaps? Well? What do you have to say for yourselves?"

People were staring at them, rangy relic and crimsoning kids, and the texters looked at each other in desperate hope of escape. Monsignor

Jameson looked down on them from his great height, and his eagle-owl eyebrows were at their most elevated, his nose at its most beak-like. After tense seconds, the texters muttered something and almost ran past him, and as they went they were forcing laughter, to show they didn't care what the loony old man said, thought or did. He looked after them, half-smiling; he would not see them again, and he couldn't help being glad. Who would want to share eternity with such?

But even as that thought came, he rejected it - after all, it wasn't their fault they were what they were. And really, who could blame young people for at times detesting what the Church had become? He divested himself thoughtfully and walked slowly back to his office through frantic crowds that parted for him, a visitor from another age.

The late cardinal (who had also been a wintry humorist) had 'asked' him years ago to take up his present important post, working with the Jesuits. It was deeply flattering to have been selected, and yet the idea had not appealed. Although respectful of the Society's history, he was not really in sympathy with its modern manifestation, which he still associated with Liberation Theology. So to sweeten his 'request', the cardinal had given him the old library as his office, and so the Monsignor had the compensation of working surrounded by shelves of morocco-bound, gilt-lettered volumes whose bindings were more often admired than their contents were consulted. The C.o.I. had taken their books when they vacated, but the Catholic theology was scarcely more readable. The Monsignor had always had an appetite for the abstruse, but even he found this literature hard going. The only religious work he often revisited was paradoxically the King James Bible, and he was never sure whether he was reading it for spiritual or literary reasons.

He always thought how amusing it was - in a way - that supposedly timeless meditations should have dated so badly - and that the newest theology seemed the most dated. Sometimes even Aquinas nodded, but at least he had things to say, and could express himself clearly - unlike the Monsignor's present *bête noire,* "Daddy Jimmy", the Church's official "Apostle to Youth". The Monsignor affected not to be able to remember the name of Jimmy's latest 'book'. He had seen a large pile of them in a Dublin bookshop, and the sight had saddened him. Where were book-burning mobs when you needed them?

The Monsignor had taught at Maynooth, and remembered the media's favourite faithful as a young diplomatist, crinkle-haired and glad-handed, effusive and non-committal in doctrine, and so marked for preferment. A wily churchman indeed Jimmy had turned out to be - veering to every Vatican and wider wind, ingratiating himself where he had to, saying whatever was sought. Even the whispers about his financial peccadillos had just slicked off his exoskeleton - although the Monsignor had gleefully reported the rumours in the relevant quarters.

The Monsignor had little time for reading in any case. His prestigious but ill-defined position meant that he had become a default troubleshooter for matters others could not, or would not, handle. This included detailed questions about doctrine, or what the Church was doing about abortion - or Church politics - or Vatican procedures - or looming scandals - or, as in this case, crazy letters. Crazy letters were, in a way, his particular province.

Although the term had fallen into disuse, it was known throughout the global Church that the slender Irish septuagenarian with the vinegarish wit was one of the select band of "devil's advocates" – senior clerics whose judgement was so respected that they were trusted to put to the test all newly-reported "miracles". It was not too much to say that the reputation of the whole Church at times partly rested on whether the Monsignor, and a few others of equal rank and learning, allowed or disallowed the supernature of certain events. If they allowed - and they generally did not - the probability was that the event would eventually be accepted as a bona fide miracle, and the miracle-workers fast-tracked for beatification, maybe even canonisation. If later this miracle was exposed as a mistake, or a hoax, not only would the Monsignor and his peers look foolish, but much more importantly so would the Church (and by extension all Christianity). The accumulated mistakes, the unworthy "saints" and misattributed relics of the long past, were difficult enough to justify to the modern world; he had no wish to add to the burden of belief, or undercut the faith to which even now his heart cleaved.

It was a weight of responsibility that could at times have been insupportable, except that such claims had become exceptionally rare. Now they came almost exclusively from the developing world, and thankfully he had not needed to get involved with one for almost ten years. So this letter had attracted his attention from the start. But this was not a "normal" crazy letter. It had first intrigued, then troubled, and eventually amazed him.

The same post that had brought the letter had also brought a note from Rome requesting that he look into the very same matter. That was quite a coincidence for a start – but it was only the first of a concatenation of coincidences – ones so extraordinary that a small bell in a rarely-visited antechamber of his brain had jangled into life. And then the matter had become even more tangled – because it had become one of the acutest personal significance. Could all these things coming together be – he hesitated, but the thought had presented itself – could they be more than coincidence?

The letter had come from a nun named Sister Mary Sheehy, who lived at that monstrous old edifice in Oldtown. It was a highly respectable convent, and that the Mother Superior had counter-signed it attested to Sister Mary's credibility. She was clearly a nun of the old school. The letter covered several weeks of extraordinary incidents, or claims of incidents, all of which revolved around her nephew. There was no hyperbole or hysteria in the letter - no extravagant claims, nothing vulgar – no mobile monuments, no bleeding BVMs, no divinities discerned in doughnuts. The detailed, meticulously handwritten letter breathed puzzlement rather than ignorant conviction.

"I realize, Monsignor, how foolish all this may seem. It seems foolish at times even to me – and yet there is something about my nephew, and these events, that rings true. The various incidents almost certainly have been exaggerated, and where they have not almost certainly have some logical explanation. But even allowing for these factors something else seems to lie behind Ambrose's activities, and what I can only describe as his unearthly transfiguration. I have tried to dismiss all of this from my mind, but find I cannot. Whatever the truth of the matter, I fear what may happen if this is permitted to get out of hand. If it were only possible to bring him to see you, it would be a great comfort to his mother, who is, you will understand, extremely worried by this bizarre affair..."

Just such a letter could have been written from Lourdes, or Fátima. It had a provincial lack of pretension – and also a sublimated hope that touched him, in a place he had not been touched for far too long. Whatever about this Ambrose, he felt he liked the writer.

That was all as it should be. The stories the letter told were almost extraneous, because they were entirely predictable. They all had logical explanations, of course. The business that had started it off, for instance, the lad drilling into his arm – the Monsignor was well aware that there were medical conditions, or narcotics, that rendered one impervious or less susceptible to pain. As a pre-seminarian, he had once fallen flat on his face after downing half a bottle of whisky, breaking his nose, and he remembered that what had seemed hilarious at the time had translated into agonising pain just a few hours later. He had come to see this pleasure = pain equation as a metaphor for the human condition.

As for what had been reported after the man had hurt himself so superbly, the tales were too ridiculous. The priest knew that people "seeing" one "miracle" often saw others. Illnesses supposedly cured? Hypochondria, or misdiagnosis, or one of those spontaneous remissions for which science did not (yet) have an answer. The boy's supposed supernatural insight, glossolalia, ability to foretell events? All rubbish - a clear and confident voice, plus resonant gobbledygook, operating on people who longed to see patterns in things. Objects moved by telekinesis? Optical illusion. Or hoax. Or both. He had leafed through these anecdotes with impatience.

There were always three possibilities in these cases – scoundrel, simpleton, blend of both. There were millions of people who saw things that were not there because they wanted to see them. And there were some who would abuse innocents' trust if they could get away with it, either for self-publicity or for money. As that old fox Barnum had said – "every crowd has a silver lining". It was more confusing when the shysters believed in themselves. (The Monsignor had never quite made up his mind which was the more interesting – the manipulative crook, or the true believer. He knew which he would rather meet socially.) But all these bogus incidents were in a way irrelevant. What really mattered were all these coincidences. If that's what they were. If that's what they were... He lit a pipe, in contempt of the "No Smoking" sign (he had disconnected the sprinklers years ago).

An apparently trivial happenstance was that the young man shared his unusual Christian name. The Monsignor had always hated his first name, and on his stationery he was simply Reverend Monsignor A. B. Jameson, followed by many academic and holy acronyms. It had always seemed presumptuous to bear the same name as one of the Fathers of the Church - and especially inappropriate for such a wasp-tempered wretch as he knew himself to be. He had given his nickname on the rare occasions he felt constrained to make any concession to familiarity. Even the cardinal called him Wolf when there was no-one else nearby. He wondered if the other Ambrose felt the same about his Christian name.

A smaller, but still more remarkable, happenstance was that a horse named Ambrosian was running the following day at Leopardstown - a rank outsider, but still... Jaded student of the turf though he was, he was superstitious enough to place twenty Euros on its fortunes.

All these little things were indeed curious. But life often threw up strange linkages, and he would not have ascribed much importance to these things had it not been for the clinching coincidence. It had been this last thing which had jolted him upright in his chair, raised silver hairs on his leathery nape, made him cough on his smoke, and turned a chain of whimsy into something like an Indicator. If this wasn't a Message, it was something that looked very, very like. This thing suddenly bore the hallmarks of the marvellous. Maybe something more than marvellous...

There had been one more enclosure in the envelope from Oldtown – a letter that had slid onto the desk when he had opened it, and which he had read only after he had read Sister Mary's letter and mentally consigned it to the courteous demurral category. The single page of handsome stationery handwritten in fountain-pen had been folded in half. He had unfolded it, and as he did so it was like finding a map of long built-over fields. His past rose out of the paper in all its contours and colours, its italicised historic sites. Central Dublin wheeled, years elapsed, and he was magicked back to his twenties, and a time just before commitment, a time when he had stood briefly at a junction in the road, unsure which way to go.

It had not been the content of the note - which was indeed very simple and generic, starting "To whom it may concern", simply supporting the note from Sister Mary. It was not uncommon for those who wrote to him to bolster their claims with testimonials from local 'names'. But this one had been written by - Letty!

It was a name he had not spoken in ages - almost fifty years - but now the two syllables breathed out involuntarily into the breathless office, unnerving him, unmanning him - warming him. There had been a time...

A time indeed... when he had wanted her, more than almost anything else in this world or the next - when he would find himself staring at her for endless moments, fixated on the fineness of her features and figure, the agility of her mind, the nobility of her soul - while she would smile beckoningly back, teasing him from below the brim of her hat, knowing well the effect those glances had, revelling in his company as he in hers, their two minds so often synchronized as their bodies yearned towards each other... He gasped at the immediacy of long-lost lust, bubbling so hotly and sweetly and unexpectedly out of this piece of stationery, on this dull mahogany desk, in this boring book-lined office, darting ceilingwards to sport among the plaster Cupids, only to lose itself with a sigh and a *pff*! along the spines and shelves, among the barren books.

Ambrose and Letitia, Letitia and Ambrose – she had once joked in all seriousness that they might as well pool their ridiculous Christian names to avoid inflicting them on other spouses. And he had laughed, and very nearly asked her then and there to be his wife. Very, very nearly... and she would assuredly have agreed... except that an even more powerful Force had also been astir in the world, and inside him, and there was an even clearer Voice calling to him above hers, calling from some even higher Place...

And in the end he had not dared to disobey that Summons. That obeying meant amputating her from his life, foregoing his physical future, had made it a truly agonizing choice, one he had put off, and put off, and put off yet again. Sometimes, he would wake very early and go first thing to Head House, determined to make the break once and for all, only to capitulate as soon as he saw her slender shape. He would go home hours afterwards, loving and wanting her more fiercely, hating himself more deeply, resenting her dominion, riddled with guilt at his want of firmness and faith.

Yet one morning, an ordinary morning probably for most people, he had done it. He had left her weeping as though her heart had shrunk to walnut size, while he descended the long drive to the iron gates feeling like he had killed her, and most of himself, and that he was bitterly alone now and forever - alone, that is, except for a host crowding at his shoulder, boiling in his brain, validating and comforting him, whispering she would recover, he would recover, that his road ahead lay clear, and at its end there lay the greatest Reward that could ever be.

And indeed, piece by piece, prayer by prayer, minute by minute, day by day, he had come to terms with that choice. That obeying the call had meant making such a sacrifice had paradoxically made the Church all the more precious to him. The love he had borne for Letty still existed, but now had a different object; lust had been transmuted into evangelizing energy.

He had gone away from Ireland, and come back, and after a while had trusted himself to see her socially (when there were others present) - and it hadn't been nearly as bad as he had anticipated. She seemed indeed to have recovered, and was again everyone's angel, consulted, sought after, desired, pleasurably lost in the aimless round. She had been charming on that meeting - cool hand extended, a social smile as she said so nice to see you again, do drop in if you're passing. Of course he never had dropped in. He had seen her afterwards once or twice, always with others nearby, and had at times been able to regard her almost objectively. Then he had gone overseas again, and thrown all his energy and will into Heaven's work, and decades had crept up on him. But he had never forgotten.

He went now to the window, her note clutched in his hand, and looked down onto the immaculate quadrangle of grass (even at this time of year), the clipped yews, the colonnade, the Carrara fountain whose central nymph tipped water from a ewer in the summer, a soothing noise when it could be heard above the cars. The quadrangle was a capsule of civilization, and seeing it normally soothed him with its loveliness, while alarming him with its smallness. There was a precision and proportion about the scene – the architectural grammar, the understatement, the nature goddess spayed into baroque ornament, spreading foliage snipped into geometric patterns through the eternal vigilance of the gardeners. It would really have distressed him if it had ever been let go – if the grass had grown long, the hedges had reverted to bushes, and the nymph had sprouted vines from her mouth and stretched to brandish her pudenda like a Sheela-na-Gig from the Hibernian half-light.

He had often philosophized serely on this vista, and written the conceit into several treatises which no one of importance had ever read, or at least acted upon. What a triumph, he had written, for Man to take the cruel luxuriance of nature and code it into patterns of perfection – to turn the groves into fanes – sin into symmetry. The pointless cycles of prehistory had become a hopeful straight line, the deities a Deity, the ghosts a Ghost, cults into culture, culture into Christian Europe, and Christian Europe into… what we had now. Every few years, he gathered his thoughts into elegant, unavailing books that would be published by tiny presses. But today, all such thoughts were revealed as trite. What were all these things compared with the profile of a woman, The Woman, the pressure of her hand, confidential conversations with someone of such abounding beauty and blood? O, Letty!

Her sure-handed words blurred. He took off his glasses and rubbed them slowly. He opened the window. Cold charged in; like him, the quadrangle was stricken with frost. But he looked through it and time, and saw again grey eyes below a well-selected hat, that hat below an August amphitheatre, he and she both there with many others in a crowd on top of a hill on a cerulean day when the Church was renewed.

Those eyes, never gazed into since – taking their fill of him one last appraising, anguished time before they were taken away to view new scenes – Nice, Monte Carlo, Gstaad, New York, Berlin, the Cotswolds, all points north of fashionable - and many well to its south, because she had been a trendsetter too.

His own new scenes had been subfusc – Douai, Rome, Manila, Dublin, Rome again, Dublin again, a plenitude of corridors, refectories, dormitories, city churches, country chapels, cloisters in small towns, book-lined offices, Pugin pastiches. They had both lived in London at about the same time, within a few miles of each other, but unknowingly, because Mayfair and Willesden did not often intersect. They had almost met one evening in South Kensington, she going to a gallery, he to a dying man - except that he had turned down another street sixty seconds before she came to the same crossroads. She had vaguely registered his retreating form, but it had been darkening, and she had been late, and after all there was no reason why she should have associated that tall priestly back with one tall priest in particular, and so both had passed on wrapped in their worries.

That day on the Head - the last time they had seen each other - had been the only other time she had seen him in clericals. Caught up in zeal, and the earnest desire not to make any mistakes in front of the Cardinal, he had not had time to rue her on the day. Not then… He had thought only long afterwards how much it must have galled her to see his so-public renunciation of her. Not that she had shown her feelings, of course – she had always had more class than was good for her. To casual observers, like the man who had taken the newspaper photograph, Letty's was just one more approving face (if an especially lovely one) in a crowd of approving faces – while he was just one smooth-haired priest amongst several (if taller), milling obediently around the plenipotentiaries and the newly erected symbol of re-affirmed allegiance.

Perhaps once or twice a decade thereafter, he would hear some rumour of her – an article in a magazine, a passing mention on the radio, reminders that she lived and breathed somewhere on this same earth, in her own hologram. There had been a marriage - and then at some stage a terrible bereavement, a dead child - although he hadn't heard about that until long afterwards. And of course he was aware that when she wasn't travelling she could always have been found at Head House – which she loved, where she had always lived, where he had once been received warmly by her family, and around whose glittering lough, beneath whose magnificent trees, he had walked and talked for hours with her so terribly earnestly, and at the end so bleakly.

But he had never called, or sought further information – and then again he would become distracted by his unearthly Mistress, whose needs and preoccupations were even more pressing than those of the most beautiful woman in Ireland. In an afterlife, his pain would turn back into pleasure - and she would be there, and understand at last.

Yet now, upon receipt of this simple note, all these matters melted, and he was again seventeen, and so was she, and all the old uncertainties arose with undiminished force. Letty – her loveliness - their youth – their love - so lost. But now she was found again, the two of them thrust together through a concatenation of circumstances, the medium of a monomaniac and now also at the urgent request of Rome. He could not help it. He did not wish to help it. He had to see the troublemaker - and through him, he would be justified in seeing - her. Faced with Fate, for what felt like only the second time in his life, the pillar of the Church shook.

OPENING DOORS

Liam Larrikin's dramatic downfall passed around the world as quickly as an ominous comet. His vast visage was so obviously steeped in shame that it was clear he really had something serious to hide. Something Very Bad indeed... He fell from public grace almost before the studio hands had bundled the contents of his office into two large black plastic bags, and sent him and them to Howth in a taxi. Some journalists started to sleuth, but most attention switched to his slayer.

Philomena had discovered she despised Liam Larrikin at the moment when Ambrose had said "goatish sins", and Liam's lower lip had dropped to disclose tiny but pointy dentition and an aperture stringed with spittle. After that, she (and not a few other viewers) had seen no-one else but Ambrose - Ambrose the accuser, Ambrose the all-seeing, Ambrose the exciting, Ambrose the strong, Ambrose the friend of icons, Ambrose the famous.

She had leaned forward on the sofa as the show had closed in confusion, and scanned every pixel of her former classmate, marvelling that she had been so blind. Such eyes he had - such striking looks! Even distinguished - in a way. How could she not have noticed in all those years? She reddened at recollections ranging from when she was twelve until she was eighteen - throwing rubbers at him, putting chewing gum into his hair, sharing in all the ragging, egging on her admirers to push him round, sending insulting anonymous messages in Valentine envelopes, leading him on through simpers before humiliating him in front of all of her friends. She suddenly appalled herself. She dwelt aghast on the last time she'd seen him, that night when she had been so cruel, the night when she had accidentally changed everything. She pictured his face as he had looked at her in that salient light - like a dog begging, then hurt, and finally destroyed, the wind whipping his seaweed hair. She recalled his too-wide smile with too-yellow teeth, his Adam's Apple travelling up and down in its scrawny shaft, his face flicking from shock to anger and finally horror, and behind those emotions other injuries too deep ever to be described, let alone treated. Shame had swept her even on the night, even as she had laughed and turned her back, and had been festering ever since. A Door had opened in the Head that night, some people said. She was agnostic about that, but one had certainly opened in her.

It seemed to her that Ambrose and she were uniquely linked. What had happened to Ambrose may well have been his destiny, as lots of people were saying. Yet somehow she intuited that he had only been up there in the first place because of her. If she hadn't answered quite so unkindly when he spoke to her, maybe he would just have gone back into the pub - hurt and annoyed, maybe, but within reasonable limits. It wasn't as if she hadn't hurt men before. But those had been such simple creatures - nothing like Ambrose. There was no one like Ambrose! Could he, she wondered, ever forgive, ever forget? What if she were to go to him, and explain, apologise? Might there be a chance of becoming friends... or maybe even...? Would she even want...that?

Impelled, enticed, confused, she made her way late that afternoon to Tara Road. So strange so ordinary a place could turn out someone so different. Cameras clustered around Ambrose's gates. There were lots of delightfully scandalized loiterers there, some of whom she knew. It was not every day, after all, that a king of couch potatoes was boiled and mashed in real time. Philomena was called to, waved at, beckoned over, but she declined all offers smilingly, preferring to be by herself so she could analyse her emotions.

Strange, maybe, that a girl so pretty, and popular (mostly with males), should not have needed to deal with such feelings before. But such was the case. She had read once that her first lover would also be her first and truest love, but that certainly hadn't been the case for her. At fourteen, she had yielded up her virginity to an eighteen-year-old in exchange for cannabis, and all she had felt about those frantic scrabblings (on his part) had been a fleeting twinge of pain - and she had been expecting that. She hadn't even enjoyed the dope. She had just wanted to try it, and bore its purveyor neither affection nor ill will. When she had given him the push, he had taken it extremely badly. He still did, she knew, because she occasionally saw him around the town, now bloated and mottled above the collar of his uniform, staring at her with sour yearning. Had she but known it, she had been one of the chief causes of Garda Rogers' systemic disenchantment. "She was the only beautiful thing there ever was in my whole life", that operative had confided to one of his fellow officers -

although he had been too drunk to remember having told him, and his listener had been too drunk to remember being told.

There had been many males since, and following the example set by her mother, Philomena had submitted to their lines and gropings with amused tolerance - sex their reward for their meals, drinks, tickets, jewellery, holidays. She had early learned how to maximize her assets and returns. She took the requisite precautions, and picked up and dropped partners with equal casualness - casualness they did not often reciprocate. She was so very beautiful - and so hard; every man wanted to melt her, and felt he was the one who could do it.

Until she had seen that footage of Ambrose drilling into his arm, she had not realized just how alike all those men had been. Or how boring. She had not noticed because their predictable opinions had also been hers - but now she found herself becoming less and less interested in bands, clothes, diets, gadgets, games, destinations, and social media. She was beginning to think there was a deepness to the world after all, and a mystery - exemplified in a tall and gawky figure in white standing in a high place, defying physical laws - and bursting a bloated beast in front of millions. Who else in her orbit had ever done anything so grand, or serious?

Fidelma's house's once-ordinary garden looked otherworldly in the late light, its plants and trees sprouting strange tokens, shining and twisting in slanting sun and a cold breeze that carried the sea. Teddy bears, dolls, leprechauns, crucifixes, Jesuses, Virgins, St. Christophers, horseshoes, rabbits' feet, ankhs, number sevens, colourful cloths, photos of big-eyed children and ill elderly, bunches of real and fake flowers, bundles of evergreen leaves, slips of paper with names and numbers, intercession slips taken from churches... She wished she had something she could add, although she would not have added it with people watching. She had a different kind of link with Ambrose... if she could only let him know. (Perhaps he already did.)

She looked keenly at the house, thinking she might see him, and him her - and that he might divine her feelings even at that distance. But the windows had remained obdurately blank, the door unopened, and the phone unanswered, and after a while in that bitter wind, the crowd had started to disperse. She had felt more and more conspicuous as even the journalists lost patience and drifted away. She felt tired and cold, and thought about going home, but the thought of her empty house didn't appeal at all - it had not been the same since Dad had died. She decided to walk once around the block, and see how she felt after that. She roamed abstractedly along the same streets Ambrose had traversed nude, and she wondered how he had looked. The image was not altogether pleasing, and so she zoomed in again on his face - the laser eyes that had cut the lard-man.

As she turned into Ambrose's road again, everyone else had gone, and she decided to walk past the gates one last time. It was almost completely dark, and chill moisture was radiating up from the paving. The Head had already been blackened out. Then lights washed over her as a powerful car pulled around the corner - a grey and beautiful Mercedes, which slid smoothly to a stop outside Ambrose's gateway. A man in a peaked cap got out smartly and opened the kerb-side back door. As Philomena neared, she saw with excited unreality that the elegant exiting legs belonged to none other than Letitia Shaughnessy-Don. She stood still, drinking in the star-studded moment. The man closed the door after Letitia had alighted, and the car moved off. Letitia smiled at Philomena, and made to pass on up the drive, until the younger woman recollected herself. "Please...!"

"Yes?" That well-modulated voice, heard so often on the media. So controlled - so kind. The woman, so beautiful, even at her age - such bone structure, poise, clothes...

"Is he in?"

"Well, I can't be certain - but he usually is at this time. I understand he had quite an exciting time of it today! Some television programme or other."

"Yes, he did!" Pause. Frost on trees. A car passing. "I used to be at school with him. We called him Catalogue. His ears, you know - a catalogue of ears! A stupid joke."

Letitia laughed softly. "Catalogue? I like that! I bet he was always a bit of an outsider. He's an eccentric sort, by any standards. Or perhaps I should say exceptional."

"No!... I mean... that is, yes, OK he was. But maybe we just didn't understand? He was always reading - always strange books."

Letitia assessed her. Philomena felt hoydenish, provincial. "I think he is the kind of person very many people wouldn't understand. Do I take it that you and he were not exactly friends?"

Philomena addressed the ground. "No, we weren't friends. In fact..."

"Yes?"

"In fact, I didn't like him. I even hated him sometimes! He was always such a weirdo; I suppose we all hated him, really. He had a hard time - from all of us. Maybe especially me."

Letitia nodded, smiled slightly. "I can imagine. And now?"

Philomena didn't reply. Her face glowed, and she was glad of the gloom. But Letitia saw, and understood. "Does he know?"

Philomena shook her head. She couldn't speak for embarrassment; she felt absurdly young, and she didn't want this woman - of all women - to find her comical. But Letitia's voce was kind and understanding. "Well, don't you think he ought to? He may need to be told. He'd probably never find out for himself. He doesn't think in the same way we do. He thinks about - well - he thinks about Other Things!"

"Other Things - yes! He's terribly different, isn't he?"

"He is indeed! I've never met anyone like him either - and I'm a little older than you! Five decades or so, I would say!" Letitia looked at her intently, then made a decision. "Why don't you come in and say hello? It's too cold to stand around here - too cold for me, at any rate."

"But I haven't been invited - I mean, I hardly know him! And it's not as if he has any reason to welcome me. You see, the last time we met, I... I..." She stopped.

"Well, there's no need to tell me! Tell him, if you feel you need to. I don't think you will need to. I should probably warn you that he is so busy thinking about those Other Things that he's not exactly easy company. But then he probably never was! Anyway, do come on in! It really is cold..." The two women proceeded up the drive, talismaned trees to either side.

"But the house is all dark..."

"They'll be here, don't worry. They use the rooms at the back, and don't put on the lights in the front. Fidelma - that's Ambrose's mother - is fed up with the whole business, and tries to discourage callers. Today has probably been an especially bad day for her."

"Then I don't want to disturb her! It's probably best if I go home. I'll come back some other day."

But Letitia was piloting her by her arm. "Nonsense, my dear! Something tells me she will be delighted to see you. And you might be just what Ambrose needs."

They had gone around the side, through a tall wooden gate, and now Philomena could see light falling from un-curtained windows, striping the black hoar-held lawn. Letitia knocked a special rhythm on the back door.

Inside, Fidelma made a face. Letitia again! Her infatuation with her famous friend had started to fade several days ago, as she had become inured to hearing that particular knock, and seeing the celebrated smile as she opened the door. In any case, although Letitia always greeted her breezily, and asked how she was, she obviously only really wanted to talk to Ambrose. Or just see him - because she seemed content simply to sit in the same room as him, sometimes for hours, just listening to what Fidelma always called "his nonsense". Afterwards, she would emerge with a beatific smile and make elegant adieux. Fidelma had once asked her whether she hadn't been bored, and Letitia had looked amazed. "Of course not, my dear! He has such radiance! We have a kind of telepathy, you know..."

Fidelma always looked especially hard at Ambrose after Letitia had been, hoping to see what it was Letitia saw. But he always looked just the same as he always had. If anything, he looked even dirtier than usual. And the terrible smells he left in the bathroom! What was wrong with her that she couldn't see what Letitia and all the others saw?

Something else that annoyed her was that Letitia had now been in her house fifteen times, but she had never been invited back to Head House - increasingly unsubtle hints notwithstanding. Didn't Letitia think her good enough to cross that invisible but all-important line?

So when she heard the special knock now, she felt almost like swearing, except she didn't want to release any more negative energy. She was very surprised to see that Letitia was not alone, and was about to get awkward when she saw whom it was. "My goodness! Hello! Come in, come in!"

"Evening, Fidelma! As you can see, I've brought... oh dear, I don't know your name! Anyway, she's a former school friend of Ambrose's."

Philomena smiled, pulchritudinous even in the kitchen's unforgiving fluorescence. "Hello, Mrs. Sheehy-O'Connor. I hope you don't mind..."

"Not at all, Philomena! This is Philomena, Letitia - as you say, she was at school with Ambrose. How nice to see you again. Won't you sit down? Can I take your coat? Will you take tea? Coffee? How do you like it? Cake? Please call me Fidelma - 'Mrs. Sheehy-O'Connor' makes me feel a million years old!"

Hospitable clichés tumbled over each other as she opened and closed cupboards, taking out things and putting them away again - conscious of Letitia looking on with sardonic amusement. What was this girl doing here? It couldn't be that she was interested in Ambrose? Impossible! But then why was she here? And there had been so many strange things lately. For her part, Philomena was quite enjoying being fussed over. Her mother had never done that.

"How has he been, Fidelma?" Letitia enquired. (It was never, Fidelma noted yet again, "how have *you* been?")

"Oh, he's fine, don't worry! Ambrose is always fine! Nothing gets to him! He just breezed in here a few hours ago, and I don't think he even noticed how furious I was with him. You probably won't believe it, but I had no idea he was going to be on that awful show. I suppose you watched it? I suppose everyone saw it! That poor man! What Ambrose did was disgraceful."

"I saw it, Mrs... I mean, Fidelma. But I thought Ambrose was awesome! When he pointed his finger at Liam, it was, like, you know - am-a-zing! I never liked that Liam, and it was, like, you know, awesome to see him being taken down. Ambrose is fab... well, as his mum, you'll know!"

Fidelma felt she would never be able to get used to people saying things like this about Ambrose. (For a second, she had even thought Philomena was about to say "awful" rather than "awesome".) And to hear this well-brought up, beautiful girl defending Ambrose's social solecism was startling, and deflating. "You did?" she tailed off lamely.

She thought of just how "awesome" Ambrose had looked an hour or so ago. The media Goliath-killer had ambled out into the garden, without shoes or trousers, shouting at some birds in Sandra's hawthorn. "Throstles of the septentrional Zones..." The birds had flown away with a frightened clapping, and he had looked after them in satisfaction, then smiled at her to say, "My message flies on red wings to the North!" She had bundled him indoors, but as they reached the door, he had stopped and looked back at the cold-clutched garden. "Come spring, this land will be filled with the song of the turtle!" She had not even bothered to tell him turtles did not sing. He would have a smart, stupid answer for that too.

Had Letitia come alone, Fidelma would have shared this further evidence of Ambrose's sickness. So disenchanted had Fidelma become with her famous friend that she always presented Ambrose in the most ludicrous possible light. She wanted Letitia to leave Ambrose alone, leave them both alone. She felt uneasy about doing it, but it was for his good. But she didn't want to deter this girl. If a girl as gorgeous as this one didn't take Ambrose's mind away from his rubbish, nothing and nobody could. Maybe it was just as well not to tell Letitia anyway; she might have found the story funny, as she had enjoyed hearing about the appalling way Ambrose had behaved towards those poor Jehovah's Witnesses. Sometimes the older woman had a cavalier disregard for good manners (and furniture - Fidelma suspected she deliberately avoided using the coasters deployed everywhere a cup might conceivably rest). She tuned back into Philomena's account. "...and then he calls him all these names - where he gets them from I don't know - and the big fat pig starts, like, to cry!"

Fidelma and Letitia glanced at each other, uncomfortable, and a moment later Philomena caught the mood. A sticky silence descended like small spiders from a ceiling. They were all thankful when the kitchen door swung open and the subject of their conversation came in like a one-prophet procession, for some reason carrying an electric torch. He fixed them to their places with one long adamantine appraisal.

"Oh..." said Fidelma.

"Oh..." echoed the reddening Philomena.

"Hello, Ambrose!" said Letitia. He scowled at her.

Fidelma smiled nervously. "Ambrose, you remember Philomena, don't you?"

He looked her over impassively. She stared back, shy for the first time since girlhood. She had forgotten how tall he was. Tall, and terrible, and stiff like a statue come down from a plinth. She saw too, as if for the first time, the glitter of his gaze. The calves' eyes of schooldays were revealed as glowing prisms, in which swirled all kinds of colours and cloud-patterns, whorls and spirals drawn from each of the planets. His voice, too, was rich and deep, not the too fast near-squeak she had once thought she heard from those same lips. And what knowledge, what magisterial language, from one of the most silent boys in school!

"Womenfolk, whither away? Hast all day to chatter? A New World awaits beyond yonder wall - an Age of such splendour and power as to confound the cosmographers, the soothsayers and alchemists of yore. Paracelsus, Doctor Dee, Bacon of the Brazen Head, Michel de Nostradame, Mother Shipton, Francis Dashwood, the Abbots of Thelema and Theleme, Catweazle - what are they? I set at naught their fiddle-faddle, their incunabula and paraphernalia - their grimoires and palimpsests, retorts and familiars and charts and unguents - their runes and cuneiform and 'book learning'! 'Tis not too late for even drabs such as thou to seek, mayhap to find! Come, come, come - let us leave the Town. Come away, come away, make haste!"

Clapping his hands behind them as if they were chickens, before they had time to think, he had shooed them all into the room he had just left, followed them in and locked the door. Letitia smiled tolerantly - Philomena was puzzled but excited - Fidelma was furious and unnerved. She thought again of his expression as he had chased the Witnesses down the drive, and shuddered. "Open that door! Open this door at once, Ambrose! Do you hear me?"

He looked at her thoughtfully, and tapped his teeth with the key - which made him look rather less thoughtful. Philomena winced at the noise - and the teeth, but forgot both again as soon as he spoke again. "J'écoute! With all my heart I permit thee to leave - but with this warning. If thou dost, thou mayst never return to my bosom!"

"How dare you, Ambrose? This is my living room! Of course I can come back whenever I like! I will come back into this room whenever I like! Do I make myself clear?"

Letitia and Philomena glanced at each other awkwardly - and Fidelma suddenly recalled they were there. She was coming off worst in this exchange, as usual.

"Mistake me not! Thy room is thy room - and thou canst enter and leave as pleasest. It is thy room, never forget! Yet thy room is but a vacuum and vacancy among many mansions. I allude not to thy room, but to thy prospects of eternity! Here for the nonce a tiny hand -" He extended a large and unhygienic one, knocking over a reproduction Tiffany lamp, which Fidelma just caught "... is extended to thee. Grasp, I entreat thee, this boon, this brand, this hand, this chance!"

His eyes were full of compassion and confusion. With a semi-sob, Fidelma snatched the key and unlocked the door, leaving it open as she darted up the stairs to her room. Ambrose crossed quietly over and closed the door again, but this time did not lock it. A moment later, his muffled voice (and only his) could be heard, rising and falling in stately cadence.

PUTTING TO THE TEST

A few days after Philomena's first of many visits to Tara Road, the Monsignor found himself sitting across his handsome walnut desk from one of the strangest-looking persons he had ever met. Some of the Church grandees who had sat in that same seat had possessed faces seemingly designed for celibacy, but none had presented such a compelling argument. To make it worse, the specimen smelt - faintly, but detectable even above the background odour of pipe tobacco. The wild thing in near-white was in startling contrast to the neatly conventional flanking women - one the nun Sister Mary, the other the apparition's mother. The latter was clearly profoundly uncomfortable, and she kept stealing uneasy glances around the huge room, with all its weight of abstruse learning in books and paintings. The Monsignor looked again at Ambrose, and summoned all his patience. He knew he was being unfair.

He had been biased against Ambrose from the start. He was always biased against self-proclaimed visionaries, of course - and had only suggested this meeting at all because he had assumed Ambrose would be accompanied by Letitia. He had asked Mary whether Mrs. Shaughnessy-Don would be in attendance, and the nun had said she believed she would. But only these three had turned up, and so the Monsignor was left with the prospect of entertaining a madman and his indulgent kin in the absence of the most enticing of all possible intermediaries. An un-required coffee cup and saucer stood sadly on a silver tray on the side-table.

He had wanted to be fair to Ambrose for Letitia's sake. He had even started to read Ambrosenet, but had given up halfway through the first article, which within three short paragraphs had linked the Holy See to El Salvadoran death squads, and both to the Merovingians and (apparently faked) moon-landings. Then he had watched the footage of Ambrose drilling unblinkingly into his own flesh. In the watching crowd, he had glimpsed dangerous things, like the puzzled rapture on the face of a young woman, who was actually licking her lips as Ambrose's blood spurted hotly into the air. He had then read a few articles about him, of which there were very many, almost all scornful. Finally, he had viewed with unexpected enjoyment the onscreen evisceration of that blimp Liam Larrikin, doyen of the disgusting, and - best of all - a long-time associate of Daddy Jimmy.

He felt he had done his duty, and had sufficient evidence for the letter he had dictated for Rome, which read simply, "After thorough consideration of the available evidence, and a personal interview, I find there is no substance to the claims re. Ambrose Sheehy-O'Connor. With brotherly love..." He had even signed the letter with his gold fountain pen, and the pleasingly heavy piece of paper with its lovely crested letterhead lay in his out-tray, only a few feet from its subject. But a lingering punctilio (or was it superstition?) had made him defer sending the note until after he had actually interviewed Ambrose - and, as he had hoped, heard Letty's reasoning. She might have swayed things, even now - if she had seen something in this prize specimen, maybe there really was something to see.

The other Ambrose had shuffled in and flopped down into the chair, staring at the surface of the Monsignor's walnut desk. No, not at, the observant priest corrected himself - into! Then at last he lifted his head as if he had seen all there was to be seen, and the Monsignor was subjected to the most disquieting eyes he had ever been perused by (not counting Letty's). These were set in an un-ignorable countenance - something about the distance between chin and brow, the black corona of hair and beard, the ears that looked like signposts pointing down untravelled roads. Once in the firing line of that face, it was quite difficult to look away - so he forced himself, and shuffled some papers on his desk. Mary and Fidelma looked at him expectantly.

He cleared his throat. "I understand..." Cough. Had they noticed he'd reddened? Get a grip on yourself...remember what you represent! "...that Letitia Shaughnessy-Don is involved with this unusual business, Sister Mary. If I may be frank, her recommendation is one of the reasons I agreed to see your nephew. She couldn't come with you today, I understand?"

Mary indicated Fidelma, who gave a slight self-satisfied smile. "Yes - that's right, Monsignor. As I have already explained, we were expecting her to come today. She has obviously been delayed by something. My sister and she are close friends, and live near each other."

The Monsignor blinked in mild surprise, noting Fidelma's clothes, and the cheap conception (although expensive execution) of her jewellery. "Oh? I wouldn't have thought... that is, it's quite a coincidence, because I used to know her years ago. What a pity..." His voice faded away. Fidelma darted an annoyed glance at Mary; she was always sensitive to slights. After about twenty seconds, the priest recollected himself, and shuffled more papers. "Anyway - to the problem in hand. Before we begin, could I ask you please to undertake not to discuss what we talk about today with anyone outside the room? These things are terribly sensitive, and prone to misunderstandings and misconstructions. We have so many enemies these days!"

Mary nodded knowledgeably, but Fidelma felt irritated at being thus co-opted into a conspiracy of the unenlightened. "Excuse me, if you don't mind..."

But whatever she was going to interject was forgotten when Ambrose lifted his head and enquired, "Wherefore thy secrecy, Priest?" It was the first time he had spoken. The Ambroses assessed each other, and it was the older one who cleared his throat and cast down his eyes. The young Ambrose seemed hardly ever to blink. The priest drummed his fingers on the table. Ambrose watched the fingers for a couple of moments. "Walnut!" he shouted, and they all jumped.

"Yes, it is walnut, Ambrose. Are you interested in woodwork?" The Monsignor knew he oozed condescension, but he couldn't help himself, and didn't much care. Ambrose didn't seem to notice anyway.

"Dost not know its cosmic significance?"

"The tree's significance?" (It was going to be a long interview.)

"I will reveal all!" and he shot up, but the Monsignor, terrified that he was about to disrobe, stood swiftly and pushed him back into his chair.

"What do you think you're playing at? Stop it - now!"

Ambrose looked mournfully at him. "Art denying the walnut's worth? Thou noodle! I allude to the timber's parabular potency. The walnut signifies the Godhead; the sweet kernel is His divine nature, the green and pulpy outer peel His humanity, the wooden shell between it the walls of the coffin. Dost not know this?"

There were times in the Monsignor's life when he felt terribly tired. He took off his glasses, and rubbed the corners of his eyes with the thumb and third finger of his right hand. "Sister Mary - Mrs. Sheehy-O'Connor - it might be best if I could talk to Ambrose in private. I think we could get to know each other more quickly. I always find that is the best way. Would you mind...?" He needed to say certain things to Ambrose that should probably not be said in front of a nun with a vocation to lose, nor an unknown housewife whose discretion could not be relied upon. She couldn't really be a friend of Letty's, could she?

Mary stood straight away, accustomed to obeying, muttering, "But of course..." But Fidelma stayed sitting. She wasn't going to be shoved around by somebody just because he happened to have grand titles and shelves of old books. She wouldn't be browbeaten by him, or anyone else. She had rights in the matter - not that a priest could understand family bonds! Her chin was squared, her lipstick like the Maginot Line in fashionable autumnal hues.

"Well Monsignor, if you don't mind I would really like to stay and hear what you say to him. I am his mother, after all!"

"I'm acutely aware of that, Mrs. Sheehy-O'Connor. It's just that these things are complicated, and so very personal, that sometimes the only thing that will do is for a stranger to look at things objectively, to take on the burden. It's the same principle as Confession - or even psychotherapy, something about which you may know more than I do!" He realised what he had said, and winced.

Fidelma started, "I beg..." The boy stared straight ahead, smiling gently at something only visible to him. Then he waved at it. The priest stared at him, then recovered.

"Good gracious, what am I saying? Please forgive me, Mrs. Sheehy-O'Connor! Slip of the tongue - that wasn't what I meant to say at all, ha ha ha. That's what comes of priestly sequestration. What I meant to say is that a lady of your education would doubtless be familiar with the works of Freud. Please accept my apologies!" Fidelma really had no choice but to nod in gracious acceptance, and retreat step by verbal step. Within another two minutes, she and Mary had been inveigled into the ante-room - a room far more luxurious than Fidelma's living-room, but under the argus eyes of a frowsty typist well past retirement age. The Monsignor came back, rubbing his hands. He was congratulating himself on the way he had cozened Fidelma into going along with his wishes. He still had it, he still had it. And now to deal with the stripling!

The stripling was standing looking down into the quadrangle, and the priest joined him. "It's a handsome garden, isn't it, Ambrose?"

"A goodly prospect, priest." The two were the same height, although the Monsignor was far burlier, with a suggestion of old strength, trace-elements of charges across rugby pitches, early grapplings with dogma. But there was something in the young man's face that made the Monsignor think of his own younger self, when he had similarly thought he had all answers. In other circumstances, maybe he would have turned out a little like him. He softened slightly; the lad was a by-product of a putrid society.

"Now, Ambrose, the women are gone, and we can have a proper chat. It's just you and me, and what is said in here goes no further. You can drop all that crap, for a start!"

Ambrose looked genuinely puzzled. "You talk in riddles, priest!"

"Now, Ambrose, don't take the piss. You can talk to me, man to man. I repeat, whatever you say to me in here won't go any further. I'm a priest, after all, and whatever our drawbacks may be, we don't snitch."

"I do not believe thou wouldst breach the secrecy of the confessional. Yet I have nothing to vouchsafe to such as thee. I am a sinner, as are we all - and yet I am as an emissary from Above, gifted with a Message that is the hope of mankind."

Time to change tactics, thought the Monsignor. "Do you know my name is Ambrose too?"

"I was not cognizant of this."

"I've always hated my name. Do you hate being called Ambrose as much as I do?"

Ambrose shrugged. "It seemeth of small significance. My name is my name; thy name is thy name. My mother's name is Fidelma. My Aunt Mary is yclept Mary..."

"Yes, yes, OK! Oh, by the way, I need to thank you."

Ambrose arched an eyebrow. "For what reason, or reasons?"

"Because on the day I first heard about you there was a filly running at Leopardstown, and her name was Ambrosian - so I had a little flutter, and she romped home! Are you a gambling man, Ambrose?"

"I detest Dame Fortune, that fickle jade! She is a flibbertigibbet - a Baphomet! The truly holy have no more need of pecuniary peculations than sensual excitations. Brother - thou dicest with devilish distractions. Forsake these ways - for thine own sake!" Ambrose clutched the other's arm, and the Monsignor bridled before he recalled his office. Calm down, he warned himself - remember the lad is either sick, or trying to provoke him.

"What's your middle name, Ambrose?"

"Roger Moore D'Arcy". Fidelma had watched *Live and Let Die* just before Ambrose was born, and had developed a crush on the male lead. The "D'Arcy" had come from *Pride and Prejudice*. Fidelma had had some vague idea that by giving him such a name he might develop sophistication by osmosis. She had still had hopes for him then. The Monsignor was genuinely amused. What chance had the lad ever had?

"Do you know, we have a lot in common! Embarrassing names, at least! Do you want to know what my middle name is?"

Ambrose's expression was discouraging, his voice almost a yawn. "If thou desireth to apprise me."

"It's even worse than yours - it's Boniface! How about that then?"

Ambrose looked puzzled. "But the Apostle to the Frisians was a most worthy and holy man!"

The Monsignor's momentary mirth was crushed. It wasn't worth trying to explain. Time to appeal to Ambrose's sense of responsibility. (If he had one.) "Do you know why I wanted to meet you, Ambrose?"

"To discredit my Message, Pharisaically? To aver I did not see that which I have seen? I warn thee, my faith is as Wicklow granite."

"Goodness me, of course not! What an idea! No, Ambrose..." He put a ham-sized fatherly hand on the other's bony shoulder, and left it there. "Quite the opposite, in fact. Quite the opposite. I wanted to see you because you had seen what you saw. So few now have the imagination. We live in a society in which far too few feel they have seen the face of God, or even wish to see it. Our age, you see, hates mystery, hates things that are secret and impressive. It wants everyone to see the same things - the same boring and ugly things - and to think the same boring and ugly way. It is because of the great rarity and beauty of what you saw that it must be handled with such care. Do you know how many people have come into this office in the last ten years to tell me they have been in direct contact with God?"

"I know not."

The Monsignor laughed - the short, lemon-sharp laugh of a disappointed idealist. "None! That was one of the reasons I wanted to see you. We live in an age with no meaning - an age that wants no meaning. So I am always interested in meeting people who *do* see meanings. But I also wanted to point out a couple of things that might not have occurred to you. You'll forgive me for saying that I have been around the block a few more times than you have." He wondered whether Ambrose knew what knowledge and experience his title of Monsignor conveyed, or what it meant to be permitted to wear the purple. He supposed not, and sighed at this reminder of his essential insignificance.

"See that man down there?" A gardener was moving across the quad, carrying a spade. Watery sun was projecting his grotesquely foreshortened shadow.

"Aye, I descry him."

The Monsignor repressed irritation. Descry! He removed his hand from Ambrose's shoulder. "Well, that man, whose name by the way is Seamus, is a unique individual of unique worth. But he is also Everyman. He carries with him all the tragedy of the human condition. See - he's even carrying the tools of the gravedigger! His whole life is like this quadrangle - small and cramped, and although it makes sense in its own terms it is only a tiny part of the world. Beyond these walls, outside this ordered square, mostly beyond his comprehension, there are vast streams of traffic pounding along wide roads, and they are indifferent to the existence of this little corner, or the life of Seamus. If they did know about this place they would probably obliterate it, not out of malice, but simply because it makes no sense to have such a place these days. Likewise, if Seamus gets in their way they will run him down, without compunction, without remorse, without even noticing. Yet Seamus is more or less happy, telling himself that whatever problems he has in this world he will get requital in another. It's the way men have always lived, since long before Jesus came along to trouble the world with His offer of escape from endless repetition, from the crushing wheels."

Ambrose sounded suddenly excited. "The wheels, yes... the wheels! In my mind I see them sometimes, rolling on forever, mowing down all in their path. I know him well, the Juggernaut."

The priest was unsure whether Ambrose was taking the mickey all of the time, some of the time, or none of the time. The safest course was to take all of his remarks, however infuriating, at face value. But an alert auditor would have sensed resentment in the cleric's reply, glimpsed danger in his hazel irises. "That's right, Ambrose. The wheels... What I'm saying, Ambrose, is that religion is a perennial impulse. But it's also a dangerous impulse, one that needs to be channelled. Religion has a social function as well as a transcendental dimension."

"Wherefore? Cannot thy 'Everyman' decide for himself?"

"No, Ambrose - Everyman cannot. Some can; but many, I'm afraid, cannot. When everyone thinks they can, there you have disaster. Religion needs to be organized, and interpreted. I'm not saying organized religion always works, but it's infinitely better than the alternative. This is why we have structures, and doctrines - hierarchies and liturgies - dealings with governments. The alternative is Babel, with every maniac taking it upon himself to decide who or what God is, and what is meant by such and such a phrase - and trying to re-mould society in their own image. Organized religion, by contrast, is the sum of centuries of experience, and it's based on an awareness of what's achievable. Now, out of all the millions of people who weigh down the world, what makes you think you've been given privileged access to the Man Upstairs?"

Ambrose looked ceilingwards, then inquisitively at the Monsignor. His eyes bulged painfully, as if they might pop. The bracket clock chimed 4pm. It was getting dark. "Which man?"

The hand that had lately been on Ambrose's shoulder balled, then un-balled again as the priest forced a laugh, and pushed the hand behind his back. "I mean God! Why do you think that you have been granted special access to Him? Why are you a latter day Moses? Why are you, Ambrose Roger Moore D'Arcy Sheehy-O'Connor of Tara Road, a brand snatched from the burning?"

"'Tis not why, but by whom."

"All right then - by whom?"

"Thou jestest!"

The response was extruded through taut teeth. "No I am not jes...joking! By whom?" But he already knew that the answer, whatever it was, would be maddening. Both hands were fists now.

"The Godhead, thou noodle!"

Control! the Monsignor told himself. You're a MONSIGNOR, a Prothonotary Apostolic, a Prince-Prelate of Peter's Church - and whatever else you do in your long and dignified career you don't lose your rag with lunatics wearing tracksuits with "Harlem Globetrotters" and tomato sauce splashed across the front! You just don't... however much you might like to knock their teeth down their scrawny necks into their anorexic guts, grab them by their unhygienic scruffs and shake them as if they were maracas! But even as he gulped down his prideful passion, Ambrose asked sweetly, "Hast heard the Parable of the Pie?"

*

His visitors had gone, and the Monsignor had re-entered his usual orbit. He was even smiling slightly. His calming process had been expedited by the whisky he kept in a filing cabinet out of sight of Miss Tighe, the teetotaller and inveterate gossip who acted as 'confidential' secretary. That angular operative was presently chattering to the Cardinal's equally 'confidential' secretary, while watching warily the door that separated her from the Monsignor, whom she had always regarded as deplorably irreligious.

"...and he was shouting in there! Shouting! No word of a lie! I could hear him even through that big thick door. And there's me, sitting here with the boy's mother, and his aunt - she's a Sister at Oldtown - nice ladies, lovely manners. And they're looking horrified, as you might imagine - and there I am, trying to pretend there's nothing uncommon going on! 'Would you like some more tea?' I says, and the mother almost bites my head off! Just as she's about to say something else, the door opens, and out comes the funny looking lad - not a pick of meat on him, face on him like a monkey, filthy clothes - but walking like the King of the World! And behind him I can hear himself fuming and swearing...and then the door slams and since then I haven't seen hide nor hair of him. I bet he's at the whisky again..."

The Monsignor was indeed downing a second tumblerful, as he recalled the ridiculous details of the interview. He was also trying to analyse precisely why, despite his obvious insanity, the lad nevertheless exerted a weird spell. One felt forced to take notice of him. Ambrose somehow surmounted his ridiculousness. He was like two diseases in one - itchy and unsightly as eczema, yet lodging under the skin like a cyst. There was a potential in the lad, as well as a capacity for great annoyance - a potential that would almost certainly never be realized in this society. Ambrose's views were a confection, not remotely serious - he was a music-hall turn, a charlatan. Yet some would always follow him, in whatever ridiculous or dangerous direction he might lead.

The cleric wondered - possibly heretically - how the real Ambrose had seemed to the Romans. Had he simply been lucky with his period, that state of human readiness? Would the young man who had just stalked rather magnificently out through that door have done better to have lived then? It was a fascinating conundrum - and one that linked the Monsignor to his own young life, those times when he too had felt he was special and singled out, a princeling destined to inherit not only the earth, but also a slice of heaven.

When he had been a novice, it had still been just possible to take the old tales at face value, take the ancient institution on trust. But could anything be taken for granted now? Was anything ever just left alone these days?

Wasn't everything always up in the air, open to question? Wasn't religion (his, at least) routinely ridiculed, sidelined, feared, detested? Could even someone as strong-minded and perverse as he knew himself to be have been able to have followed the same trajectory if he had been born twenty-three rather than seventy-three years ago? Or would he have been a little like the young maniac who had just left, leaving only a faint smell of dirty clothes?

His tried to imagine how Ambrose must have lived before his 'conversion'. He saw the young man swimming in empty space - living without purpose, or belief, probably without friends, in that boundless boring wasteland whose miles of roofs sprouted aerials specifically to capture a senile civilization's sonic sewage. What it must be like to be young and imaginative now, to live rootless and without hope, alone before the face of history... all that thumping music, that pointless computing, those intoxicants ingested! When every need had been met and all authorities discredited, what more natural than that the sated should pick at the scabs they called souls, itchily yearning for release?

As for the boy's perfectly-groomed mother - what could someone so shiny ever have known of her boy's inner life - or public culture's failings? What help or sympathy could someone like she have offered someone like Ambrose, a complex lad who would need complex answers? Poor bastard; it must have been a hard kind of comfortable life for him. He guessed Ireland would be hearing more of Ambrose; and in a way he hoped so.

But now, there were other matters to deal with. The first was to date the letter about Ambrose he had written earlier, and mark it for "Immediate Dispatch" to Rome. Then he took out of his top drawer - for about the two hundredth time - Letitia's note, and laid it flat on his desk. He read it all over minutely yet again, and then his eyes flicked once more to the telephone number at the top. He touched the telephone gently, almost stroked it, took his hand away. Then he stood abruptly, crossed to the door and pulled it open swiftly. He had the satisfaction of seeing how guiltily Miss Tighe muttered something and replaced the receiver, before turning towards him with a half-smile. (He knew how much she disapproved of him.) Before she could speak, he said in the ultra-brusque manner he reserved for her and for modernizers that he had several telephone calls to make, she could take the rest of the day off, he would lock up thank you - and goodnight, Miss Tighe! She sniffed, but started to assemble her accoutrements - and just two minutes later was saying "Goodni..." as he pushed the door closed.

He waited until she had definitely gone before he picked up the receiver, and stabbed the numbers with slightly frantic fingers. Too frantic, because he got a voice saying the number had not been recognized. He took a breath and another amber swig from his Waterford tumbler, before trying again. This time it rang six times, which felt like sixty as he half-hoped, half-feared pick-up. And then it was.

"Hello?" He had heard the voice only yesterday on the TV, but he had been focusing on how she had looked. But now he recalled just how distinctive her voice had always been - so precise, so fluting, a hint of Joan Greenwood huskiness. In an instant, he was nineteen again.

"H-Hello, Letty. It's me."

A moment of agony, a swoop in his gut; a catch at the other end, a startled inhalation. "*Ambrose?* It can't be!"

His heart boomed like a Lambeg. He had to keep clearing his throat. His hand was tight on the receiver. (So was hers, on hers.) The connection was wonderfully clear, and he could hear every respiration - visualize the air travelling down her still slender throat. "It can, and it is!"

"Goodness! I don't know what to say! It's been an age! What must it be...? Let me see...forty-five years? Forty-six? Seven?"

"By my calculation, it's been an age too! How are you?"

"Oh, fine, fine - well, I mean, where do I start? And why am I starting? What on earth made you call? And why today? I mean, it's lovely to hear from you and all that, obviously - but why now, why today? You must have some ulterior motive. It can hardly be for auld lang syne...can it?"

The Lambeg was less furious now. "Ha, well, I suppose you could say it's a coincidence - a rather extraordinary one. It's all to do with a young man who came to see me this afternoon. In fact, you were supposed to have accompanied him."

"So *you* are the Bogey-Buster-in-Chief! The people at the Archdiocese wouldn't give Fidelma or even Mary the name of the person who would be dealing with him. Seemed to be a terribly sensitive business. They sounded almost embarrassed to be talking about it. Well, I never! Trust you to get such an interesting job! An important one too. If I had known it would be you, of course I would have come. But I'm afraid the idea of sitting across a desk from some grim-eyed Torquemada glaring at me as if I were insane just seemed too much. On second thoughts, maybe even if I had known it would be you, I wouldn't have come. Ambrose is someone who needs a heck of a lot of explanation!"

"He is indeed. That woman isn't really a friend of yours, is she? She hardly seems the type."

"Poor Fidelma! Well, I wouldn't have said there's a natural magnetism. But tell me what you think of him! How did it go?"

"Ha! Do you want me to be honest? No - of course you do! Well, then, I think he is interesting. I think he is annoying. And I think he is mad. I gave him short shrift, I have to say. But then he gave me short shrift too."

Her old, young laugh - alive with melodic mischief. How much he had longed to hear it, without knowing how much he had missed it. His palms were sweating. Nineteen again, indeed. "I bet you did! Had I known it would be you quizzing him, I wouldn't have dared write. I can just imagine what you made of him."

He laughed too, at first shortly, then long and richly as the image of Ambrose rose up before him again. This was not his usual snorting and sarcastic laugh, but one that welled up from some unpolluted source, a place where joy bubbled unselfconsciously all by itself. He gave her the edited highlights of that afternoon's encounter, and she exploded and empathized in all the right places. She had always been an excellent listener. But when he had finished, she said, "But seriously now, seriously. Just for a second. Of course he's eccentric. But don't you think there's something more to him that that? There is something really very unusual about him. You can tell by looking at him that he was made for something out of the ordinary."

"I wouldn't disagree that he looks out of the ordinary, Letty." He liked saying her name. He liked the fact that they were slipping easily into their old mode, when serious things would be said in light ways. He liked reverting so easily into the old humour, the astute observations, the shared thoughts and tastes. But he wished they could talk about something else. "You see, Letty, it's just that - well, what can I say? I don't want to argue with you now, in our first conversation in forty-eight years."

"Forty-nine - in fact, almost fifty. I've been working it out."

"Forty-nine, as you say. That makes me even more reluctant to argue. But there is something else I've needed to say to you for a very long time. I hope you don't mind my mentioning this - but I was terribly sorry about James and the boy."

Silence, just her breathing down that preternaturally clear line.

"I would have made contact at the time, but I didn't hear about it until almost a year afterwards. I was on retreat, you see, miles from everywhere, nowhere near phones or newspapers. And then by the time I did hear, it seemed much too late - and I guessed it would just distress or embarrass you to hear from me then. But I'd like you to know I was thinking of you. I was always thinking of you, really, but never more so than then, when I came down from the mountains all recharged, only to hear that while I had been away my oldest and dearest friend had been through such suffering."

"Thank you - that means a lot! I mean it. I did wonder whether you had heard. I remembered how you would go for months paying no attention to the news, or what was going on in the world. I used to tease you about it, didn't I - always so busy looking at distant horizons! So I wasn't surprised not to hear from you. But thank you for saying that now, because there isn't a day when I don't think about them. Especially little Jackie... It will never quite heal, I'm afraid."

After a half-minute she spoke again, her tone determinedly brisk and cheery. "But we mustn't dwell on this subject, now must we? What's happened has happened, and today should be a day for celebration. Two old friends finding each other again in a wide world - now that doesn't happen every day."

"You're right, it doesn't! Look, Letty - why don't we meet?"

"I knew you were about to say that. I even hoped you were - in a way. But, Ambrose, is it wise? It's been such a long time. And I know we're not supposed to worry about that kind of thing, and to search for spiritual beauty and all that sort of rubbish, but - well, to be honest, I look every bit of my age. Every bit..."

"Well, I saw you on the TV yesterday, so I already know the worst. And you know me well enough to realize that I am not being gallant when I say you don't look a day over sixty! As for me, I now resemble a Norwegian promontory."

"What a silver-tongued rogue it is! Well, as you have already seen those awful pictures, maybe we could meet - although the off-screen reality is even worse. But then between old friends these things probably shouldn't matter." There was a strange old-fashioned static burst, like a valve radio broadcast from Athlone or Hilversum. "But it's not just a question of how we look, is it? It's about everything - our whole lives, and the marks they have made on us. And I ask again - is it wise? There is a part of me which says mightn't it be better to remember how things used to be, how we used to be so easy? What if we were to meet, and find we now dislike each other? Or even worse, if we had nothing to say to each other? Can you just imagine us sitting somewhere, and we're both fidgeting, and wondering who will be the first to say 'Is that the time?'"

"Come off it, Letty, you know that wouldn't happen! We were never short of things to say to each other..."

"That was then, Ambrose, back when... well, when there were things still to look forward to, things to hope for. Things are different now... we can never rewind that tape—if they still use tapes these days, which I doubt."

"Well, yes, things are different, Letty. But you're not completely different, and I'm not completely different. I'm not talking about rewinding any tapes, either - by the way, they use CDs and DVDs these days! It's just that we were once such friends - and still can be again, I believe. Don't you feel that, somewhere below this conversation, we still know what the other is thinking? At least, I feel that."

"I do - at least I think I do... but it's just... oh, I don't know..." It wasn't like her to flounder. He took command of this conversation, as he had once taken command of a similarly significant conversation years before, on a lovely afternoon beside a lake. Their last real conversation.

"Letty, look - let's put it this way. If we don't meet now, then when? If we don't meet soon, maybe we never will. At least not on this side..."

"Let me think about it," she said at length. "Of course I'd love to see you. I'm madly curious! But can we go back to Ambrose for a moment? I feel I need to explain about him. I know very well how bizarre he seems - how bizarre he really is. And of course, as you know much, much better than anybody else, I am not naturally religious. Or at least, not since I was very young. Funny, really - I remember almost skipping up the aisle at First Communion. Do you remember that horrible blue glass in St. Fechin's - the way it made everyone look like they had been poisoned? Then - well, like all teenagers I thought I was some kind of rebel." She stopped, gulped slightly, spoke again, haltingly, embarrassedly. "Then - well, when things happened - or rather didn't happen - you know, with us - I blamed God for taking you away... That was desperately unfair, I know - stupid, and childish - but I was so unhappy, for such a time..."

The line thronged with almost-history, wreathing regrets. "Ah..." he breathed, "were you? Were you really? I... I also... I mean..." A very loud motorbike dashed past the Monsignor's office, and luckily broke his side of the spell. She too seemed to gasp slightly back into life.

"I never understood how you could believe all those things, set all those cold and invisible things above things you could touch and that could touch you back. They just seemed unbelievable, and unnecessary - and you seemed merely perverse. And you know, you are perverse!" She was trying to lighten the tone again.

"Ah, it's a fair cop!" he replied, mock-flippant to help her. But she slipped back into seriousness almost at once.

"But then there was the crash, and everything was ripped away in an instant. One tired lorry driver not paying attention - he wasn't even scratched, of course. And ever since then, I've been wondering whether you weren't right all along - that there must be more than what we can see or feel. That a world without meaning would be just too cruel a joke. This is why I find Ambrose fascinating. It's as if he's plugged into some high-power cable. He gives off sparks. I know all those stories about healing and so on are rubbish. I know there's nonsense in him - and play-acting. But that's not really the point. Despite all the nonsense, he has a kind of pure power - and an innocence. You sense somehow a Purpose, a Presence; it feels as if there's someone breathing warm down all our necks... oh, I'm not explaining it very well. But there it is anyway - that's how I feel!"

The priest visualized Ambrose again, standing beside him, looking out of the window before turning those troubling eyes onto his - a vivid presence indeed. But "pure power"? And if there was any "innocence" in him, it was the innocence of ignorance. And Letty (so sceptical, so shrewd) had fallen for it. Because she wanted to believe in something. Because even such as she were always vulnerable in certain circumstances.

"Letty... I'm sorry, but I can't agree on this. I'm trying to be fair - really. I don't think he's a bad lad; in fact, I was just feeling sorry for him, and the kind of life someone like him must lead these days. But what I saw in him was 99% nonsense and playacting. All those ridiculous words - his clothes - that hairstyle - not to mention the ignorance of his followers. You are almost certainly the only intelligent person who sees anything in him. I admit he does have a bizarre sort of presence - but just listen to what he says. Look at the calibre of his fans! I saw some of them interviewed yesterday, with the journalist trying not to snort with laughter in their simple faces. You're the only reason he is being taken seriously by some. That, and the fact that he accidentally demolished that television creep."

She sighed, but she had always been impossible to offend. "You were always unfair, Ambrose Boniface Jameson - and impatient. That was why... well, let's just say you were always unfair and impatient! You're doing him a disservice. Maybe yourself too. He makes some very good points."

"Humph."

"Don't 'humph' me! That's not an argument; it's just a noise. And not a very intelligent one either! You'll have to do better than that."

He laughed. Nobody else would have mock-scolded him. Nobody else had ever spoken to him in such a way - not since childhood. And he liked it. It made him feel untried again, but full of confidence - as if he was back again trying to push beefily through the scheme of life, talking to her in that lost garden, batting aside all obstacles en route to the central Truth that would explain the entire universe. With her new capacity for belief, and his for disbelief, it felt like they had swopped places. If she had been such a believer when they had last seen each other, and he as disenchanted as he had become, maybe everything would have worked out very differently. But that wasn't an avenue he wanted to explore. He laughed again, short and citrus-sharp once more.

CAPTAIN OF THE NATIONAL SOUL

Captain Bosco Buggy (Retd.) was watching one of Ambrose's webcam meditations with great absorption. Curiosity, perplexity, impatience, irritation and wonder followed each other across his gingery visage - until eventually they coalesced in cunning surmise.

This attentive watcher was considerably younger than the "Retd." suggested, being in his early forties, and physically vigorous. He was, however, extremely proud of his erstwhile commission, and invariably used it in his many letters on many topics to many editors. And yet he had *been* retired, greatly against his will.

He might conceivably have got away with shooting up the guardroom that Sunday morning - after all, no-one had been hurt - had his defence of stress-related mental strain been given credence. But it had been undercut by the discovery of an empty *uisce beatha* bottle under the bunk in his billet - just one of many which had been abstracted over several months from the Officers' Mess. To add to his disgrace, he had allowed a Mess Orderly to be blamed, and demoted. It had been a sad coda to the career of a man whose C.O. had once declared he was "one of the most promising young officers in the Defence Forces". Sometimes when Bosco was in his cups (and he was rarely out) he would bemoan the injustice of the military in thus discharging the greatest patriot he knew. In his blackest moods, he would speak of trumped-up charges and cover-ups.

But whatever he thought about the personnel occupying high positions, his opinion of the machine itself was abnormally high. The army was, for him, the incarnation of the nation - and the nation the incarnation of Divine destiny. His dream had always been to lead the former to the glory of the latter. His tragedy was that any possibility of this consummation seemed to be receding almost hourly. Yet deep within him he cherished a faith, against all the evidence, that there was an incorruptible core to the Irish people - and that given the right signal at the right time, they might yet rise up and... and... do something really radical. In a decaying world, he at least had always stayed steadfast; he sometimes boasted that he hadn't changed his mind about anything since he was twenty.

He limped very slightly with his left leg, and without ever actually saying so, would let new acquaintances believe that he had sustained the injury while serving with the Ranger Wing in a covert operation. He would say, with significant winks - "Oh I'm afraid I can't talk about those days, if you know what I mean". Sometimes, he even persuaded himself that he really had been present in secret ops. He had in fact been a Catering captain, and the limp had been caused by the shrinking of the skin on his calf and shin after he had spilled a deep fat fryer. But he preferred not to dwell on details. He felt he owed it to Ireland to jazz up the story. He was, after all, a guardian of the national soul. Maybe the only true guardian... The political class needed to be swept away, and he was flexible as to the means.

During daylight hours, there always flew outside Wild Geese Hall (a pebbledashed council house in Finglas) the tricolour and the Papal flag side by side - except on G.A.A. days, when the Papal emblem would be temporarily replaced by the golden harp of Leinster and the burning castles of Dublin. He took G.A.A. so seriously that he had got into trouble the previous year, when he had led a small group of patriots against the house of a Cork native who lived nearby. The judge had taken a dim view of the shouting, window-breaking and urination which had enlivened the Finglas small hours, and levied a substantial fine. This had been augmented by a contempt of court fine, after Bosco had told the judge that he was an Establishment stooge. But at least the Corkonian had left the area. Bosco felt this was one of his finest achievements to date.

He wished he was as successful with his other campaigns. For a man so naturally ardent, and with so much spare time, some fifteen years ago he had felt duty bound to take up arms against a sea of foreign and domestic troubles, some of which were real. So he had founded Public Interest Salvation (P.I.S.), the "P" belying its level of support, and whose acronym occasioned regrettable jokes. Bosco was mercifully oblivious to irony, and on the wall of Wolf's Lair (his bedroom), just above his alphabetized country and western CDs, was a framed local newspaper profile entitled "Taking the PIS all the way". Some of his many baiters ran a website called PIStakers.com, but Bosco always refused to look at hostile sites because, as he had told one interviewer, "It'd be a waste of time, d'ye see, as I am always proved right!"'

Utilizing his military experience, he had launched a political-cultural offensive - almost a one-man war of national liberation. He had a staggering array of enemies, and this was as it should be - it proved he was right, and it would make his eventual triumph all the more epochal. Alexander and Napoleon had also had seas of enemies. Thanks to his highly public espousal of the anti-gay marriage cause, he had been instrumental in losing them the campaign. Other causes included contraception, dog excrement in Finglas, drugs, England, the EU, feminism, fluoridated water, fractional reserve currencies, Freemasons, halal slaughter, import duty on alcohol, Kennedy cover-ups, kosher slaughter, moon landings that hadn't happened, Muslims, planning controls, the absence of planning controls, political correctness, pornography, Protestants, public drunkenness, single mothers, taxation, Travellers, the UN, usury, Vatican II, vegetarians, welfare (except that extended to ex-soldiers) and Zionists. His ingenuity in linking these apparently unrelated subjects was unparalleled, if usually under-appreciated.

His devotion to the public weal had been, and remained, personally demanding, even after he had given up on the street demos. There had been a Mrs. Bosco Buggy, but she had ghosted somewhere along the way, along with little Bosco. Her most memorable comment during all their years of wedded bliss had been when she had accused her husband of being "more interested in libations than liberation". Bosco occasionally wondered how she and Bosco Junior were getting along, but there was always some reason why he couldn't look into it immediately, and so the days had lengthened into years without news. It was a decade, maybe twelve years, since he had seen either of them. But this was a sacrifice he had to make, and that would one day be acknowledged. In the meantime, it was pleasant to think that somewhere out in the sinful city there was a straw-haired, foxy-faced facsimile of himself who could one day carry on his crusade (if still required). If only his letters to editors were more frequently published, and his website more visited by a higher calibre of people, he could have been quite content. Although society would still have been sinking, at least his protests would have been registered, and future historians would notice, future generations thank. Sometimes after whiskies, amber-tinged tears would start to his eyes as he pondered the patriots of the future and saw the statues they might erect - and then he would sit up straighter, envision a monumental bronze of himself seated at his desk of Destiny.

Life wasn't fair, he often reminded others. Here he had been, plugging away for years with minute resources and multiple enemies, telling truth to power, and that power replying with lies and slander. Sometimes he felt loftily sorry for them, leading such unenlightened lives, never seeing their puppet-masters. But not too sorry. They had always had it easy - not like him, not like him at all, who had had to struggle for everything, make every penny count, combating classism and underprivilege at every stage. His life had always been, would always be a battle. And all this effort for this decaying country, this depraved metropolis, disguising its disease beneath lights like rouge smeared on a smallpoxed face.

Bosco was one of life's enthusiasts, capable of being sincerely shocked ten or twenty times a day, and alternating sometimes within sentences from profoundest depression to unreasoning optimism. Every New Year's Day, he would inform his contacts that the tide was turning, that this would be the year. But by the 2nd or 3rd of January, this would be forgotten in the aftermath of some news item, or in the fierce joy of faction-fighting with those too stupid to agree with every aspect of his worldview. Once a month or so, 'Bosco juice' to hand, he would e-mail a female confidant in America, enchanted by her avatar, and pour out the contents of his susceptible heart. He never guessed that his lucubrations were being gleefully recirculated by a nineteen-year-old (male) hoaxer.

Bosco might have self-immolated years ago, had it not been for the companionship and patronage of retired civil servant Horatio Mutton, who lived loyally in the damp-spotted bedroom adjoining Wolf's Lair. His (always modest, now severely straitened) private means had often meant the difference between meeting or not meeting The Movement's bills. He was also quite good at getting things down from high shelves.

Otherwise, his day-to-day assistance was frankly not all that useful. He would sometimes send out misspelled press releases to the wrong lists, ring people then forget why he had phoned, and occasionally get Bosco into trouble by repeating something supposed to have been confidential. He would sometimes pick up the National Hotline on the infrequent occasions it rang, and say "Eh? Hello? Who's there?" or nothing at all. This did not give the right impression at all - although it did confuse creditors. Bosco also felt that some of the videos he had shot would have been better if Horatio's face did not sometimes loom up suddenly from the sides, grinning in admiration. At public meetings, Horatio would always sit proudly in the front row, leaning forward, unmissable with his long, grey, curly locks, thick-framed 1960s glasses and scurfy shoulders. Sometimes he would read a magazine during the speeches, although he would always laugh at the right places (if sometimes also in the wrong ones). He would applaud wildly, sometimes for too long. Bosco often had to glare at him to get him to desist. That this amiable object had been named Horatio was really the most remarkable thing about him. The meat-minded Bosco privately called his comrade "Scrag End", and occasionally would even address him as that, but Horatio never seemed to notice.

Oddly enough, it had been Horatio who had first drawn Bosco's attention to Ambrose. Unusually for a man of his age, Horatio was addicted to Twitter. Viewing the footage of Ambrose on his phone, he had been fascinated (and faintly aroused). When he had eventually shared it with his Friend-Leader, Bosco had at first been unimpressed. He was instinctively resentful of this upstart. Who the feck, he had asked Horatio, was this fecker from the fecking suburbs - this "Ambrose" (whose name reeked of privilege) - who had materialized out of nowhere, bullshitting about God, being believed by celebrities, and within a fortnight becoming the talk of the town? This was not just surprising, but also, Bosco added, deeply suspicious. "A classic Establishment safety valve!" he pronounced. Ambrose was also enviably tall - Bosco registered bitterly how Ambrose had loomed over Liam Larrikin, now bundled into such precipitate and mysterious retirement. (Bosco had only just been tall enough for the army; now, he wore discreetly built-up brogues, an old but very high-quality pair of Irish-made shoes that had belonged to his father, a department-store sales assistant who for reasons lost to time had always been passed over for promotion.)

But he had quickly become convinced that Ambrose was sincere. Ambrosenet was too bizarre for him not to be. No joker would have come up with a worldview so insane. And at about the same time, some of Bosco's contacts, especially in America, had started to ask him about Ambrose. It had got to the stage that, in order to retain his credibility with them, he had started to claim that he and Ambrose knew each other - that they were, in fact, friends. In reply to one e-mail from a donor, he had gone so far as to aver that he and Ambrose were working together on "work of national importance". His gratified contact had immediately made a medium-sized donation "on account". So now he really had to meet Ambrose. But in any case, Ambrose might well be the Something he had been seeking.

Bosco had for years been working on a Plan - and at 2.07am one more than usually restless Tuesday it occurred to him: the looney could be the key! Bosco was dazzled by his own brilliance as he blinked at the streetlight-oranged ceiling. Of course! A gift - a man who could attract attention, channel it - then be channelled. The perfect front-man. Why the feck hadn't he thought of it before?

Ambrose, with his profile and contacts, was surely the ingredient he had been missing. If he wasn't, who was? It could work - it really could work... Bosco saw at once how their double-act would operate - Ambrose bamboozling and blinding with sheer effrontery, while Bosco would direct from behind, a great strategist, a grey eminence, marshalling the nation's columns and marching with them - Robespierre to Ambrose's Danton, ready to supplant him when the time came. The great strategist quivered at his own ingenuity, and reached out for the lamp-switch so he could start making notes - but spoiled the mood when he knocked over the smeary glass that housed his lower denture, and it spilled over the beetle-crunchy carpet.

He began systematically to monitor Ambrose's output, to get inside his mind. He saw it as psychological warfare. In so doing, without realising it he started to fall himself under Ambrose's strange spell. Whole hours would slip away as he watched Ambrose's presentations, delivered in that pleasingly well-educated baritone. He started to mimic Ambrose's voice, and ape his mannerisms - first as a joke, then as an experiment, then without noticing. So ridiculous - so fascinating... Yet he retained at least some critical distance, and at times would tune back in briefly to hear effusions like -

"...fifteen and ten are the numinous numbers. The calculation is a simple one. There are eleven celestial spheres and four elements. Multiplieth these by the ten categories, and this leads to 150 natural habits. Furthermore, ten commandments multiplied by fifteen virtues equals 150 moral habits. But what are these fifteen virtues? There are first the three theological virtues, and four cardinal virtues, then seven capital virtues - which makes fourteen. There remain two other virtues - religion and penitence. Certes, thou wilt have observed this comprises sixteen virtues..."

Ambrose paused to let the dreadfulness sink in, before resolving the conundrum triumphantly. "But as temperance of the cardinal series is identical with abstinence of the capital series, we are back to fifteen! Each of these is a queen having her nuptial bed in one of the divisions. Each word representeth one of the fifteen perfections of the Godhead, and also a precious stone, and is able to drive away a sin, or the animal representing that sin. Then there are the branches of the tree which carrieth the blessed ones; the steps of a staircase. One word signifies innocence and the diamond; it driveth away pride, or the lion representing pride. Another denoteth wisdom and the carbuncle; it driveth away envy, symbolized by a black dog. The sloth of course represents Sloth!"

He stopped for a chortle, before continuing inexhaustibly. "Consider the similarities with the Assyrian system..."

Bosco shook his head to clear the mist. He turned to Horatio, who had just come into the room, jumper sleeves still rolled up after having cleaned the downstairs toilet. "Turn that feckin' thing off, and get him on the phone!"

"Who? Bosco, I wish you didn't swear so much!"

Bosco not only ignored his lieutenant's small-mindedness, he deliberately larded his next sentences with words that would offend him. Subordinates sometimes needed to be reminded that they were subordinates. "Now who the feck do you think I mean, Horatio? Fecking Santa? The Easter fecking Bunny? Tinker-fecking-belle? Mr. Fecking Wonderman Ambrose Sheehy-O'Connor, you clown! For feck's sake! And have you washed your hands?"

"Of course, Bosc... Captain!... eh, what's his number? Shall I wash my hands now?"

"Now how should I know what his number is? Get it, man, get it! Directory enquiries, or whatever... don't bring me problems - bring me solutions! And wash your hands first - I don't want filthy germs all over the furniture."

"But Directory Enquiries costs a Euro a time..."

"Well get it on line then! For feck's sake, Horatio! Do I have to hold your hand all the time? And don't forget what I've told you - when you get these people on the line, remember to address me as 'Sir'. It's all about giving the right impression from the get-go. Remember, every moment is a defining moment. What did I just say?"

"Every moment is a defining moment, every moment is a refining moment..." Horatio's knobbly fingers skittered over the keyboard, while Bosco glared out of the back window. Beyond the rubble-strewn, breeze-block bordered garden, there was an expanse of scrubby grass looking towards a shut-down factory, and a boy was riding a scruffy pony from left to right. A net curtain of rain was trailing sadly behind. Bosco wondered if he had time to go out and box the rider's ears, but he probably didn't - and in any case, the last time he had done that, the local tinkers had pelted the house with stones. Poor Horatio had been quite badly cut when his bedroom window had shattered - although he had cheered up when Bosco had wiped his tears and blood on the corner of a tricolour, and renamed it The Martyrs' Banner. "The first of much such blood!" he had promised Horatio as he bandaged him up.

That proto-martyr had found the number. Bosco found this slightly surprising, but the simple reason was that Fidelma received so few phone calls that she had never bothered going ex-directory. He waited impatiently to be connected. This could be a very important conversation. Scrag-End was making a hash of it, as usual. He looked down on the grey cranium with scorn as Horatio spoke.

"Is that his house?... Ambrose's?... Oh... I'm sorry. Your house! I see... You're his mum, are you? Good morning. Is he in? Who am I? Well, I'm Horatio Mutton... Eh?... Well, I'm calling from the National Headquarters of Public Interest Salvation. Yes, that's right - Public Interest Salvation. We're... a campaign group, and we - you know - do campaigns. I am personal secretary to Captain Bosco Buggy himself - he's our leader, and by the way a close personal friend - and he wishes to speak to your son about work of national importance! So can you put him on please? Quickly now, please, if you don't mind - the Captain's a very busy man."

Bosco could hear an annoyed buzzing, and snatched the receiver. Horatio was smiling broadly and put his thumbs up in jubilation at his success in getting through. Bosco turned his back in disgust. "Good afternoon. Is that Mrs. Sheehy-O'Connor? I'm so sorry about that. He's new here. We have a big operation here, and sometimes - well, you know how it is, you just can't get the staff!" Horatio looked crestfallen, but Bosco didn't see, and if he had would not paid much attention. He was focusing on placating this difficult (and socially superior) woman. "I do appreciate that, Mrs. Sheehy-O'Connor. Sometimes, we all need time to be by ourselves, for a little private prayer and contemplation." He kicked Horatio, who had turned on the TV, yanked the plug out of the wall, pointed sternly to a chair, and mouthed "Sit!"

"It must be terribly difficult for you, Mrs. Sheehy-O'Connor. All this sudden pressure from the media - it gets all of us down some times! People who think for themselves - people who do things - people who care - we've always been hated and feared by the Establishment! We need to stick together, to help each other, be team players, but also be able to work on our own initiative in a supportive framework. A good team is a happy team, I always say!... Absolutely! You're so right!... Well, as I was saying, maybe I can help him in some way. There have been similar issues in my family. My Uncle Fintan used to say..." And eventually he had worn her down, got past the defences. He downed a double Bosco-juice in one go, and motioned to Horatio to get another.

Ambrose descended into the hallway at Fidelma's insistence that he speak to this charming and understanding man who could help with some kind of important work. "Good morrow. This is Ambrose speaking. I state at the outset that I am merely a Mouth. A Plenipotentiary, if you will."

"Eh? Oh, good morrow to you too! This is Captain Bosco Buggy speaking. You've heard of me, I suppose."

"I think not... err, Colonel."

"Oh! Well, in that case I must explain that in my way I am also a Plenipotentiary in my way. "

"You intrigue me strangely. Art an Adept of the Left or Right Hand Paths?"

"Oh, I'm as Right as can be; don't you worry about that! I represent the Irish People, a noble and holy race long denied a voice by the New World Order." ("Fecking headcase!" he mouthed at Horatio, who giggled at his wit.)

Ambrose breathed understandingly. "Ah, the Novus Ordo Seclorum which was foretold."

"Yeh, by the Federal Reserve!"

"I comprehend not thy drift, General Duffy."

"Buggy - it's Buggy! And I'm not a Gener... never mind! Look, my drift's this - the words Novus Ordo Seclorum appear on the back of the US dollar bill, along with other Masonic emblems. Now do you see what I'm getting at?" He could hear a strange sound - it sounded like snapping fingers - and a kind of snorting laugh.

"Nay, my friend - I alludeth to Revelations... and Old Mother Shipton, yclept Jezebel."

Bosco swallowed down a thunderflash. The lad was even more sincere than he had expected. He wondered whether it was worth continuing. He could just put down the phone, and let the eejit go and drill another hole in his head, or whatever - and it would be no loss to anyone. His hand tightened on the receiver, his wrist twitched in anticipation of the order. But... he thought in a millisecond of insight, if he did hang up, give up, what happened then? What was the alternative? He looked over at Horatio's irritating face - saw piled-up newspapers, letters from creditors, empty bottles, the mouse-trap by the skirting board, wallpaper in the worst 1980s taste - and through the window the same boy riding the same pony under the same trailing rain for decades to come. In that second, he knew he had to launch himself once and for all out of there, and into myth. So he swallowed pride, inhaled, and spoke again, conscious that every word he said and every thing he did could have the most momentous consequences for himself, and the country. Everything now was a means to a great end, and so he swallowed, and spoke the first tactful words he had ever uttered. "Yeh, right. Anyway, I think we're singing from the same hymn sheet! The reason for my call is that we can help each other. Your great brain, plus all the resources of my organisation, could make a winning combination. May I tell you what I have in mind?"

"I am agog, Field Marshal!"

BOSCO'S PLAN

Bosco's plan was one of Irish history's most elegant designs. The more he thought about it, the fewer flaws there seemed to be. It was risky, but then, men like him had always thrived on danger - and the country was surely ready. During a recent planning meeting with Horatio, he had referenced *Julius Caesar* - "There is a tide in the affairs of men, which, taken at the flood, leads on to... to... good luck, and if missed... something, something, something.... shallows and miseries." Horatio had clapped, and for sweet seconds Bosco had felt he had already thrown down his enemies. The squalid room was a stage in the Square, Horatio had been a malleable throng, his applause a great explosion that had rippled out and collapsed the post-1960s world. He had in those sweet moments hear singing, welling up from within, coming from the stones of the Square, up from everywhere, a warrior song... "And is the country ready, my bucko!" he had exulted aloud. But then Horatio had spoiled the mood, by wrinkling his nose, and asking, "Is it?"

Bosco met Ambrose the evening after their phone conversation. The proposed venue for the Summit was a respectable-looking pub named Oscar's in a town backstreet, a place Bosco had never visited, but which looked clean and well-maintained. He did not have all that much choice anyway. He was a bit too well known in the central Dublin pubs, and there were quite a few he couldn't go into. Oscar's looked like the kind of quiet place he and Ambrose could talk discreetly, while Horatio took notes which would one day form the basis of a significant Chronicle. "They also serve who only sit and write..." he had remarked to Horatio as he pushed open the door, in an excess of kindliness.

He had been surprised by the volume of the music. ABBA bounced around the low-lit, tastefully-appointed interior full of men drinking quietly - or noisily. It was hard to tell because of the music. He was just wondering whether he could prevail upon the management to turn it down when he noticed that some of the men had more earrings than was quite usual. Then it struck him that for some unaccountable reason he was attracting hostile glances. One man with very short hair sitting near the door jerked upright when he noticed Bosco, and whispered something to his companion - and hostility seemed to spring from table to table, until almost all of the people there were scowling. But by then Bosco had already seated himself, and Horatio had come carefully back from the bar, although not quite carefully enough, because Guinness slopped over the sides of Bosco's pint, and his half-pint (Bosco expected him not to drink too much when on duty). Horatio grumbled, "I had to get Guinness, because they only had weird foreign beers... and I think the barman may be - you know, one of them..."

He hadn't quite finished his limp wrist gesture, before the large and well-built barman was there, his hairless cranium looking like a medicine ball. The music was suddenly switched off, and the silence was a menace in itself. Everyone in the place was glaring now. "If I'd known you and that fecker were together I wouldn't have served you! You two get out!"

Bosco bristled. He would never get used to the ingratitude of those whom he was saving. "Now listen here, my good man - you clearly don't know who I am!" For answer, the barman merely threw down the coins Horatio had paid for the drinks, some of them rolling off the table and onto the tiled floor. Horatio immediately went down on his hands and knees under the table to pick them up. Mild grumbling came from out of sight. "Dear, dear... ah, I've found a Euro... now where is that fifty cents?" Someone started to snigger at the sight of Horatio's spindly legs and buttocks in their comfort-waistband slacks - and Bosco came out in goosebumps of indignation, and fear. "What's the meaning of this? You can't turn away a customer! I'll have the law on you! I know my rights! You don't know who..."

But the barman broke in. "See?" Bosco followed his finger, and saw a large rainbow flag on the wall. "Get it? Now get out, or I'll throw you out!" Bosco looked around and saw a wall of glares. He pushed back the chair and pulled himself up to his full height so that he could stare the barman full in the... chest. He took a master tactician's swift appraisal of the odds, and walked over to the street door and out, draped in a toga of dignity. As the door swung to behind him, inside Horatio emerged from under the table, smiling in glee as he held up a tiny nickel disc. From outside Bosco heard a cheering roar, and a moment later Horatio was manhandled through the door, his glasses crooked, his hair hanging wetly and his scurfy tweedy shoulders tidelined with Guinness someone had poured over his head. It took all of Bosco's leadership qualities to talk his lieutenant out of going home, but Horatio eventually stopped sniffling when told that his presence would be invaluable - and that, besides, beer was excellent for the hair.

There was a cold breeze on the corner as they waited, and Horatio began shivering. By the time Ambrose turned up, thirty-nine minutes late, Horatio had started to sneeze, and all the rest of the historic meeting was punctuated by stupendous trumpetings followed by apologies that annoyed Bosco even more than the sneezes. Luckily, Ambrose seemed not to notice.

"Wonderful, wonderful. It's such an honour to meet you!" Bosco lied patriotically. He had the unnerving idea that Ambrose wasn't wearing anything underneath his tracksuit. (He was correct.)

"Verily, Colonel, a momentous moment for such as thou, and... this person!" Ambrose gestured vaguely towards Horatio.

"Captain only, I'm afraid! Captain! The top brass - fecking feckers - weren't quite ready for me to get my colonelcy! Anyway, we've changed our mind about the pub - it isn't as nice as we had been told. How about that place over there?" Ambrose bowed (bowed!) and they crossed the road - Bosco and Horatio with care, but Ambrose just sauntering out without looking to left or right, as if his safety was beyond his control. The road was luckily empty, so there was no way of seeing whether his supreme confidence was justified. The other pub was much more traditional, with a reassuringly poor choice of beers, and they found a table at the back near the dartboard (no-one was playing). Ambrose pointed at the dartboard and laughed. "The sportsman's eye is sharp and keen, But death's darts hit their target, I ween!" Bosco wondered yet again if he was wasting his time.

The barman looked on Ambrose and the dishevelled Horatio with disfavour, but grudgingly served up a pint and a half of Guinness (and whisky chasers) and two packs of peanuts (the patriots had been too busy to dine). Ambrose declined anything. The trio sat down, and two said "*Sláinte*", while Ambrose pursed his lips, and muttered something which sounded like "spirituous liquors..."

"Eh? What's that?"

Ambrose pointed at the glasses and said, "The Sun has not yet entered the Lion, yet already in the morning, you wander about seeking wine in taverns instead of coming together to greet the Sun of Justice. Quaff not, friends!"

"But it's not the morning, is it? Cheers!" The delegates quaffed deeply, while Ambrose sat with a look of wooden virtue. Bosco was fixing every detail with quick eyes. Ambrose wasn't as comical in person as he seemed on screen. Notwithstanding the bizarre clothes and coiffure and the irregularity of his features, he possessed an indefinable dignity - a sort of stillness that commanded attention. He began to see why Ambrose had attracted some considerable supporters, notably that Shaughnessy-Don woman everyone went on about. It was all to do with Ambrose's background, Bosco felt - economic security gave him a self-assurance that could carry off any eccentricity, and gild any dung. Ambrose had the confidence to be himself, and to be able to take risks with his reputation. Bosco had always worried greatly about his. (And where the feck had it got him? he asked himself, not for the first time.)

He hated Ambrose on principle - and yet, Ambrose's face was so large, and so marmoreal, with those blue soul-stabbers, that he could not help falling into it. And then when its owner spoke, with his pleasing accent and expansive vocabulary, you felt constrained to listen, even though you were well aware that he was mad, and a mummy's boy. Bosco's resentment hardened as their conversation was interrupted several times by normal-looking people, clean people, mainstream people - who came over to ask Ambrose for his autograph (but never Bosco for his!). Whatever compunction Bosco may have felt about using Ambrose for his own ends - and it had never been much - rapidly evaporated. He'd use the bastard, take him down, and enjoy it...

Horatio made dutiful, useless notes as the visionaries conversed. Bosco would never look at the notes, but it gave the right impression to have one of life's underlings noting down his table-talk. "Well, it's excellent to meet you, Ambrose! I'm probably your greatest fan. Isn't that right, Horatio? Aren't I always saying that Ambrose is the real deal?" Horatio nodded. Bosco waited for a return compliment, but Ambrose was staring into the corner where the wall met the ceiling, and he seemed to be winking at something that wasn't there.

"Anyway, I wanted to meet you because as I said on the phone, you and I are on the same side. You and I both want to help Ireland get back to the old-time religion - and I think that our skills are mutually complementary."

No reaction.

"It's so important that people like us should stick together, and work together. Don't you agree?" Ambrose still said nothing, but he moved his head in a way that might have been a nod. "I thought we should organize a large public meeting in the town - a prayerful public meeting, a launch of a crusade to save Ireland from the devils that beset it." Another anomalous movement of Ambrose's head. Bosco felt like punching him, but checked himself with an effort of will.

Patience, Bosco! he told himself softly. When he had done what he planned to do, he would no longer be ignored. The Plan was what mattered... *Tiocfaidh ár lá*, Bosco me boy - and all that carry-on! He told himself yet again of the essential soundness of the Irish - daily disproofs notwithstanding. They were only awaiting the right signal, sent in the right way, at the right time. They only seemed comfortable and content; he was certain many secretly shared his views, and would follow if only he was allowed to lead. Some, after all, were born to command, predestined to the purple.

Bosco's grandfather had commanded an IRA flying column against the Brits, then the Free Staters. His grandson cherished a sepia photo showing Grandpop clad dashingly in fatigues, puttees, peaked cap and bandoliers, a Lee Enfield cradled carelessly in his arms, as ancient oats bristled in an Offaly background. His grandson had such mettle in him too, if only he had the chance to prove it. He had made an excellent psychological start by replicating that photo, with the help of army surplus clothing and a realistically-painted rifle-shaped stick cradled in just the same casually threatening way, against an identically oaty backdrop. The photo had been blown up and now hung opposite his bed - highly agreeable to see first thing every morning (although his wife had never appreciated it). He often wished he had a real Lee Enfield - yet what he did have was even better.

Just before his grandfather had been demobbed from the army of the living, he had left most of his modest effects not to Bosco's father - for whose respectable career path and inoffensive persona he felt unbounded contempt - but to his more vigorous grandson, who had always been so captivated by his Civil War anecdotes. Among his things, Bosco had discovered a locked wooden box stamped with German lettering, and when he opened it he had found to his inexpressible delight two Mauser machine pistols and ammunition. The guns oozed oil and peril in equal satisfying measure, winking up at him from purple velvet plush padding. They gleamed of high adventuring in the past, and even more importantly, a fantastic future time.

Indiscreet by nature, he had nonetheless contrived to kept the existence of these guns a deep secret, compensating himself by visiting them regularly late at night in their attic cubbyhole, taking them out to caress and careen, looking at himself lovingly in a mirror as he posed with them -

hefting their broom-like handles, sighting along their greenish-grey barrels, pretending to blow smoke off the barrel end after dispatching in imagination the current symbol of decline - the Taoiseach of the day, some journalist, some trimming priest, Gisela Mildew. He had maintained the weapons religiously, and had taken them up the Scalp to do some target practice, with satisfying results. He had a steady hand, although of late it had seemed perhaps less steady (yet another reason to prosecute the Plan with a degree of urgency).

The previous year, he had taken Horatio into his confidence, after threatening him with expulsion from the Movement if he told anyone. But he had known Horatio would not tell. For one thing, Horatio didn't often come into contact with other people. Besides, Horatio had been satisfyingly impressed, and he would sometimes entreat a none-too reluctant Bosco to take out the guns so that the two men would sit across the table from each other in awed silence, each fondling a gun, each with shining eyes, each their own vistas of personal and national redemption. It was time for these splendid things to come into their own, to do what they had been designed to do. Even as he buttered up Ambrose, Bosco was thinking of them, waiting in their plush-lined box, metal predators, national liberators... He returned, with some reluctance, to the matter in hand.

"So you see, Ambrose, what I have in mind is this. In a few weeks' time, it will be Easter - a time of great significance for your... our religion, and of course our country. What better way of celebrating than by having a Day of National Penance and Reaffirmation in the centre of town, near the 1916 memorial? With your profile and speaking skills, and with all the resources of our organisation at your disposal - I would also give a speech - a short one, no more than forty or fifty minutes - I think we could bring off a really top-notch event that would catapult our concerns to the centre of the national stage. The whole world will sit up and see that here in this blessed plot there still beats a sound heart - and that the people of that place still thirst for truth, for law and order, for real leadership." He paused, and quaffed yet again. "Get some more in," he instructed Horatio. He leaned forward matily and tapped Ambrose on his noticeably knobbly knee. Then he waved his arm to encompass the pub interior, as if he were flinging back a theatre curtain. "Sorry, my friend!" he said to the man whose drinks tray he had just missed. "Cool, yeah?" The man glared, but let it pass.

"Picture it, Ambrose! Just picture it... A lovely spring morning, the whole town gleaming in the sunshine, flags flying everywhere, and the streets crammed with people who have come to hear you tell them all about yo... our religion, and to see Ireland renewed! And there you are on your stage, and you're telling them all about... about the Assyrian numbers, and they're all shouting and stamping their feet, and waving their flags. They're there because they want to be nowhere else in the whole world! They're there to hear you - and to know what you know about Jesus! They're *moved* by you, Brother Ambrose! They carry flags and pictures of you, and they wave them in the air and roar until it seems like a forest has come into town! They're hanging on your every fecking syllable! They're up for it, Ambrose - and when you give the word, they'll disperse in all directions, carrying the flame of your words to all the cold fireplaces of the country. Your words - are you getting all this, Horatio? - will flow from you, and sink like gravy into the mashed spuds of the public mind! Can you see that, Brother Ambrose? Can you see it?"

A commotion came to Ambrose's face, as if he too was on that sunlit platform, on a glorious morning when the whole world could begin again. But he spoke very quietly. "The scenario delineated is not displeasing. Couldst guarantee a multitude, Major?"

"*Captain!* And yes, I could guarantee that there would be a big crowd - thanks to the considerable resources we control, and the excellent organisational abilities of myself and Scra... Horatio. We have a leadership team second to none. Isn't that so, Horatio?"

"Eh? Oh, yes, yes indeed!" Horatio's claim would have seemed more credible had it not been for his beery and bedraggled appearance. He, too, was thinking of the Mausers, and how it would feel to have one of them secreted under his coat, ready for brandishing when Bosco made the signal. In fact, he had just drawn a tiny gun in his notebook, just below the words "prayerful", "Assyrian" and "excellent". (The page was otherwise empty.) But Ambrose seemed content to take him and his boss at face value, and again made that anomalous movement of the head.

Bosco was watching Ambrose very closely, and smiling inwardly. He had got him where he wanted him. Christ, the fecker was mad in love with himself! But what did that matter? The key thing was that he would come, and hundreds, maybe even thousands, would come because he had come - some to laugh, to heckle - but others because they were soul-starved patriots looking for a lead, hoping for hope. There would be an angry, hungry atmosphere in that square, and hopefully a few leftwing protestors, raising the temperature even further as they hurled anti-Hibernian hatred onto the heads of the restive crowd.

And of course there would be cameras, and in large numbers - the cameras usually denied him, but which on that day would witness much more than they had expected. It would not just be Bosco's speech they would record and transmit, but his manly and decisive actions to save Ireland, and the purposeful ripple that would race through the crowd at the climax of his oration, as he announced regime-change and carefully-selected activists took control of the crowd - and took care of any Gardaí. Oh, it was one of History's most elegant designs, all right!

The country being the way it was, the world in such a state, all it would take would be his carefully-chosen words, a few pushes and scuffles out in that ocean of people, and - if necessary, as it almost certainly would be - a few shots that would ring through the world in real time. A few would get hurt - but they would be so worth it! That was the way of all revolutions. He sat up Ranger Wing-straight, shrugged his shoulders to signify regret at the sacrifices that needed to be made, and then made an involuntary air-punching gesture to mark the strike. Ambrose watched this pantomime impassively, immobile except for an index finger systematically exploring one nostril; but Horatio - who saw a little of what Bosco saw - was wriggling in excitement.

ORDER OF BATTLE

Beer had followed beer, whisky after. Then there had been a port and lemon "for the *bóthar*". Then there had been another. An hour passed, deeply pleasurable at least to Bosco. Then Ambrose (who had refused all drinks) suddenly stood in the middle of one of Bosco's lengthier anecdotes, and said decisively, "I must needs make an exodus". He walked out without looking back, not even when an elevated Bosco had called after him, "Do one for me too!" After his departure, all tension slackened as Bosco congratulated himself on his machinations. The *bóthar* was forgotten, and the two insurgents sat on while the pace of their drinking picked up. This morning, even Bosco's head bore some impress of the heroic ingurgitation. Horatio also felt more confused than usual, and he had a sore spot on his scalp. Towards closing time, darts had started to fall amongst them (they had forgotten the perilous location of their table), and one had stuck in his head for a moment, like an arrow in an old Western. In the exhilaration of that evening, Bosco had forgiven the throwers, and had persuaded Horatio to laugh it off. His sidekick was rubbing the spot ruefully as they sat delicately down to instant coffee in stained mugs - but he was also wielding a foolscap pad and business-like biros in different colours.

Bosco placed the phone at his own elbow, and dialled the numbers of the names as Horatio read them out. As each answered, or each answer phone clicked in, he would give the same curt message - "Nimrod calling. Nimrod calling. Operation Summer Storm is go. Operation Summer Storm is go. Confirm status. Confirm status. Over." There was a slight hiccup at the fourth call, when an annoyed woman had demanded to know who was calling, and what was all this malarkey, and if you want Joe why don't you say so instead of all this play-acting, and besides he was out, and no he didn't have a mobile. But most of the other calls went directly to personal mobile numbers, thus avoiding such difficulties. They rang twenty numbers, then they sat looking at the phone and each other in anxious silence for about sixty seconds, and then it started to ring. Horatio sat across from his energized Friend-Leader and watched him with a thrilling sense that he was watching History being wrought.

Bosco had long ago hand-picked trustworthy lieutenants from among the people who had passed through the PIS purview. Truth to tell, it was a smallish pool, and most of the people concerned were activists rather than intellectuals. And "activists" in this context mostly meant "troublemakers", many of whom were known to the Gardaí for non-political reasons. But although Bosco would moan to Horatio about the calibre of his followers, it secretly suited him, as it meant they could never be rivals. Of the twenty notified, twelve called back - and one of these was clearly looking for an excuse not to participate. But that was only to be expected; and Bosco wouldn't need all of them anyway. Better they fell away at this stage than later. He shouted at the backslider - "You haven't got the feckin' balls!", and then hung up. "Scratch Big Con from the list" he said to Horatio. "He hasn't got the feckin' balls! I never trusted that bozo anyway."

Bosco was thinking about his Speech. He often thought about it. These were some of the pleasantest hours he had ever known - hours which would sometimes become entire days. He had always given a good speech - everyone said so - and this would be a Speech with a capital S. People would still talk about in a hundred, two hundred, three hundred years. It would be up there with Gettysburg, the Proclamation of the Republic, the Dublin coach's exhortation just before the 1983 GAA final against those Cork bastards. It was entitled "As long as there are Irishmen (and women)". The two parenthesized words were a recent amendment, over which he had agonized for months. He wanted to be inclusive and modern, to connect with the younger generation who would have to carry on his world-historical struggle after he had been cortèged to his vault in Glasnevin. He had even added in some quotes from pop songs the youngsters would appreciate. The times they really *were* a-changing! And things could only get better! He had been refining the text for years, and had even marked the places where judicious interjections from planted allies would stoke up crowd fury. These places were marked with multiple asterisks - the more asterisks, the more passionate the response. By page 30, there were almost as many asterisks as text. Bosco started to read it yet again, and as he whispered the words, his headache vanished, and the snail-sticky kitchen dissolved into an oriflamme arena.

*

Ambrose's head was so busy that he had quite forgotten the name of the foxy little man and his servant - but he remembered the idea and the date they had decided upon. He updated Ambrosenet, and almost immediately began to receive expressions of enthusiasm and promises to attend. For a time, these outnumbered the ridicule and threats. He had no need to work on a speech - his problem was that he always had so much to say and so little time to say it. And every time he opened a book there were more things to weave in. The universe was full of possibilities as well as certainties. There was free will, but also a Great Structure - a massif pointing Man's attention upwards, a Hill of Hope forested with pines. He sat considering these things and more as bright moons orbited around him.

One of these satellites was Letitia, and she became very thoughtful when she heard about this plan. She knew Ambrose had many calumniators, and that a surprisingly large number of people would take unaccountable pleasure in seeing him humiliated. Many more would turn up just to make fun of him. She could not bear to think of this happening; he was such a child, so in need of shelter. She thought of him almost as often as she still thought of her Jackie - with whom had ended not just her own dreams, but the name of Shaughnessy-Don - a name that had slashed its way through the national consciousness since the early Middle Ages at least, all now jumbled up in the ground with his little bones. When she joined him in the family vault (who would put her there?), a chapter in Ireland's history would close - and she was ashamed that it should have been she who had let that story end.

Meeting Ambrose and becoming involved - giving interviews, acting as spokeswoman, dealing with some of the correspondence, trying to edit some sense into his articles - had helped her forget that old preoccupation for afternoons on end. Some of her love for her dead son had been transposed to Ambrose. She had, in fact, become fiercely protective of him. It had been bad enough seeing him jeered by passers-by. She worried that this event would attract too many people, and of the worst kind. She had found that human beings were reasonable enough as individuals, sometimes almost rational - but that when they got together in groups, they too easily became something quite different, something seething and malignant.

She had also noted the hatred that many now felt for any hint of Christianity - and many people did see Ambrose as a Christian, albeit an offbeat one. There were people who would hurt, or even kill, to extirpate anything that was old, or hinted of any kind of Authority. This hatred came across strongly in many of the messages left on Ambrosenet, and in some of the media coverage. Ambrose, the ugly babe, the lanky lamb, had through sheer innocence made himself all kinds of enemies.

By himself he might have got away with minor unpleasantness - jeering, jostling - but the presence on the platform of that little foxy fascist was a guarantee of mayhem. His last meeting had closed down the centre of Dublin for a whole afternoon, as he and four followers had been escorted by hundreds of Gardaí through hundreds of protestors. Even if Ambrose by some miracle didn't say something unwise, Bosco Buggy certainly would - and she had a horrid vision of a mob in motion, urgent animals uncaged, things flying through the air and striking Ambrose, him falling, brilliant blood bursting from his brow, his so-bright eyes screwed shut in pain.

It was her clear duty to raise the subject with him, although she knew it would do no good. But all he would say, in his maddening, endearing way, was "It hath been so ordained", after which he would change the subject in his bewildering way. She knew there was no point in talking to Fidelma, who had never had any power over him, and had in any case been in a daze ever since that TV show. So she went to Oldtown Convent.

Letitia and Mary had only met twice, the first time when Mary dropped in unexpectedly to see Ambrose while Letitia was there. But they had got on exceptionally well - better, Fidelma thought resentfullly, than she and Mary had ever got on together. Letitia had subsequently made a prolonged visit to Oldtown. Letitia liked that Mary had never alluded to her celebrity (whereas Fidelma was always asking things like whether she had met so-and-so, or whether some celebrity was gay).

But Mary wasn't troubled by Letitia's concerns. On the contrary, she seemed excited about the rally, and planned to attend, hopefully with all the other Oldtown sisters. She smiled and clasped her hands, looking for a few seconds like a little girl. "It reminds me," she said, her eyes brimming with quiet fervour, "of the events they used to have in the old days - there is almost a kind of medieval flavour, don't you think? There hasn't been a national day of prayer since Goodness knows when - years, decades. I can't remember any such thing - at least not since His Holiness's visit. And there won't be one again in my lifetime."

"But, Mary, it's not official - the Church doesn't endorse the rally. The only speakers advertised so far are Ambrose, and this ghastly little Buggy man. I don't see how you can construe that as being a national day for anything - except maybe trouble-making! It will only discredit Ambrose, maybe even endanger him."

"I'm sure you're worrying unnecessarily. But if it happens, it is beyond my control - or anyone's control. There will be Gardaí there, and they will do what they can, but if bad people want to make trouble, then they will make trouble! It may yet be declared official by the Church - there are weeks to go yet - but even if it isn't we are within our rights to go as private citizens. I somehow don't think we'll be the only good Catholics there! No - things must be as they will be. I can't help feeling they've been ordained!" It was only then Letitia realised how like Ambrose Mary could be.

Letitia's only remaining recourse was the Monsignor. Since his phone call on the day he had interviewed Ambrose, she and he had spoken almost every day - feeling their way back to former footings, falling agreeably into old conversations. They had not yet met, but to him their conversations were a very welcome distraction from his tedious round of correspondence, meetings and occasional flights to Fiumicino.

"What ho!" he answered her, an allusion to their love of Wodehouse.

"What ho to you too. How is work?"

"Oh as you might expect - dull but essential to the smooth operation of the cosmos."

"Ambrose, I'm very worried about your namesake. Very worried!"

"You always mention the urchin when you call - and you're always worried about him. If I wasn't a priest, and he wasn't a lunatic, I could become quite jealous. What's he done now?"

She told him the details.

"Buggy... Oh, yes. Foxy fella, fascist, bit of a nut. I've seen him on TV. Wrote to me once - can't remember why. Not sure I ever answered."

"I think this'll cause trouble for Ambrose. Wherever that Buggy goes, there's trouble - usually violent trouble. I've told Ambrose he's making a mistake, but he doesn't want to know. He just looks at me with those eyes and makes some gnomic remark. Fidelma has no sway over him, and Mary wants the thing to go ahead. I think she really believes in him, or is on the cusp of doing so. I'm not sure whether she would have any influence over him anyway. So what I want to know is what you can do to dissuade him?"

The Monsignor chuckled. "Letty, I have no power whatsoever over the young harum-scarum. I've only met him once, and as you know it wasn't exactly a success! I don't appreciate people taking the piss out of an ancient and dignified religion which just happens to be my one - and I told him so, and he just smiled and said... oh, what does it matter what he said? If I think about it, I'll just get angry again."

"You're one of the very few people I have ever met who is really serious about something. That's your best quality."

"Your old flannel won't wash, Letty! And even if I felt inclined to help, nothing I could do or say would make the slightest difference. The lad's on autopilot; he doesn't know what day it is, and his so-called religion - in case you've forgotten - is a farrago of falsehood, fairy tales and crap from computers. You were saying that no one is serious about anything these days - well, your long Barnaby Rudge of a friend's a prime example! Let him alone, Letty, let him alone - let him get his comeuppance sooner rather than later, so that he can drift back down to earth without damage. Let him go on his damn-fool march or parade, or whatever it is, and get himself arrested, and have done with it. The lad needs to get it out of his system."

"If I didn't know you, I would say you're being a callous brute. I would add that you are very boring! However, as I know that you are neither of these things, all I can say is that regretfully on this occasion you are suffering from a major failure of imagination. Ambrose needs help, and you might be able to give it to him."

"But how, Letty? What can *I* do? I told you - he doesn't know what he's doing. He's living in his own universe. He's not going to listen to me, or anyone like me. He doesn't even know who I am."

"You're wrong there. He's mentioned you to me more than once, by name. I can tell you that *means* something! He knows who you are all right, and what you represent - and in some part of him he respects that. He's not anti-Church - it's just that until now he hasn't had any outlet. And what can you expect, with a Church run by people like... what's his name... the Arch-Creep?"

"I do hope you aren't referring to our most Reverend Apostle to Youth!"

"That's the swine! Just think what it would be like to be an imaginative person like Ambrose, born into a church that gives high office to a mollusc like that. Is it any wonder that he's gone off on his own tangent? And then what about his mother? You met her, didn't you? Poor woman, thinks she's terribly sophisticated, but she's a child. Not even a child - a doll... He...oh, maybe I'm wasting my breath! But I'm just trying to explain why he's the way he is, and why he deserves sympathy and help."

"OK, OK, Letty - but what can I do? If he's said he'll do this thing, then he'll do it, no matter what anyone says or does. You know I'm right."

"That's what's so frustrating! You're right. He'll be there, and therefore I'll be there, in the hope that just maybe I can be of help, or stop something worse happening. But I just wondered if... if... No, I suppose it's not fair to ask..."

The Monsignor rolled experienced eyes, and prepared to capitulate. Whatever she wanted him to do, he knew he would do. It had always been that way - except for that single significant exception, beside that sad lake, all those years ago. "To ask what? Don't go all coy on me now."

"Well, all I was... no, no... no, it's not fair of me to suggest it. It'd cause too many problems for you. And it probably wouldn't do any good anyway. I'm sorry - forget it!"

"You want me to go along to this jamboree? To keep an eye on the lad, or something - to make sure things don't get out of hand - to use my legendary tact to defuse any tensions that may arise! Is that your master plan?"

"What a brilliant idea of yours! I knew I could rely on you. But seriously now, I was going to ask you to do exactly that - but as I was about to ask you, I realized of course you couldn't be seen at such an event. It's not as if you're a free agent, is it? Of course you couldn't go. I'm sorry - I should have thought before I blurted it out. Forget I mentioned it. Of course you couldn't go... officially."

She changed the subject, and they talked on for almost an hour about other things. But at intervals through the remainder of that afternoon, and those that ensued as the days started to stretch into spring, he found himself thinking a great deal about Ambrose - wondering what might be in store for that poor puzzled boy, this poor puzzled country.

LIFE AND SOCIETY

It was an evening. Or was it afternoon? Maybe even a morning. Even in the old days, the o'clock had seemed largely unimportant to Ambrose, and now all hours merged into one long elevated state, when he was neither asleep nor fully awake. He had taken to resting standing up, or leaning at 45% on a plank propped against the wall. Being uncomfortable was *ipso facto* good, because pleasure and pain were the same. It was also good to be that little bit closer to the Great Texter. Indeterminacy was essential; he needed to be able to drift between dimensions.

His bedoom curtains were almost never opened, except when Fidelma ventured in during his rare absences, on a hunt for things to wash. (There were always plenty of these, which he would cram out of sight under his bed amongst the 'clean' clothes.) He would rush over and close the curtains again as soon as he got back to the room. But even so he was still troubled by noises - dawn birds, cats, dogs, foxes, doors banging, dustbins being emptied, cars and motorbikes, passers-by, and during the daytime, the murmur of visitors outside the gates, chatting, sometimes chanting. At nights, he watched dubiously the car-light lozenges that rolled across the ceiling and wondered what they signified. "Who *are* you?" he would whisper. "What do you want?"

The webcam was always on, its tiny red light like a sanctuary lamp in the perma-gloom. The moment he 'awoke', he would click on a lamp accidentally angled to make him appear heavy-browed and prophetic, and start to repeat whatever he had heard when 'asleep' - sometimes speaking for several hours, or until he next fell out of consciousness. Sometimes he would stop mid-word - and resume in the middle of a different word. It didn't seem to matter. There was a narcoleptic delight in sliding in and out of the world, to try to catch it unawares - and a pleasant delirium in physical stress. Less pleasant were the creatures that would come and roar in his ears, and disappear before he could ascertain their type. Yet again there were times when everything connected - double-shot espresso moments when his brain felt preternaturally alert, and insights streamed unstoppably.

A Modern Journey

The lately Spartaned cell was re-filling. As well as the computer, lamp, bed and plank, there was the plaster tableau and new books, stacked and strewn on the straw-strewn floor. He had been inspired by finding a tatty old copy of *Napoleon's Book of Fate* - and the notebooks in which he had been recording his shortcomings (how horribly quickly these accumulated!) were now also studded with tables, formulae and lines of dots giving the answers to the same questions that had vexed the Emperor of Europe. Ambrose had tried the questions on himself, and the results had been generally encouraging. It seemed he would obtain his wish, and he would succeed in his cause. Other answers were less obviously applicable - which patient would be healed? What prisoner released? Himself? Perhaps these secrets would be vouchsafed in time.

He had discovered that everything had its numinous side, a secret spiritual life. He had been so clodlike! To think others even now didn't know, couldn't understand, even after he had explained at length! They who thought themselves so real and rooted - they saw nothing, knew nothing, except what was immediately in front of their muzzles. But then he too had harvested on earth as if it would be his abode for ever. As soon as he had opened himself up to all possibilities, his mind had expanded until it accommodated all. The world was full of windows and wormholes, and everyone moved (usually without noticing) through a meteor-storm of ciphers, codes, signals, symbols, talismans and tokens. Spirits sighed among us, constantly brushing our skin and kissing our brows in cold regret, heralds bringing messages we rarely read.

Death was often present in the tableaux Ambrose was shown, sometimes just a distant dart that left white scratches in the sky, en route to some other target. But other times Death was a figure in many guises, garbed for different ages - classical robes, doublet and hose, black leather and motorbike boots, metallescent garments from some other planet's far future. When seen so often, the Great Equalizer started to seem almost companionable. And in any case he was only one of many who called on Ambrose - brownies, guardian angels, fauns, little men, tiddy folk, gnomes, kobolds, hobbits, dragons, yales, hippogriffs, and far too many others to taxonomize. Ambrose moved among them with wonder as they glided and flew and ducked and whistled and chuckled in and out and under the heather, the gorse and pines, down the hill, girdling the Cross in pagan patterns, scattering out over the sea and vanishing in concentric waves of light. He strode boldly from room to room in a mansion of marvels, kicking open doors, facing down foes, picking up power packs, accumulating points as he mounted towards the top Level.

Mingled in with these were people he knew, and many he didn't - asking things, doing things for or to him, clustering messily like magnetized filings, parting like oceans - interchangeably angry, anxious, contemptuous, contorted, delighted, disconcerted, earnest, eager, hate-filled. And there was antiphonal chanting heard (or was it just hoped for?) - "Ambrose! Ambrose! Lead us! Lead us!" Or was it "Ambrose! Ambrose! Loser! Loser?"

Some of the faces that jostled and jabbered around him seemed to have escaped from old paintings - such as that of a fat, fair man he had met once, sitting opposite Ambrose in a very bright room, perspiring in the heat of strong lights and whipped by the imps of his own noxious conscience. That face had seemed eventually to melt into paste.

Also oddly un-alive was the most familiar of faces - his mother, omnipresent yet never quite in focus, as if she had been peered at too closely and her pixels had unresolved themselves. He wished to do her honour, but when he tried to connect no sense would come from his mouth, or hers, and she would look back at him in dumb reproach, pitiable but forever beyond help, like a hunted hind expiring in some long-ago forest.

Then there was a truly lovely face, a girl he recognized from the different days. She seemed to be with him often, and for many hours, a pale form prone in the dim bedroom. But she rarely smiled, and her eyes often looked always tired and red. What is your name, and why do you cry? If he ever asked, and if she ever replied, it never registered. He wished he could be to her, and all people, whatever they would wish him to be.

More vivid by far than these three were many moiling new faces, animal-fast eyes surmounted by wild hair, persons whose garments marked them out as poor in the flesh. But it seemed that their natures were rich, and they lived more in one minute than others in lives. "Blessed are they... blessed are you," he would murmur as they offered shabby but sincere gifts, and they would bend their heads in acknowledgement and something like adoration. They touched him deeply. So kind... wonderful... delightful...

There were two more phantoms, ancient but impressive - a man, a Temple Elder, of his own height but much broader, a man of predatory physiognomy, a man easily enkindled, with whom he had once stood ages ago looking down on an ancient sunken garden across which a tiny man had been walking with his shadow. He and the Elder had argued, almost fought - and he could still pick up occasional old transmissions from their encounter, fading in and out again, as if racing through radio-waves at the extreme edge of the solar system.

A woman of similar age also often featured, her eyes the hue of the Bay in Decembers, and with something of its restlessness - a person of economy of movement, whose fine-lined face pleased him, and whose mellifluous voice sometimes penetrated the rushing and roaring, and lodged things in his head. Now she was here again, and she was pleased and excited, and some of her words broke through. "... fantastic opportunity... you to explain... respected... influential... in front of the whole country...see you as we do..."

He smiled approvingly at her as she spoke and fussed, pushing him into a coat, brushing his hair. No, it wasn't her brushing his hair, it was the lovely girl - and she was also kissing him on the mouth, pressing her body against his. How kind and good some people were! It was for such as them that he was doing such as he was doing. What is your name? (Had he asked out loud?) He protested mildly - but he did not mean it - at being bundled out of his cell, and downstairs towards an open door through which could be seen the toxic radiation of the city. His blood flooded in the knowledge that he was sallying forth to do battle with its orangeness. He hardly registered his mother looking on - a bisque doll with folded arms - as he exited between Letitia and Philomena.

Later (when?) - a brilliant room, stifling, with fidgeting, chattering, tittering atoms agglomerating into an audience, and shades shifting around him with clipboards and booming voices. Only studio technicians would have recognized it, but it was in fact the same studio that had until recently hosted L.O.L., re-configured as the new locus for television's leading cultural discussion programme, *Life and Society*. The primary colours of the old set had been discarded in favour of pastels, cheery plastic chairs for intellectualism-evoking black faux leather armchairs with chromium feet. There was a smoked glass table with carafes of water where Liam's epicurean board had groaned. And there were grave-looking people sitting to either side of Ambrose, speaking courteously to each other around him and making churches with soapy fingers. What they were saying rushed through Ambrose's head as if he were intercepting someone else's signal - but an undamaged indexing system on the right-hand side of his brain was quietly clicking, registering their identities.

There were four of these, umpired by the much-awarded-to Fitzroy Nevin, there to do courteous battle on behalf of realer religions against this interloper arisen Alien-like from Ireland's entrails. Without really liking each other, they were allies for an evening, willing to put aside their own agendas until they had swatted away this affront to their respective dignities.

Most important by far - although he was too polite to point this out - was that chevalier of neo-Catholicism, whom even Nevin called "Daddy Jimmy". But then, even Vatican insiders had to think for a few seconds before remembering his surname. He was a middle-aged, grey wavy-haired man with a seasick tinge to his skin, as if he had been experimenting with vegetable dyes. He specialized in social relevance, as could be seen by the butterfly tattoo on his neck, and that he combined clericals with running shoes. A gold stud spangled in one lobe as he looked sagely from one friend-in-faith to another. He looked to Letitia, watching from the front row, ridiculous yet sleek, a wolverine waiting to be unleashed. His dog-collar reminded her of a napkin. Was he about to feast on Ambrose? She had heard him lecture once, and although she had managed to contrive an early exit, had seen enough to know that he concealed shrewd calculation behind his veneer of friendly flamboyance. He saw her looking at him, recognized her of course - and made a curious gesture that combined elements of equality and obsequiousness - smiling and wiggling his fingers, while his thickening body half-rose out of his chair in a sort of semi-bow, one social force acknowledging another. She looked away, faintly disgusted, thinking of Mr. Collins in *Pride and Prejudice.*

Representing a younger, but if anything even more respectable religion, was a middle-aged Church of Ireland rector named James Saxon - a bachelor of misleadingly athletic build, whose mien and interest in clerestories and the Boys' Brigade had early marked him out as ideally suited to a denomination which combined Low ideals with social pretensions. The shrinking number of woman parishioners who had marriageable daughters would often point them like torpedoes in his direction, but he seemed more interested in Fair Trade. A truly good man, so dedicated, the parishioners murmured among themselves, slightly sorrowfully, wondering about his private life. His religion was reasonable almost to the point of disappearance, but sometimes when he peered down from his nightmarish nineteenth century pulpit onto all those politely upturned faces he wanted to kill them and then himself.

A religion much older than Anglicanism, but very new to Ireland, was represented by Abdul Abdullah Abdul, a paunchy greybeard whose light grey suit shimmered with cheapness. He was a chain restaurateur from Tunisia via Tallaght, a husband of two, father of twelve and uncle to fifty-plus. In his very limited spare time, he ran the Muslim Mission to the Infidel, which he always referred to diplomatically as simply "the Muslim Mission", and worked towards a time when all of Europe professed his faith and patronized his restaurants. He had assimilated fully into Irish culture by developing a secret drinking habit. His views were as incandescent as they were ill-informed, and he was widely respected.

Older by far than all the above - if again, startlingly new to Ireland - was Hinduism, whose representative was none other than Dr. Kumiswaramy. Fidelma was very surprised to see him sitting among all those Establishment representatives. He was arguably a controversial choice, with all the awful things that had been alleged about him recently by a newspaper and across many websites. His camel-like countenance was impassive, but even someone with his enchantingly imperfect English must have been aware that he was the object of much prurient curiosity. Fidelma felt terribly ashamed of Ireland sometimes; it was disgraceful how prejudiced some people could be, and how the good that was in the world was so often met with evil. Some women were their gender's worst enemies. She rubbed her cheek reminiscently; Dr. K's cream was doing marvels, eliminating epidermal badteria, and plumping her peptides. The idea that someone so wise, so kind would do what they were saying he did! He was so brave to face them down! She admired his deep and sincere commitment to the massively important cause of advancing the wisdom of the East.

Nevertheless, the rumours distressed her. They made her think of incidents and sensations during his treatments that she would rather not have called to mind - things that even at the time had seemed weird (albeit pleasurable) - but which she had dismissed until a couple of weeks ago as merely reflections of her own dark imaginings, her provincialism, maybe even unworked-through racism. It might be best, she had very recently concluded, if she were to keep away from him for a while - until he had cleared himself fully. She desperately hoped Ambrose hadn't heard any of these stories. He had such an obsession with sex. He might do to this most distinguished of Indo-Irishmen what he had done to that creep Liam Larrikin. To repeat any of these allegations on live TV might be slanderous...even worse, it would be terribly vulgar. Sandra Gulliver would never let her live it down.

The Monsignor was also watching, sipping whisky in his grace-and-favour apartment on one of Dublin's handsomest Georgian thoroughfares, its Augustan proportions the perfect setting for a small collection of old paintings in which the female form featured frequently enough to offend the woman who came in to make breakfast and pass a vacuum cleaner over the carpet. These paintings were the personal property of the Monsignor, as were a great many well-bound books, almost none of which pertained to religion. It was unusual for him to watch television, but he made an exception for "Life &" (as people called it). He felt it incumbent on him to keep an eye on contemporary thinking, to see the myrmidons of modernity in close-up and hear their rationales - in fact, to remind himself precisely why, despite everything, he remained in the Church.

He also lived in the hope that one day Daddy Jimmy (a frequent guest on Life &) would tumble very publicly from grace - so far that he would never be able to rise again to snuffle the social truffles. The Monsignor had always been disappointed. But this time it really could be different. Ambrose, as he knew only too well, was a law all to himself. He might do... anything! The idea of Ambrose's wildness awed him. Jimmy would have no idea what Ambrose was like - no-one who had not met him could imagine that - and faced with him for the first time it was not beyond possibility that even so smooth a bastard would lose his temper. The Monsignor lifted his tumbler in ironic salute.

Ambrose sat still while the studio revolved around him, sizzling slightly like a dormant volcano, as Fitzroy Nevin explained to the studio and worldwide audience that religion had been around a long time, and was still around, human need, profound questions, incompatibility with modernity, is there still a place, distinguished panel... "Get on with it, man!" expostulated the Monsignor, but Nevin opted to ignore this astral plane interruption, if he ever received it, and turned to Ambrose only after he had sucked every shade of unmeaning from his own words.

Nevin was Ireland's most eminent presenter of other people's ideas - a brilliantly-burnished, well met glad-hander who could insert himself into anyone's front room thirty Saturdays of the year and make himself entirely at home. His voice was low and West Brit; his silver hair (an integral ingredient of his brand, laved with Scandinavian shampoos) betokened learning as well as lustre. His clothes were bespoke, his opinions off the peg. He exchanged Happy Holiday greetings with Gisela Mildew and the presidents of several countries, some of them large ones. Their cards in reply were framed, and formed an impressive display in his all-white Ballsbridge living room. The son of a senior diplomat, whose children were at Clongowes, he was celebrated for egalitarianism and atheism. *The Irish Gentleman* had just granted him the coveted "Ireland's Most Dignified Man" award.

"Welcome to Life &, Mr. Sheehy-O'Connor. I'll call you Ambrose, if you don't mind. You see, you are one of that very small number of people whose single name is a national brand, so widely recognized as to make your surname superfluous - like Madonna, or Elvis, or maybe even Jesus! Or even Daddy Jimmy! Isn't that right, Daddy? Ha ha ha." Daddy Jimmy puffed up his plumes in modest acknowledgement of being name-checked in such company, and grinned the winning grin that always made the Monsignor wish they had met on a rugby pitch (opposing teams). Ambrose said nothing, but levelled a look of calm contempt at his host, who affected not to notice. The Monsignor felt greatly heartened.

"We've invited you here this evening because your new religion has made quite a stir. We have all seen the footage of you on the scaffolding self-mortifying yourself. We have all looked at Ambrosenet and –" he just avoided smirking "- marvelled at its contents. Am I right in saying that it is presently Ireland's most visited website?... Sorry? I thought you said something... No? Well, OK, Ambrose. OK. Anyway, as I was saying, you've made quite a stir, and we are all fascinated by you. And now of course you are planning a National Rally. Perhaps I should start by asking you a simple question - why?"

"Why what?"

The Monsignor smiled in pleasure; Letitia's lips curved upwards; Philomena gasped in admiration; Fidelma winced.

"Why, ha ha, I would have thought that was obvious. Why did you start a religion?"

"I initiated no religion. I inherited and have since sought to revivify an immemorial faith. I may" - he simpered - "have refined and sifted, but the ingredients remain unadulterated. The same ingredients as have been abused by creatures such as yonder poltroon." He pointed at Daddy Jimmy, whose gently superior smile froze. Nevin injected disapproval into his voice, although inside he was exulting. This could be a TV classic-in-the-making, destined for YouTube immortality.

"Tut tut, Ambrose! Less of the personal stuff, if you don't mind. Can we stick to the issues, please? I'll ask again one simple, slightly rephrased, question - why did you decide to start - or, if you like, revive - a religion? What was it that made you arise up out of the comfortable suburbs to evangelize - or re-evangelize - the country? We've heard that you had visions on the Head. You are, to me, a modern on a hill. But was there also a book that inspired you? A film? A piece of music? A crisis of faith? A personal crisis? Were you unlucky in love? Or was it just one of those existential moments when you realize that you and the Gleichshaltung are out of kilter? You know, you remind me of Kierkegaard."

"That is many questions, not one, Silvertop. Which wouldst you have me answer?"

Many in the audience were grinning, and Nevin wasn't used to that. He decided he didn't like it much. Nor did he like this guest. "All right, Ambrose - all right! Why don't you tell us in your own words what it was that switched you from being a normal, modern Irish person to some kind of Old Testament prophet?"

"I thank thee for this opportunity to expound my doctrines at length on thy televisual infotainment. Accounts of my transfiguration atop the Head have indeed been widely broadcast, as thou vouchsafest at the onset. Sufficeth it to say that on that eve and in that place I was afforded entry into a sacred space that subsists below quondam consciousness." A current of derision and disapproval passed through part of the audience. Others were smiling in anticipation of yet greater insanities. But a few were leaning forward eagerly - maybe hungrily.

"The vision was of such immanence I knew immediately it was my bounden duty to speak out to a nation athirst. I could not do otherwise - I knew it was my duty to speak as I had found, to offer hope to the hopeless, and advertise the return of the King."

There were audience sniggers, drowned out by angry "Ssshs!" Some in the audience shifted, eager to be offended. But Ambrose continued talking, impassive and impressive, like a long river rolling at last to its delta. Nevin and Daddy Jimmy stared scorn, James Saxon was clearly wishing he was anywhere else, Abdul Abdullah Abdul looked puzzled and, although a vegan, Dr. Kumiswaramy was carnivorously chewing the inside of one cheek.

"We dwell in a domain sunk in sin, chastised by crime, plagued by corruption, abased by economics, the plaything of evil forces. We career in carnal and wild courses, ingesting sulphurous air, rolling in liquid fire, plagued by infernals and terrific forms. The powers of darkness assail us keenly, denying us admittance to that place where the living fountains play. And these merry-andrews..." - he pointed at Daddy Jimmy and James Saxon - "...proffer no medicaments. Their currencies art milk-and-water medicines, placebos, flatulent flummeries, bread and circuses, grave nonsenses, and carnal extravagances. There is no mission in them - no commitment to outcasts, the underprivileged - the sex workers, the whoresons, the publicans, the thieves, the politicians, the attorneys, the politicians, the Level 1 players. They art but fatted calves, bloated maggots battening on rancid flesh, liver-spotted lackadays, molly-boys, inveterate cock-fighters..."

"Now hang on, Ambrose! Hang on! We already agreed, no personal attacks! No offensive remarks!"

"I did not agree to thy conditions, Ash-Bonce - thou madest that assumption."

Much tittering in the audience. Anger, too. Nevin turned swiftly to Daddy Jimmy. "Daddy Jimmy, perhaps thou... you would like to come in at this juncture? What do you have against Ambrose, specifically? I mean, isn't his religion as good as anyone else's? Doesn't he have a right to freedom of conscience?"

"Of course he has a right to freedom of conscience! But to speak frankly, Fitz..."

Ambrose interjected, rolling his eyes and clucking triumphantly. "The first time is oft-times most difficult, thou Pharisee!" There was a huge audience laugh. The Monsignor noticed a mottled purple flush spreading across Daddy Jimmy's face, and grinned in admiration of Ambrose's gift of the goad. Daddy Jimmy retorted with real hurt and anger.

"That's where you're wrong! Dead wrong! I am no Pharisee! I am against the Pharisees, against the System. That's why there are so many young people here tonight - many more so than usual, I think I'm right in saying, Fitz? As I was saying, Fitz, people have a right to make a fool of themselves! And I'm afraid that's just what young Ambrose has done - although no doubt for the best possible motives, like highlighting climate change or anti-Roma discrimination. But we in the responsible community also have a right to challenge him when he emerges into the public square to stir up trouble, to set faith against faith, to bring religion into disrepute.

Nowhere in the Good Book does it endorse his literally sickening views! Ireland is aghast - the world is aghast!"

To the delight of one third of the audience, and the horror of another, Ambrose was snapping his fingers at him and saying "Fie fie, folderol!", but Daddy Jimmy ploughed on, speaking loudly, his face burning. The Monsignor and Letitia were laughing out loud. Philomena was perched forward, not yet laughing, shocked by and proud of Ambrose's crazy bravery. But Fidelma was shocked and silent. This was worse than anything she could ever have imagined.

"You see, Fitzroy, religion is in everyone's DNA; it's like our species' signature tune, our Top of the Psychology Pops, and this is why it's so crucial that at the end of the day we communicate the awesomeness of God to..."

Daddy Jimmy faltered as he sensed the audience was ignoring him, and only then noticed that Ambrose was staring threateningly and muttering outré insults - "Cobnut, wingless lizard, extinguished firedrake, woolly bear, pteranadon, genital louse..."

High seas of hilarity were heaving around the studio, and the technicians were grinning as Camera 1 zoomed in on Ambrose's face, set in grim determination of a kind never seen before on Life &. Fitzroy Nevin had raised a cologned hand, for him a sign of the deepest perturbation. "Ambrose, Ambrose! Some respect for the cloth, pulleeease! Give Daddy Jimmy a chance to speak!"

Daddy Jimmy looked stonily at Ambrose, who subsided into a sarcastic smile, to the disappointment of most of the audience. "As I was saying, that's why it's so crucial to let everyone say their say and walk their walk, take their own personal pilgrimage, but at the end of the day I have always been clear that in the final analysis whatever you believe is fine, so long as you don't diss others. And that's the problem with Ambrose - he's not only dissing Jesus, he's dissing the nation, he's dissing you and me, folks!"

Ambrose interjected again. "Those who oft go on pilgrimage rarely become saints - so sayeth Thomas à Kempis! There, there, I have spake my piece! Blow on, brother, blow on!" He waved his hand airily, and pointedly turned his back on Daddy Jimmy; the latter mastered himself and then continued gamely. But everyone was watching Ambrose, who had now switched his attentions to the increasingly uncomfortable James Saxon, immediately to his left.

A Modern Journey

That sensitive Fair Trader was not happy with Ambrose staring severely at him from only about three feet away. He passed his hand uneasily over his hare-like features, sweating slightly - sharp, tapering face, big, brown eyes with long lashes, a suggestion of nervous activity. He had never had a congregant like Ambrose; he didn't think even the Primitive Baptists had ever had a congregant like Ambrose. He had never met, or even heard of, anyone like Ambrose. He smiled shyly, ingratiatingly, hoping to see some softness enter those eyes. But none came; Ambrose was nodding, as if in confirmation of something he had long suspected. "Aye, I am perusing thy person, mannequin. I ask thee - what hath thee done of late to recall the dead to life?"

"The dead to life...? Sorry...?" The astonished Saxon thought vaguely of *A Tale of Two Cities*.

"The dead faith that thou and thy dittoheads hath smothered in serviettes! Who wilt be thy church's resurrection man, and cleanse thy chasubles?"

The vicar's mouth opened and closed again helplessly, and Fitzroy Nevin broke in with obvious irritation. "Ambrose, Daddy Jimmy's talking! Wait your turn! And don't be so rude to our distinguished guests!"

Ambrose glanced at him briefly, then pointed to Daddy Jimmy with superb scorn. "That is not talking, that is uttering! A parrot might utter such - click, clack, cool, faith, flutter, seedcake, bananas, relevance, who's a pretty boy then, click, clack!" The last few words were delivered in an energetic approximation of a parrot's squawk, and the audience broke up in delight. Fitzroy Nevin tried not to show a sudden urge to throttle his guest - the first atavistic urge he had had in at least two decades - and only those who really knew him (if anyone did) would have realized the significance of the rapidity with which his Adam's apple was ascending and descending, like a lift in a shopping centre. Meanwhile, Daddy Jimmy's face was puce and his hands clutched the arms of the chair as if he was about to pick it up and cast it at his tormentor. But the eternal diplomat beat down the instinctive man. "Now, Fitzroy, can't you keep the poor lad quiet for just a few moments so we can have our little say?"

Ambrose's eyes were much clearer and colder than any quartz had ever been. "Thou hast had thy say for many years, Jammy Diddy - and where now is Mother Church? Descending yonder toilet! And why do you—" - Ambrose turned savagely back to the Rev. Saxon, who face-palmed - "...let his ilk prostitute the faith? Mayhap thou possesses no faith of thine own?

Thou whited sepulchre, with thy *whist* and *strawberry teas* and *beetle drives*! Where, oh where is thy shame at such backslidings?" Whist, strawberry tea and beetle drives were ejected with a venom that had probably never before been applied to such inoffensive objects, and the minister blinked.

"But..."

"Butt, thou sayest! Butt! Aye, thou art the butt of all jokes - thy sect a comic coterie of cushion stuffers and shirt lifters!"

"Ambrose, that's enough! I've warned you before! This is the last time! We've invited you on here to explain all about your religion and your views, and all you have done is to abuse our trust in you, and make homophobic remarks, and insult all our valued guests. How dare you? Don't you believe in democracy?"

Ambrose smiled disarmingly. "But I have not insulted all thy guests! There are yet two others..." He pointed at the Milesian-Muslim and the Hiberno-Hindu, who had been watching the inter-Christian argument with mystification, and some complacency. Their smugness vanished, and most of the audience rocked in joy - although one heavy-accented voice rose up, shouting "Insult not the Prophet!"

"But..." said Abdul Abdullah Abdul.

"But..." said Dr. Kumiswaramy, and at that Ambrose was standing, his arms thrown out and almost hitting Fitzroy Nevin in the face, sending a carafe of water arcing through the air. Then he was grappling at his waistband, and his white jogging bottoms were around his ankles, revealing cod-white skinny stalks sparsely interrupted by weirdly dark and long hairs. Moved to some of the profoundest emotions he had ever experienced, Fitzroy Nevin covered his mouth with his hand - while the panellists recoiled, and blanched as much as their melanin permitted.

"Butt! Butt again! Art obsessed by butts? And so I present my butt - to thou, Everyone's Daddy - to thou, Episcopalian faintheart - to thou, Mahometan mountebank - to thou, Hindoo hornswoggler - and thou, silvertopped loon..."

Men moved in, cameras showed "We Are Experiencing Technical Difficulties".

COMETH THE HOUR...

Letitia was already awake as Easter Sunday shuffled in, carrying a gull-grey rain-system that dripped dankness all along the coast. As she looked out through the webby casement she felt as though all the cheerlessness of the universe had been concentrated in one corner of one county in one country. But it was supposed to get brighter, and even if it did not, it would be a memorable day. Hopefully not *too* memorable!

She dressed swiftly and made an infinitesimal breakfast at the kitchen table, leaving the bowl and cup-and-saucer, before slipping almost noiselessly out the back door and down the damp-hung lime avenue. A song thrush was signalling his endorsement of this day, and this particular territory. Letty was pleased to hear him; there had always been thrushes here, and she hoped there would always be.

Her thoughts were on two men divided by a common name - yet who nevertheless had odd similarities. Between them they had broken her rest with turnings, mutterings, pillow-plumpings, glasses of water she didn't need, wanderings to the uncurtained window to see if the Head was still there. Of course it had always been, still was, when she could see it through the cloud - and now so too were the thrushes, and things seemed somehow more manageable.

As her feet moved over the weedy gravel and her mind through the past, one of the objects of her thoughts was dressing with care, in elegant, understated garb, with no clerical signification. As he fastened his gold cufflinks with the Jameson crest - a parting present from a grateful seminary, since shut - he wondered yet again whether he was doing the right thing in going to the rally. For someone so senior in the Church to be seen at such an event could undercut his whole calibrated career. In theory, he could go home after he and Letty had had their reunion. But she had understood he would accompany her to the rally afterwards. Surely if he was discreet - and wasn't he almost always? - there could be no harm in it. He was going as a private person, as moral support - and maybe physical protector - for an old friend. He would be able to explain away his presence if challenged. In any case, he was really curious. Even if the rally passed off entirely peacefully, it would make excellent theatre. There would be interesting and comical faces in such a crowd. Furthermore, Daddy Jimmy was going to be there, with the anti-Ambrosian demonstrators. If there was trouble, even someone so sly could easily get caught up in it. Crowds were like seas, and even very careful men can find themselves suddenly swept off their feet. Jimmy might even get... hurt. The idea of the Apostle to Youth falling under flailing fists, ideally those of his allies, made him snort in hope.

  He wished to see Letty more than anything else in the world, or (he sometimes thought) the next. This was, he knew, terribly wrong. And yet he was a man too. Not that he would do anything he should not. Yet he was drawn inexorably towards her as she was towards the deluded lad, following in her wake as she followed in the boy's. Curiosity and love were good things, Godly gifts in fact. So he reasoned yet again as he stared at himself in the mirror, and remarked (*O, vanitas!*) how the decades had chased across his face like weather-front. Who was that ruin, about to walk out into hard daylight to rendezvous with his youth? Who had bleached that chestnut hair, intaglioed all those experiences across his forehead?

"You damned fool, Ambrose Boniface Jameson..." he said softly.

*

The other Ambrose made less elaborate preparations. In those days, he never really dressed or undressed, or washed. He never really ate breakfast either - especially not now that he was experimentally confining himself to roots and tainted meats, in emulation of certain stylites. He didn't relish this new regimen. He had thought these foodstuffs would heighten his dreams, but they seemed to be distracting him from them instead, as his stomach was racked with cramps, and he kept throwing up. He wished he could do without eating, but he had early on discovered the disadvantages of relying on oxygen and hydrogen alone. He chewed without relish on a green rasher, from the secret store sandwiched inside *Napoleon's Book of Fate* - focusing his mind on the trials of the world-historical day ahead.

*

Fidelma was looking in her mirror at the same time as the Monsignor. She wrinkled her nose in puzzlement. Where was that smell coming from? It was starting to pervade the whole house. Ambrose was behind it, of course, but he was on one of his silence kicks, and would not answer questions. He had stalked angularly into the kitchen two days ago, and stated without preamble, as he had done two or three times before, "The

Sun has entered the Lion. I must needs enter the haven of secure taciturnity." He had then stalked out, and since then he had said nothing at all, even when she wished him good morning. All she had elicited in reply was a loud and sibilant "Sssssh!" hissing out from behind wagging fingers and googling eyes, a response which both startled and infuriated. It was a struggle at such times to remember that he was sick - assuming he really was.

She wasn't sure how much longer she would be able to keep it together. This thing had gone beyond the pity stage, and the joke stage (not that she had ever found it funny). She had been marvellously patient, but she couldn't help thinking that Ambrose could help it. Any mental health issue - and weren't we all mentally ill, in one way or another? - *could* be overcome these days, she told herself, through therapy, drugs, positive thinking. Today was a big day for him, so she would let it ride today - but from tomorrow, she would start thinking about her options. (And his.) This couldn't go on indefinitely. She wanted to do what was right - but if things didn't improve... well, she also had rights.

*

Neither trepidation nor bitterness were in evidence at Wild Geese Hall, but great good humour - even though all its windows opened onto scenes of pebbledash, flyover and electric wires, presented under the same glowering gloom that was enmiring the town. Certainty and celebration were the watchwords of the day, carried by the Captain downstairs into the kitchen, and strewn with almost orgasmic release upon Horatio's ovine curls as that valued sidekick stood in front of a frantic frying pan, his quasi-military outfit protected by an old and faded PVC apron bearing the words "Mafia Staff Kitchen - you breaka da eggs I frya dem".

"Good morning, good morning, good morning!"

"Oh, it's you. Good morning, sir." Horatio didn't know why he had said "sir" this morning; it just seemed natural. He sniffled and breathed all over the bacon, but on such a day who could have minded? Not the Captain anyway, whose Napoleonic brain had been whirring all night, rehearsing the details of the day, and whose lips had been whispering out into the darkness the words that soon would be roared - those words so long in gestation, those words that would rescue the nation... turn the world onto a new axis. "Good morning, good morning, good morning!" he called out again, forgetting or not caring that he had already said this. It was a day for words - The Day, The Words! It was his day to outdo Grandpop! He sat down, feeling he was floating above the table, and as the greasy strips of bacon slid down his throat, they tasted a little like ambrosia.

*

Oldtown was disgorging its devout. The nuns had gathered en masse - *en masse*! thought Mary wistfully, as she looked at the nine lined brides of Christ, wrinkled as winter apples, milling excitedly outside the grand portico as they waited for the minibus. They had never all been out together before, and they would almost certainly never all be out together again. For the first time since its foundation, the convent would be without nuns that afternoon, and there would be nothing to stir up echoes down those echoing Italianate passages. The sanctuary lamp would still burn in the chapel, powerless to illuminate the in-need-of-cleaning Zurbarán that was one of the convent's two great secrets, but its tiny twinkle would find no empathetic eye, warm no womanly heart. Yet as Mary told herself yet again, it was entirely possible that today's events might reignite something at risk of being utterly extinguished here and everywhere. Maybe when the ten of them returned that evening, buzzing and chattering, they might carry with them some spark that would allow them all to rededicate and rejuvenate.

A spark made by *her* nephew... it was still extraordinary to think of Ambrose in such a light. To think that someone as shallow as Fidelma should have produced someone so deep! To think of Ambrose growing up in that house, awkward and unappreciated, a seed out of place, yet somehow not dying in that unwatered earth. It made Mary almost cry to think that she had been one of the first to see him for what he was, or could be. So must the Baptist's earliest followers have felt as they saw their star rise ever higher in the heavens, and known where it would lead; it was pride, but it was a disinterested pride, a pride formed of love and fealty. She wallowed in the warmth of her ideas, and mouthed a prayer for the day, for the Faith, and for herself.

By midday, a relenting sun had dismissed the dismalness and gladdened the centre of town. It also gladdened other parts of the world, but at present the world's media seemed less interested in those. "Ambrose weather!" someone said, and the meteorological meme passed through all present, to sniggers or smiles. Many people there - the majority - seemed content to loaf good-naturedly until they could be entertained by the main speaker, who had so legendarily distinguished himself twice on live television. What might he do today? Many of them had bought "Ambrose masks" from an enterprising vendor who had bought the entire stock of a closing novelty shop, and had now found a serendipitous outlet for his Herman Munster merchandise. There were many camera crews and freelancers, set up close to the speakers' platform in front of a bronze United Irishman who had been born in the town, and was now destined to stand forever in the square facing down the easterlies that whistled up the river, his improbably muscled biceps shielding a national maiden who was either becoming, or had already been, a swan. The bird's outsize wings in turn arced over the man's head, and town wits had christened the confection "Old Birdbrain".

But there were also small groups waiting to be united, wanting to be led. Flags and placards were leaning against buildings or rolled up under arms. Men and women of all physiologies and persuasions, all socioeconomic statuses and degrees of disaffection, fidgeted and talked and looked around for someone to tell them what they would soon be shouting. Coffees, cigarettes, sandwiches and beers were produced and dispatched. Pigeons pecked around sandaled or booted feet, or perched vigilantly along the arms of the United Irishman, occasionally sending down little ammoniac parcels to mottle and moisturize the stage. Sound engineers were testing the microphones. "One, two, one, two," boomed the speakers, and once a half-heard swear word that made one or two of the older onlookers shake their heads at the awfulness of the age. Gardaí were moving metal barriers in a choreography of crowd control.

The reason they were in attendance in such large numbers was at that moment addressing his followers just half a mile away - the same pub, in fact, in which he had met Ambrose. Three who had promised to come had not come. One had rung Bosco nervously with an excuse about the buses being on strike, and had winced as Bosco tore him off several sarcastic strips - "Now isn't that a terrible state of affairs, Pádraig? I wonder how the feck none of the rest of us have heard of this strike! What do you take me for? OK, OK, feck off then, ya chicken bastard! But just think of this, Paddy my lad, as you sit there scratching your arse - what will you tell your childer? I was *almost* there on The Day We Saved Ireland? Go on home to your filthy hovel, and your teledevilvision and your - your potato crisps. Leave it to the buckos! The men - the *statesmen*! And now get the feck off the line as I need to keep it clear for important calls! I always knew you were chickenshit."

But he was not disappointed with the other soon-to-be-statesmen. On the contrary, he surveyed them with proprietorial pride as they sat around the pub table for the Final Briefing. "The Final Briefing!" Bosco exulted - although he kept his face impassive, de Valeran, Wellingtonian. How often he had rehearsed this in his mind - although admittedly in his imagination the venue had been somewhere more imposing. The Guinness-slops on their table's black surface, the sodden beer-mats, the empty pork-scratching packs, the canned laughter on the large TV, the beeps and bells from the fruit machines - he was already editing it for posterity. Maybe one day this table would be preserved in a museum. And he was fixing his followers too - where they sat, their determined features, their anoraks, their earrings, their scars and tattoos - and he loved them like little brothers.

This would be the last time, he assured them, absolutely the last time they would have to enter a place like this fecking shithole. From now on, you, P.J. - and you, James - and you, Larry - and you, Phelim - and you, Sean - and you, Horatio - from now on you will no longer be ordinary Joes. Whatever you've done, whatever trouble you've had - it'll all be forgotten. You'll be able to see your kids again, P.J. - and you, Larry - and Phelim. That little business with the tax boys, Sean? Forget it! As for your little misunderstanding, James - I think the authorities might take a different view when *we're* the authorities! Eh? That's right! He banged James on the back in rough solidarity. What you do today, boys - and how you do it - will mark you out, will make the difference, will change the country, the world, the future. History is standing behind us all, we band of brothers, and her hands are on our shoulders. Now is our chance to get the bastards, to nail them down so tight they'll never get up again.

The group erupted in cheering and table-thumping that for a moment drowned out the TV. When the cheer died down at last, Phelim could be heard saying to P.J. - "That Ambrose *mooned* Fitzroy fecking Nevin!"

*

As Bosco strode along backstreets towards the square, his flag-carrying retinue a few steps behind, he attracted growing and gratifying attention. Also less gratifying attention. The stares were balanced out by glares, and a man spat pointedly on the pavement in front of Bosco's bulled boots. Bosco knew it would be beneath his dignity to engage fully, so he contented himself with staring coldly into the man's eyes and saying, "I'll remember you, me bucko..." The man grinned, and Bosco blenched at

A Modern Journey

alcoholic fumes and crooked teeth. The man then fell sideways out onto the road, forcing a car to make an emergency stop, and he lay there kicking and cursing. Bosco marched on, sorry the car had stopped in time.

The alley Bosco turned into was narrow and lined with tall old warehouses, and it began to sound as if he had an army behind him, as more and more footfalls and murmurings bounced back from the nineteenth-century brick. Shouts too, business-like shouts, menacing shouts, intoxicating shouts, even some intoxicated ones. He heard his name, and he heard it repeated, and yet again. He did not need to look back - he must always look forward now, now that he (almost) had to consider the good of everyone on this island.

He would be magnanimous, let old grudges go - except for those gobshites at Finglas Garda station. And the Traveller boys who had stoned the house. He still had their faces in his mind's eye, could pick them out in any line-up. And maybe... but no, Bosco, this was not the time for detail, for he was moving to his appointed place - leading the Irish up from bondage, Israel out of Canaan - and all the time in his trench coat pocket there reposed a deadly smiting stick, the time for whose revealing was almost at hand.

As Bosco neared the square - he never wanted that approach to end - there was an almighty bellow from just a few hundred yards ahead. Bosco realized that Ambrose must at that moment have entered the square from the other side. He stopped for a moment to collect himself, analyse his thoughts at this epochal moment. He stood so straight that he felt as if he were falling over backwards, stuck out his chin yet further, swallowed even harder, and appropriated some of that crowd energy, which was, he felt, his by right. After all, this thing, this stupendous thing, was happening because of him, a cashiered Captain from the wrong side of the city - and really had very little to do with a mentally deficient mummy's boy who had always had everything, and now wanted to steal what belonged rightfully to the Irish people.

But he - Captain-General Bosco Buggy, heir-apparent of the High Kings, and Brian Boru - would fix him, and soon. Deliciously soon, Bosco me boy, Bosco me fine fellow, oh Bosco, now is the hour, the time to taste the sweets of success, now is the hour towards which your life has been pointed like a heat-seeking missile... He gulped at the greatness of the moment and stepped out at last into the square, into the blinking brilliance of Ambrose's weather, his arms upraised to accept a Nation's adulation.

Derek Turner

A ROW IN THE TOWN

About two hours before Bosco turned into that alley, the Grand Hotel had been doing a typical morning's business. There had been a pianist in the lobby, travestying a 1950s melody for the benefit of four dry-powdery women clustered around one of the tables swapping malicious scandal over delicate tea. The only other table occupied was that of the Monsignor, who had arrived ten minutes early, even after circumnavigating the block four times. He felt absurdly jittery - he who had sat straight-backed and insouciant through endless rarefied occasions, debated abstruse points of doctrine with leading intellectuals, sat in stern judgment on backsliders - but he was enjoying the long-forgotten sensation. He might never have this feeling ever again.

He was glad that the odd-looking musician - whose mullet was surely held in place by hairspray - wasn't singing. The lyrics to that tune were, he remembered, more than usually inane even by 1950s standards, and besides no good sound could ever have emerged from such lips. God wasn't *that* kind. And yet the tune's cheddary innocence was in fact appropriate, at this moment when he was about to renew acquaintance with his young self, that time when it had been possible to believe music could not get any worse - and that soon there must be Renewal.

He had seated himself hastily at the table nearest the door, only to stand up again immediately afterwards and move to another - and when the nice young waitress came to ask if he would like a drink, he actually stammered. He downed a double Scotch, one gulp per measure, and she asked smilingly if he would like another. He declined, but from then on she watched the tall and spare septuagenarian with mild interest. There was, after all, no one else to look at apart from him, and the matrons, who were regulars. Her interest became acute when the revolving door admitted the unmistakable form of Letitia. But the waitress's excitement was inconsequential compared with that churning inside both cleric and icon, as he stood, and they looked each other in the face for the first time in forty-nine years. Forty-nine years! Letitia wanted to cry and laugh. Still superb! thought the priest, swallowing hard. He appraised her progress across the

Fermanagh carpet, and was pleased beyond measure to see her movements still queenly, her spine still straight, as she stared up into his face, analytically, but also slightly imploringly, entreating him silently not to find fault. And he did not - he could not - he never would. He took her calf-gloved hands, and kissed her chastely on both tremulous cheeks - and neither could think of anything to say. It was she who spoke eventually, with something like her sprightliness. "A fine articulate welcome from an old friend - and one who is generally regarded as one of an ancient institution's finest thinkers! I thought you were never short of something to say!"

He started to laugh, then noticed the heroine-worshipping waitress hovering, anxious to fetch and carry. "I... ahem... that is... what will you drink?"

"I see you have already started the party! You know, I think I'll have one of those too - and he will have another one, my dear." She nodded towards the whisky tumbler, and the waitress bore it exultingly away. They sat across from each other, and Letitia's eyes were dewed, but they were also dancing as they had done ages before. He wanted to mention her eyes, but couldn't. She wanted to tell him that he was still handsome, but didn't.

"I, em..." said the Monsignor. She willed him to go on, but he seemed to be stuck. Then the waitress arrived providentially with whisky, olives and peanuts, which she deposited on the table before departing awestruck, and grateful for a very generous but un-showy *pourboire*.

Then the pianist started a Sixties hit they had heard when it first came out, and they smiled simultaneously at its badness. "Do you remember..." the priest started, then stopped, and a smile broke across both faces - smiles too small to signify all the pleasure that lay behind them. At just that moment, the street seen through the wisterias was doused in sudden sunshine.

*

It was still sunny an hour or so afterwards as they exited, the waitress almost curtseying as Letitia drifted past in a cirrus of celebrity. Philomena had undertaken to bring Ambrose to the square, so Letitia and the Monsignor had time to sample the pre-rally scene.

There were very large numbers of people in the streets as they neared the square. A few people carried the posters designed by Bosco and proofread by Horatio - a huge and fuzzy picture of Ambrose taken from the web, showing him cutting into his arm, above a simple message:

A DAY OF NATIONAL PENINCE AND REAFIRMATION
AMBROSE and CAPTAIN BOSCO BUGGY (Retd.)
to SPEAK
Come and here history
The Square, The Town
Easter Sunday, 2pm

The Monsignor grinned to see one wire-haired pedant in a bad blazer who had corrected the mistakes with felt-tip. Some people had devised their own posters - poorly-designed, with creaking sentiments - like "Ambrose speaks for us!" and "National Healing" - while serial moral marchers had recycled posters from other demonstrations for other causes, most of them lost. The Monsignor slightly wickedly pointed this out to Letitia. But she didn't care; this was the right place to be, whatever happened, or did not happen.

A few minutes later, they came across the Oldtown contingent, sitting on benches, sipping tea from flasks and eating sandwiches. Mary darted over in pleased surprise. "Monsignor, I had no idea you were coming! How delightful!"

"Hello, Sister Mary, and I hope I find you well. Thank you for your kind remarks, but could I ask you to keep it down, please? You see, I am here incognito; I'm just an observer. I am here really as a favour to Mrs. Shaughnessy-Don, who is, if you remember, an old friend."

"I see! Of course! Sorry, Monsignor. Hello, Letitia. Are you well?"

Letty pressed her arm, and smiled warmly. "Yes, thank you, Mary. Well, it looks as if there'll be a good turnout. Any idea how many are expected?"

"No idea. But there must be thousands here already! It seems strange, but I don't think anyone has really *organized* anything. It's all sort of organic. It's been done informally on the internet and by phone. I believe there were also some articles in newspapers and on the television. But essentially it's been a word-of-mouth affair. I rather like that. It's the way things would have happened the first ti..." She noticed the Monsignor's ironic eyebrow, and coloured. "Anyway, it's a nice old-fashioned way of doing things, don't you think? And there are a lot of young people, aren't there?"

"I suspect they may not be here for the same reason you and the other sisters are here, Sister Mary. Look at the placard that one is carrying - I say 'one' because I can't tell if it's a boy or a girl - and that one over there. I'm afraid they are almost certainly here to demonstrate against your man, Sister Mary - or to make fun of him."

"*Our* man, you mean!" broke in Letitia, laughing. "Isn't that right, Mary? And now, Mr. Incognito, I think I shall take you away before you say something else disagreeable!" Letitia beamed brilliantly at the nun and led the Monsignor away. Someone like her could not melt into any crowd; people nudged and muttered as they noticed her, and a little girl in what looked like a First Communion dress asked lispingly for an autograph, which was provided gladly. Even some anti-Ambrosians had themselves photographed with her, notwithstanding her association with him. She charmed all with her ease and approachability. The Monsignor felt proud to be with her, and did not notice that he himself was also the object of admiring glances.

The wind died away and the sun continued to strengthen until the statue in the square shone as if it were really capable of guarding a nation's interests. Even the river threw back light to freckle the quays. "Ambrose weather!" someone said aloud, and a ripple went through the vicinity - irony, scorn, sniggering - but also belief. People shifted and grumbled as the Gardaí segregated them. Chants and handclaps started, and stalled. There were quiet laughs and crackling police radios - people eating hot dogs and drinking beer - swearing, muttering, journalists asking inanities, and a group of about ten kneeling in prayer. When had *that* last been seen in the town, the Monsignor wondered. That sight by itself almost made this foolish enterprise worthwhile. It would offend the kind of people who so enjoyed being offended.

Hands male and female, slender and broad, calloused and delicate, gripped wooden poles on the ends of which were (according to taste) plaster saints, plastic Virgins, Sacred Hearts, crosses, devotional texts, fraternal order emblems, tricolours, the banners of small political parties, anti-Catholic slogans, warnings against Islamophobia and homophobia, threats against bankers, complaints about spending cuts, effigies of Bosco dangling from gallows... The Monsignor found the Hogarthian spectacle very engrossing. It was long since he had experienced ignorance in such quantities. "It's like being inside a Bosch painting!" he marvelled to Letitia, and she smiled.

Two young men who were holding hands saw Letitia, and one squealed "O. My. God!" She and the Monsignor moved on hurriedly, only to almost bump into Daddy Jimmy, surrounded as usual by presspersons. They tried to get past without hearing what he was saying to them, but could not help overhearing the words, "The world is aghast..." It had been a near thing.

Fidelma was with Tom Gulliver, whom she had met by chance just a few moments before. She had been pleased to see the familiar apple of his face atop a larger apple whose curves were emphasized by an inadvisable T-shirt and a pair of white trousers that clung too closely for his (or anyone else's) comfort. "Hello, Tom! How nice to see a familiar face among all these strangers!"

He had clearly felt embarrassed to be found ingesting a processed-cheese sandwich and pint of Coke, and tried to dispose of them in the quickest possible way by eating as he replied, "Oh...Mrs. Sheehy-O'Connor!" [gulp] "I should have known you'd be here." [slurp]

"Are you here by yourself? Your mother...?"

He glanced away, remembering his mother's anger when he had told her that he might, you know, take a stroll down to the town, just to, well, take a quick look at what was going on, and see whether there would be, you know, any trouble. He had not realized until that moment just how much his mother hated Ambrose and, for some even less fathomable reason, Fidelma. Stopping only to pick up his provisions, he had left her glaring at the town out of a steamed-up kitchen window, consumed by resentment at the paucity of celebrities in her life.

He murmured polite demurrals now to Fidelma - idle curiosity, thought he'd see how his old school friend was getting along. But the truth was that he had also become increasingly engrossed by what was taking place next door, and the contrast between that life and his much less colourful existence. He even felt grateful to Ambrose for providing such relief from accountancy, as if his neighbour had taken up all these exciting activities specifically for his benefit. Tom had always wanted to break out, but knew he did not have the initiative to do it himself. It seemed to be only through Ambrose that he could get intoxicating whiffs of a wider kind of life.

Once, when he was sixteen, Ambrose had allowed him to toke at a joint, and for about thirty minutes of mingled delight and concern, Tom's world had reeled and raced around his toppled form, and everything he had always thought important looked ludicrous, and vice versa. Something equally giddying was happening again now, as he watched Ambrose gelding celebrity stallions and defying the assembled forces of Aghast-dom, making audiences rock with scandalized laughter, actually mooning

Fitzroy Nevin, having the super-confidence to hang with extremists like Bosco Buggy without worrying how it might look, or what danger it might mean.

Ambrose may have been a nerd at school, but he had in some unique way also been slightly cool - at least, so it seemed to Tom, who had never been either. Ambrose, the lifelong loner, had always had sufficient company in himself, or so it had seemed to Tom - and now it began to seem as if he had some strange supernatural sanction too. He was starting to look upon Ambrose with something approaching awe - as if his neighbour walked mantled in some towering spirit. So despite the awkwardness caused by his sandwich and Coke, he was rather pleased to come across Fidelma, in case he could be of help to her, and by extension her enigmatic, enviable son.

Then Letty and the Monsignor arrived. Tom felt absurdly shy, and he wished devoutly that he did not have a small trail of pickle on his shirt - that he was not pudgily clasping a vast empty Coke carton - and that there was something other than book-keeping or others' sporting achievements he could converse about with her and her imposing friend. Luckily, some students close by started a chant - "No to theocracy! Yes to democracy! No to theocracy! Yes to democracy!"

The Monsignor had to bend and speak close to Fidelma's ear in order to be heard. "Not much of a chant, is it, Mrs. Sheehy-O'Connor? But at least our young friends make up in volume what they lack in euphony or originality."

But she didn't smile back, or even reply - and he straightened again, slightly annoyed. He was about to make an excuse and pilot Letty onwards and away, when Fidelma unexpectedly put her hand on his sleeve, and stared up at him pleadingly. What a small and useless hand it seemed to him; he couldn't imagine it holding anything for long. Her eyes looked touchingly girlish, but he could see the ghosts of lines beneath her make-up. And he suddenly had a too rare kindly impulse and pitied her - so awfully alone, so out of her depth here, so out of her depth everywhere.

"Yes, Mrs. Sheehy-O'Connor?" He almost had to bawl to be heard, and he did not want to bawl at her, because she looked as if she might snap in half.

"What do you think will happen? Everyone's saying there's going to be trouble..."

"It's very difficult to say. Maybe nothing at all. These people near us seem to be in a bad mood for some reason. But then I suspect they're always in a bad mood. Young people tend to be these days - and occasionally they are right to be."

She nodded. "Could I ask a favour, please?"

"Of course. And if I can help, I will."

"It's just that - if you see Ambrose in trouble, could you help him? He's not strong, and he doesn't know what he's doing most of the time - and looking at some of these terrible people..." Her eyes roamed unhappily over the idealists, whose noise was getting intolerable. He had to emphasize his shouted words with a powerful squeeze on her forearm that brought tears to her eyes, but balm to her heart. Ambrose would have at least one powerful protector.

"Say no more! If I see anything, and can do anything, I will. There are lots of Guards here today too, and they will also be looking out for him. Now try not to worry too much!"

Letty told Fidelma where Mary was, then she and the Monsignor walked on. But there was yet another familiar face nearby - Molly's mother Mairéad, her badger hair marking her out even among a multitude of bad dye jobs. She was smiling hugely.

"Is it yourself, Mrs. Shaughnessy-Don? I'm delighted to be seeing you - I am that! And to meet you, Monsignor. I hoped you wouldn't keep on talking to that auld eejit. She's a right stuck-up cow - if you'll excuse me, your reverence!" She nodded in the direction Fidelma had gone, then made a slight obeisance to the Monsignor. He liked her at once - the true Irish stock, rock of the Church, living on the edges of a society which despised her, and which she despised in return. If only more Irish people were a little more like her and a little less like Fidelma, he thought, how much better the country would be, how much sounder the Church.

"It's funny," Mairéad went on, "how someone like that auld hoor - if you'll excuse me, your reverence! - can have a son like that. He's a grand fella, don't you think, Father?"

He was saved from answering by a commotion. An elderly woman who was actually wearing a hat, and carrying a poster of an aborted foetus that had last seen daylight during the final unsuccessful rally of 2013, was standing in front of the chanting group, and her cracked voice rose for a moment in an approximation of a hymn, before she was drowned out again by the chants of "No to theocracy! Down with Ambrose! No to theocracy!

Down with Ambrose!" Then one of them bellowed "Get your cruets out, love!" and the chanting broke up in rough laughter.

The Monsignor empurpled, and stalked back towards the group, which momentarily quailed. His age notwithstanding, he stood several inches above the tallest of them, and his eyes blazed like a peregrine's. His voice, too, was deep and sonorous, cutting through the racket for a moment, like Siegfried cancelling out the choir. "Aren't you ashamed of yourselves, you filthy little children? How dare you address a lady like that?"

A red-haired man looked quickly to either side for back-up and then spoke in nasal tones underpinned by long-held psychosocial grudges. "And what's it to you, old man? Why don't you mind your own feckin' business?"

The priest stepped forward, nineteen again and willing to risk a life's accumulated respectability, but suddenly Letitia was there, holding his right arm, and Mairéad the other. "No, your reverence! Don't! That's just what the gurriers want!"

Letitia hissed - "You mustn't draw attention to yourself!"

The Monsignor saw that they were right, and as he subsided, Red Hair laughed scornfully and turned triumphantly back to his comrades, and their chant began again. The Monsignor stood there for a couple of seconds, breathing heavily, before he was frogmarched away by Letitia and Mairéad. Behind them rose a sneering cheer, and Letitia patted his taut arm sympathetically.

"Never mind those feckers - if you'll excuse me, your reverence!" Mairéad added, and he had to grin. The woman with the hat stayed where she was, with heavenward eyes tightly closed - she did not seem to have noticed either the insult or the would-be avenger.

Mairéad peeled away to find her family, and by the time the others got to the square, just before two, everything looked focused and business-like, with barriers up and people segregated according to their faith, or lack thereof. There were the Ambrosians in the centre - several thousand, mostly older and dowdy, but with hopeful faces. Beyond were the anti-Ambrosians - a few hundred, mostly younger and grungily-dressed, with scornful faces. Beyond these was a much larger, less cohesive agglomeration of loafers hoping for laughs, or for a fight in which people would get hurt so they would have something to photograph. There must have been at least ten thousand people there, the Monsignor estimated. The centre of the square was an island of belief in an indifferent ocean, burdened with banners, posters, figures and flags that spoke of unreasoning devotion. The Monsignor was surprisingly moved to see all these faithful in one place, and Letty said softly - "Well, isn't that something...?" It was, and they passed into and through the crowd with ease - a combination of the crowd's politeness, the Monsignor's stature, and especially Letty's fame. She gave the Ambrosians a pride in themselves, as a crowd that someone like her could join.

Just as they had made their way to the foot of the platform in front of the statue - Ambrose's ambo, the Monsignor called it, showing off his useless, much-prized knowledge of ecclesiastical furnishings - a stiffening and roar passed through the assembly, and they shifted and bent as one, like starlings in winter. He's here! He's here! The words came like a cold incoming tide, clarifying, cleaning. With an effort, part-plea and part-push, the Monsignor propelled Letty up the few steps, so that she could take her allotted place behind the main attraction. Once elevated, she gazed in the same direction as everyone else, and stood there clapping wildly and cheering with all the assembled Ambrosians. The Monsignor felt jealous he could not join in with the emotion. He and the lizard-eyed media crews were the only people in the immediate vicinity who were not applauding rapturously - while beyond there had arisen a tempest of jeering and laughter. The noise was batteringly stupendous. It dizzied and distressed, even as it excited him. King Mob, here you are again, he thought!

The people parted and Ambrose was suddenly there, a few feet in front, wafted in on a wave of exultation - white-clad and unhealthy-skinned as before, but looking, if anything, even wilder and dirtier. His beard was longer and curlier than when he had visited the Monsignor's office, his Adam's apple bulgier, the nails on the hand on his staff rimmed with black - and yet a strikingly pretty girl stood adoringly behind. Ambrose caught the priest's regard, and they exchanged a several-seconds glance, during which the Monsignor felt once more the ill-at-ease feeling, as if the boy really was more than a boy, and he the only one who simply couldn't see it.

Then Ambrose spoke, half-smiling. "Hail, priest! Well met. But I must needs mount my ambo. We shall meet again, I hope!" He turned and mounted the steps with unfaltering feet. The Monsignor was startled by his use of ambo, a word he had never heard anyone else use. Had something profound just been telegraphed between them? Or was it, once again, simply that troubling thyroidal intensity of Ambrose's eyes?

As Ambrose processed onto the platform, there to be welcomed by renewed raptures, and handshakes and kisses, the priest watched with a kind of envy. Now his namesake approached the battery of microphones, and stood for a couple of seconds looking out over the crowd, as they swelled towards him. He was smiling. At what justifiable pride, or private joke? Was he really looking out over that horde of cheerers and jeerers, or over some vast interior panorama? He seemed to be swelling up with their energy.

Ambrose launched at last into a speech, although the audience was stamping and singing so loudly no one could possibly hear what was being said. The Monsignor could hear enough of it to feel that it was just as well for Ambrose's reputation. The speech was, in truth, so preposterous that in a sane world a mob would have rushed the ambo and strung up the orator.

Orator, indeed! Ambrose's vocabulary was too large, his references too recondite, his 'logic' full of holes, his 'facts' incorrect, his voice a mumbling monotone - and yet this rapture! What had the Church done to forfeit such fervour? He was shaking his head when he caught the eye of one of the reporters, and they smiled at each other in wry conspiracy - two of the few. It was at that precise moment the Monsignor sensed a change in the crowd.

Ambrose and the Ambrosians were being increasingly drowned out. "...seven supplications...["BOO!"]...seven beatitudes...["SCUM!"]...penitential psalms...["FASCISTS!"] of the Passion...[jeering]...sacraments...[guffaws]...seven deadly sins...["SCUM!"]...each represented by seven animals...["WHICH ONE ARE YOU?"]...seven diseases...["AMBROSE IS A KNOB!"]..." The pro-Ambrosians were trying to shout back, but they were not good at it - intrinsically more reserved, less morally sure. It sounded like football fans had irrupted into the square. But the mood was still essentially good-natured - until the floozie Fate thought it would be amusing to lead Captain Bosco Buggy's (Retd.) bulled boots to the precise place in the crowd where Ambrose's most fervent Traveller followers had arrayed themselves, a lump of hard reality between a huddle of lady Redemptorists and several superannuated Knights of Columbanus.

Travellers had no reason whatever to like Bosco, who devoted much time and energy to denouncing them in the strongest terms that were congruent with race relations legislation. To worsen matters, these particular Travellers were related to the Northside horse-riding boys whose ears Bosco had boxed. In a final unlucky twist, the man standing closest was from a noted bare-knuckle boxing clan. Several Nollaigs came together for that gallant, as he saw one of his people's most prominent persecutors materializing magically and unguarded at his elbow, ripe like russet fruit.

Pausing only to call out, "Calf's head, woman's face, poxy leprechaun bastard!" he pulled back his mighty right and put all his inherited insight to practical use. Bosco lay down at once, without any fuss or scarcely even a sound - although any sound he might have made would in any case have been drowned out.

The next thing audible was Horatio's indignant "Oh!" as he darted in to help his Friend-Leader, only to join him unconscious on the cobbles - but then P.J., Phelim and the others powered in, their careful plans forgotten in booze-fuelled loyalty to Bosco, and the delight of the fight. The Travellers yielded at first to the PIS phalanx, but the square was too crowded for them to be able to fall back far, and in any case they were up for this! And so they bounced back boxing. Baseball bats and hurley sticks were plucked from somewhere, and very quickly made their presence felt on P.I.S. pates.

Waves raced out into the crowd, and people were pushed increasingly roughly against others, and the others against yet others. "Oh"s and "Oof"s became "Watch it!" and "Who do you think you're pushing?" Then the angry and alarmed pushers told those they had fallen against whom they thought they were pushing, and the pushes started to become punches, traded with interest - even by people who had only come to laugh. Violence radiated out in seconds far into the middle of the assembly, and before they knew what was happening, highly respectable pilgrims up from the country and even some from overseas were being rumpled and roughed up, before they started to go down like August barley - although some stood their ground valiantly, one African nun wielding a "Prayer is the only answer" placard to great practical purpose.

All started to war with all - Country People attacked Travellers and Travellers attacked Country People, Traveller clans worked out old scores against each other, atheists attacked Catholics and Catholics atheists, leftists assailed Bosco's men and Bosco's men leftists, husbands defended their wives and wives their husbands, men their girlfriends (and sometimes boyfriends), while Gardaí steamed in, the Dark Side of the Force, to restore democracy at baton-end. Even the uncommitted had swiftly to choose sides, because one side or other had chosen them - and so all sides folded in on each other in a multitude of private combats. Ambrose's voice continued to boom senselessly through the speakers for a time as all else became bedlam, and old and new Ireland fought back and forth briskly and without reason across the faces of the fallen.

Around the ambo, the chanting and cheering of the Ambrosians had faltered, as all except Ambrose craned quizzical heads, and the savage jeers of the antis were suddenly shockingly loud. Ambrose was still speaking, but everyone else was looking at what was taking place behind him, worried, then horrified as the tsunami rolled towards them. Letty turned her head to search for the Monsignor, and smiled when she saw him, taller than everyone else. Then the stage shook as the riot struck, and masked men appeared to spring up from the ground. They started to rock the platform, and Letty and the others rocked with it. There were screams from all except Letty and Ambrose, who was still speaking, holding onto the microphones for support - and then Letty and several others fell over and out of sight. At this signal, the momentarily paralyzed Monsignor was released.

He exploded into ferocious life, and then - Heaven be praised! - he saw the red-haired young man who had cheeked him earlier, masked but clearly him with that carroty coiffure, in the centre of the whooping group shaking the stage. The priest did not hesitate, but with a few berserker bounds he was there amongst them, and his fists were in flailing motion, connecting with chins and cheeks, mashing noses, and his fingers were closing windpipes and crashing craniums, crushing enemies and making way. Nineteen again, and he still had it - nineteen again, taking on nineteen enemies and winning, descending like Jove to rid the land of Red Hair and his ilk. He was by now grappling Red Hair in person, holding him as humanoid shield against counterpunches and feet, and eventually holding him (such was his strength) by his booted feet and swinging him round in a circle, as other masked men and one woman toppled and succumbed. As they stood up groggily, they were set upon by massed Ambrosians, wading in with sticks and umbrellas, even hymnals.

The Monsignor stood recovering his breath for a few proud seconds, before he forced his way onto the respited platform. Chaos was in command there, with everyone on the deck, including Ambrose, prone with his eyes closed, but still speaking through a microphone although now no one at all could hear him. "...it is time for the Lightworkers, weavers of the Chakra..."

A Modern Journey

Letty was sitting up, thank God unharmed - and so was the pretty girl. Letty smiled to see him standing there above her, even smeared as he was with others' blood - or perhaps because he was smeared with others' blood - stretching down huge hands to help her. Even in extremis she retained poise, and even as she and Philomena were getting to their feet, she solemnly introduced her to the Monsignor. Then she realized what she had done, and she sat down again, laughing at herself, and the Monsignor laughed too - just the two of them in the whole violent vista seeing how ridiculous the world was. Philomena did not join in; dazed, she yet retained enough presence of mind to throw her arms around Ambrose, and kiss and stroke his head.

The platform shuddered again, as fresh anti-Ambrosian forces arrived, mostly younger men beating down mostly older women. A knot of nuns was surreally at the centre of the rear-guard, and at their centre was none other than Mary, laying about her with Counter-Reformatory zeal. It was an inspiring as well as amusing sight, and the half-smiling Monsignor launched himself back onto the ground with a spring that would have done credit to a man decades his junior. With his help, once again the anti-Ambrosians juddered to a halt before breaking and falling back. The Monsignor found himself standing next to Mary for a moment, and saw (a) that her nose had been broken and (b) that her eyes blazed with rapture. "Isn't this *grand*, Monsignor?" she shouted in broadest Corconian tones, before they were separated by the press of people - and it seemed to him it was. This - this sanctified soldier spirit - this was what had pushed the Church to the ends of the earth, and its absence was why it was now rolling it back in on itself.

And there by his side now too was Letty - no longer immaculate, but a tigress elegantly alive, clawing at the eyes of enemies, returning blow for blow, not flinching when their blows landed, or when their or her blood stippled her skin. He and she fought on and through towards one side of the square, leaving far behind them Ambrose and Philomena on the now overwhelmed platform - leaving behind even the Amazonian Mary - leaving behind them a seething Sargasso of bare-knuckle boxers, spinsters breaching public order, perspiring policemen, infuriated idealists, thrilled reporters, hundreds of insects struggling in a sticky mess of their own excretion.

*

Bosco tuned back into the Square after some time spent patrolling some other solar system. He had rarely been so uncomfortable. His face was sticky and numb, the back of his head still ringing with the impact of the pavement. Worse even than these, he was confusedly aware that he had been trying to do something important, but had failed. There was a terrible noise all around. He closed his eyes, and considered the possibility of lying quietly for a little longer, but at that moment the thing he was lying on spoke. "Ooof - gerroff! Gerroff!"

Bosco obligingly slid to one side, wincing, and perused his late perch. Horatio! That stalwart's curls were larded with blood, and his glasses had gone.

"Who's that? I can't see a thing! Oh, it's you! Have you seen my specs? They were on my face!"

Bosco found them, but one of the lenses had cracked, and the thick frame was twisted. "Here!" and he thrust them into the other's hand. He pushed himself into a sitting position, and passed his hand over his eyes. What he saw banished his bleariness in an instant - and he kicked his lieutenant smartly on the knee. "Look, Horatio! Look at the feckers!" Horatio squinted through smashed specs, monocular like his famous namesake.

The feckers were fighting - fighting as if for life, fighting for the hell of it, fighting confusedly and pointlessly. Other feckers were fleeing or trying to flee, but they were being headed off by yet others or kettled by Gardaí advancing like angry ants from several directions at once. As they reached grappling knots of people, they passed over them, and the knots would cease moving. The noise Bosco had registered on recovering consciousness was resolving itself into its components - shouts of anger, pain, command - sirens - breaking glass - running feet - batons beating on shields, sticks breaking on heads and backs - dogs barking - and a terrible feedback whine from unattended microphones. And that noise in particular helped Bosco to gather his thoughts. The mummy's boy! Where had he got to? And then he finally remembered what he had planned, and he groaned. Full recall followed, and he saw again that huge fist that had turned out his lights. He scrambled for his Mauser - still there, thanks be to Jaysus!

Nearby were other groaners, and two unconscious men. Bosco stood with an effort, and swiftly examined the nearby fallen. Phelim lay among them, for once oblivious to the Cause. His open mouth displayed a bloody hole which until recently had been occupied by quite a decent set of teeth.

Horatio started to help in this audit of allies, then heard a squeal of triumph and turned around to see Bosco kicking and spitting on a prone figure. "Horatio! Come here a sec! It's him! The tinker scum! Hold his mouth open!"

Horatio made his dizzy way over and without having time to wonder why held open the Traveller's mouth. He was amazed to see Bosco unzip himself and direct a stream of urine into the open aperture - and annoyed at being splashed. The man choked and started to splutter and moan. Bosco finished and zipped himself up, then kicked his assailant back asleep. Then he turned to his lieutenant with a deeply satisfied smile. "There! That settles a little score - and now, Horatio, that we've got our personal vengeance out of the way, we can still turn the day around. Where's your gun?"

Horatio had forgotten it, but there it was, in its shoulder holster. He nodded shortly, painfully. In a way, he wished he didn't have it; it didn't seem like such a good idea now that they were actually here, and the day had turned against them. Maybe they had never been meant to succeed. Bosco divined his thoughts. "We can still do it, Horatio - just you and me, if we can't wake those eejits. Look at the square! Look at it! That's the sight of an Establishment dying, a country being reborn, rising from the ashes like... like one of them birds that rises from ashes. A pelican! And we can rebore it. This is our chance - our one and only chance! The whole system's breaking down - the system! We've still got our guns, and above all we still have our unshakable resolve! One bold move now, and our gunfire will go round the world like...like gunfire! Come on, *a chara*! Let's give it what we've got! Let's make such a name for ourselves as will give us immorality!"

Horatio's resolve was much shakier than he would admit, and didn't Bosco mean *immortality*? But the Mauser's broom-handle butt made him feel a great deal better. And in any case he had made a promise. He always kept his promises. Now was not the time, he admonished himself - NOT the time for second thoughts, backing out, backing down, betraying Bosco! "I'm with you!" he said, and in that moment he meant it. (What else did he have, anyway?)

"I know you are, Horatio - I know you are!" Bosco looked at him with something that looked almost like warmth.

"Shall we rouse the others? Phelim? P. J.'s over there, and he's moving. Can't see the others..."

"No time - leave them. Swift's the word! Let's go, just you and me - like old times, like it's always been! Follow me!" So Horatio stumbled and shambled in Bosco's wake as they zig-zagged across the square.

Bosco's fertile brain was boiling, thoughts bubbling frantically up and bursting. Two simple notions were uppermost - that he needed to do something grand, and he had the means to do it. Something - or someone - would present itself as sacrifice and symbol. The means was in his hand - and his right thumb stroked the safety catch. He glanced down at the gun, and loved it more than he had ever loved anything else. There was nothing nearly so deadly anywhere else in the square, probably in the town - except for one more just like it, and that was borne by his bondsman, just behind him, ready to die with or for him. As he hurtled towards the thickest crowd of strugglers, he sensed his youthful grandfather keeping pace with him, risen up out of the resonant past to help deliver the future - and he thought with fell delight that with his blooded face, torn clothes and death-dealing device he must look to the crowd like an avenging angel, a saint from the earliest Church sweeping all heathendom before him. His teeth flashed in a skull-grin, his boots sprouted wings, and with a menacing, meaningless war-cry he crashed into the crowd from behind.

Thanks to sheer impetus, even his smallish body made headway, and his onrush was lent power when Horatio concertinaed into his back. But this made Bosco stumble, and once again he felt himself falling, this time forwards rather than back. He could not use his hands to save himself, because he needed to hold onto his gun with one, and the other had embarrassingly become tangled up somehow in someone's groin. His chin cracked as it took his (and Horatio's) weight, and a front tooth took the opportunity to escape. A petite and recently-pristine woman who had been nearly knocked over by the two men kicked at their bullet heads in fury - Fidelma, as no one had seen her before, or would again.

Her nameless dread had been realized when the trouble started - shouts, a sort of shudder, jostling, then - terrifyingly - missiles passing over - bottles, chunks of wood, bricks, stones. Some of these found soft targets nearby - a blue-rinse woman a few feet away had gone down, and Fidelma had not seen her since, nor been able to get to her. Being such a large mark, Tom Gulliver had also been found by incoming, but even being showered in glass had not deterred him. Blood was branching down his chipmunk cheeks from wounds on his temples and scalp. Even in that uproar, Fidelma found time to be surprised by the look on his face, usually so ox-like. But now his bone structure was visible for the first time in at least a decade, as if his whole body had been sharpened. There was a furnace in his face, and a firmness to his chins which suggested that if any anti-Ambrosians were to find themselves encompassed within his stubby arms, they would not relish his embrace.

But the missiles were being aimed chiefly at the platform, and especially at Ambrose, lanky and beige, yet wonderfully dominant - the word *kingly* flashed into and as swiftly out of his mother's mind, and for a second the projectiles looked like arrows, and him like a legend. Everyone around him had fallen or taken cover, and he looked incredibly tall, a megalith on a plain, with projectiles falling around like hail. She loved him in that moment with all the power she had - oh, son! - but no emotional forcefield could avert the piece of paving which sliced him on the temple. Even from where she was she could see a small explosion of blood, and she screamed something that had always been screamed in such moments by human and animal mothers. Then the missiles thickened even more, and she and those around were shoved flat. When she had battled at last back to her size 5s, Ambrose could no longer be seen.

There was a ruckus around the base of the platform, and for a few grateful seconds the pressure eased, only to be renewed, released and then renewed again. For a marvelling moment she glimpsed the Monsignor, parting the crowd with main strength, his long arms like paddles, and then wielding some reddish object to create passageways. She, less powerful, found it very difficult to maintain her footing, especially as she was treading upon things (things? They were people!) that were yielding and uneven. The ground resounded, the crowd foamed, and was buffeted now from one side, now from another. Ambrose was out of sight, almost certainly hurt, and she had failed to protect him, failed him his whole life. Her handbag was missing too, and she had been elbowed in the nose. She was shouting and crying, and there was blood on her shoes. Small wonder that when Bosco and Horatio burst in from an unexpected direction she should have visited on them her fear and anger at the turn of the day, and the savage guilt of fifty-something years. She had no idea who they were, but she could see what - one of them was holding a gun! It was scum like these who were to blame for what was happening - who were misusing her sick son to further their sicker agenda - and so she kicked out furiously again and again, for a few moments a she-wolf, a cruentous Queen out of the savage times.

Derek Turner

STREAM OF CONSCIOUSNESS

The river that ran through the town rose hopefully in a trembling moss in the mountains before sinking in stages down a glen, through bog cotton and tufted fields before eventually entering the conurbation, there briefly to pick up filth before expelling it with relief into the sea in a flurry of gulls and graffitied concrete outfalls. And Ambrose was in it.

Buses and cars were passing by on the far quay, pale passenger blobs staring through windows in wonder at seeing him there, and the scenes being enacted in the square. There were many shouting and struggling people, and some were still hurling things at Ambrose's head, the only part of him presently visible - execrations, eggs, vegetables, dog and human excrement, sticks, placards and rocks. Some of the partisans of both sides were now joining him, pitched in like him into the river of history, to be baptized by the flood of Fate - and the opposing forces were being charged by yet another force, clad all in Kevlar, banging on see-through shields with batons, driving a Centrist wedge between Left and Right. Ambrose watched this thrilling scene with interest when his head was not under the water - so much interest that he did not even really notice quite how cold the water was, or register the bloated dead cat that bobbed indifferently by, destined for disassembly beyond the groynes and beneath the stars. Confused armies clashing by night, the epic struggles of the End Times... This was his major achievement - to have taken a people enmired in ennui and rouse them to rage against the dying of all lights!

The Light had descended from up there on the Head, and he turned his head south to look at the rounded massif, in the process swallowing a little too much of the oil-striped waters. His examination of that geographical feature was interrupted when a badly battered young man with red hair clinging closely to his round skull floated by chance into him, and when he saw that it was Ambrose, punched him unceremoniously in the face and shouted "Wanker!" before his mouth filled with water and he gagged. Panic displaced the hatred in his eyes as his head went under, but Ambrose steadied him with a surprisingly strong arm, and with apparently no effort piloted them both into the left bank. He dragged the young man out onto a concrete flood defence, and checked his breathing before he sat back on his haunches to survey the battleground of celestial forces. He addressed the unheeding young man. "I am like unto one of the Great Generals of Old."

There they all were, shouting, spitting, running, pushing, punching, kicking, biting - strangers all, but not strangers, because no one was really a stranger in this small world. He even recognized two faces - that of the little ex-soldier who had wanted him to do something or other, the other the little ex-soldier's friend. He watched Bosco indulgently for a few seconds as the Irish Bolivar hid behind an elderly woman bearing a poster of the Virgin, and then ran away from the Guard who had just felled her, shouting something that could have been "Feckin' cowards!" Horatio stepped in to defend him, only to be steamrollered under several beefy men in uniform. But whether Ambrose recognized them or not, whether they were on 'his side' or not, they were all, he knew, children of the same God, playing out appointed parts in the Cosmic Choreography, the Great Dance. Even those who had pushed him into the river were only doing what they had been born to do, and he smiled on them, and blessed their artlessness.

The prostrate Red-Hair was looking up now in hate and wonderment. He sat up, gasping and coughing. "Fuck!" Then - "You saved me! But why?..." Ambrose's face was ecstatic. Even the blood that was issuing from his nose seemed to be running with unusual force.

"Thou wouldst have done the same for me, mayhap. Or e'en if not, thou wouldst have been merely fulfilling thy appointed role. Thou considerest thyself an autonomous agent, I warrant - yet you are but a toye and plaything of Providence, doing what thou was biddest to do long afore ye were born. I bear thee no malice!"

The man closed his eyes. "Fuck!"

"Open thine orbs, mine late opponent! The final game plays itself out! Consider the dispositions of the opposing forces - the camp of the godly beset by - saving thy presence - swarming goblins. But both thee and we merely execute our appointed steps in the dance. We all seek to resolve dilemmas as old as Time himself. And even now we are kept asunder by the hoplites of public order, Pilate's men, the peelers, the bobbies, the bluebottles, the filth, the fuzz, the Old Bill, *les flics, les cochons, der Polizei!*" The young man was staring with wondering eyes.

"Observe now, caitiff - it is an objective term - observe how they charge once again along the embankment, cracking ribs, breaking bonces, crushing the stones of both sides, doling out condign punishment to impose once again on the world dullness and irresolution! It is beyond goodly to see how they are opposed by the forces of the living - how the Light of Heaven runs up their plastic shields from the smashed bottles, Greek Fire to singe the Romans! Behold, mine sometime enemy!"

The other shook his head, swallowed, shivered and covered his face with trembling hands. He was close to crying. "You're fucking mad, you know that? You... you gobshite!"

Ambrose looked at him a little sadly. Perhaps he had overestimated his new friend. But understanding might yet come. "There, there!" The young man twitched his shoulder away angrily from Ambrose's consolatory hand, and fought to his feet. Without looking back at Ambrose, he staggered away, and climbed painfully up a steel ladder and onto the embankment. When he had gone, Ambrose removed and wrung out all his clothes - a distressing sight for passengers on the stationary No. 76 bus - before replacing them, and ascending in great state. His hair clung to his cranium in a clammy curtain; his tracksuit clasped in chilly embrace, and even elevated as he was, his body could not help massive shivers and racking coughs, during each of which he was reminded of just how polluted the river was.

As his head appeared above the river wall, the Gardaí had just charged again, this time breaking resistance utterly. Looking to his left, he could see a line of business-like backs, beetle-black except for white block capitals reading GARDA, as they moved quickly away, trying to get in a few last vengeful thwacks of their late taunters. Where they had trodden down the protestors, there was now just a quayside bespangled with glass, and littered with bricks, pieces of wood and placards dropped by retreating partisans. Tiny licks of flame curled up from expiring petrol bombs, and random words and phrases shouted for attention from the cobblestones - "Salvation!" - "Smash" - "God bless Ireland" - "Clerico-Fascism" - and he smiled at their earnestness. Better these placards than none. Better clarification than quietude. Better violence than a slow sinking. This day would go down in the annals. Christ's blood was streaming now in the firmament, and one drop would save them all.

A hand touched his shoulder diffidently, and he turned. It was Philomena, somehow there in this scene of strife, small and tremulous, her eyes brimming, her coat torn where someone had tried to hurt her for some reason neither she nor her assailant would ever fully understand. He focused in on her in an instant of brilliant clarity, and her face was suddenly as sharp as a sniper's target. "You here, Philomena? But how? And where are we anyway?"

"Oh Ambrose, you know me! You *know* me!" It felt like the second-best moment of her life - and she was putting up her face with tightly closed eyes to be kissed as he had kissed her a few days before, when another hand descended on Ambrose's other shoulder, and another voice interrupted.

"Ambrose Sheehy-O'Connor, I am arresting you on suspicion of endangering public order and incitement to riot, public indecency and..." Ambrose turned and looked into the clammily triumphant countenance of Garda Rogers, who had blood issuing from his ear, and more on his visor.

The Guard relished the moment of recognition, and then a millisecond later he noticed Ambrose's companion. Philomena! With whom... once... the only beautiful thing... but... then... now she... with *him*! The only beautiful thing... A life's as well as a career's pent-up rage impelled his hand, and propelled his baton deeply into Ambrose's unresisting kidneys. Ambrose folded, and started to fall, and he seemed to be the only thing moving in all Ireland when an ominous sound cracked through the square.

*

Fidelma and Mary had been standing side by side, slightly unsteadily. In those few unguarded moments, they looked more alike than for many years. Their father's features for a few moments predominated in both faces, as did his mind - quixotic, romantic, quietly savage. There was a fineness to both women's features that suggested what they might have been. They had been lifted out of themselves by sheer physicality - the simple intoxication of action. They panted, ached, exulted. Fidelma felt she had been transfigured. Those fiercely focused few minutes, when everything had been erased except rage and love for her Ambrose, had been terrifying, but they had also been wildly thrilling. Her body even now thrummed with lust of lashing out and connecting with enemy skin. It was the joy of clarity after fog. Her high-heeled shoes had surely been made for stabbing insteps, their pointed toes for pulverizing penises, her lovely nails for rending red stripes on the faces of those who had tried to hurt her boy. For a few heedless moments, she had been able simply to be.

Mary had always prided herself on her spiritual singularity, her distance from her sister. But even she had been in danger of forgetting her Purpose during the long eventless years. But at last, at last, all the cold waiting had been forgotten in a burst of glorious activity, when for a wonderful while the Enemy had been made manifest - and punishable. She had fought, fought for what was right... for the Truth against Error. All doubt, all guilt had been wiped clean. Even the fact that at her shoes' end there moaned an actual ordained priest, a senior one too - a sleek sacred with a butterfly tattoo on his neck, and wearing running shoes, whom she had toppled before clawing, did not cause a second's concern - because of all the unworthy representatives of her most worthy Church this creature was the worst.

Around the two sisters were many recumbent people, and others sitting with heads in hands, a man standing with his hands on his knees coughing up blood, a woman feeling dazedly for something, Tom Gulliver with a dreamy sort of smile - representing all the factions that had clashed, all the frictions of modernity, all the classes of contemporary Ireland. The square was confetti-ed with posters representing all political positions, and bits of brick and wood that had lately served as debating aids. Fidelma had thought she knew the square - but now could see that she had only ever scratched at its true nature. But then she saw the stains on her shoes...

Gardaí were sweeping efficiently towards them, still two hundred yards off but nearing quickly now that almost all resistance had been crushed. Others were approaching from a different direction. It was a well-organised operation that was reassuring to watch, even for those on the downward slope from berserk bliss. Fidelma watched them approach with cool acceptance rather than her customary vague dread. How strange that in that compromised moment, when she was at her nadir of respectability, with her clothes and even her hair clotted with blood, her conscience felt clearer than ever before. Whatever would come, it had been worth it. The sisters looked at each other, and half-smiled - seeing each other as comrades for the first time since girlhood. It had been superb. But now... "Ambrose!"

They spun as one. But there was no one on the platform, no one even around it, except a woman's bare legs protruding from under the twisted scaffolding. The whole construction sagged heavily where history had kicked it in passing, and the ring of posters advertising National Penince and Reafirmation had been torn and disfigured. In between the fuzzy images of Ambrose and the now even more cryptic references to "...ional Pen..." or "...firma..." drooped torn tricolours, some of which had become bicolours. There was a lonely howl of feedback from an unattended mike. Fidelma gazed around in a kind of panic, and saw there was still scuffling taking place down at the quayside, several hundred yards away. Then the

Gardaí charged along there too, leaving behind angular litter - beaten-down people, their broken belongings, their banners and badges of affiliation.

There! Wasn't that Ambrose? It must be - it was - a long pale person, looming up apparently from the earth, clear and infinitely dear for a few thankful seconds - oh, my son, now I *know* you! Things will be different from now! But before she could move she could see people closing in on him, and then there was - oh Christ, a gunshot - which reverberated everywhere, while with everyone the sisters flinched and flung themselves down. When Fidelma dared to look up a few seconds later, everyone was running, converging on a woman screaming her soul's blood, and someone beside her, lying terribly lightly on the ground.

DUTY BOUND

As so often in his life, the Monsignor was going against the flow of humanity. But this time, Letty was with him. He wrapped himself in that idea, as Garda cars, ambulances and voyeurs raced in the opposite direction. After clearing the square, they wandered almost at random for a while through oddly empty streets, listening to the diminishing hubbub, recovering their breath. Both of them were old, after all, although for several glorious minutes they had not remembered. Even now, they were coming down from their high, and the sight of each other caused merriment - Letty crimson, bleeding from an earlobe from which had depended an antique gold and pearl hoop to match the one still in her other ear, and with a large rip in the front of her dress - the priest, battle-lights still rising and falling in his eyes like waves after a storm has blown itself out, gore on his jacket, and his shoes badly scuffed. But they stopped laughing and stared at each other in dismay as they heard the appallingly-unexpected report of a gunshot.

They stood in an agony, dreading more. None came, but they turned as one and headed back as fast as they could go. There was nowhere else a priest should be at such moments. They were stopped by a line of grim Gardaí, some wearing bandages. The Monsignor identified himself, but a young policewoman told him very respectfully that not even he could be let through. She added reassuringly that so far as she knew no one had been shot.

So they turned around again, feeling inordinately weary, and now starting to register minor hurts. The priest's upper body and arms ached abominably, and he had a bite mark on one of his cheeks - the mark of Red-Hair. Letty's shins were paining badly where she had been kicked repeatedly, and now they were swelling up. Neither felt like subjecting themselves to the paramedics, where they would probably have been interviewed by the police, and no doubt the press would latch onto Letty. The Monsignor had to avoid giving his name and job title to anyone. There was only one possibility. "Couldn't we go to yours to clean up?"

Letty looked uncharacteristically unsure.

"What's wrong?"

"Oh nothing - nothing! It's just that.... no one's visited for a while, and it's in a bit of a mess."

"For goodness' sake, Letty, I don't mind if it's a bit untidy. Since when did you ever worry about things like that? It may have slipped your mind that I have been there before!" His voice gentled. "But if you'd really rather not..."

She touched her lip with her right index finger - a pensive habit he had entirely forgotten - and then decided. "No, no, of course it makes sense. Of course you must come. In fact, I'd like you to see it." She started up the road without saying anything else - the same road, in fact, that Ambrose had once barrelled along, fleeing from the quondam life. The Head rose proud at the end of the road, its windswept summit shrugging itself clear of a stole of Scots pines. The Cross seemed to be glowing softly - some trick of the light.

Presently, they came to the gates of Head House - ten feet tall, cast iron, rusted but still crested with the family griffins that also featured on the town crest. The tumbledown place where Ambrose had scaled the wall was a hundred yards to the right, but Letty let herself in through a pedestrian gate at the side of the main gates, and then they were in the park.

Her companion noted with surprise that the drive was thickly weeded, and the avenue of limes had run rampant. When he had last been here, the trees had been neatly lopped, and between them there had been great sweeps of lawn. But at some point in the intervening decades, someone had opted for wilderness over garden, and now the limes were swathed in ivy, elder and honeysuckle, and self-seeded sycamores and hawthorn were colonizing the gaps. The effect was disconcerting to a man who so valued human order. So many places were too tidy, he said kindly to Letty, guessing she felt embarrassed. She said nothing, and as they came around the sharp bend in the drive, he realised what was really troubling her.

From here, the House was visible for the first time, prominent on a small mound that overlooked the large lawn called the Chase, and beyond the Chase the little wooded Lough Beag, pike-patrolled, with a tree-clustered island and eighteenth century Prospect Tower. The trees around the Lough had always been called the Jungle, and now they deserved the soubriquet, as they were all overgrown and leaning, with dark and tangled undergrowth. The trees on the island, too, had grown up, and almost the only thing that could be seen of the Prospect Tower was a tiny reflection of the sun from one of the windows of the observation deck, where the family (and he) had once gathered for long dinners lit by massed candles and the moon. It was plain the island was no longer visited, and he couldn't even see the boathouse with its Temple of Diana portico, so swathed was it in sallow. Then his gaze travelled to the House itself, but he already knew what he would see.

The long, grey, granite range of the south elevation scintillated slightly with mica even from several hundred yards, and its mellow beauty still filled those who saw it with a regret for a time when to the very rich, at least, the world had seemed intelligible as well as harmonious. Windows threw the Chase multiple reflections of itself - but not all of them, because in some of the first floor window openings there were dark rectangles where there should have been light - missing glass - and as the Monsignor marvelled, a pigeon flew out of one of these openings and onto the roof, which was tinted green-yellow by guano. There were green patches in some of the interstices between windows, and a large one where guttering had failed. The famous Orangery was also missing panes, and even its door. Letty had walked on, and he hurried in her wake.

They passed the mulberry tree on its crutches - that at least looked the same - and entered the house through the huge Ionic portico. The priest looked up in sad wonder as she rooted in her bag for the key. From up close, the decay was very apparent, with mould inside the fanlight with its rippling old glass. Even the burglar alarm looked rusty; the Monsignor guessed it didn't work. The opened door displayed the once familiar hallway, whose elegant proportions were unchanged, but which had been emptied of almost all of its furnishings and appointments. The Louis XIV wood-gilt hall chairs and matching consoles were missing, there were cardboard boxes piled up along one wall, and there were darker patches on the panelling where paintings had hung. Stray sun slanted in from the fanlight and the door's flanking windows, and molecules and animalcules sported half-heartedly in the beams.

The priest tried to remember what the paintings had been. Letty, divining his thoughts - as always - pointed to the nearest discoloured patch. "Lorrain - classical landscape with Saturnalia. Poussin opposite - Arcadian shepherd and shepherdess. Over there was a Domenichino - then there were various Dutch still-lifes, rather horrible pictures of hares and herons all hanging upside down beside the rifles that killed them. They were the first to go."

She pointed to a recess near the stairs. "My favourite was over there. St. John in the Wilderness by an unknown sixteenth century Italian. That picture used to fascinate me when I was little. I'd spend hours staring at it - a near-naked man all by himself in a gloomy wood, pointing to a shadowy figure in the background. What, I always wondered, would motivate someone to go out naked into such a hard world? Who called him? What voices whispered to him beneath those trees? What eyes winked at him along the branches? Who was he pointing at? And how could he be sure that it was real? And this is the funniest thing of all - in fact, it's a bit spooky - Ambrose looks like him! Although in all honesty, I have to say that John was more handsome."

"Well, that wouldn't be very hard, now would it?. I'm afraid I don't remember that picture. But this explains your infatuation with the lad - it's like your picture has magically come to life! A little bit of your childhood..."

"And there he was, living just up the road. It still seems like too much of a coincidence to be a coincidence. When I first saw him in the street a few months ago, the similarity knocked me sideways - even though I had not seen that painting since it was sold twenty years or so ago. I stood still in the middle of a busy pavement, and felt like I'd woken into some dream."

She was smiling embarrassedly. "Then poor Fidelma spoke to me, and I woke up - partly, anyway. There I found myself, a foolish and lonely old woman, staring at the back of a spotty twenty-something who had clearly been spending too much time on the internet. But still... still, I couldn't help wondering. And so I decided to meet him properly. And now, here I am, months later, still wondering!"

"Well, even I wonder sometimes. He is a phenomenon, there's no denying that."

They parted while Letty went to change her clothes. The priest laved his face and hands in cold water in the downstairs lavatory, tried to disguise the damage to his shoes, then walked quietly about the house for a time, opening doors and peering into rooms he remembered, only to see the same dusty disuse, covered chairs pushed against walls, mouse-chewed carpets, webby windows. There were empty niches where there had once been classical statuettes, unfeasibly huge fireplaces piled up with newspapers, sticks and even a dead nestling whose downy flesh had dried into cartilaginous fluff. He closed each door sadly after him, and their still smooth mahogany action underlined how magnificent the house had been.

A Modern Journey

She called, and he followed her through dwindling rooms at last into the kitchen - clearly the room where she spent most time, because it was warm and well-organized, and perfectly clean. She was immaculate again, except for a discreet bandage on her earlobe, and poured tea from an old Spode pot. Sandwiches appeared, on a mixture of heavy old plates. There were some good paintings in here, one very good - a Connemara watercolour whose frame seemed to be finding it difficult to contain such a fine, wide country. She nodded at it affectionately. "I still have the Paul Henry, anyway. So now you know the awful truth! The last of the Shaughnessy-Dons squats in the ruins of her house - a lesson to The Ages!"

"But what happened, Letty? Everyone thinks you're a millionairess! So did I, by the way."

"So that's why you're here!" she smiled. "It's not much of a story, really. No rakes gambling away the estate or anything like that! But we also always liked buying lovely things, and then there were houses in Paris and Rome to keep up, and for a time even in New York. When Grandfather came back here, we already had huge debts. And like all the old houses, this one was already unmanageable. Then he and Father were always giving money away, to all kinds of people - ancient retainers, hard-luck story merchants, good causes - that was why Father was approached to help pay for the Cross." She inclined her head uphill, although the Cross could not be seen from there.

"It was the last time we could afford to give away money like that. So it all went, even though all the other houses were sold off - losing the place in Rome was a real wrench, because the family had lived there since 16 something, when we were exiled with the Stuarts. I suspect we didn't get a good price for any of them. And what money was spent here was badly spent - a lot of shoddy workmanship, all now buried anyway in brambles. Daddy was never a hands-on kind of person, as you know - too interested in his books and genealogies. Mummy was the only one who ever looked at the accounts - and when she died, Daddy took up with a succession of seriously unsuitable fillies - most, I'm afraid, into his money. And of course the name."

"Yes, it's always been a name to conjure with, even in our sainted Republic..."

She smiled, and sipped tea. It was good tea - jasmine blended with Assam. "It's a lot to live up to sometimes! Anyway, we always seemed to owe money even with selling off the odd chair, or table, or painting. The one thing Daddy would never consider selling was land - he was a peasant in that way. I'm glad about that. He was a bit of a snob too, and hated seeing old estates being swamped by Noddy houses. But he wasn't prepared to do anything practical. The Shaughnessy-Dons have never been quite cut out for the world, and now the world has become so small and ugly."

The Monsignor sighed. "I know what you mean - no room for big houses, or big people, or big ideas..."

"When James came along, it seemed providential, being from a banking family and all that. And he was a good man. I was terribly fond of him. He might have made a difference if he'd had time - but then of course he and Jackie were killed..."

She was gazing at a framed colour photograph in a silver frame on the windowsill - an open-faced man in his early forties and a boy of about six, standing with a palomino, both smiling with vast confidence into the lens, their hairstyles and James's suit suggesting the early Eighties. The Polaroid was discolouring slowly in the sun, curling at the corners like an old sandwich. "Shouldn't you move that, Letty?"

"I've wondered about that, but it just seems - it's stupid, I know - too sad to face it away from the light. Jackie was so outdoorsy. That was taken over in the Bishop's Field - you remember, near where the tinkers used to camp. It's all bramble and thistle these days - you couldn't keep a mare like Pallas there now."

So like her, reflected the Monsignor fondly - masking pain with practicality.

"Anyway, it all just became too difficult for me, rattling around in this place all by myself. What, really, is the point of keeping up a building that no one else can ever really know, let alone love? The chain's been broken, and it can't be fixed."

Universalist though he may have been in theory, the Monsignor knew pride of race, and he nodded sympathetically. He was stunned by the thought of all the years Letty had spent in unpeopled rooms.

Letty tidied away the plates and cups, and brushed a hank of grey from her eyes. "Anyway, ever since I've been sitting up here like Miss Havisham, but managing to keep up appearances. I hire a car and chauffeur when I go out, because it somehow seems expected. Every year, a little man in a van comes to take away some more stuff to London, or the Far East, to sell. He's terribly discreet - highly efficient in a ferrety sort of way, well worth his 20%. I allow the world to think what it likes. I don't actually lie to people, I dissemble. It seems to have worked - I remember one newspaper called me 'the embodiment of unacceptable inequality' That tickled me! People seem to think I live surrounded by valuable *objets d'art* - to the extent that there have been two burglaries in five years. They didn't find much worth taking - but obviously they couldn't tell their story to the press!"

The priest felt greatly concerned. "How do you bear it? I know you're brave, but it really could be dangerous."

"Don't be so bloody patronizing! I am, in case you have forgotten, the last of my line, making a last stand in the ancestral acres. What else would I do? Where else would I go? This is where I *belong*. Besides, I had really quite a nice chat with one of the burglars. Such a life he had led! I felt quite sorry for him. I can still see his little pointy, scared face in the torchlight. I gave him a meal and he thanked me very sweetly, and promised he wouldn't bother me again. And he hasn't - honour amongst thieves, and all that!"

The priest threw back his head and laughed loudly, a sound that had not been heard in that room for decades, and raced through the hollow house awakening echoes. Ambrose was forgotten as they reminisced for hours. Letitia served a simple meal accompanied by a bottle of Chateau Musar somehow saved, fetched up by the priest from a cellar white-whiskered with mould. Pleasant tiredness had come over them both as a reaction to that day's exertions. Sunlight peered in and moved from window to window, as she told him what she had done and where she had been since they had last seen each other.

She unfolded a gazetteer of glamour and good living, interspersed with anecdotes that would never be heard by gossip columnists - how this famous person had been shorter and with worse skin than imagined - how this heartthrob had had halitosis - how these brilliant youngsters had destroyed their brains with medication or ideas, or without writing the great book or music that had always been expected of them. Family and friends were translated to fading photos, or relegated to footnotes in histories that would never be written. So many remarkable people she had known - brilliant, beautiful, fun-loving, inspired, experienced, loving, loved, dead. And with each loss, her vision seemed to have become sharper. Maybe now at last (the Monsignor thought) she saw the world for what it was, had always been. An agreeable charade. Aimless. Seductive.

Pointless. A wasteland. His younger self had been wise after all, when it had told her there was more depth to things than she guessed. As he listened, it seemed he had been right to reject her kind of life - even though it had meant such a sacrifice. Did she see that too, now - now, when it was too late?

But then it came to his turn to talk, and the strangest thing happened. His own life seemed scarcely more satisfactory. In some ways it seemed even less adequate. He had bypassed so many of the everyday experiences that everybody else had - all those possibilities of instinct, and love. His life had been distinguished in so many ways, and spent in the service of an ancient and admirable institution. He recalled grand ceremonies - intellectual heights scaled - books published - aperçus exchanged with the equally erudite... all against a background of refined architecture and great art. But how cold these things all seemed now that he had been asked, so freezing and vinegarish that his mouth shrivelled as he spoke. When eventually he faltered to an anti-climax, he couldn't look at her - she with whom he had always shared his inmost thoughts, and might have shared even more in some multiverse. He stood, stretched, and went to the window. He heard her exhale in the silence, and knew they were both tasting the same acrid flavour.

The sun had declined behind the Head and the tangled Jungle - and he noticed a fox slinking along the edge of the Chase, shining for a second in a stray beam before it disappeared in darkness and dappling. The strain of the day was telling heavily; his arms ached with a lifetime's accumulated effort. It was Letitia who switched on the radio to find out how the world had got on in their absence, guilty that she had not thought of doing so before. She gazed pensively at her oldest friend's back, which stiffened as they heard the end of a headline "...during a day of violent rioting, Ambrose Sheehy-O'Connor has been killed".

MAGIC BULLET

For years afterwards, the more impressionable among the Ambrosians would insist that the sky had cracked open that Easter Sunday. The Mauser's 7.63 bullet, carrying doom at a little over 800 miles per hour, seemed to them emblematic of Ambrose's own urgent trajectory, the way he had flashed onto all radars and as quickly off again. It had been almost like an arrow sent by the gods to reclaim one of their own.

Except that the divine bolt had missed. The bullet, which had issued forth somehow from Horatio's gun, to his surprise and consternation, as he dodged to escape the downwards slice of a nightstick, had gone nowhere near Ambrose. It had also easily avoided the red-haired man Ambrose had pulled from the water, Garda Rogers, Philomena, Fidelma, Mary, the safely prone Daddy Jimmy, and a plethora of other deserving or undeserving recipients. It had admittedly passed very close to Bosco, zipping past his right ear at a distance which shrank the more often he reminisced about the affair - but what happened to it after that was unknown, and the mystery of the bullet that never landed would add greatly to the Ambrosian legendarium.

The little lead lump had in fact made straight for a tall building bordering the square, once a warehouse but now an advertising agency, angling up with every micro-moment towards a thirty-foot-wide poster for barely-there lingerie that had been the subject of hundreds of complaints by mutually shocked Catholics and feminists. It hissed in hot joy for one last millisecond before it plunged into the image and went out, but not until it had penetrated right through the wooden board and an inch into the brick behind - giving the alluring giantess a perfectly placed third nipple with an aureole of splinters. It was an accidentally well-aimed broadside against public near-nudity, but it was very high, and no-one had been looking in that direction. The workmen who the following week pasted up the next poster (history does not record whether it was beer or margarine, or some financial product) were so busy reprising the *Banana Boat Song* that they never noticed anything out of the ordinary.

Yet Ambrose was indisputably dead, his sharp cadaver successively gaped at, screamed over, checked for vital signs, despaired of, cordoned off, photographed, and carefully removed for autopsy. The fatal instrument had been the baton wielded by one of the most prosaic men ever to wield a blunt instrument against a pointy-head. Garda Rogers had hit Ambrose deep - much too deep - in the solar plexus, with all the viciousness and carbohydrate-power at his command. Even at his present level of fitness, Garda Rogers' blow could still persuade, and this skill had been much prized by his superiors. This time, with the assistance of a hard and small-headed stick expertly held, the power of his arm had persuaded Ambrose's soft tissues to shudder, to move, to part, to absorb, to rupture and hæmorrhage their oxygenating, mineralizing, soul-carrying fluids into parts of the body they had no business to visit. Bubbles of blood and waves of hurt fleeter than any bullet had raced round Ambrose's body in a massive physiological panic, over-stimulating glands, distorting muscles, shattering nerves, bursting through tissue walls and running the wrong way up veins, and each new, rapidly-succeeding, tiny trauma had carried unbearable agony. But it had been only for a few seconds, during which time Ambrose's even speedier synapses vouchsafed one last grand vision - cobbles bursting up from the quay towards him, opening up the earth to let him in.

*

This bullet that had not actually done anything had yet other portentous effects. When Horatio let it off, he had automatically assumed he must have hurt someone, and suddenly saw that he had never wanted to. So he had reacted as if the gun had bitten him, and he let it fall before he fled, leaving it to be picked up a few minutes afterwards by a wondering policeman, who loved its lines and, seeing he was unwatched, on an impulse slipped it inside his jacket and took it home - after which it passed out of all chronicles (at least for the moment).

Horatio was very lucky that so many people were hiding from expected future firing, and that there was so much panic and confusion - also that his appearance made him the unlikeliest looking of assassins. So he had escaped from his situation - and his old allegiance. The way Bosco had behaved during the last few crowded minutes had been truly revelatory, even to his longest-serving adherent. The fleeting warmth of his feelings for Bosco, just before they had made that last charge across the Square, had dissolved instantaneously as he had yet again been subjected to the violence of strangers with whom he had no quarrel - and as he had suddenly noticed that Bosco had a knack of somehow managing to avoid the worst of the violence to which he was prepared to expose everybody else. Horatio had seen to his shock a terrified-looking Bosco actually step aside from the furious onslaught of a tiny woman with perfect make-up, thereby exposing his loyalest lieutenant to that woman's small but sharp foot, which had made crippling contact with a exceedingly delicate area of his anatomy which even now was streaked with white agony. But even if he had not had this sudden insight into Bosco's character, the sheer terror of having fired a gun that could have *killed* someone - and condemned him to the rest of his life in Portlaoise - would have been enough to break the old enchantment. He had been *such* a fool!

Disabused, desponding, panicking, he raced away as quickly as sixty-year old limbs could convey him. Miraculously, he secured a taxi a few streets away, and raced in it back to the Northside - thankful for once that the taxi driver spoke almost no English, and needed to be directed. Arriving at Wild Geese Hall after a fraught and frustrating journey through heavy traffic, he instructed the driver to wait for a few minutes. The large and mercifully incurious African shrugged and slumped in his seat, with rap playing at full volume.

Horatio opened the five locks on the petrol-scorched front door, his hands trembling, and let himself into the so-familiar hallway. He was greatly relieved to be there alone this last time; he had worried all the way that Bosco might somehow have got to base before him. After seeing what he had seen in the square, it would not have surprised him in the least to find that Bosco had simply abandoned him and dashed back here for Bosco-juice. But no, and so Horatio stood just inside the door for a few seconds, inhaling the old bouquet - dampness, old take-aways, mice, and some more obscure ingredients possibly relating to the hard-pressed local sewerage. He knew this was a hugely significant moment in his life, and he was not naturally decisive. Where could he go? What could he do? And with whom? His future lay at his feet like a crevasse, and for perhaps a minute he teetered on its edge. But self-interest clicked on at last, forcing itself through the shock and disillusion of the day - and he started to move unusually swiftly from room to sordid room, collecting his appurtenances. He did not, however, enter Bosco's bedroom - even though he knew that there would be some, perhaps many, of his belongings in there. Just the other day, his old tortoiseshell hairbrush had vanished, like so many other things over the years. He had, of course, always known in his heart what had happened to these items - Bosco used some of them quite openly - but this was the first time he had confronted the fact. He hated himself for having been so weak, so stupid, and he didn't want to see the compromised objects again. Bitter words that even now felt almost like treason rolled out - "Let the bastard have them then!" - and he finished his gathering-up, expecting every tense moment that the front door would open and the familiar voice would call his name. If this happened, he did not trust himself to be able to stick to his resolve.

But at last he was done, and downstairs. As he left the building for the final time, softer feelings flowed back for a moment. He had invested so much in this place after all, and the remarkable person who haunted it. He stopped and peered back myopically along the hall. Wistful eyes ranged over last year's leaves, the year before's mud, the year before that's newspapers, unused posters, and at the far end, one of the big blown-up photos of Bosco, taken on the day of his passing out parade at the Curragh - young, trim and smiling in those days before the guardroom incident, and his long slow slide into dipsomania and disappointment. The sight stirred some kind memory, and Horatio smiled slightly and actually saluted, before taking a fifty Euro note out of his wallet and leaving it on the hall table, a final Bosco-juice voucher to be urinated away by the former Friend-leader. He turned swiftly and left before he could change his mind, locking the door almost lovingly, the slight draught from his exit moving a few of the crinkled leaves for a moment.

It was well after dark when Bosco returned to the cold and cheerless HQ, breathing heavily in the chilly Finglas air. It was clear, to use one of his favourite phrases, that he had been "seeing his old Greek friend Silenus". Prior to that, he had helped the Gardaí with their sarcastic enquiries, but they had not been able to detain him long, because he had after all been the first victim of the day's violence, and he had been given no chance to say anything inflammatory. When they had searched him they had found nothing incriminating either, because immediately after Horatio fired, his fast-moving brain had made the prudent decision to shy his own unfired gun into the convenient river.

Seeing that small but significant splash had been a wrench, but it had also been a moment of clarity. Maybe his scheme had not been as well worked out as it might have been - although if he had had higher-calibre followers it might have had a chance. There would be another Day. And there were other guns in the world - and he knew fellas who could get them. The true tactician was flexible and broadminded. For now, he had outwitted the authorities effortlessly, thanks to sheer intellectual superiority - turning a potential fiasco into a character-building exercise. He throbbed with aches and pains, but there was still a suggestion of swagger in his unsteady stance.

At the moment that he inserted his key (after several near-misses, and much muttering) into the fifth lock of the front door of National HQ, he was feeling kindly even towards Horatio, even though he had blown it so badly and decamped, leaving him to face the music. Not everyone, he reminded himself charitably, was made for leadership. They'd have a little drink, and he (Bosco) would tell him (Horatio) not to worry, that it wasn't his fault, that the odds were against them, that maybe if the others had had a bit more cop-on they could still have swung the thing. And there would, above all, be other days. That was, he knew, the essence of leadership - ensuring that key members of the team always felt valued. "Horatio? Horatio? Shite!" He had tripped over a table while feeling for the light switch, precipitating a pile of old election addresses onto the snail-stickied electric blue nylon. He flipped the switch, and the bare bulb obligingly came on. But Horatio did not come out correspondingly obligingly.

"Horatio? Horatio? Where are ye, for feck's sake? I'm not angry about the way you fucked it up!" The fecker was sulking! "I've got some Bosco-juice!" But even this most powerful of arguments did not draw forth the familiar whiffling snout. This was plain disrespect now! Now, fair was fair, but at this stage he needed to assert his authority. In his recruit days, the corporals would kick open the door of the billet in the middle of the night and order a full kit inspection, or even a night run in the rain. It was sound psychology - it kept the recruits disoriented and hating the NCOs, and so built camaraderie. So he picked up a placard pole, and mounted the stairs with some excitement (also some stumbling), prepared to visit righteous as well as rational wrath on the door of Horatio's room, or even better on his person.

But the bedroom door was already open, the semi-dark landing (the landing light bulb had gone months ago) giving onto Horatio's even darker dormitory. Bosco fumbled and found the switch, and filled the room with as much brilliance as forty watts could manage. It was enough to see that it was unoccupied - and more than unoccupied. Bosco went over to the melamine wardrobe with the gold-coloured knobs and pulled the doors.

The wardrobe was so empty and unsubstantial it almost toppled over. A single sock - grey, acrylic, stale - had been overlooked in Horatio's rush, and lay curled in one corner like a sulking snake. The matching chest of drawers was equally empty. The whole room showed no signs of ever having been lived in, except for that sock, which seemed to Bosco's alcohol-sensitized eyes almost to lurk at the back of the wardrobe. He bent down to pick it up, and he actually felt slightly worried by it, even though it lay innocently over his palm.

Horatio had made time in his packing to strip the bed, and fold all his dirty nylon sheets into a pile to be brought down to the laundromat. And that was *it*! No note, no explanation, no apology. *Nothing* after all those years of comradeship, and intellectual stimulation! Nothing - except a single sock (standard issue, grey, unwashed, foot for the wearing of). On a sudden thought, he checked the Mauser box, and found it empty, as he had guessed it would be. So he had taken the gun too. It wasn't really a surprise, although it was a disappointment - after all he had done for him, after putting up with his ugliness, ignorance and incompetence for so long, out of Christian duty. So this was the thanks for all that! Why, for feck's sake, did he bother?

He sagged onto Horatio's squeaky bed, with his elbows on his knees and his head in his hands, looking morosely at the window, through which he could see a ragged line of so far unsmashed orange lights dotting the footpath across the ex-meadow. The lights seemed to sparkle on a carpet of glass and syringes. He stayed there for a few minutes, as the house's breathless repose sank into him, its intrinsic coldness - and he felt older and more tired than ever before.

He knew he should do some work - Ireland wouldn't save herself, after all - but Horatio's treachery had been so terribly dispiriting. He looked at his watch, which had once been Horatio's father's - too late to start any work now. He would make an early start. For now - and he brightened - if he hurried, he could catch last orders at the Northside Arms. He had noticed that some donor had left a fifty Euro note on the table on the hallway. With anticipatory pleasure, and a hint of old elasticity, he rose and snapped off the light. Forty-five seconds afterwards, the front door smacked shut, and was locked five times. Wild Geese Hall slid back into its own time zone.

IN ABSENTIA

Mary and Letitia organized the funeral with great efficiency, while Fidelma sat mostly in Ambrose's room, refusing to see anyone except them - not even the Monsignor, who called three times. He felt abominably guilty, because he had promised her that he would look after Ambrose. But the only person she blamed was herself. She could not find it in herself even to hate the Guard, now facing disciplinary measures. If she had done more for Ambrose, been there for him, tried to understand him, she kept thinking, he would not have been the way he had been, and none of this would have happened.

The media had come and gone repeatedly, always going away unanswered. This did not stop them printing or broadcasting all kinds of stories, and Mary and Letitia were careful not to have the TV or radio on too loudly, or to leave newspapers lying around where Fidelma could see them. But the most persistent callers were members of the Traveller community. In the last few days before the funeral, the CCTV system at Tara Road had monitored a stream of delegates from that semi-detached segment, handled with finesse by Mary and Letitia, as they came bearing communal condolences and gigantic floral tributes.

One of these was in the semblance of a pair of hands fashioned from pink roses, cradling a heart made of crimson roses, with WONDERMAN picked out in white roses across one of the vegetal ventricles. Another was even more striking, and Letitia thought it best not to let Fidelma see it at all - what was fondly supposed to be Ambrose's head, a six foot high, sleep-discouraging physiognomy in pink, scarlet and dark blue roses (the latter representing hair) plus cornflowers for eyes, the whole creation rising like Baron Samedi from a ground of moss and ferns. The ears had their own specially strengthened wire framework. Even Mary, who had never been known to express views on aesthetic matters, blinked in distress when she saw it. The confection was hidden in the cupboard under the stairs, once almost making Mary scream when she opened it in search of the vacuum cleaner.

The Travellers made generous offers, all graciously refused - a horse-drawn cortège, an honour guard of bare-knuckle boxers and Irish dancers, tin whistles and *uileann* pipers (Ambrose had always despised folk music), specially printed black T-shirts with white letters reading SLÁN LEAT, WONDERMAN, a professional DVD crew to record the whole proceedings for a very competitive price. Mikey Walsh himself offered to burn all of Ambrose's belongings, to signify Ambrose's high status, and Letitia needed all her diplomacy to decline without offending him. Fidelma remained luckily oblivious to all these kindnesses.

During those long, miserable days, she had been going through her son's legacy. A sad thing it seemed to her who so wanted to find evidence of greatness - books and pamphlets, his begging-bowl, his staff, the remains of food so rotten she could not even begin to guess what it might once have been. But there were unexpected things too, including a box of little identical notebooks filled with the same black-inked neat sentence - "I have sinned again", followed by a time and date, and a small symbol she did not understand, like a stick with three twigs. And then after one more delve amongst the detritus under the bed, she understood.

She found, with a violent repulsion, a small penitential whip, with knots along its length, and signs it had been well and recently used. The cotton had once been white, but had dulled into rusty brown, and there were grainy residues, miniature flakes that did not bear thinking about. She had put the horrible thing quickly into a plastic bag, and carried it downstairs in her finger tips, and out into the back garden where the dustbins were kept. After briefly wondering whether it could be construed as garden waste, she had opted for general rubbish.

Mary had been in the kitchen as she passed through, but Fidelma had ignored her. No one, Fidelma told herself over and over, must know about this! On her way back through the kitchen, she had washed her hands for almost ten minutes with powerfully fragranced soap, again ignoring Mary. So moved had Fidelma been that Mary had felt almost afraid of whatever had been in that plastic bag, but curiosity won out, and as soon as Fidelma had gone back upstairs she had the contents of the bin spread across the garden.

Her reaction to the whip was utterly different. As she looked down into the bag's opaque depths, she gave a slight smile of satisfaction. For her, it was yet another testimony to Ambrose's sincerity. It seemed to her a testament to the human spirit, almost like a relic. It was gruesome, and she shivered as she touched it, but it was also a piquant token, a votive offering, a link to greater days. She brushed potato peelings off the parcel, and secreted it in her handbag.

*

The sight of a nun rooting in rubbish bags went some way to recompensing Sandra Gulliver for recent slights at Fidelma's unknowing hands - especially when she saw what Mary had uncovered. She felt it was her citizen's duty to inform the local newspaper and RTÉ News. Such public-spirited activities also had the happy effect of taking her mind off the bizarre behaviour of her son.

She had noticed a fever in his face when he had come back from the riot, cut, bruised and untidy. She had presumed it was just shock, and all he needed was a good meal. But he had barely touched his food that night, or since, and was already losing weight. Admittedly, there was a good safety margin before he ran any risk of malnutrition, but it was a worry. Not only this, but she had found him reading a book. A hardback book. When Tom was out of the room, she had taken the opportunity to hide it, for his sake.

He was also starting to look slightly scruffy, even for work, the smooth egg of his face now slightly shaded around the circumference by a suggestion of stubble, his suit slightly wrinkled, his shoes slightly dull. And just that morning he had announced that he wasn't going to go into work that day, as he did not feel well. She couldn't remember the last time he had been ill - and yet he had almost angrily refused her offers to fetch a doctor. He had almost *sworn* at her! Lucky for him he hadn't, she thought grimly - his childhood acquaintance, the Smooth Stick, still reposed under the stairs.

*

Fidelma had been mute and numb at the funeral, a mourner in the classical mould - well turned-out, wan, dried out from crying, erect and tiny, hearing but not absorbing the words she had last heard at Fergus's funeral, and before that her father's. She yearned to be by herself at home, in any place without people, where she might be able to address the outline of Ambrose. And all her failures.

The parish priest, a man she had never spoken to before, although he had been in post ten years, had been kind and thoughtful. He had researched St. Ambrose, and in his homily tried hard to find parallels between him and his awkward namesake. He glossed over Ambrose's eccentricities and stressed his energy and sincerity. The Monsignor, in civvies at the back of the crammed church, thought what a shame it was that the priest had such a high-pitched voice, so pink and shiny a face. There was no real authority there, and old-school authority was what was needed as a coda to this jejune outbreak. But the priest was trying hard, and he was young, and maybe this authority would come in time.

"Saint Ambrose," said the priest, "is supposed to have been the originator of the phrase 'When in Rome, do as the Romans do' - but of course in his life he did just the opposite. He spoke as he found, and he was never afraid. And our Ambrose was like that too. He spoke as he found, he was never afraid..."

The Monsignor wondered who was listening - really listening. His poor mother, stricken for what might have been the first time in her prepacked life? Look at her rigid back, grief graffitied in every line, a jelly held together by clothes - even she probably isn't registering a word of this kindly and ingenious homily. All those scholarly references were probably wasted on such an audience, on almost any audience nowadays.

"...death as a good. He flew from this world, just like his predecessor, and we are the worse for his passing..."

"Humph!" and this time it must have been aloud, because one or two people nearby gave the Monsignor disapproving looks. He turned it into a cough, and looked down at his shoes, whose leather he had carefully re-balsamed after they had been so badly scuffed during the fighting. A faint reminiscent smile moved on his face, and then he stood with everyone else to sing (haltingly, because it was unfamiliar even to him) one of the songs the saint was supposed (probably incorrectly) to have written. The last verse ran -

"New hope his clarion note awakes,
Sickness the feeble frame forsakes,
The robber sheathes his lawless sword,
Faith to fallen is restored."

But of course it had been the lad himself who had fallen. And how ironic that it should have been a lawful "sword" that felled him - or at least one wielded by a lawman, although for how long he would remain a lawman was a moot point. That oaf would be no great loss to the public, and once the furore had died down, he would gravitate into some other job where he had the opportunity to bully people.

As for restoring faith to the fallen, it had to be admitted that Ambrose in absentia had attracted a large crowd - and that these disparate and mostly unpromising-looking people were sharing some sort of spiritual or at least semi-spiritual experience. He spotted a badger-haired head, and saw Mairéad staring at the nave floor and rocking with sobs. Rock of the church, he thought pityingly - she had *really* believed!

The parish priest's highly researched words were indeed lost on Fidelma. So too were the several thousand mourners outside the church, the cameras, the microphones, the brief car journey to that grim death-field whence Fergus had preceded their son, the way the sun tried to burnish the black marble headstones... all these things raced away into dreams and distance, into insignificance. All she really registered were the tears in the corners of Letitia's oceanic eyes, and others coursing down Philomena's lovely face - those, and the way her own legs felt as if they were about to fold and precipitate her into the greedy grave. The top of Ambrose's coffin onto which she cast stony municipal subsoil looked like a door leading into the black heart of reality. She tried hard to think of Ambrose continuing on in some other guise, in some other dimension, as some insisted he always would. But she simply could not see it, or him. He was out of focus. He had always been out of focus. Oh, Ambrose...

On that same evening, alone at last, rain cloaking the coast, she looked long into the front garden. She scarcely saw the longer-than-usual lawn over which, in normal seasons, she would roll weekly on a ride-on mower, as if Nature was a personal affront. Now, long stems were daring to unfold themselves, and delicate seed heads to nod and whisper, softening the space for the first time since a developer had seen the ancient meadow and dreamed of coating it in concrete. In the last few days, some of the trees had suddenly sported a new type of tinny talisman - little bullet charms, or maybe they were real bullets, dangling on chains, twisting and glinting in all weathers, symbols of Ambrose's speed and spirit. Fidelma stared semi-hypnotized at their gyrations, and remembered a strange little boy she used to know - an awkward, arrogant, embarrassing, rude, selfish, ugly, ungrateful boy, but one who had also been loved (had he ever known that?), and was now gone. Deleted. Erased. Vanished beyond afterlife - or communication - or recall - or remorse - or repair. Her certainty that all was nothingness almost strangled her, and made her limbs unable to carry their own weight. The sky seemed to lie very, very close upon the garden, and she felt she was being squashed between the two, breathing through a tiny hole, the eye of a needle. Misery moved through her in long, slow, endless pulses.

*

A week after the funeral, she left the house neatly and quietly, hours before Mary was due to arrive. She was wearing what were for her scruffy clothes, although they were very clean - jeans, a jumper, an anorak, sturdy shoes. The sun was pewter behind a curtain of mist. It had been an unseasonably cold night, and frost-remembering droplets weighed down all plants, and glistened on the trinkets in the trees. She walked quickly in those heavy shoes along Tara Road, and then uphill through similar thoroughfares until she reached the old iron gate that marked the footpath up to the Cross. The gate was always unlocked, and beyond it the sticky-muddy track snaked up, first between gardens, then alternating between deciduous woodland and more open patches of gorse and heather.

This was the way most people ascended the Head these days, although it was not the way Ambrose had gone - and there was a lot of litter along the path. Fidelma felt pain in her plexus when she spotted an old local newspaper, crumpled, torn and dirty, blown or dropped here, on which she could see part of a headline "Ambr..." She turned it over with her toe apprehensively-hopefully, but the rest had disintegrated into the trampled muck. She moved on quickly.

It was absolutely silent except for the squelching of her feet, and birds or perhaps rodents itching and twitching invisibly among the greenery. A blackbird swooped suddenly across her path, and she wondered if something had frightened it. She looked nervously around, and could not help recalling stories about the Head she had heard when she and Fergus had first moved into the area. She had laughed them off, obviously - but she had never forgotten them. How could she have - with the Head so omnipresent, its shadow lying always across the town? Cloud still stuck clammily to the summit, dankly dispiriting - not at all the lambent morning she had hoped for.

In the smallest and most sleepless hours, just before the light jemmied its way in, it had come to her that she must climb the Head. She had confusedly felt that by staying in the house she was in some way keeping closer to Ambrose. But now it came to her that he had always been unhappy there - and that if she wanted to understand the way he had been, she needed to see something of what he had seen, up there on the roof of the county. The exercise would also be good for her. She was surprised that this hadn't occurred to her before.

Now, her hamstrings aching, her breath short, muddy, mentally exhausted, and ill-at-ease among all this Nature, she was starting to think she had made a mistake. But she went on, hoping at any moment that she would break out from these trees, the cloud would quit, and there would be long, long views across the coast and into Ambrose's heart. She longed to see some other early walker, to break the uncanny aloneness. But no one came, and things she couldn't see seemed to be able to see her, and still the fog closely followed the Head's contours, thicker in dips, enlarging those things it didn't conceal, drenching her fringe, making her cheeks cold. She slipped, falling heavily forward onto her right knee. When she stood gingerly again, the knee felt stiff and sore, and the hands she had thrust forwards to save herself were slimed with mud, and grazed from protruding granite. Tears started to tired eyes - of physical pain, and frustration. Why was this path so *hard*? It wasn't *fair*. And there was so far still to go. Trees marked the track upwards and down, an endless enfilade. She stood undecided.

Someone was coming! Down below, coming up from the town just as she had done, she discerned the shape of a man - a stocky outline, progressing more steadily upwards than she had, but looking down at the ground so she couldn't see his face. He must be deep in thought; he didn't seem to have seen her. But as he got nearer, she was disconcerted to see that he was wearing an odd-looking garment - almost like a robe - and that he was muttering to himself. She was therefore relieved when he looked up and they recognized each other. "Tom! What are you doing here?"

He started, looked shifty. He'd lost weight, she thought - quite a lot of weight. It wasn't a robe he was wearing, after all - just a long coat. He was also wearing white trousers. He looked distrait, slightly guilty. "Oh! Hello! You gave me a shock! Normally there's no one up here at this time."

"Well, I haven't been up here in years and years! I'm only up here today because... because... well, I need some fresh air. And why are you here anyway? I never knew you went on early-morning walks. Funny to think you can live next door to someone for so many years and never know something like that!"

"Well, I don't usually - I mean, I didn't until recently. I'm trying to lose some weight, you see." She watched him closely, knowing there was more. He gulped, and then gabbled embarrassedly, in the manner of a man unused to saying meaningful things.

"You see... you see Ambrose made me think about things! Things I'd never thought about before. Like my own life, and how damn boring it is! I started to realise that I hate my job - and a lot of other things too. Things about myself, mostly. And I realized that we only get one life, and, well, it's very short, isn't it?"

He looked at her with embarrassment, but also defiance. "So every morning for the last three weeks I've been coming here - just to have some thinking time. And as I say it's good for me in a physical sense. I've also given up eating meat - much to Mum's disgust! I feel much better; I think I may even go vegan. I remember once you told me I should!" He tried to smile. So did she.

"Shall we climb it together, then?" she asked. "To be honest, I'd be glad of some company. This place gives me the heeby-jeebies!"

They proceeded wordlessly, except for an odd "It's this way!" from him whenever they came to a fork. She needed all her breath for the ascent; Tom already seemed quite fit. The mist made her hair flop into her eyes. They stopped for a moment, to catch their breath, ingesting the miasma. "Ambrose didn't come up this way, you know," he told her, as he wiped his brow and recovered his breath. "He went up the most difficult side. But that means going through Shaughnessy-Don land. Besides, I don't know if I'm up to anything harder than this. Later, maybe, when I'm fitter..."

"The most difficult side? That was so him!"

"It was! Ready for the last bit then?"

They toiled upwards once more, again in silence, except for the whistling and jumping of birds, now not at all unnerving. After twenty minutes more, just when she was thinking she needed another rest, they got their first glimpse of the Cross on top of the highest hummock. They emerged at last at its foot, but the cloud had come all the way with them, and they were cocooned in silvery-yellow, with nothing further than fifty feet away visible. Fidelma could feel the fingers of the sun as they pressed down on the grey envelope, and for a few seconds the day promised to brighten, but then the fog pushed back.

She felt more than usually hollow - and then came a much worse emotion, as she noticed recent graffiti on the plinth of the Cross in tall scarlet spray-paint. "AMBROSE IS A FUCKEN BASTERD!" and a large caricature, all eyes, ears, buck teeth and grossly swollen sexual organ. She felt a falling inside, and warm tears trickled down her chilled cheeks.

"Aah!' said Tom. "I'd forgotten about that... Sorry!" He watched with his head slightly on one side, while she rubbed fruitlessly at the plinth with paper tissues. "Do you know what he looks like?" he went on after a moment. She didn't hear, she was so fiercely focused on rubbing. "The Cerne Abbas Giant! Saw that once - we were on holidays. Always remember it. It was the first time I'd eaten curry." After another moment, he added more thoughtfully, "I suppose it's the same kind of thing in a way - a sort of weird tribute." She wasn't listening; she was pressing her hot forehead against the plinth.

Five minutes afterwards, she raised her head. The caricature was unaffected by all her exertions, and she looked quickly away. Tom was standing about twenty feet off, gazing eastwards, his face keen. She cleared her throat, and spoke huskily. "What are you doing?"

He was excited. "I think the wind's changing! There's a definite movement there that wasn't there before - and I can smell the sea." She could smell it too. "We might be able to get a view after all," he went on. "I really hope we do, because it's fantastic from up here. And there's a special feeling about this morning! Do you feel it?"

But she could not see or feel anything unusual, peer anxiously everywhere, stare as strongly as she might. It was just fog - cold, uncomfortable, totally explicable. It was just her luck that it should be here on this day - the one day when she had thought to come, this one day when of all days she had needed to see something invisible from below. "Listen now!" said Tom, with a thrill. "Listen!" he hissed. And she did, but could hear nothing. There were not even any birds up here on the treeless crest.

"Listen to what?"

"Sssh!" he had his hand up commandingly - a gesture she would never ever have expected from someone like him. "I think it's clearing a little - over there! Yes, it's definitely clearing!" He swivelled, clumsy in his coat but intensely alive, and faced back inland, down to where the town would normally have been visible. And indeed it seemed for a moment as if the cloud really was in flux, swirling, thinning, as if something was pushing hard to break through, and the grain of the morning were going to be burned away. She stood with her mouth open, her right hand half-covering it in excited fear, and she willed the wall to fall. Tom was pointing, his arm taut, his finger trembling, and it looked as if his remaining hair was standing up in unconquerable joy..."*There!* Do you see? There!" She knew it was terribly important that she should see, and she held her breath, her eyes bulged, her brain thumped with strain...

And then the fog fell back down again, weightier and wetter than ever, and she turned towards her companion. He was standing in the same place, but his pointing hand had fallen to his side, and his body so lately poised looked limply fat as usual. Yet there was wonder in his face when he turned towards her - a hungry flame that seemed to singe her, even at that distance. "Did you see it? Did you *see* it?" He seemed exorbitantly excited.

"I *think* so," she said cautiously.

He was staring at her in bemusement. "You can't have done! I mean, you wouldn't be talking about it like *that*!"

"Like what? What do you mean, Tom? I've seen the Financial Services Center before - and to be honest, I can't even be certain I saw it at all. Perhaps I only imagined it."

He gaped at her. "The what?"

"The Financial Services Center - you should know it better than me! I think I saw some of the industrial estate too."

He blinked, then blinked again, astounded. "That's not what I'm talking about at all! That wasn't the *Financial Services Center*! There's no comparison - no comparison at all!" She had never seen anyone looking so shocked. Then his shock turned into profound pity, before he looked away and stammered. "I... I don't know what to say! If that's all you saw just now, then all I can say is that I'm sorry - really sorry for you!... So you never saw any of it? The most wonderful city..."

She felt quite frightened by such intensity from so unemphatic a young man, but she felt she had a duty towards him. She needed to tell him the truth, however much he might dislike it. This was how Ambrose's problems had started - seeing things that weren't there. "Tom, listen to me, please. I'm sorry, but you did imagine it! There was nothing there. It was just the Financial Services Center - and as I say I can't even be sure I saw that. The light plays funny tricks sometimes, you know, especially on a day like this, especially in creepy places like this." He was still staring away, breathing hard and loud, creating his own mini-mist. She changed her tone, to talk him down. "And speaking of the Center, shouldn't you be thinking about going back down and getting changed? If you're not careful, you'll be late!" He span round to stare at her for a long moment, tiny in her mist-disarranged make-up, and emitted a laugh of infinite scorn.

*

A Modern Journey

A few days later, Mary invited her sister to come and see her at Oldtown. Fidelma had agreed gratefully, out of a new appreciation of kinship. Mary was so kind, and was besides her only remaining family. And getting out of the house for a few hours - even to the convent - would do her good. She had to shake the inertia that had flopped back down over her since she had climbed the Head. She had not been out of the house since then, ordering groceries online to avoid having to go down among people, who were so unpredictable and unsatisfactory. She looked at the TV with indifference, and had not even been able to summon much interest when she had seen the coverage of Dr. Kumiswaramy's arrest, on numerous sex-related charges. She could not know that Mary, with the special permission of Oldtown's Mother Superior, was about to let her into a great secret.

It had been her first time in the car since Ambrose had gone away - and although normally a skilled and impatient driver, she had at first driven clumsily, changing gears against their will, creeping along well below the speed limit, a nuisance to drivers caught behind, who could not guess at her identity or state of mind. But after a near-miss at a crossroads, she jerked into greater consciousness, and by the time the car swung up the steep hill towards the convent's great gates, aristocratic closures to the road so recently made suburban by housing, she had been regaining confidence, and starting to notice things once more. In the huge, immaculately lawned, dull house immediately beside the gates, two blond boys were playing at some chasing game of the kind children had always played - except, inevitably, Ambrose - who had always preferred drawing maps of imaginary countries, and then dropping tactical nuclear devices on them. Fidelma marvelled at their innocence and health, envied their mother, exhaled, and passed on through the gates.

Fidelma and Mary had talked desultorily for several minutes, when Mary said, with a curious semi-suppressed thrill. "Fi - I invited you here today for a very special reason. Do you want to know what made me choose the life I chose?"

Fidelma tried hard to summon interest. "Hmm? Oh yes, please, I suppose so."

Mary didn't notice her lack of enthusiasm, too caught up in her own. "Well, it was because the inconsequentiality of death was demonstrated to me in the clearest possible way - the irrelevance of the frail sepulchre in contrast to the eternal soul." This unexpectedly portentous turn slightly embarrassed Fidelma. Sisters probably shouldn't speak to each other about such things, or at least in such a direct way. "It's something you should maybe think about, Fi. It might help you. Ambrose understood, you know - without needing to be told! That was how I knew he was special!"

Fidelma lifted her head. "What do you mean?"

"I mean you're still locked into the modern way of thinking of Ambrose as having been purely material - chemicals and nerve-endings, gases and genes. This idea is pretty horrifying to you. It is to anyone! But I think I can prove to you that death doesn't really matter. It's not the end, Fi!" Mary gazed at Fidelma, her head tilted like a terrier's. "I think you're ready for this. I think you need to know this. Come with me!"

She took a vast bunch of keys out of her chatelaine. It was not that there were many keys on the bunch, but the ones there were were substantial chunks of ironmongery contemporaneous with the building. Fidelma did not much like the look of them - they hinted of secrets, shadows, distrust, a dark view of humanity. With the heavy, hand-cut utensils swinging so surely from her fingers, and in her habit, Mary looked not just older than her older sister, but almost like she had dropped in from some other century. The Keeper of the Keys... a figure from some old story.

They walked echoingly along corridors and cloisters, a blur of Romanesque arcades and Romantic curlicues, last gasp of the high age, wind-chilled ways of saintly statuettes, texts and exhortations, lapidary limestones bearing messages like "Sister Sheila - Fell asleep in The Saviour's arms, 6th July 1954". Repetitive doorways and arches framed the fountain, flowerbeds, the fountain, flowerbeds, the fountain, flowerbeds - then there was a dazzling vista of the Head for a moment, through some light effect appearing to hover a little above the land. Then Mary stopped in front of an ornate iron gate of floriated design, in a sunless part of the complex Fidelma had never seen before. Through the openings in the gate breathed bone-chill. Above the gateway was a cartouche with QUIS SEPARABIT? chiselled in italics. Mary nodded upwards. "Romans 8:35."

"Oh?" What else was she supposed to say? What was Mary up to? Fidelma waited slightly irritably, while her sister bent to fit the most serious key Fidelma had ever seen into the most serious of locks.

The Italian architect of the convent had travelled extensively throughout southern Europe, including Augsburg and Palermo. He had always taken a keen professional interest in the religious as well as the ducal architecture of the places he visited, and so when he had landed the commission to build Oldtown, he had decided to incorporate certain features that were popular on the continent, but rare in the British Isles. It was one of these architectural flourishes that was now opened to Fidelma's astonished eyes.

It was a long, high space, although this was not immediately obvious because it was lit and ventilated only by the door piercings, and by one tiny barred window high up opposite. Those sources were just enough to reveal the room's design of facing bays, each lined with stone shelves and separated by Ionic columns. They also revealed the chamber's contents. Fidelma's eyes needed a moment to adjust, and when they did she was astounded and appalled.

Each of the shelves contained tidy lines of spherical objects, and long, dry-looking bundles, colourless and characterless at first glance, looking like faggots of firewood – and similar bundles stood up at the base of the columns. Stood up - because Fidelma now noticed with disbelieving vertigo that each bundle was a corpse. To be exact, a skeleton, each one clad in a habit identical to that now being worn by Mary. And each of the spheres on the shelves was a skull.

They were the first skeletons and skulls Fidelma had seen in real life, and they were inexpressibly horrible - especially as they had been arranged with such fanatical neatness and organisation. Even worse, with macabre humour, because someone had made looped chain-like decorations and charnel-house coats of arms out of tibias and ribs. Mary's voice cut in, quiet, proprietorial, as Fidelma swayed. "So here we are, Fi - the Oldtown Ossuary, which is we think the only one in Ireland. It's something almost no-one knows about. We don't think people would like it very much, so we keep it secret. Some of the ladies in here are over 150 years old! There's something about the air in here that slows down decay. When they were building those horrible houses a few years ago, we were worried that they might damage this place, because some of them are built right up against the wall, big fancy rooms with computers and jacuzzis and the like, I bet. Funny to think that just a few yards away from Sister Sheila..." she patted a skull fondly, an awful echo of girlish playfulness, "...with just a few bricks between them, there's probably someone watching television! They'd get quite a shock if one day the wall collapsed and she rolled in among them to say hello!"

Fidelma was stupefied with horror. Those little boys - this charnel-house! Sister Sheila, she noticed with near-terror, still wore a circlet of withered flowers, and there was even some loyal hair - a few stray strands of old ivory that had last seen full daylight on 6th July 1954. Mary noticed her sister's state, even in that light, and put a supposedly reassuring arm around her quivering shoulders.

"You see, Fi, how little death means! To us, this place isn't horrifying, or frightening - it's just a place where the unimportant bits of us rest after we've finished with them. To me, the women who once used these are still here, living alongside us, following us to Mass, walking with us through the corridors, eating and sleeping and washing alongside us, talking to us and giving us advice. They're all still members of our community, don't you see? And Ambrose knew this - he saw this! Don't you remember him describing this place to me? How could he have known, Fi - how could he have known... unless...? Could he have had a bit of Mummy's gift?" She was massively excited, even if her question suggested she was seeking validation for herself as much as for Ambrose. Fidelma had never seen her like this, would never have thought it was possible for Mary to be like this. How little she knew her sister! How little you knew anyone in life!

Mary turned back to the undercroft. "The dead have always greatly outnumbered the living, so why should we be afraid of them? Look, *he* isn't afraid!" Fidelma followed Mary's finger and saw a tiny bird hopping in from outside through the barred window, the stubby silhouette of a sparrow on a hunt for spiders. But its sparky activity, heard rather than seen skittering and flitting among the tenebrous tympanums, instead of soothing made her feel even more distraught - because its scratchy plumage and dry skinny legs reminded Fidelma horrifyingly of the nuns themselves. "They nest in here, and we don't mind."

For a dizzy second, Fidelma thought that Mary had meant "we, the dead" - then realized she meant "we, the nuns". But in any case, the idea of warm eggs and bald brood-patches, and chicks cracking into consciousness among these things was absolutely sickening. How could any kind of life subsist amongst so much deadweight, hop with bright eyes among these horror-film props? It was as indecorous as you could get. And how could any human - and especially her own blood! - contemplate this scene so cold-bloodedly, stand looking at these sacks of sticks that were all that remained of people, clicking her keys so casually? It was *monstrous*! Mary at that moment seemed terrible, a trader in death - and then she inclined her head, "That's my shelf over there!" She was proud - *joyous*...

"Excuse me!" Fidelma pushed her way out of the catacomb, through the iron gate with its mocking representations of flowers, into the cloisters she had thought cheerless but which now seemed like passageways in Paradise.

There was the Head again, now again anchored to earth; there were the flowerbeds prinked with pansies, like sweets that had just tumbled from the air. She sensed pearls of perspiration on brow and cheeks, and her heart bounded fiercely as if to disprove what she had seen. She pushed her brow against never-sunned stone, heedless for once of dust. She felt like retching - and then she did, slightly, an acid trickle down her front that left metal in her mouth.

She had always feared death so dreadfully - much more than most people seemed to. She had always made strenuous efforts never to think about it at all. Her phlegm at funerals was not acceptance, but refusal to consider what awaited (or wasn't awaiting) her and everyone else - what could take her at any moment, as it had taken Ambrose, her Daddy and Mummy and Fergus, and would soon sweep Mary off to her waiting shelf - so many billions stacking up in rivalry with the living, whom they would always defeat. What she had just seen, so unexpectedly, so closely and in such quantity had made death seem even more awful and undeniable. Those filthy things in there should never even be seen, let alone handled - let alone celebrated!

She heard Mary locking the gate. Why lock it if the dead were safe? Her sister's soft steps beat like timpani on the hollow flags. Mary spoke, and she sounded like her old sisterly self again. "I am terribly sorry, Fi! I didn't think for a moment you'd react in that way! I just wanted to show you how unimportant bones are - they're just lumps of nothing, compared with the Inner Life. And please, Fi, remember - Ambrose *knew* this - he saw this place in his mind, and he knew what it meant. Think of that - please - think of that, and take comfort!" She took her sobbing sister by the elbow, and steered her back towards the light.

REVELATIONS

"Do you know what date it is tomorrow?" Letitia demanded as the Monsignor picked up the phone on the walnut desk.

He glanced at his desk calendar. "I think you mean what date it will be tomorrow! It will be the 15th."

"And therefore, you deathless pedant, the fiftieth anniversary of the dedication of the Cross on the Head."

"No! Well, well. Is it really?"

"Yes, really! And what do you propose we do to mark the anniversary?"

"Err, go up the Head?"

"Be here tomorrow, at 11am, and bring some sensible shoes. That is - if you think you will be up to it? You *are* getting on a bit."

"Oh, I'll be up to it, all right. Just try and stop me."

He put down the receiver smilingly. It was an excellent idea - but then her ideas almost always had been. He could really do with a devotional day, a day away from all this - he surveyed his desk with distaste - and the weather was predicted to be sunny yet again. He would always now think of such weather as Ambrose weather! It had been a stunning summer, and as he had driven to and from the office he had often looked wistfully at the shimmering silhouettes of the Three Rock, Two Rock and Kippure. Whilst in Rome he had spent many holidays hiking, following the Via Francigena and interlinking smaller routes, striding from holy site to holy site, measuring his day's distance as much as possible by magical locations, from chapel to shrine to grotto and well - delightful solitary days of unending heat and pleasant effort, ranging in search of religion, hoping some of the accumulated hallowedness of these places might stick to his boots. A little exercise of that kind now would do him a power of good.

He rubbed a leg ruminatively, thinking of that day's headlines about the Guard who had inadvertently killed Ambrose four months before. He had been dismissed from the force, of course, but he had received a surprisingly lenient sentence from the judge. In his summing up, the judge had spoken of "...the disgraceful scenes, and confused and highly charged atmosphere in which this tragic event occurred - an atmosphere for which the deceased was himself unfortunately largely responsible. It is to be hoped that such disgraceful scenes are never again witnessed in this country, and that nobody else will ever have to die because of irrational, medieval superstition".

The Monsignor had lingered over this last phrase. It seemed almost certain, he thought, that the judge would be vindicated by non-events. Ireland would soon be like all other European countries - a land cut off from its history, without hope, without sacredness or seriousness.

In truth, Ambrose was rarely far from his thoughts. The Monsignor was haunted by his failure to protect him. But there was much more to it than guilt. His story had refused to die. The poor deluded lad had been elevated by his death, purged of much of his grossness and comicality, his sins forgotten, his ugliness less striking. And the more time that elapsed, the purer and higher he would seem to those who remembered him at all. Even the celebrated mooning of Fitzroy Nevin - which had already been viewed several million times on YouTube - might come to be seen in time as a brave defiance of pompous temporal authority. Yet again, the priest was forced to confront a deeply disquieting possibility - that some of the saints he venerated might have been a little like the lad.

Some said that Ambrose had changed nothing. The Church had ignored him - and the Monsignor's conscience was clear about his role in that. But even if it had been foolish enough to have embraced Ambrose, it would probably still have continued on the same precipitous plummet. The Church's future course was hinted at by the rumour that Daddy Jimmy was in line for a mitre. This was entirely predictable. He would be a safe, politic choice. Almost the only choice, really, for a Church that had after all usually adapted itself to the world. He had met Jimmy at a function a few evenings ago, and told him mischievously that he was sure Jimmy would lend his new role the same dignity and aplomb he had always lent everything. The other had just looked back at him, and there had been little in the way of Christianity in that look. How typical, thought the Monsignor ruefully, that Jimmy would continue to flourish. People like that always did well - and if they were swiftly forgotten once they were gone, then so were most others. At least Ambrose had given them a run for their money. He smiled to himself yet again as he thought once more of Fitzroy Nevin's face as Ambrose bent over in front of him.

Yet there were still redoubts, which in some totally unexpected way Ambrose's blood had helped to cement. Although Jimmy was on the upwards slope, so were a few others. It was just as well that the Cardinal-to-be had not recognized his assailant in the confusion of the riot, because otherwise she might not have been appointed as Oldtown's new Mother Superior when the old one had finally claimed her ossuary shelf (the Monsignor was one of the few people who knew about the existence of that interesting architectural feature). Mary had already had an impact. There were several novices at the convent now - attracted by the new Mother Superior's rigour and excellent reputation, so Miss Tighe had told him with a sniff.

*

The day came in as beautifully as had been foretold, and shortly before eleven the Monsignor passed in through the gates of Head House and up the drive, enjoying the late summer signs - limes, oaks and horse chestnuts under full sail, rosebay willowherb shedding seed, profuse grasses, dragonflies zipping up from the lough to hawk the open rides. In such kindly light, even the dilapidated house seemed drowsily content, its dereliction under injunction as long as the lazy weather prevailed. Letty was waiting outside, finishing off a cup of tea in the sun - and from a distance (and even from quite close), she looked almost the way she had looked when she was twenty. He saluted her chastely on each cheek, and they set off around the house, sloping gradually up, getting into their strides, companionably quiet, content just to look at the long-grassed loveliness. Dandelions at different stages were everywhere, the youngest and yellowest really looking like tiny lions in a great greenwood. The Head stood in their way, taller by the second, and the Cross was pointing higher still. She looked at him with a conspiratorial kind of smile. "Ready?"

"Lead on!" he said, and they went through a small old gate into the wild. This was still part of the demesne, but it had never been gardened or farmed, and it was a mosaic of old undisturbed habitats unusual so close to Dublin. She pointed out several deeply personal places as they ascended - a few of which he remembered - but some of which he had never known, or noticed, before. Girlish places, full of innocent whispers, that she would never have owned up to when she had been closer to girlhood - but now could re-embrace as her life wound down. He saw a side of her to which he had never ascribed enough importance - Letty as explorer, prospecting by herself, content to be alone, and quiet. To be, in fact, nearer to God...

He had been too wrapped up in what he had always thought of as higher things (or himself) to notice that she too was a pilgrim, more like him than he had thought - and he wished, he wished... well, what did he wish? At any rate, he had been far too dismissive of that side of her. But then he had always been too hasty and obtuse to be a truly good Churchman. She looked at him, teasingly like the old days, archly amused. "You're very quiet. Out of breath?"

"A little," he lied. To cover confusion, he pointed to a glade where oaks bent to stare at themselves in a rivulet and Scots pines stood like exclamation marks, and asked if it had a name.

"Tinman's Meadow. Mairéad - remember her? - belongs to one of the families that have been visiting here for decades, maybe even centuries. They're ever so good - never any trouble, never any mess, and they tell us what's going on."

"I liked her. A lot. It struck me when I saw her she is the kind of person we need a lot more of."

"Who's we?"

"Well, Ireland, obviously, but I really mean the Church. She makes me think of all those people who have kept the Church going over the centuries. She's the unshakeable type, the kind who...what are you smiling at?"

"Didn't you know?"

"Know what?"

"She - and therefore the rest of the Walshes - have joined one of those happy-clappy churches. They go every Sunday to that huge barn of a place on the Hibernia Road - I think it used to be a factory - where they listen to some American talking the most awful rubbish. Or perhaps I should say shouting the most awful rubbish... And as for their songs... She told me she thought it more respectable! They're socially ambitious, you see." The Monsignor was momentarily irritated at having been so wrong, but then he grinned at their and his absurdity.

Letty went on thoughtfully, "Of course, that doesn't stop them thinking poor Ambrose really was rather wonderful - almost a saint, in fact! I don't know if you have recently passed where Ambrose was killed, but it's a kind of shrine - covered in flowers, and there are little handwritten notes, people asking for help, all that sort of thing. The council clears them away, but within a few days they're all back again. There's a young man named Tom - we met him at the rally, you might recall - who seems to organize it. He runs the website too. Mairéad told me she goes there often. I find that rather sweet, don't you?"

"Me too. Good for her!"

"I wonder who will play her in the film?"

"The film?"

"Ah - something else you didn't know! Fitzroy Nevin was talking about it on the radio. It seems he's an expert on Ambrose now. 'A modern John Wesley', he called him. 'We didn't always see eye-to-eye, but in a way maybe we needed him!'" She impersonated Nevin's voice quite convincingly.

The Monsignor shook his head, admiring Nevin's adaptability. "Well, if they do ever make that film," he said, "there's one vital consideration. Who'll play Bosco Buggy? I bet he'll have strong ideas on that subject..."

She laughed and they kept climbing, their flesh protesting, but their spirits unaccountably high. And what a walk it was, he felt, the best he, at least, could remember - and he had Ambrose to thank for it, for being here on this morning of mornings! He was walking in the best possible company, miraculously restored for a short time, the last time - and everything around them was so lush, hinting at growth and renewal going on for ever.

In a clearing, trespassers had raised mountain-bike tracks out of mud, with ramps and jumps and twists, and it looked like some buried monster which might at any second re-emerge. There was an area of recently burnt gorse, desiccated charcoal sticks in a bed of grey powder - but there were already hints of replacements, bulging green lumps starting to unfurl upwards. The trees were striped and warm to the touch, and between them cloud-shadows chased each other over parti-coloured fields. Lichens bearded branches in dry reds, purples, greys and greens, and gave feathery softness to grey rock. There were ladybirds everywhere, landing, taking off, rolling helpless on their backs until the humans righted them - black and scarlet bumps on wood and rock, medieval in their heraldic hues. "Did you know," asked Letty, looking at them like they were her own creation, "they're called *bóin Dé*?" He had not, but it didn't surprise him. He could imagine them in some mellow Old Master - "Madonna of the Ladybirds", perhaps, Nature's tiniest toys garlanding the resplendent Queen of All, while Sienese towers clustered on a hill behind.

A walk indeed, in which muscles didn't matter nor shortness of breath, in which the present was all, that summer sufficient - and yet which was also a peregrination back over fifty years and beyond, to a more innocent age. And that was before they came blinking out from under the trees at last, and there stood the Cross, and the sun, and the bones of the slumbering land. They stood at its flower-festooned base, and drank in glorious prospects as they recovered their breath.

"Fifty years! Makes you think!" Her face was keen, glowing.

"It certainly does, it certainly does..." He looked around, found the place where he had been standing as the Cardinal aspersed the Cross, and the place from which one woman in particular had watched the holy proceedings, watched him walk away from her, and from her kind of life. That same woman was talking now, as easily as if they had been talking every day ever since.

"But it's not just about the past, is it? Not just our past, I mean. It's also about poor Ambrose. I often think of him here on that night, in that awful storm - exactly here, where we are now, all alone except for his unhappiness. No wonder he came down with Somebody else! And yet, don't you think that in a way he was only seeing what we saw all those years ago?"

"Sometimes, Letty, sometimes!"

She smiled brilliantly, and pressed his huge and veiny hand. "I'm glad!" She was silent for a minute. "You know, sometimes I think Ambrose may even have a future! I bet an awful lot of people are thinking about him right now..."

They looked down together on the ever tinier town - and it seemed to them that they were almost back to where they had been decades before, with the world and sky to choose between, yet both somehow the same.

*

At the same time, only about a mile and a half away by thunderbolt, was the summer-subdued High Street, and unending cars grumbling hotly past the open door of a charity shop. There were only two people in the shop - one an elderly female attendant, whose pleasant face was wrinkled in worried conjecture as she gazed at the other. That other was young, but startlingly unfashionable - moustachioed, and wearing tweeds, woefully inapt for so broiling a day, and such a society. He was unaware of her askance, absorbed as he was in adding to the tottering heap of hardback books he had pulled from the shelves with mounting excitement. His lips moved as he muttered to himself, and devoured the marginalia inserted by an earlier owner. The books were by all kinds of authors, and on diverse subjects, but all bore on the flyleaf, in a showy script, the same, significant words - Ambrose Sheehy-O'Connor.

*

Just a few doors down was a tired shoe shop - the same in fact, in which Philomena Cogaidh had passed, and was still passing, excruciating workdays. She was sitting in the little staff room having lunch, conscious that she needed to eat well now. She was starting to feel uncomfortable again, and it was not quite as easy as it had been to attend to customers - to reach the highest shelves, to bend down and then straighten up again after tying the laces on the shoes of cross and kicking children, to patiently await their mothers' verdicts - while all the time she was wondering how she would be with her own.

Beneath even her lightest clothes, her breasts felt heavy and chafing, and the bump was starting to show. Already she could not wear some of her old clothes. Soon she would need to tell people; already she had surprised surmise in the shop-owner's eyes. Increasingly often, she felt a tiny tremor intimately inside as if it - he! - was anxious to be out, and as active in the world as his extraordinary father had been. She wondered what her son would make of that world, and it of him. She smiled absently at dithering mothers and their squalling brats, and forced herself to concentrate. She sweltered - she felt sick - and fantastically excited.

*

As that propitious day splashed news of its demise across the west, and a stiffish wind picked up from the sea, Fidelma was trying to renew old interests. She was eating properly again, watching the news, starting to think about what things there could still be in her future. She was young(ish); she was healthy; she was solvent; she was intelligent, still attractive. And now she could do exactly what she wanted. Her job had been kindly kept open, but there were so many other things she could consider now. Now that there were no ties. Now that there was nobody to care for - or care for her...

She had been greatly helped over the last few months by the professionals at GriefManagementProcess.com, and her anonymous letter to the editor had been one of their Star Letters. She had then tried to develop an interest in the radical designs shown in *Tomorrow's Interiors* - although she had lingering doubts whether 32 Tara Road would really wear the New Aesthetic. She was toying with the idea of selling the house, in any case. She was so free now...she hoped some day she might be able to feel excited by that idea. (When had she last felt excited about anything?) She paced the house over and again, restless as a prospecting mouse, trying to visualise each space in ochre and ecru, containing this admired sofa or table, the walls bearing enviably eclectic art.

Yet however busy and future-focused she kept herself, the past would creep up on her, and bellow in her head. When she was most sleepless, or dyspeptic, or deadest at heart, or just chanced across something that reminded her even more sharply of... that reminded her... she would find herself staring into space, or waking with wet eyes, her body powerlessly heavy, saying things she didn't understand. (Had he had these identical feelings, of lassitude and confusion - heard those same shoutings in the darkest hours?) Trying always to turn her thoughts, she had cleared the things people had tied to the trees in the garden - where once again the lawn was sterilely smooth - putting them in boxes in the shed. She wished people would let her forget, let poor Ambrose lie quiet - but still some people would turn up outside, or call at the door, or chatter about him on the TV and radio. She avoided going into town, because of all the constantly renewed flowers at the Place. Probably it would be necessary to leave, she told herself - start somewhere new and clean. But start what? And why? Impossible, really, ever to move on here where the Head stood so tall in all vistas, and the past crowded in so claustrophobically close however much she tried to paint it out.

She looked up at the Head now, one side brilliant, one side black - at Gisela Mildew on some show and somebody else on some other - then back out into the garden where night had inked in the air under the leylandii, and still she could not settle. She thought she heard a door close upstairs and although she knew she could not have done, nevertheless went into the hall. "Ambrose? Ambrose?" she called. But there was nothing and nobody there of course, although the hall felt half-alive with eyes. She shook her head, and turned, retreated into her room and closed the door - but all the while outside, the pines fidgeted and frisked as if many strange spirits were passing.

Glossary of Irish Words

a chara - friend (formal salutation, sometimes used in official letters)
asarlaí - sorceror
bóin Dé - lady of God
bóthar - road
buachaill - boy
dochtuir - doctor
Nollaig - Christmas
Our gathra, who cradgies in the manyak-norch...etc - the Lord's Prayer in Traveller gammon
sláinte - good health
slán leat - goodbye
tiocfaidh ár lá - our day will come (Irish nationalist slogan)
uisce beatha - literally, water of life (whisky)

Printed in Great Britain
by Amazon